A BAEN BOOK

For: Frank Taylor, the first editor who told me I could write . . .

Astere Claeyssens, the teacher, whose positive criticism has always helped me to see the forest without losing sight of even the smallest tree . . .

Noel Loomis, the writer, (in memoriam), who taught me the rules so I would know what I was doing if and when I choose to break one.

AUBADE FOR GAMELON

A Baen Book

Baen Enterprises
8-10 W. 36th Street
New York, N.Y. 10018

First printing, December 1984

ISBN: 0-671-55924-9

Cover art by James Gurney

Printed in the United States of America

Distributed by
SIMON & SCHUSTER
MASS MERCHANDISE SALES COMPANY
1230 Avenue of the Americas
New York, N.Y. 10020

BY THE FARTHEST BED, A HUDDLED FIGURE SAT

Racklin said softly, "Slim Boy, this is my brother Lon."

The figure on the stool turned its head slowly, and Gamelon recognized the young Indian who had come into the five-and-dime the morning before. The man looked at him steadily for a long moment. Then he asked Racklin calmly, "He know all about this?"

Racklin shook his head.

"Can he take it?"

"He'll see it like I do: clinically, objectively, questioningly."

Slim Boy turned to look Racklin dead in his amber eyes, his own black ones unwavering. "O.K., if you say so." He shrugged. "He ain't *my* brother."

"No, this is," Racklin grunted, and threw back the sheet.

On the bed were two other Slim Boys, sleeping on their sides facing each other. They were connected at the chest by a membrane of flesh alive with tiny red veins. As Gamelon watched, the membrane began to truncate in the center. It became narrower and narrower and then, as though pinched between invisible fingers, it became only a string, then a thread. Then, a second later, it parted—and the two resulting tags of flesh subsided gently into the breastbone like melting butter fading into hot pieces of toast.

Slim Boy reached out and touched each of the sleeping figures on the forehead, the lips, and the chest where the heart would be and said softly, "Welcome, Little Brothers."

By the same author

THE SINGER IN THE STONE

From the program notes for the Los Angeles Philharmonic Orchestra Concerts of May 26-30, 1986

AUBADE FOR GAMELON
For Viola, Tenor, Chorus and Orchestra
By
John Frederick Sevrinsky

For this, the world premiere of his latest large scale work, the composer has supplied the following comments:

> The *aubade*, or morning song, is defined as "a piece sung or played at dawn as a compliment to someone." I believe the concept is as old as Man himself and was probably realized originally as a crude hymn to the rising sun, to the morning, to the return of day and light—in essence, a song to welcome the return of life with its continuing cycle, always constant, always slowly changing.
>
> Who or what is Gamelon? For purposes of *Aubade*, let us just say that Gamelon is that force which insures that life does continue. In doing so, that force, that power recognizes neither light nor darkness, good nor evil, truth nor falsehood, beauty nor ugliness, as Man defines them, but only the necessity for that life, with its peculiar combination of stability and change, to continue its slow upward progress undisturbed.
>
> I have been asked why I chose the viola and the tenor voice as soloists . . .

JULY 21, 1984

La Playa, California

The flooding light of the full moon helped, but still he was having difficulty finding his way along the faint path through the scattered chapparal and stones.

"Evening, Mr. S."

John Frederick Sevrinsky stopped halfway in from the highway and looked toward the dunes at the top of the beach. A tall, lank figure stood there, black against the light of the westering moon, lazily waving a flashlight.

"David, is that you?"

"Yes, sir."

"Well, I'm coming right along. Bear with me."

The man on the dunes lowered the light and threw the beam on the path ahead of Freddie Sevrinsky. It helped him to maneuver the rest of the distance to where Deputy Sheriff Sorensen stood waiting for him. He took off his bedroom slippers and emptied the sand out of them, rolled up his trouser legs a couple of turns, stuffed the slippers into his back pocket and said, "Silly of me, I forgot to put on shoes. You have a problem, David?"

"Will you come down the beach with me, please, Mr. S.?"

David Sorensen was and had been many things to Freddie. He was as closed-mouthed as he was bright, as gentle and considerate as he was strong. As a young criminology student with an uncanny flair for logic, he had more than once set Freddie's seminar in aesthetics on its ear with but a single pointed question. He was still the strapping surfer who strolled on the beach with Freddie on occasion, board under arm, listening intently and questioning incisively. To this day, Freddie had trouble seeing him, the village policeman in his uniform, as anything but an overgrown boy dressed up for a masquerade.

Nonetheless, Freddie followed him obediently down the beach, the sand beneath their feet becoming firmer as they neared the ocean. Sorensen's big light picked out the tangled piles of stranded kelp as they went so that Freddie would not stumble over them.

When it was impossible to go any farther without walking into the Pacific, they stopped. Sorensen stood silently gazing out toward the swelling horizon for a moment or two, then said, "I'm sorry to get you out at this hour, Mr. S., but there wasn't any help for it."

"It's all right, David, quite all right, but now that I'm here, what *can* I do for you?"

It was the time of the month for the spring tides. The flow of the ocean reached higher, the ebb bared the beach farther out. "There, Mr. S., watch right about there when the surf pulls back again," Sorensen said as he stabbed the water with his light.

A breaker collapsed a few feet from them, strewed its foaming crumbs at their feet, then dragged them back again across the glistening beach. Sorensen's light held steady on a turbulent spot where the water swirled and gouged at the sand around what looked to Freddie like slender joints of driftwood. He said as much to Sorensen.

"No, Mr. S., I'm afraid not. You're barefoot, so you won't mind coming out there with me, will you?" Without waiting for Freddie's answer and heedless of what the salt water would do to his polished boots, Sorensen strode into the gentle surf. Hiking his trousers, Freddie followed.

He came up with Sorensen just as another breaker was pulling its parts back into the sea again. The young man's light held on the churning spot. The water disappeared, the blow holes of tiny sand crabs began to pockmark the sand at their feet. The two men stood looking down. "Mr. Rogers, the man who lives in the brown shingled house up the beach, was running his dog about an hour ago when the tide was all the way out," Sorensen said. "The dog found her."

"Her!" Freddie gasped.

What Freddie had taken for elbows of driftwood were the rigid, bent arms of a woman, all of her that showed above the sand.

Handing his light to Freddie, Sorensen said, "Hold this, please, Mr. S." He rummaged in his pocket and came up with a set of large fingernail clippers. As the deputy leaned down, Freddie noticed the plastic packet floating on the surface for the first time, rising and falling with the water. It was tied to the woman's left wrist by a length of heavy twine. Sorensen snipped it off, took the light from Freddie and held the beam on it. "Can you help me with this, Mr. S.?"

Freddie took the packet, held it at arm's length to make up for the glasses he had left at home and read through the clear, wet plastic, "To: John Frederick Sevrinsky." He looked up at Sorensen and said, "I won't know until I see what's inside."

David put the nail clippers back, fumbled up a small clasp knife in its place, slit the packet and handed Freddie the note it contained scrawled on the blank side of a printed form. Freddie unfolded it and started to read in the beam from the flashlight:

Mr. S.,

This is the last piece of the hell I've lived through these past weeks. Maria's death was the first piece. Yet, it is only the end of the beginning. Please forgive me for leaving it on your doorstep, but I must.

You may not realize it at the moment, but you have almost all that's needed to reconstruct those weeks, that hell, fill in what's missing and fit it all together. And, you have the only mind I know capable of comprehending what you'll find when the patchwork's complete. Whether you'll understand, agree, disagree, I don't know. But someday, someone may have to try to explain, and, as I said in my last note, any poor soul, no matter how depraved, who is heading into the unknown perhaps never to return would like to feel some single comrade in the human race will remember him.

I doubt we shall ever see each other again, Mr. S., and I think you know how much I'll miss that. In the end, all the words and thoughts we exchanged over the years couldn't help me. I had to take my own terrible stand on the meaning of truth, on what beauty really is. Pray for me that what I did as a result was the only thing that could have been done.

With deepest respect and affection,
Gamelon

The final words blurred before Freddie's eyes as he handed the letter to Sorensen to read.

When the young deputy had finished a quick scan of it, he turned his attention to Freddie again and said softly, "Mr. S.?"

Freddie did not answer.

Sorensen shook his arm gently. "Mr. S., you all right?"

Freddie nodded slowly.

"Mr. S., *do* you—comprehend—this?"

"David—" Freddie's voice broke. He cleared his

throat. "David, yes, I think I do, but it will be awhile before I can string it all together and begin to try to relate it to you. I don't know that I can ever explain it because I'm not sure I ever will understand. One man cannot explain something to another which he does not fully understand himself. Yes, David, I'll try, but not right now, if you don't mind."

Sorensen did not press him. He took the elderly man's arm, turned him out of the surf and steered him up to the top of the beach. He helped him on with his slippers, then walked him back along the path to his battered, venerable Cadillac at the edge of the highway.

Freddie settled behind the wheel and sat quite still. When he made no move to start the engine, Sorensen leaned down and asked through the open window, "You sure you're all right, Mr. S.?"

Freddie took a deep breath, nodded and turned the key. The engine caught, and he paused again, then looked the young deputy straight in the eye. "David," he said, "I believe you're one of the very few who could comprehend it all, too. You see, there's been only one student I've ever had who was as bright or perhaps even brighter than you. He was a few years ahead of you, thank God! I don't know how I'd have coped with the both of you at once. I haven't seen him for almost three months now, not since just before his Maria died, and I haven't heard from him in—about two weeks. His name was Gamelon Waugh.

"But, David, as he suggested in that note, there's a Grand Canyon between comprehending and involved, sympathetic understanding.

"I'll give you a taste of what you'll be up against trying to reach that understanding. I'm only making what you'd call an educated guess right now, mind you, David, but I think when you start taking fingerprints and checking records and whatever else you do in a situation like this, you're going to find that the woman out there in the sand has died before."

Freddie put the car in gear and it shot out into the deserted highway, the churning back wheels showering Sorensen with sand. The deputy stood for a moment on the shoulder watching the car's taillights disappearing toward the south and home. If he had been Roman Catholic instead of Mormon, he would have crossed himself. As usual, John Frederick Sevrinsky, renowned composer, conductor, teacher, philosopher and La Playa's most famous citizen, was driving hell bent for leather and smack in the middle of the road.

La Playa, California
July 25, 1984

My Dear David,

Since we parted in the wee hours of last Sunday morning, I've mulled it over and have decided how best to relate to you what I know. With commissions to fulfill and a hectic conducting and teaching schedule, I haven't time for any lengthy, consolidated report. That's your department. Yet, I'm sure you'll need some kind of record to consider when I'm eventually done, so I'll begin where I think the beginning needs to be made and write everything down for you as time allows. I'll see that you have the "pieces" in some sort of order. What other "order" we ultimately make of them will have to be up to each of us individually.

In the long run, all I'll be able to tell you, really, is who Gamelon was—as far as I know—and why *he* believed he had to do what he did. I have no idea where this may lead *you*, David, you and the law you work for, or what actions you and that law might take as a result. Even though I'm said to be a philosopher, I doubt I'll ever be able to establish whether what Gamelon did was right or wrong. If anything, it was probably both—or neither.

Beginning, I choose to begin with Gamelon himself. How shall I say it? He was deceiving? No, that has a negative connotation and that's not what I want. Let me just try to tell you what I mean.

For example, he was burly, built like a heavy construction worker or a middleweight wrestling contender, but had no interest in sports or other physical endeavors as far as I know, and was gentle and quiet. Still, there was something about him that seemed to whisper to others' subconscious minds with a soft smile, "Don't tread on me."

Rather strangely combined with all that bulk and muscle was superb red hair and magnificently translucent skin. I've never seen the combination anywhere else except in the lovely women in the north of Ireland. (I suspect a heady colleen in his lineage somewhere!) Altogether, it should not have fit, but it did, gracefully and without a hint of softness. I remember wondering once if he had an Irish redhead temper and what might happen if someone drove him to discover it.

He sometimes appeared plodding. What he was was dogged. He seemed shy, but he was only reserved, and capable, on occasion, of a rare warmth, even gregariousness. I have seen a look on his face that implied, yes, stupidity, but I learned over the years that when he looked that way he was exercising a rare ability he had: he could shut off his mind, as it were, to let it rest and refresh itself. He could get that look, true, but he was brilliant and he was curious almost to a fault.

His genius was genetics, horticultural genetics. He only attended my graduate aesthetics seminar because that curiosity of his was never satisfied when it came to what constituted beauty, and, some say, therefore truth. Perhaps it was the happiest of combinations: a man who devoted his mind to experimenting with the mysteries of life with a soul so deeply concerned with the definition of beauty. You must remember this, David. It has all the bearing in the world on what is to come.

Now to Maria. I think I should tell you what little I know of her because of Gamelon's mention of her in the letter.

The one and only time I saw her was the last time I saw Gamelon. Always in the past when he had come to see me, he had just popped in. That time, he phoned ahead, all apologies for disturbing me, and asked rather formally if he could call on me with a friend. It didn't occur to me until after their visit, but it was as though I'd been asked to give a father's blessing on the woman he loved. And, David, he loved her. It was splashed all over him like cologne. He loved her, and he was pouter pigeon proud of her.

Maria: a vibrant, mercurial girl some years younger than Lon—in her very early twenties, I judged—with great gray eyes and honey-colored hair halfway down her back. Her face wasn't beautiful, only pert, and, I thought, liable to go bird-like with age. Her body wasn't beautiful either, in the way the media standardizes what bodies beautiful are these days. She was tall, on the lanky side, except for deliciously full breasts, and, I thought, liable to go top heavy with age and children . . .

MAY 18, 1984

Los Angeles, California

"Lon—," Maria purred in his ear, "don't go yet." She held his head tightly in the circle of her arms and locked his hips against her with her legs.

"I won't if you let me breathe," Gamelon mumbled.

Maria laughed and relaxed her arms enough for him to lift his face out of the pillow. He took a deep, leisurely breath and exhaled slowly.

"Better?"

"Better."

"Not better," she said with sudden pout.

"What?"

"It's not better when you're even that far away from me."

"Get used to it. I'm going to be three thousand miles away from you for several days. You'll have to get along without me."

With a sudden vehemence, she released her hold on him, shoved him roughly off her, rolled over and lay silently on the edge of the bed, her back to him.

Gamelon was a little surprised; it was not like Maria to be obtuse, and particularly not right afterwards, but he made no move, no sound to communicate with her.

Finally she said softly, "Lon—"

"Hmmm?"

"Do you really have to go?"

"Don't you want me to?"

"Yes, well, of course I want you to, but—"

"But what?"

"But I don't." She sat up, flipped her long straight yellow hair over her shoulders, cradled her breasts in her hands for an instant as if they were too heavy or as if they hurt, then stood up and turned toward him. "I feel like I smell bad," she announced, then turned away and disappeared around the room divider behind the bed and into the bathroom. Gamelon heard her depress the reject button on the phonograph as she passed.

There was a soft clap as the record dropped, then the needle touched and the sad strings of the opening bars of Sibelius' *Swan of Tuonela* began to murmur all around him. When Maria was unhappy, which, thank God, was not often, she played that haunted piece. That she had prepared to play it while in the jaunty mood that had preceded their lovemaking bothered him more than the piece itself always bothered him. It was the only composition he knew whose bleakness and hopelessness made him feel he might start sobbing without any reason.

Today, there was a reason.

The English horn began the piteous song of the black swan that circles endlessly in the river surrounding the world of lost souls, plaintively mourning for them in their despair. He rolled to the edge of the bed in his turn, stood up and walked naked to the chair where his jacket hung. He fumbled in the pocket and drew out his father's letter. For the fifth time since it had come in the early morning mail, he read it:

My Dear Son,

It has been said when one recognizes and accepts something as inevitable, when it finally comes to pass it is easier to meet. In my life, I have found this to be as often false as true. I have learned to live with the inevitability of winter's coming, with the rain inherent in summer thunderheads, even with the certainty that love is nothing more than lust codified and condensed into leftovers of respect and habit. But, I have never succeeded in preparing myself to accept cruelty, even when by some stretch of the imagination it is required; or artifice, even when fully justified by the needs of those upon whom it is practiced; or death, even though I believe there is a firm assurance of a life beyond this world.

Forgive me, Son, for rambling on so. Perhaps it's just my way of postponing for you and of shielding myself from the pain of telling you sad news.

It has been almost a year, now, since I've heard from your brother. Even though, as you know, his work often took him away for long periods, he always managed to stay in touch with me regularly, even if it was nothing more than a note or a brief call from wherever in the world he might be at the time.

Gamelon, I can only assume your brother is dead. Inevitable, perhaps, but why just yet, dear God, why just yet? He was pursuing something of extraordinary importance to him and what, exactly, I don't know.

Knowing how close the two of you were up until the last five years or so—opposite sides of the same coin, it's true—I know this thought will hurt you as deeply as it does me to share it.

Please come up to New England to see me if you can while you're in the east receiving your honors. My love to you . . .

For the fifth time that day, Gamelon roared inside at the knowledge that his brother, Racklin, might be dead, as the song of the swan faded and disappeared amidst pianissimo violins.

Maria stood behind him rubbing at her wet hair with a hot pink and lime green beach towel. "Your turn," she mumbled through the flopping terry cloth.

When he made no move, she stopped twirling the long hanks of hair in the towel and peeked out through them at his thick neck, his heavy, sloping farmer's shoulders and broad back, his hard buttocks, his slightly bowed, knot-muscled legs. "What's the matter, Lon? Come on, honey, you'll miss your plane."

Gamelon turned toward her, his warm brown eyes blank, his rugged face haggard. Maria was so taken aback she could do nothing but stare at him for a moment. Then, dropping the towel, she came quickly to him and pressed close: "Lon, Lon, what is it?"

In a voice as flat as his eyes, he said, "My brother is dead." Aggressive, obsessed, bright, wild and winged Racklin was dead.

She pulled his head down and kissed him gently, expecting no response and getting none. "When, Lon?"

"I don't know when. I don't know how or where or why or even if for sure. All my father said was that he had to assume him dead."

"Why didn't you tell me when you got here? I didn't know Racklin, but you've talked about him so much I feel like I did. You knew I'd want to share something like that with you."

"I was going to tell you. On the way to the airport. I didn't want to spoil our morning."

Maria kissed him gently again.

Gamelon stood as he was for a moment letting her roving hands soothe away a little of his hurt and anger, then turned to put his father's letter back. As he slid the envelope into his jacket pocket, his fingertips reminded him of the other letter there. He smiled with one corner of his mouth, and for a second, the warmth and softness that were usually present in his eyes flickered.

Maria, tuned like sympathetic strings to his every subtlety, sensed the tiny changes at once. She stood looking at him with raised eyebrows, hand on one cocked hip. Then, she hooked the gaudy towel off the floor with one big toe, ducked forward under it so that the falling towel covered her head and shoulders and trailed down her back. "How's that for a lady who hated girls' soccer almost as much as 'clean-everything-off-your-plate-including-the-rutabagas?!' " Then, her face and head still hidden under the towel, she began dribbling an imaginary basketball in a tight little circle around the center of the room.

As Gamelon began to smile in spite of himself, she dribbled off, bobbing and weaving, around the end of the room divider, going "thoomp, thoomp" every time her imaginary ball hit the floor, pressed the reject switch on the phonograph in passing, dribbled out around the other end and back. She stopped right in front of him, jogging in place high on the balls of her feet, her bare breasts jouncing up and down, the towel still over her face.

The brawl of Copland's *Rodeo* split the silence as she demanded in the gruffest voice she could muster, "OK, pahdnuh, what else ya got in thet thar coat pocket?"

Gamelon's sorrow for Racklin flushed away for the moment in the river of joy that was his love for this delightful girl. He grabbed her to him, held her so tight she squealed and buried his face against her neck.

A moment later he straightened up, rubbed at his eyes with the backs of huge, red fists and smiled at her. "Like you said, I'm going to miss my plane if I don't get a move on," and he made to go around her.

Maria swung onto his arm. "Oh, no you don't! One little snuffle isn't going to get you off the hook. I'm the sheriff on this hyar county, an' I wanna know what's in that pocket, ya' hear?"

"It's just a letter from Mr. S."

Maria metamorphosed instantly from frontier policewoman to pixie. "Oh, Lon, may I read it? You know I love his letters!"

"You may not!" he said indignantly; it was his turn to play-act. "It's addressed to me, not you! I'm saving it to read on the plane."

He dodged as she swung open-handed at his bare butt, danced around her and made it successfully into the bathroom.

Maria sat close to him in the cab, her arm linked through his. She was as quietly elegant dressed as she had been boisterously capricious naked thirty minutes before. He never could figure out how she could make the transition so quickly. Pale, pale blue cowl-neck knitted dress with a sleeveless dark blue vest, boots and beret. The long string of gold beads he had given her was knotted between her breasts—a chastity belt, of sorts, she seemed to imply by the knot, that she would wear until he returned.

Gamelon sighed; this was as good a time as any if he could find a way.

A billboard flashed past: beside a twelve-foot-high man's face crammed with too many teeth and wearing a ten-gallon hat, "Sho nuf, Padnuh, you'll buy your next used car from a man named Wally."

He had it.

Without turning toward her, he asked in a casual tone, "Would you buy a used car from a man named Gamelon?"

She looked up at him with the same questioning glance that had been on her face when she first suspected Mr. S.'s letter in his pocket. Then, her face broke into a wide smile, then an even wider laugh dispelled his "elegant" view of her altogether and knocked some of the wind out of his self-confidence at the same time.

"I don't know why the hell not!"

He collected himself, then asked just as casually as before, "Well, would you marry a man named Gamelon?"

She dropped her head and appeared to consider, and began to mutter to herself, "Maria Waugh . . . Maria Waugh." Then she raised her head suddenly, stared straight ahead and said in a voice so loud the taxi driver glanced in his mirror to check conditions in the rear seat, "Maria Waugh! You would have me give up a magnificent name like Maria Rundqvist and go through the rest of my life as Maria Waugh?!"

He was attempting to frame a bluff reply when she went on severely and with a wagging finger, "And me marrying a redhead? I don't know about that. I'd be afraid to have children. Mixing genes with you, I'd probably give birth to the world's first case of incurable sunburn! Now, if you could clone a couple of you's and one or two me's like you do with your roses, I might consider."

"You know I don't 'clone' roses. Leave that to the orchid growers. My infrequent days in the lab are strictly confined to attempts to modify the DNA structure of the rose cell to enable it to do all sorts of things it can't do now like picking up certain chemicals from the soil so it will be more resistant to disease." He went on with his own brand of mock severity, "What we want here anyway are new varieties, not copies of the old ones.

The tried and true methods are the only way to get them. Hybridizing in horticulture and—" he leaned close to her ear and whispered passionately, "—screwing—" then in a normal voice, "in humans." He laughed. "Anyway, what would the world want with another copper-maned horticultural geneticist and another skinny, emotionally unstable, honey-blonde graphics designer?!"

"You hair's only 'copper,' " and she drew the word out dramatically, "when it's wet. All of it, I might add—" and it was her turn to whisper, "—right down to the little ringlets around that commodious—"

He stopped her mouth with a kiss.

She never did actually say yes, but, as the cab swung off the freeway and into the thrust and screech of Aviation Boulevard and the last few miles to Los Angeles International, she curled close to him again while the two of them laughed and devised imaginary children—everything from a willowy, strawberry-blond faggot with an out-sized chest who was the world's greatest ocarina virtuoso, to a hulking, hairy, mad lady scientist who devoted her life to creating gene mutations in peacocks just to catch the changes in color.

His father's assumptions about Racklin were the farthest thing from his mind.

In the waiting area, they were met by two delegations of one.

The uninvited delegation was Sam Coleman. Tall, lean, bronzed, a lawyer and the perennial president of the San Marino Rose Society, "Mr. Rose" of Southern California was there to pound him on the back, to congratulate him on his pending honors from the All-America Rose Selections for his new varieties "of superior quality and marked distinction," and to let him know without the slightest trace of courtroom diplomacy just how grateful he should be for his, Coleman's, support in his work.

Beyond a perfunctory nod, Coleman did not recognize Maria. He was heading off into a one-man dissertation on his own views of rose horticulture when Gamelon interrupted him to introduce her.

It was her turn to be perfunctory.

Coleman was about to pick up where he left off, but Gamelon said, "Sam, I have something here I think you'll appreciate. Jorge—" He beckoned to a small swarthy man in tan work clothes who stood quietly a few feet away.

Jorge Gonzales, the invited delegation, was Gamelon's "dirt man" and his friend. It was Jorge who tenderly nurtured the plants that were the result of Gamelon's imagination, ability and patience. He came forward shyly, but with a huge smile for Maria. She had joked with him in the flower fields, admired his work in the greenhouses, and he had come to love her in his own way. Maria stepped out to meet him, and to his embarrassment, flung an arm around his neck. She bussed him warmly on the cheek and asked about his children and his wife, whose name was Maria, too.

Gamelon's eyes were shining as he said to Jorge, "One *did* come in today!"

"Of course, *Señor* Lon. Why else would I be here? You told me not to come unless one did." Jorge's words were tinged with a bit of accent and a hint of mystery. He handed the long, thin object he was carrying wrapped in heavy waxed paper to Gamelon deferentially.

Gamelon took it and motioned those in his little group to silence. He drew himself up and looked around, his smile so broad, his face so radiant that for a moment Maria was jealous that anything else could make him so happy.

She forgot the feeling when he turned the smile on her and said, "Remember, Maria, what I said about the old tried and true methods. They always produce the most exciting results because those results are always completely new. I think Jorge and I have produced something with those methods this time that's beyond anything either of us could have imagined, and we weren't even trying for it."

Coleman, the true rose fanatic, anticipating the revelation of a new variety, was almost panting with expectation. "Whatever it is, Lonnie, I've got to have it! If it's new, I've got to have it!"

"We're two years of grafting, field trials and all the rest away from that, Sam," Gamelon said without taking his gaze or his smile from Maria. "For you," he said, and handed the slender package to her.

She took it and painstakingly peeled the paper back to reveal one perfect rose.

Coleman gasped.

"Lon," Maria said in an awed voice, "It's—it's blue!"

On a long, straight, black-green stem, its foliage the color of crushed mint, the high-crowned, half-opened blossom was the flawless reproduction of the cloudless sky on a deep summer afternoon.

Very softly Gamelon said, "For you, Maria, the world's first blue rose, the 'Maria—Waugh.' " Then, he took the exquisite flower from her and handed it back to Jorge who rewrapped it almost reverently. "I'm sorry," he said, "but the plant patent hasn't been applied for yet and we don't dare let it out of our hands."

Maria watched longingly as the rose disappeared again inside its paper covering, then she turned to Gamelon and said so the others could not hear, "Lon, suddenly the possibility of a case of incurable sunburn doesn't bother me in the least. The sooner we get to it, the better." She kissed him lightly on the cheek, frivolous again. "But for now, you'll have to excuse me. You know how I am when I get excited." She started off around a nearby bank of baggage lockers and in the general direction of a sign reading "Women-Damas" high on the wall beyond them.

Just as she was about to disappear from sight behind the lockers, she shot Gamelon an impish look over her shoulder, did one quick, almost imperceptible dribble, and was gone.

Coleman was suddenly all hail-fellow with just a sliver of menace behind his parting smile. "You will let me see more of that—'Maria Waugh'—when you get back, won't you Lonnie boy?"

Gamelon was careful not to commit himself. He returned Coleman's farewell wave, then turned to Jorge. "Aren't you going, too?"

"I thought the *Señorita* might like to ride home with me instead of taking a cab. It's only a little way off the freeway for me." Gamelon put his arm around his small friend's shoulder and said, simply. "Thanks." Then, as Maria had not yet reappeared, Gamelon suggested they go across the waiting area and sit down and be comfortable. It was still a good twenty minutes before his flight was due to be called.

They crossed the broad empty space together to where the brightly colored molded plastic seats were bolted in rows to the floor. Jorge sat down gingerly and held the waxed paper package before him as though it were a reliquary containing a fragment of the True Cross.

Gamelon sat next to him, slid down, kicked out his legs, locked his hands behind his head and did something he did only when he was very relaxed and happy, a trick he had taught himself as a boy: he put his eyes slightly out of focus. This gave everything in his line of sight a certain softness and he could keep it that way as long as he did not blink. He sat, waiting for Maria, the hard lines of the baggage lockers and the "Women-Damas" sign blurred to a pleasant inconsistency, and let his thoughts drift back to what she had said earlier that day about her idea of a perfect morning . . .

". . . brightness, sunlight all around, a baby's breath of a breeze, the sound of water trickling in a fountain, rich, black coffee, love nearby—but not right in your pocket—and Brahm's *Liebeslieder Waltzes* playing in the background . . ."

Maria came slowly around the end of the lockers into his furry vision, her head down, puffing lightly at the back of her beret with one hand. Then, just as she was beginning to drop her hand and raise her eyes to look for him, she seemed to sidestep as though blown off balance by an unexpected gust. His heart was just beginning to smilingly tell him she was treating him to one last dribble when his brain broke in to communicate that she was not recovering from the movement.

Gamelon's legs came under him of their own free will as his eyes came unwillingly and cruelly back into focus.

The bank of lockers seemed to heave a great sigh, then swell, then begin to come apart in a huge, silent, slow-motion eruption of tearing gray metal chunks and flying suitcases, bursting as they came and ejaculating underwear and shaving cream cans. A locker door ripped from its hinges, laid straight out, flew towards Maria's rising head, severed it from her shoulders, upended, and threw it, blood flinging from the ripped throat, against a concrete pillar. It ricocheted back into the oncoming mass of screeching debris tearing outward, outward, reaching for destruction on a million trajectories within the terminal.

Gamelon was flung backwards over his bright plastic chair by the blast just as his brain began to refuse the horror his eyes had no choice of seeing. His head smashed into the terrazo floor giving him into the merciful hands of temporary oblivion.

He sat cross-legged poking aimlessly at the litter around him with one finger. He turned up a bent pair of eyeglasses with one lens still intact. He put them on and sat quite still for a moment enjoying the magnified view of the textured back of the plastic chair through one open eye. He wondered casually what smelled so bad and looked down to discover he was sitting in his own excrement. It made no more impression than the distorted plastic.

A trembling hand began to stroke the nape of his neck. Jorge murmured in his ear, "*Señor, Señor* Lon, come on now, we're going home."

Gamelon turned dumb eyes toward his friend. He seemed to have lost something, but he could not remember what.

He noticed the blood seeping through the fingers of Jorge's left hand. That hand still held the treasured blue rose, its wrapping intact, but the little man had gripped so hard in his terror, the thorns at the base of the stem had pierced his palm through the layer of wet cotton and the outer paper.

Seeing the rose, he began to remember what he had lost. As Jorge helped him to his feet, the black swan began its mournful song again.

La Playa, California
August 9, 1985

David, My Boy,

I am sincerely sorry for having been so long in writing again in the matter of Lon Waugh. You doubtless saw in the gossip column of the village weekly that I was in the east for the world premiere of my third string quartet, the one commissioned by the Helen

Sprague Coolidge Foundation. I must say the young fellows who make up the Guarnari Quartet did it justice and a half, but I find I don't like the work myself as much in reality as I did in my head. I may revise it.

But, all this is certainly not to our point.

Going back to late spring: Maria's death seemed so brutal, so tragic, so utterly senseless to me. You may recall the public was being subjected to a rash of "airport bombings" at the time, the responsibility for them being claimed by any number of poor, desperate people either alone or in misguided little psuedo-political groups. The perpetrator of the crime that killed Maria wasn't found, which made her death even more senseless.

I didn't learn about it for several weeks. I had no reason for concern at the time; as I intimated in my last letter, Gamelon's letters and visits were sporadic. Sometimes months might elapse between them. When I finally did hear of her death for the first time, it wasn't from Lon himself . . .

JULY 2, 1984

La Playa

The small, swarthy man in tan work clothes stood well back from the door, one hand shading his eyes from the bright, mid-afternoon sun. He peered under it at Freddie and said in a low, respectful voice, "*Disculpa me, Señor. You are Señor* Sev—, Sev—"

"Sevrinsky, yes. What can I do for you?"

"Nothing for me, *Señor,* but perhaps for *Señor* Lon you can do something."

"*Señor* Lon—ah, Lon Waugh! What is it he wants?"

"He does not know, *Señor.*"

"He doesn't know?"

"No, *Señor,* he does not know what he wants and he does not know that I have come here to ask you to try to help him find it."

Thoroughly confused, Freddie stopped the conversation, invited Jorge into the house, found out who he was, and asked him simply why he was there.

"Because somebody's got to try to help *Señor* Lon. I tried and I can't seem to do it. I don't know who else can help. Then I remember your letters and how *Señor* Lon and *Señorita* Maria, when one comes, they laugh over it sometimes, sometimes they sit for hours speaking very seriously about what you say, then they laugh. I figure you're his friend like I am, *Señor,* so I go to his desk and I find one of the letters with the address on it and I get in the truck and drive down here to ask you to help."

Freddie learned of Maria's death then and sat stunned as Jorge went on.

"*Señor* Lon, he don't laugh anymore. He don't do much of anything anymore but walk in the rose fields pickin' at this, pickin' at that. One day I even find him sittin' in the middle of a row of bushes crying by himself. Can we help him, *Señor* Sev—, Sev—"

"Sevrinsky," Freddie whispered.

La Playa, California
August 11, 1984

Dear David,

You have Miss Altenbäumer to thank for that last letter. Never hire an elderly German spinster as a part-time secretary. The efficiency may well be the death of you! I had to stop before completing my last note, so stuck it in the envelope I'd already addressed to you until I could get back to it. In swept Fräulein Altenbäumer and, assuming as she always does that I am absent minded, sealed it, stamped it and mailed it dead in the middle of a paragraph. I apologize.

I believe I had just told you about Jorge's visit when I stopped the last time. I promised him I would drive up to the nursery in Wasco, near Bakersfield, to see Gamelon as soon as I could. Unfortunately, that couldn't be until early the following week after the Fourth of July weekend. As it turned out, though, I never went.

I'd set the 9th aside for the trip. On the morning of the 6th—I remember quite well as I was jotting the final bars of that quartet for the Coolidge Foundation—the phone in my study rang. It was Jorge, who managed to explain in his own inimitable way that Gamelon had gone away, that he, Jorge, did not want *Señor* Sev—, Sev— to come all that way to see nobody but himself and to *disculpa me* himself many times for causing *Señor* Sev—, Sev— any troubles.

I didn't know where Lon had gone or why. I didn't find out until some two weeks later when he wrote to tell me what he had found on his journey and how it troubled him. I have that letter somewhere, but I can't put my hands on it right now for the life of me. I shall sic Fräulein Altenbäumer on the problem when she comes in next Tuesday and drop you a photocopy when she finds it—and she will!

Best regards,
J. F. S.

JULY 5, 1984

Wasco, California

In the heavy, deeply scented silence of the hybridizing house, Gamelon sat alone, his head bent over the cross list. Around him, parent plants in smock white pots, buds tight and defiant, waited stoically for his mating decisions. Stretching away into the soft light at the far end of the greenhouse, those that had already undergone his gentle surgery, tagged, small brown bags hiding the ripening secrets within their swelling hips, waited, waited. In the soil and sand-filled seedling benches behind him, the results of earlier experiments sprouted or leafed or bloomed in delineated groups, each group the different children of the same parents, some disappointing, some showing great promise. Beside a bright orange miniature with surprising rust-colored edges grew a white, the sickly shade of a fish's underside, on a stem too weak to support the blossom, and beside it a vigorous, bright green bush that did not bloom at all. A single insect tunneled through the quiet. There should be no pollen carriers in a hybridizing house, but the spray can of insecticide at Gamelon's elbow went untouched.

For the twentieth time, Gamelon read "7532-'Winterset' X 'Starburst' (28)" and strove to recall what he had been trying for when he had pollinated the hearty little white with the big blousy yellow. What had he wanted? A yellow that opened more slowly? More disease resistance in a bigger white? Longer stemmed yellows with a more compact blossom? What? He never performed a cross just for the hell of it, never without something specific in mind. And in what part of which seedling bench had Jorge planted the twenty-eight seeds? He could not remember and could not motivate himself to check all the squares in the benches' checkerboards until he found the proper identifying tag.

He was reluctant to become aware of the disturbing shuffling sound at his elbow. He raised his head wearily and glanced out the corner of his eye to see Jorge standing near him, a bit pale beneath the warm brown of his skin, his eyes shifting, twisting nervous hands. It took a moment for the realization to grow in him that all was not well with his friend. When it finally did, he shivered off his desultory attempts at recollection, rose, went to Jorge and put his hands on his shoulders. He stooped slightly, looked into Jorge's eyes and asked, "What is it?"

The little man looked at the trodden earth floor and shook his head.

"Come on, what is it? Is something wrong with your wife—one of the children?"

"No, *Señor, estan bien*—as always."

"Well, what's bothering you?"

Jorge took a deep breath, straightened, then drooped again, put his hands over his eyes and murmured, "*Ay, me engañaran los oyos.*"

"Come on, what trick did your eyes play on you?"

Jorge let his hands fall, looked searchingly at Gamelon, then asked, "*Señorita* Maria, she is dead, is she not, *Señor*?"

Gamelon took his hands from the small man's shoulders and turned away to lean on his arms on the desk. At last, in the mouth of another, the truth of the fact overwhelmed him just as the refusal to accept it had nearly drowned him for the last six weeks. Now at last he lowered his head and whispered his acceptance of it as much to the flowered, perfumed stillness as to Jorge, "Yes, Jorge, *Señorita* Maria is dead."

For a long moment, there was only the fragrance of the flowers and the sunlight filtered through the white-washed greenhouse roof between them, then Jorge said in a low voice, "Then it is all right, *Señor* Lon. Everything is all right."

"Yes, my friend, it will be now."

"I am happy I came to you, *Señor*. It is true. My eyes played a trick on me. I did not see *Señorita* Maria at the airport after all."

It was too cruel. Now, after all the dimensionless weeks when he had finally accepted her death, it was too cruel. "You did not see—what did you say?"

"At the airport. I had to go there with the special shipment of cuttings for the growers in Conn—, Conn— you know, *Señor*."

"Connecticut, yes."

"I left the box in the airplane freight and came back outside to go to my truck when a taxi passed me."

"And?"

"There was a lady inside. That was when my eyes played the trick on me. I thought it was *Señorita* Maria."

It was too cruel. He turned slowly toward Jorge and asked, "What made you think it was—my Maria?"

Jorge shrugged slim shoulders and replied, "As far as my trick-playing eyes could tell, it was her. Why else would I think it?"

"Did you—did you see her close up?"

"Of course, *Señor*."

"Well?"

"I ran behind the taxi until it stopped and the lady got out. She was in a big hurry. She took her baggage from the driver and ran inside. I ran, too. We both ran all the way. She came to one of the places where one gets on the plane and stuck out her—*boleto* for the man to see. He just nodded to her and she went past and down toward where the plane was. I could see it through the big window. The man, he just goes on talking to the—the—thing in his hand, the *microfono*, about how it is the last time they will call the plane—"

"Did—the woman—see you?"

"*Si*—a funny thing, *Señor*. Right at the end of the tube that slides out to the plane, she turned real quick and, *Señor* Lon, I swear by the Holy Mother herself, she looked right at me. My heart jumped because I was sure she would know me. But she didn't know me."

Oh, God, couldn't it be ended? But he could not stop himself from asking. "Was it Maria, Jorge?"

"My eyes told me it was, but that could not be, could it? You said it out loud yourself, *Señor*. *Señorita* Maria was—killed in that place six weeks ago."

It was over. It had to be over. "Yes, Jorge, you must have seen someone who looked a lot like her. My Maria is dead."

Morning after morning he had fought awakening and once awake had cursed the coming hours of nothingness underlined by recollections of Maria all over a dull, throbbing ground of pain. Night after night he had begged for sleep to come so that he could forget he had nothing to remember and had fought it at the same time so there would be no slide show of her terrible death flickering throughout his dreams. It was too cruel to have even the smallest hope struck alight on the heel of his life.

And yet, could it have been *his* eyes all those weeks before, first blurred with happiness then flooded with horror, that had played tricks on him instead of Jorge's today? He did not want to ask. He tried not to ask, but he could not help himself. "Did the man say into the *microfono* where the plane was going, Jorge?"

"*Si.* First it would fly to Phoenix, then to a place called St. George—is that like San Jorge, *Señor*, the saint who killed the dragon—then up one more time to Salt Lake City."

The light coming through the hybridizing house roof was just barely that, but Gamelon made no move to switch on the lamp on the desk. He sat alone as Jorge had left him two hours before, staring at nothing.

At first he had tried to convince himself that he believed what he had told Jorge: " . . . must have seen someone who looked a lot like her. My Maria is dead . . ." He had not been successful, and so he tried disengaging his mind completely for a while to let it rest or seek, undirected, some new footpath to the tomorrows, empty though they might be, but dawning nonetheless. Again, he had been unsuccessful. Questions surrounding Maria's death insisted on rising through his attempts at solitude like sluggish bubbles, one by one, from the depths of his wounded memory. At last, there were too many floating exposed on the surface for him to discount them any longer, and he cursed out loud—himself as much as the persisting questions. How could he call himself a scientist if he assumed anything based only on what he *thought* his eyes had seen in a single flashing instant?! The only excuse could be that until now considering anything except the gruesome finality of Maria's dying would have seemed an exercise in futility, could not have changed anything.

In his disgust with himself and the sudden seeming urgency to corral the thoughts that followed, he did something he would have fired any one of his small staff instantly for doing: he scribbled those thoughts across the X's and variety names and numbers on the open page of the precious crossing records:

Airport. My eyes blurred. Stress. Horror of explosion.

I suffer concussion. Hospital in shock almost a week.

I so "sick" myself, never return to her apt., never ask any quests. No knowledge of funeral. Not like me.

Another woman in blue with beret?

Maria only hurt? Amnesia?

Where did plane go?

What Maria say about where she was born? "Where is Nesset? Well, it almost isn't, but if pressed, I'd say it was north of St. George, south of nowhere, off the beaten track and almost in the desert. Some dinky airline has a flight from here to Salt Lake City with a pit stop in St. George—but Lon, honey, if we ever decide to go there—Lord knows why we ever would—but if we do, let's drive. That way we could camp out one night in the desert on the way—in Vegas . . ."

The pencil slipped from his thick blunt fingers as his powerful frame sagged forward against the desk.

". . . we could camp out in the desert—in Vegas . . ."

Maria, oh, Maria. How I loved you. How I love you.

Slowly he straightened, turned on the desk lamp and almost unconsciously began to erase his scribbling as carefully as he could from the crossing record page. Then, he dug a chewed ball point and a yellow legal pad out of the desk drawer and began writing quickly in his all but indecipherable scrawl:

7/5/84 7PM

Jorge,

I'm going away for a few days, maybe a week. Pls. take care of everything. Don't water that field planting of the red, 6792. I want to check the drought resistance. Let the front office know I'm going—I don't know exactly where, so there's nothing more to tell anyone if they ask. I'll call in.

Don't worry about me. It's all right now.

Lon Waugh

He could live now without Maria, but if there was the merest chance his eyes had played the trick, not Jorge's . . . His love for her was so boundless, so endless not even he would be able to contain it, much less suppress it or transfer it if the possibility still existed of sharing it with her whatever the circumstances. He could live without her, but not without the certain knowledge that he was without her.

JULY 26, 1984

La Playa

Freddie coaxed the sheaf of papers out of the big manila envelope. Paperclipped to the edge of the top one was a note in David Sorensen's big, painful, uphill printing:

7/24/84

Mr. S.,

Attached: copies of my report and the coroner's.

Don't know you'll want to read it all, but am providing for information. Department records. Pls. return.

In essence: death by drowning—in salt water. Fingerprints on file Sacramento with DMV not only match, they *are* those of one Maria Rundqvist, deceased May 18th. Further check underway in other states, with U.S. Gvmn't, etc. I see what you meant about understanding.

Respectfully,
D. Sorensen, Deputy

JULY 27, 1949

Washington, D.C.

"Who's getting it tonight?"

"Nobody much tonight, but wait 'til later tomorrow or early the next morning."

For several minutes, the Weather Service meteorologist, one coming on, one going off, stood together silently studying the synoptic weather patterns on the charts before them that together covered the area of the world from mid-Pacific to mid-Atlantic and from Alaska to northern Mexico.

The relief grunted, then said, "I see what you mean." He leaned down over the surface chart and tapped a large "L" in the Gulf of Alaska, the symbol for a cyclonic storm with its attendant frontal systems. Then he looked at the upper level chart and studied the trend of the contours which indicated warm, moist, unstable air swirling up from the south southwest guided inexorably by summer's high-riding subtropical jet stream. "I see what you mean," he mumbled again as he let his finger trail across the surface chart until it stopped to circumscribe an area of southern Nevada, northwestern Arizona and southwestern Utah.

"Uh-huh," his companion muttered. "That's what I figure, too. Typical for this time of year."

Sometime tomorrow night or early the next day, the area would be hit with possibly devastating electrical storms as the weather systems moved through the area. There would be torrential rains, flash floods, perhaps, in the canyons. Livestock, summer hay and canning crops, orchards could be severely damaged, even lives lost.

The man going off duty tightened his tie and slung his jacket over his shoulder as he said, "Why don't we take the wives and go out there sometime? I've always wanted to see Bryce and Zion and I hear the fishing's pretty good on parts of the Virgin River."

"If we do, it sure as hell won't be this time of year!"

"No, in June maybe. That looks like the best time out there, all things considered."

"Yeh, OK, we'll talk about it—anything I have to take care of you didn't get to?"

"Not that I can think of. All the advisories are out. The Meteorologist in Charge for the Yucca Flats Project was in. He got all our latest."

"Yeh? Another Big Bang out there soon?"

"Tomorrow. He flew out tonight."

"First I heard about it. I can remember when those tests were hot stuff."

" 'Night."

" 'Night."

The new duty meteorologist remained where he was, his finger still lazily circling the area of the coming storms. Beautiful country, he had heard, dramatic even, but hemmed into nowhere by deserts and mountains, really. What with the often violent summer heat thunderstorms and the frequent frontal passages in winter, he did not think he would really want to live there. As always, his eyes wandered eastward across the chart and hovered longingly around Key West, Cuba and the string of tiny sub-tropical dots bowing away into the Caribbean.

AUGUST 8, 1952

Near Nesset, Utah

Karl Rundqvist closed the bedroom door softly and crossed the big kitchen to where his wife, Pia, stood staring out the window at the night and the storm. As he came up behind her and put an arm around her shoulder, an axe of lightning cracked the night. For a long instant, the trees writhed and the rain twisted in ghoulish, undersea light, then all was a dark void again with nothing but the tortured groanings of the storm to fill it. They stood silently side by side until the thunder snarled at last.

"That one must of come down over around Olsen's," Karl said.

Pia, deeply stranded in her own thoughts, did not hear him, and said, "It's almost as bad, maybe even worse this year than the summer I was carrying her," then lapsed into silence again.

Karl left her that way for a moment or two, then gently took her hands away from the curtains. He turned her into the room away from the window and the storm and walked her to a chair by the scarred but dignified table-of-all-work at the center of the kitchen. He sat on the edge of the table and bent his head to kiss her cheek. "We've got to talk about it," he said firmly.

His wife made no reply; instead she raised her hands to cover her eyes and sobbed once deeply.

"We've got to get in touch with Doc Remson and get him out here to look at her!"

Pia dropped her hands and looked straight at him. "No! No, there's nothing he can do. You can't call anyway, the lines are down. The lines are always down this time of summer."

"I'll go for him in the truck."

"No! Oh, please, Karl, don't leave us alone here! A tree could fall across the road and you mightn't get back. I don't want to stay alone with her—please."

"Then we talk about it."

Pia dried her eyes with the tips of her fingers, folded her hands in her lap and looking past her husband said with as much conviction as she could muster, "There's nothing wrong with Maria."

"Pia, she's been asleep for over a day! Now, something's got to be wrong! What is it, something you've seen before and don't want to tell me about? Pia, now answer me."

Still gazing beyond him, she began nodding her head and speaking as though to convince herself, "I was a nurse, and there is nothing wrong with her. She has no fever. As near as I can tell her pulse is normal for a sleeping child. She smiles in her sleep when I call to her. There's nothing wrong with her except—she won't wake up."

"That could be some kind of sleeping sickness, now couldn't it, Pia? Like you say, you were a nurse."

"No. The pulse and the breathing, the skin color would all be different, and there'd be wasting."

Karl stood up and circled the big table, running his fingers through his thick blond hair. He came back to stand over his wife and asked, "What is it again she said when she went for her nap Tuesday?"

"She just said, 'I'm lonely, Mommie, almost all the time.' It is lonely here, Karl, with nothing until you get down to Olsen's place the one way and Nesset ten miles in the other direction. *I* get lonely when you're out in the fields. Think how it is for the child. She's forever making up imaginary friends to talk to and play with, and sometimes I don't think that's real healthy."

"All little children make up friends." Karl hiked at his trousers. "I don't care. When the storm lets up some, I'm going after Doc Remson."

With sudden unexpected firmness, Pia said, "You can't, Karl. I won't allow it!"

"You won't allow it?! You won't let me try to get what help there might be for my own daughter?!"

"I—I don't want anybody to see her."

"In God's name, why not?!"

"You can't bring anyone!" Pia flung out of the chair and across the room, hurling her words at her husband through the thin veil of control that still hid her rising hysteria. "You can't! You won't want to! You haven't seen yet! It was dark when you went in there tonight and she's under the covers. It's like nothing I've ever seen, like nothing anybody's ever seen. It's like—it's like she's—she's spreading out." Pia giggled chokingly. "Flattening and spreading out like thick pancake batter on a griddle that's not hot enough." Then, her voice constricted a childlike treble screech, she cried, "Your daughter's turning into something horrible! You can't bring anybody! Ever!" and she fell to the kitchen floor sobbing uncontrollably.

MARCH 18, 1956

Kayenta, Arizona

The constant bleating of the sheep down in the corral south of the hogan annoyed her. The lambing would begin tomorrow or the next day or the day after that and the good ewes were still in with the poor ones and the wethers.

Good, plump ewes with much milk would accept their lambs willingly, but still bore watching, Roberto had always said, and he had lost fewer lambs than most. Poor ewes with shriveled udders would drop their lambs and walk away. The orphans had to be saved and cared for if it was possible. The wethers, the young castrated males, must be cut out and penned to themselves or put out to graze until the lambing was done lest they trouble the ewes in labor or trample the newborns.

Old Bead Woman could not afford to lose lambs to restless wethers or ewes to some little complication in bearing that an alert eye and a knowing hand could set right. Old Bead Woman was too poor.

Long Silence, the dumb son of her sister, might come to help if the lambing of his own flock was done. It should be, it would be if he had let the rams in early in *Gah'ji*, the Parting-of-the-Seasons, when the rams were supposed to go among the ewes.

Old Bead Woman snorted. Slim Boy, her only daughter's son, had dallied on the range that past fall. He had not brought her meagre flock to Mucho

Jim's rams until early in November, *Nlchi' tso'si*, the Time of Slender Winds, when it was almost too late, when the antelope breed, not the sheep.

She snorted again. The rams' service had cost her two wethers and a set of turquoise earstrings and still, because of Slim Boy's lack of attention to the seasons and the ewes' skittishness, a third of them were slender and spry now instead of heavy and sedate. All the more reason she could not afford to lose any sheep this year.

The mounting sun cleared the top of Red Mesa and shone full on Old Bead Woman's long seamed face. She leaned back against the rough log wall of the hogan and thought about the earstrings. She still rued having had to part with even that small portion of her precious little hoard of turquoise. Some said she was rich because of it. She always maintained that she was not, even when she went visiting as she was going to do that morning and wore all the strands like a sky blue breastplate.

She was poor, poor.

She had the grazing rights to her land, it was true, and her small flock and her turquoise, but, ah, she had but one daughter who had no daughters, only sons. What would become of the grazing rights, the beads, the sheep when she was gone?

If only her daughter had come back to her mother's land when she had married and brought her husband to work some of it and tend the sheep as it had always been done since the Holy People came up into the Fourth World! But no, Only Daughter's Husband had gone to the war and had learned to write with machines and now made money doing it in Gallup and would not come to tend sheep and plant corn.

At least, Only Daughter and her husband had given her Slim Boy without her having had to ask for him. She had only just buried her husband, Roberto, after he died of the watery chest the winter before when they appeared with the skinny, big-eyed child, the youngest of their five.

He had ridden all the way from Gallup in the back of the truck and was shaking with the cold in spite of having been buried in sheep skins all the way. Even inside the hogan beside the fire, he had continued to shiver and stare in silence.

Old Bead Woman had accepted him calmly. He was her due. It was the way of the Navajo. As the head of the family, it was only right that she should have someone to gather her firewood, carry her water and tend her sheep. Her well-being would be Slim Boy's responsibility as long as she lived.

It was her due.

It had not crossed Old Bead Woman's mind then and it did not now to wonder how heartsick, how lonely, how lost the small boy might feel so many miles from his family, so far away from other children. He was hers to serve her. All she must do in return was feed him and see that he had clothes and shoes to wear.

But now, with the lambing so close, with rails to put back up on the corral to the southwest of the hogan, the wethers to cut out from the ewes and the poor ewes to separate from the good, what use was Slim Boy to her if all he would do was sleep?

The mission bus had once belonged to the Army and had once been a dull gray green. Once it had run strongly, if loudly, and idled smoothly. Now, its insides were on the verge of disemboweling themselves and its outside had been blasted to a uniform rust. Years of plodding back and forth between the mission hospital and Kayenta twice a week or more through the burning summers, the freezing winters and the sand that flew with every wind had put it beyond redemption long before its time. And now, with only the third son of Long Silence's second daughter, who did not care much one way or the other whether it lived or died, to care for it, it did not have much longer to go.

Long Silence's grandson began calculating as soon as the bus started down the long hill outside Kayenta. He was running empty except for his great grandmother's sister, Old Bead Woman, who seemed to know without knowing just what days he would come into the town so she could cadge her rides both ways. He wondered again if she was a witch.

He would not have to stand up on the worn out mechanical brakes until the big clump of ocotillo almost at the bottom of the hill if he was going to stop in time to let her off where the path to her hogan meandered off across the range.

The ocotillo came, the brakes went on with a rotating scream and half a mile farther down the narrow road the bus finally wobbled to a stop and stood gasping and heaving on the rock strewn shoulder. Its shivering and quaking was so bad Old Bead Woman had to clasp her woven bag and the blanket around her shoulders in one hand and use the other to steady herself on the seat backs so she could make her way forward without falling.

As she climbed down, she shouted over the clanking of the engine to the great grandson of her sister, "Tell your grandfather to come and help with the sheep if he can. Don't forget."

The young man only nodded slowly, his eyes still on the road ahead.

The bus door closed and with a gnashing of gears, it ground its way back onto the road and north again in the direction of Monument Valley and the mission hospital.

Old Bead Woman waited until the dust of its departure had blown by her in the light, late afternoon wind, then crossed the high crowned road.

As she began to plod slowly along the faint path across the desert range land toward her hogan, she grumbled to herself, head down. She had grumbled to herself all the way out on the bus. She had grumbled while she squatted in the shade of the post office waiting for the bus to be ready to go. She had been grumbling ever since she left Stick Leg's hogan two hours before.

He had been wild when he was young, but also the best there was at breaking horses. Then one day he had yanked the mouth of one as wild as he too hard and it fell on him and crushed his knee. The knee did not heal right and ever since his left leg had had to be swung in wide circles when he walked or stuck straight out in front of him when he sat on the ground, as he was when Old Bead Woman approached his hogan on the edge of the town.

Stick Leg and Old Bead Woman had had little to do with each other. He thought her to be mean and tight-fisted in a world where supposedly nobody owned anything. She had her suspicions about the Godgivenness of his abilities and had often thought he took to diagnosing ills and prescribing cures for others too suddenly after he learned he could not break horses anymore, as a lazy way of helping to provide for himself and his family. She snorted when she thought of the size of that family: a leg was not all that had been stiff through the years and three wives!

But, she had sung the few chants she knew over Slim Boy without any result and she had not been able to wake him to take any of the medicines she had brewed. She needed Stick Leg's help for what it was worth. Whatever it was worth, it was too much, she muttered to herself.

In spite of all this, she approached him as befitted his reputation, real or fake, as a hand trembler. She knew exactly how to do it. She had learned much from her own father who had been one of the great singers of his time.

She presented her gifts in precisely the right manner and order; the prayer stick, the unscraped ash bread—which should have been gift enough to bind his services she thought to herself—the pollen, the bits of sparkling rock and, grudgingly, because it was so dear, the tobacco in a pouch made from the skin of a buck that had never been wounded.

Stick Leg did not take his eyes from her as she presented her gifts. It was almost as if he wanted her to offer something wrong or to give it in the wrong order. If she had, the powers would have been put out of balance and he could have either refused outright to help her or pleaded "the press of other business."

But, no matter how closely he watched, he was not able to detect the slightest flaw in her presentation. After a long moment and without a word, he rose and walked into the hogan with his queer gait. He did not invite her to follow, but from where she was seated outside, she could see him take his place on the floor facing the doorway and the east.

He stretched his hands out slowly and placed them on his knees and let his head drop forward. He sat that way, completely motionless, for what seemed hours, then suddenly, his whole body convulsed violently, his head snapped back and waves of trembling seemed to pass through him from his feet to his head. They soon passed and his left arm went up, its hand shaking as though with palsy. He was rigid except for the palpitating hand. Its quivering kept up for several moments until, just as before, his body convulsed and he fell over on his right side.

Old Bead Woman knew to do nothing. She stayed as she was, squatting before the hogan's entrance, the warm spring sun beating down on her.

Again it seemed as though hours passed. Then Stick Leg stirred on the hogan's pounded earth floor, groaned softly as he pulled himself to his feet and came back outside, shielding his eyes from the light with one hand. Again he took his seat with his back against the rough hogan wall, his body in the shade, his maimed leg ramrodding into the sunlight.

Old Bead Woman waited.

At last Stick Leg said in a thin, grating voice, "He has walked where the lightning struck. He is now as one struck by lightning. He has disturbed the power of that place. Until the balance is restored, he will sleep.

"Very few singers know the proper chants. They are very long and very difficult and not much sung now. I can think of only one who could perform them right. He is very old if even he is still alive. The last I heard, he was living with his granddaughter near Window Rock." And Stick Leg fell silent.

Now Old Bead Woman knew there was nothing more to wait for. She rose, gathered her blanket around her shoulders, turned her back on Stick Leg and started off toward the town proper and the post office, muttering under her breath as she went.

Still grumbling, her eyes on the path watching for rattlers and stones, Old Bead Woman trudged toward her hogan. At her back, the setting sun drenched the walls of Red Mesa with blood.

She knew.

She knew who the old singer was, and she knew he was still alive as of last week and living with his granddaughter south of Window Rock.

More than anything, she knew what it would cost her to have him come and perform the Lightning Chant for Slim Boy.

There would be the gifts for him and his helpers: sheep, lambs, corn, of which she had none, perhaps even more of her precious turquoise. Then, she might have to slaughter half her wethers just to feed the rest of the crowd that would come. Some would come to help, but most just to be present when something so rare as the Lightning Chant was sung. She could have a hundred people to feed for all the seven days and nights it would take to perform the sing! And she could not deny them. Not only would she be thought inhospitable, but it could disturb the powers and the whole sing would be for naught.

No, she shook her head, as she began to climb the slight rise to where her hogan stood, she would not send to Window Rock to ask the singer to come: it was too dear. She would just have to try the few chants she knew again and hope for the best for Slim Boy. At least she knew now what was the matter with him, why he slept: he had unwittingly walked where the lightning had struck.

"Grandmother!"

Old Bead Woman stopped short, her head came up with a jerk. The light from the setting sun struck her full in the face and blinded her for an instant. Even so, in that instant, she saw there was a thin trail of smoke rising through the hole in the hogan's top and remembered she had left no fire.

Her heart lept up. The light child's voice calling, the smoke rising: Slim Boy must have wakened from his strange sleep on his own and be back to doing his chores. She would not need to feel any remorse for not sending for the old singer!

"Grandmother!"

Old Bead Woman shaded her eyes against the dying sun's last brilliance and looked up to where the hogan stood black against the paling sky. There, alongside the house, she saw the slender silhouetted figure of Slim Boy, an arm high above its head, waving to her.

"Grandmother," the figure called to her, "I have brought water from the well. The fire is going." Then, just as she began to hurry forward up the shallow rise, she saw a second figure, exactly the same size and shape, detach itself from the dark mass of the hogan and put its arm about the shoulders of the first.

"Yes, Grandmother," the second figure called, "everything is ready! Please hurry. Come and fix some supper. We are so very hungry!"

JULY 6, 1984

Nesset, Utah

The art nouveau lady carved on the stele cradled a heavily patinaed plaque in the crook of one arm. Her languorous body was wrapped in her sorrowing tresses, her eyes were downcast. The oval plaque itself told of Nesset's grief for the one and only of its sons who had gone to fight in The Great War for his country and the right and never returned: Warren F. Simpson.

Gamelon wondered what the "F" stood for; a proper name like Francis or some revered family name, Frome, perhaps, or Faraday? He always wondered what the initials in people's names stood for. When they appeared on headstones, it annoyed him. How could anyone so thoughtlessly cheat the dead? After all, their full names were all most had to leave behind to attest to the uniqueness that had been their life.

He raised his eyes from the sad stone, and shading them against the brilliant early morning sunlight began a more thorough study of what lay beyond the small, weed-choked square. From what he could see, Nesset really was not anymore. Whatever it might have been could have begun to die about—he glanced down at the base of the stele and quickly translated the Roman numerals carved there—1919. Nothing in the storefronts or the housefronts facing the square, except perhaps the Kresge's five-and-dime, showed evidence of any style having filtered through to Nesset since the memorial to Warren F. Simpson had been raised. The Kresge's was the worst of styles the early 1930s had had to offer.

All stood slowly but invisibly cracking in the dry, light, high desert air. If it had not been for the two battered '50s pickups parked bumper-to-bumper between potholes along the south side of the square, Gamelon could have easily convinced himself he had followed the almost undecipherable direction signs into a village frozen almost sixty years ago, well before The Crash and the cowed bitterness of The Depression that followed.

Nesset: south of nowhere, off the beaten track and almost in the desert. Gamelon found it hard to believe it could ever have been the market town for the rich, carefully irrigated farms he had passed on his way in at dawn. He could not picture Maria buying barrettes for her hair at the Kresge's as a girl or coming in from the farm on a Saturday evening for a movie or a Sunday morning for church. And he did not know whether she ever had or not; they had never spoken of it. He could only guess that even then, when she was young, importance must have already shifted to the more cosmopolitan St. George, leaving Nesset to slow, shrivel and finally all but stop except for its post office.

He was weary.

He had pushed the battered Fiat through the night. First it had been up, up, high into the Cajon Pass where the winds never slept, then down, slowly, but forever down it had seemed, to the desert valley where Las Vegas never slept.

The smudgy loom of the city's billion neon tubes had come toward him with the speed of a slug dessicating the length of a leaf as he and the Fiat had plodded through the black, barren wastes. Then, as though it had leaped out to smother him, he had found himself surrounded by the gauche, screaming brilliance.

Just as suddenly, it had been behind him. Only an occasional, automatic glance in the rear view mirror had served to remind him of the garish boil throbbing alone on the desert valley's floor.

Then, up again, through the torturous Virgin River gorge, its sides so high at times the stars were lost. Under a paling sky, a sleeping St. George had slipped by on his left, its Mormon Temple firmly standing its ground with its back against a butte. It had showed light gray instead of its pristine daylight white against the butte's pale pink and the darker gray of the yet-night sky.

North, still north, then briefly east, following the dilapidated signs that made him think the state of Utah must have forgotten it, to Nesset, just as the sun had broken free of the surrounding mountains and stroked the sky to a light, bright blue.

He was weary and he was famished.

According to the third-grade handwriting on the specked and stained butcher paper banner in the Kresge's window across the square, the soda fountain still served shakes, malts and breakfast all day. It was the only oasis in sight. He struck off diagonally across the square through the cocklebursand sword grass.

The inside of the archaic dime store was as dilapidated as its exterior, and everything—the dull metal racks of rhinestone trash, the plastic combs, the cheap toys left over from more than one Christmas—everything seemed coated with a superfine layer of dust and surrounded by an obbligato odor of bacon grease. The only sounds were first the slapping of the door closing behind him on worn-out hinges and then his solo steps across the hardwood floor, splotched almost beyond recognition by the spilled colas, coffees, pink face powders and orange blossom-scented eau de colognes of decades.

Unconsciously, he brushed at the linoleum-covered stool before he sat down.

He ordered coffee, two scrambled eggs and white toast from a thin-haired, thin-shouldered boy behind the counter who looked as though he would scream uncontrollably at nothing if the springs at the corners of his mouth were suddenly released.

The boy rocked off like an ancient with twisted, aching feet and Gamelon let his eyes follow down the scarred, grainy counter, around an ell and into a blank wall. There, as though that dead end was his rightful place, sat a man remarkable, it seemed to Gamelon, for nothing but incongruities.

His vintage, narrow-lapelled gray jacket looked new, showed not a wrinkle and fitted his shoulders as if it had been tailor made. The starched, pressed white shirt beneath the jacket, however, was badly frayed and so deeply grimed at the collar it would never come clean again. The bright striped silk necktie he wore, tightly and perfectly knotted even on that warm morning, bore a pathway of dribbles.

The man's thick, bristling gray hair was sharply cropped in the style of P-38s and Pearl Harbor. His turd of a nose squeezing out of a collapsed brown bag face was a fresco of lace blue veins. Bleary, worn eyes behind bifocals in chic designer frames shot Gamelon a glance over a crockery coffee cup that shook so much the man seemed barely able to hold onto it.

Gamelon's own coffee came, steaming, rank from too much reheating. He sought some salvation for it through the application of generous quantities of sugar and cream, even though he preferred it black. As he did so, he felt sure what cup the man at the other end of the counter sought at the other end of every day.

The eggs came, and the toast. The eggs were papery and tasted like they had been cooked in peanut oil. He was sure the bread had come from the baker's day-old shelf at least a week before. He tried to keep his mind on his hunger as he ate so his gorge would not rise and reject the mess. Still, he could not keep his eyes from closing every time the fork neared his mouth. It seemed those of his senses not absolutely involved refused to have anything to do with the food.

During one open-eyed moment between bites, Gamelon glanced again toward the end of the counter to find the man there watching him. The man quickly lowered his eyes to his copy of the Salt Lake City *Deseret News,* but not before Gamelon caught the look in them: Just for that instant, the rheumy eyes had seemed to long to tell a tale or to share something, anything. Gamelon was sure they would, sooner or later.

He washed the last of the oily eggs down with the last of the brackish coffee, praying the whole conglomeration would stay down long enough for his over-taxed digestion to win the day.

About then, as he had expected, there was a rustling and folding of the *Deseret News* at the other end of the counter. Some very small change was slipped under the crockery cup and the man rose and started along the counter in Gamelon's direction with the frontal unconcern of the burned out who must cling to their belief in their vanished importance in order to stay alive.

He had to start somewhere. Why not with this variety of town drunk, the common variety, who firmly believes he is the only one who knows he drinks? Gamelon knew such men had other secrets they longed to share riding tandem with the ability to assure themselves they never divulged even the most sacrosanct. In advance, Gamelon pitied him, but knew his malady was beyond control and getting worse with every lonely evening swim in bourbon or brandy, or, God forbid, gin. But, he had to start somewhere.

Gamelon wiped his mouth, put two ones and some silver on the flimsy tab in front of his plate and managed to be rising from his stool just as the man came abreast of him.

As though completely astonished at Gamelon's sudden materialization, the man stopped short in front of him and smiled broadly. His glistening, perfect dentures clicked once with the effort. "Well, well! Haha! Well, good morning," he said in a voice as scarred and grainy as the counter top. "Remson's my name, C. C. Remson, Cal Coolidge Remson, C. Coolidge Remson, M.D." He seemed to deflate and cave in a little. "'Doc,' just 'Doc.' Everybody calls me 'Doc.'"

Gamelon opened his mouth to return the introduction, but did not get beyond the intake of breath.

"Don't practice much anymore, though—used to be busy day and night, mostly night, it seemed at the time—" He drew one quivering fist from his trouser pocket and buffed Gamelon lightly on the shoulder. "—what with all the girls for miles around—good Mormon girls mostly—having babies after the war. Haha—making up for lost time, haha, and doing it mostly at night. But, being good Mormons, war or no war, they were doing their duty!" And again he laughed his strange burping haha and punched Gamelon's shoulder.

Gamelon had wanted to speak to the man, but he withdrew instinctively from the forced camaraderie.

"Nice to meet you, Doctor, I'm—"

"Great war, the second one, but after all the fire and brimstone, I was glad when it was done. Came here right after, in '46. Wanted a quiet little place to settle and open a practice."

Finally Gamelon got in a complete sentence: "Where were you during the war?"

"Where? Why everywhere! You name it, and almost always right on the front lines!"

"Field surgeon?"

"Uh, well . . ."

Behind Gamelon, the front door of the dime store creaked, then slammed on its bad hinges. He looked over his shoulder.

A strikingly handsome young Indian in Levis, boots and a dark blue sateen shirt had come in and stood motionless just inside the door. Then, without seeming to take any notice of Gamelon and Remson at the counter, he began to move soundlessly, even in his high-heeled boots, across the spotted floor to another counter where a clerk slumped. As he went, he removed a jet black Stetson from raven black hair tied tightly at the back of his head with a white cotton band. Gamelon could not help but notice the beauty with which the man moved but also could not escape the feeling that, though on the small side and lean, he was extraordinarily tough and hard.

Gamelon turned his attention back to Remson, but it was as if the doctor had forgotten him completely. He watched the Indian with a fascination that seemed to Gamelon to be only a few steps removed from fear. Even when the man stopped and began to thumb through some gaudy bandanas, Remson continued to stare at him.

Gamelon took advantage of the opportunity to get a word in edgewise. "Doctor, my name is Lon Waugh—Doctor?"

"Uh, yes." The doctor seemed unable to return more than half his attention to Gamelon. "What was it you said?"

"I'm Lon Waugh."

"Pleased . . . pleased." The old man made a move to take a trembling hand out of his pocket to shake, but thought better of it. But, the reminder of his affliction was enough to re-erect his facade. The bottom half of his pleated face again opened to display his shining dentures, and he was off again. "Haha! Well, what brings you to Nesset, my boy? And don't tell me you're just passing through." He leaned close to butt Gamelon's shoulder with his own. "Haha! I'd have to come back at you with a 'bullshit!' Nobody passes *through* Nesset. Nobody ever did much. There's no place to go beyond it and nothing to go for except thirst and starvation—unless you're a Navajo on the long way home. Haha!"

Suddenly Gamelon wanted to get out of the musty dime store, outside where the air was fresh and clear. He turned and made as though to start for the door thinking the old man would automatically stroll along with him. But Remson's attention had gone back to the young Indian.

Gamelon put a hand under the doctor's elbow as much to regain that attention as to perhaps steer him outside, as he said, "No, Dr. Remson, I'm not just passing through. I'm here for a purpose. I'm looking for someone."

"Uh—what was that?"

"I said, Doctor, I'm looking for someone." The two of them began to move slowly toward the door.

"Oh, yes? In Nesset?"

They made it to the door and Gamelon shouldered it open and navigated them through. Outside, the brilliant light forced the doctor to extract one quivering hand from his pocket finally. He hastened to shade his eyes with it.

"I don't know if—she's in Nesset."

"She?"

"Yes, Doctor, 'she.' I'm looking for a young woman named Maria Rundqvist—or somebody who looks like her perhaps."

"Rundqvist?"

"Maria Rundqvist. She was born on a farm around here somewhere and grew up there as far as I know. Would you know if you've seen her here lately?"

"Why . . . you interested?"

"I—I love—loved her."

"Loved?"

Lord, Gamelon thought, maybe the desert sun really did have the power to suck up brains. Ever since they had come out into it, the old man had become like a four-year-old with a "why" for every "because." He was getting exactly nowhere.

"Doctor," Gamelon shook his arm, "Doctor, where are you headed?"

"Headed?"

"Yes, where would you have been going when you left the five-and-dime?"

"Going?"

"Where is your home, Doctor, or your office?"

"Home . . . office?" The words seemed to stir some recollection. "Why do you want to know?"

"I thought I might walk there along with you, get us out of this sun."

"Good idea, good idea. Sun's hard to take at my age."

And in your condition, Gamelon thought. "Which way, Doctor?"

Remson jerked his head to the right. "A block down and just around the corner on East First South."

So even insignificant little Nesset had been laid out on the great characterless Mormon city grid.

"Yes," Remson went on, seeming to brighten a bit, "why don't you stroll along—"

Suddenly, Gamelon felt the old man's arm tighten under his hand and he turned his head to follow Remson's gaze. His chin thrust forward, Remson was staring intently at a rusty pickup parked a hundred feet up the street on the opposite side next to the square. Inside, in deep shadow, Gamelon could just make out a heavily-bearded man in bib overalls without a shirt, a battered Stetson tilted over his eyes, who seemed to be drowsing behind the wheel.

Remson wrenched his arm free of Gamelon's fingers. The *Deseret News* flapped to the cracked sidewalk from under his arm as he wrestled his other hand out of its pocket and up to help with the shading of his eyes. Then he leaned forward until his nose was only inches from Gamelon's and searched Gamelon's face through the lower half of his bifocals with eyes that looked to Gamelon as though they were trying to deny the ultimate truth of a revelation. Then he asked in a low voice that shook as much as his hands, "What'ja say your name was?"

Gamelon recoiled from the wretched combination of mouthwash, stale liquor and bile that accompanied the question as he answered, "Waugh, Gamelon Waugh."

Remson reared up, threw his hands in the air and, head wagging, began to back away from him. "Ooooooh, no," he muttered, "oh, no!" And he turned and hurried off down the street, his hands making a visor for his eyes.

It took a second for Gamelon to collect himself in the light of Remson's strange behavior, then he called after him, "Doctor, your paper! Doctor Remson, don't you want your paper? Doctor—"

The old man's only response was to raise his hands above his head and waggle them violently along with his head, then clasp them momentarily over his ears and finally put them back above his eyes as he continued to stump and stumble away from Gamelon at his best possible pace.

The sun, rising inexorably toward noon, seemed to pull an intense heat up from the pavement and the storefronts. It seemed to drag it up and out of the earth mercilessly as if repudiating its promise to leave it stored there from the day before. Gamelon could feel tendrils of heat curling around his ankles and exploring up his pants legs as he stood tapping the folded *Deseret News* against his thigh and wondering what a man could do or be or what could have been done to a man to make him into such a disjointed waste as Calvin Coolidge Remson.

Dear Sweet Jesus God, but he was tired.

His shoulders settled. The *Deseret News* hung from his fingers. For a few moments he stood that way in the prying heat, his face immobile, his eyes blank.

If he knew closet drunks, Remson might be more tractable later in the day. Perhaps later in the day he might find out more about the man's private shipwrecks as well as more about what he had driven through the night to either bring to life or put to rest forever.

But now, it was he who must rest. He remembered a faded "Room To Let" shingle he had seen on a house a little less exhausted than most in Nesset. He stirred himself and started off across the street in the direction of the Fiat on the other side of the square.

Only the eyes moved under the tilted down brim of the tired Stetson as the bearded man watched Gamelon tramp doggedly through the cockleburs and sword grass. Only after the Fiat had disappeared did he start the rusty pickup. He threaded the truck carefully through the potholes—the shock absorbers and the rear leaf springs were long gone—and drove off in the opposite direction.

In his benumbed state, Gamelon remembered almost too late to keep the door between his nakedness and Birdie David.

"Mumblin' from the pillow ain't good enough," the tall, knobby old woman said through the crack. "Man's got to be on his feet and movin' before I'll take his word he's up. Had to rouse enough ranch hands still drunk from the night before to know that. Now then, it's four o'clock."

Before Gamelon could swirl his tongue around enough inside his mouth to be able to say thank you, Birdie had turned away and started down the stairs, her shivering touch of what Gamelon supposed to be Parkinson's Disease jerking her head erratically now and then and whipping the knot of yellow-gray hair on top of her head.

About three steps down, she stopped and turned back toward the cracked door where Gamelon still stood motionless trying to get his eyes to focus fully, and called, "That girl you asked about when you first come: I've been ruminatin', and I remember somethin' about the family at least. When you get your jeans on, come back to the kitchen and I'll say what I remember." Birdie swung around and marched on down.

That he might finally be on the verge of finding out something about Maria helped Gamelon wake more quickly. He went to the sink in the corner of the room and splashed water in his face, then retrieved his clothes from the heap on the floor where he had let them drop before collapsing on the bed, and hauled them back on. Five minutes later, after a quick stop in the bathroom at the far end of the hall, he, too, was on his way down into the gloom of the first floor.

Birdie had all the windows closed and the shades drawn against the afternoon heat. The first floor was cool but stuffy. Gamelon groped his way along a hall that led toward the rear of the house where he supposed the kitchen to be. At the end, he pushed open a swinging door and looked around.

The kitchen, too, was dim, and for a second he could not spy Birdie. Then, a squeak of furniture led his eyes to her, rocking slowly in a corner and snapping green beans into a bowl in her lap.

"Come in, come in," she said a bit impatiently. "There's chilled sun tea in the ice box and a glass there on the table. Get some and set."

Gamelon helped himself from the big pitcher in the old Kelvinator with the coils on top, pulled out a chair, sat in it and waited for Birdie to speak.

The rocker creaked for a few moments accompanied only by the soft, regular popping of beans until she said, "Well, now Mr.—what'ja say that name was?"

"Waugh, Gamelon—Lon Waugh."

"Well, now, Mr. Waugh—funny, can't quite see the spellin' of that in my mind—but no matter. That name, Rundqvist, rung a bell right off when you said it, but I didn't want to say nothin' till I'd had a chance to mull it over proper. Besides, you was too tired to talk when you came anyways.

"First thing you ought to know is there ain't any more 'round here as far as I know. Hasn't been any for, oh, I suppose, goin' on twenty years now.

"Never was many—only the one family I ever knew of. Came into the valley here, oh, must of been somewhere in the '80s—before I was born, you understand. They was part of a little bunch of folks come original from Norway or Sweden or one of them northern countries, latter day converts, as it was, to the Church of the Latter Day Saints." She chuckled to herself. "There was some Olsens and some Petersens, and some Sorensens and that one family of Rundqvists. They all kind of settled together out southeast of the town.

"Last Rundqvist I knew of was a man named Karl. I know he went to the war as a young man—come to think of it, so'd the girl he married, one of the Sorensens. She'd been a nurse, I think.

"I recall seein' the two of 'em once in a while here in town right after they was married—oh, Lordy, that'd have to been in the real late '40s, early '50s. I remember how handsome they was together, both of 'em bein' so tall and big-boned and blonde.

"A couple years later they had a little girl who *was* named Maria, after the Sorensen girl's ma.

"Now, from there on, things is a bit muddled. And, I have to own, my mind wasn't much on the goin's on in the surroundin's right then."

For a moment or two, there was silence. Not even beans popped. Then Birdie cleared her throat and went on, "Then's about when my Johnny started with the cancer, you see—but never mind that.

"Things, like I said, is a bit muddled about Karl and Pia Sorensen Rundqvist from then on. I know there was something about the little girl bein' real ill—oh, '52, '53, somewhere in there—and I recall Coolidge Remson went out to the farm to see her.

"Now, if there was ever an old natter, it's Coolidge, was even in them days. But, the funny thing was, he never said one word about that little girl and what the matter was with her. Wasn't like him. *But*," the beans snapped at a great rate, "if I was to be allowed a guess, I'd say it was just about then he took to drinkin' a little more'n he should've.

"Then before you know it, they was up an' gone! The Rundqvists was up and gone! All of a sudden one day signs appear in the stores and on the fence posts that all they owned was to be up for auction the following week. I wasn't there for it, but I heard they took a lickin' on everything—never did sell the farm itself. Some of the others over that way farmed this and that piece of the land from time to time, but the buildin's stood idle and fallin' down. I hear tell the Park Service bought it up some years later, so that's all the farm is now—park—and that's all I know. That's all anybody 'round here knows, unless, o' course, it's Coolidge Remson. Gettin' him to make any sense *these* days ain't hardly worth the tryin'. Don't know what good whatever you did get out o' him would do you now anyway."

Again there was silence except for the complaining of Birdie's rocker. The brown paper bag beside her was empty and the bowl on her narrow lap was mounded high.

"Now, then, young man," she said finally, "I've told you all I know and I think it would be fittin' if you told me just exactly why you're so interested in the first place."

Gamelon lifted his empty glass and motioned toward the Kelvinator while looking at Birdie with raised eyebrows.

Birdie nodded and Gamelon went to get himself a refill of sun tea.

When he had settled himself at the table again, he held his own silence for a few moments. His first thought was to tell the old woman the whole story. It would be good not to have to go on living alone with his griefs, his unknowns. Up to then, there was only one person he possibly could have shared them with: John Frederick Sevrinsky. Now, for some reason, he felt drawn to the straight-out old Birdie David.

But he decided to wait a while before loading her down with it all, if indeed he ever decided to do so. He said simply, "Mrs. David, I love a girl or the memory of a girl named Maria Rundqvist who was born near Nesset. Now I know from what you tell me she didn't grow up here. Either she's dead or she's disappeared. But, there's just a chance she's still alive and that she might have come back here for some reason. All I want to do is find out."

"Birdie, son. Just Birdie'll do fine." She set the bowl of beans on the floor beside the empty bag carefully and got up out of the chair stiffly in connected sections. She came across the dim room, stopped beside Gamelon's chair and stood looking down at the top of his head for a moment, admiring his bright auburn hair, which sheened even in the gloom of the shaded kitchen. Then she patted the back of his neck and said softly, "The combination of truth huntin' and love's reason enough for anybody to do anything, boy."

She cleared her throat as she moved away from Gamelon's chair, then went on, "Now, then, before you go off to try to make some sense out of Coolidge Remson, as I suppose you're bound to do seein' he's the only one hereabouts might know something more'n I do, I want you to know supper's served sharply at six around here. There'll be them fresh beans done in pot liquor with new potatoes and carrots, cold sliced ham and a good rice puddin' with raisins and whole cream. It's all part and parcel with the room."

Gamelon told her he would try to be back in time, but asked, if he was not, would she please leave a helping of everything for him there on the kitchen table. Even cold, it would be better than rancid-tasting, flaccid eggs and bender board toast.

Birdie said she would leave him a covered dish if he did not show up by a little after six.

That morning, Gamelon had resented Remson's buffeting and his stinking breath. As he left the kitchen, he could not help but think how welcome by contrast the touch of Birdie's cool, fragile hand had seemed on his neck, how refreshing the sharp, crushed-green smell of it had been in his nostrils.

East First South ran at the back of her property, Birdie had told him. He could either cut through her orchard and get on it that way or go out the front, over four blocks along the east side of the square and down a block. Coolidge Remson's house was the second on the right after the corner. Even though he didn't practice much anymore, his shingle was still out. Gamelon couldn't miss it.

In his room to retrieve his slim excuse for calling on the doctor, the copy of that morning's *Deseret News*, Gamelon happened to glance out the rear window and saw the big neat square of trees. He decided to take the shortcut through the orchard.

He had no sooner stepped into the speckled shade than it struck him that strolling among the trees was lovelier than contemplating doing so had been. There were damn few things one could say that about.

The peaches would be ready for the jam jars in less than a week he figured. The fruit on the one great, great-grandfather nectarine would not be far behind. The apples had a way to go yet; they were still small, hard and green, but promised to be no less bountiful a crop.

It was so still, even cool there. On some other summer afternoon he could have stretched slowly on the ground under the venerable nectarine and dozed, aware but undisturbed by the sounds around: the last bees hurrying about their final collections among the blooming grasses before calling it a day and arrowing back to the hive; the clicking and grunting of a flock of thieving blackbirds as they made their supper from what they considered their fair share of the succulent loot in the peach trees. Even the distant clatter of a truck with bad leaf springs passing along the east side of the square a long country block away would not have bothered him. He could have stretched and dreamed and let the day go its implacable way and end without him.

He came to the gate at the rear of the orchard Birdie had warned him about. He put his back into it, heaved, and swung it open on its one decayed hinge just enough to let himself through.

East First South had no sidewalk, no curb. He dropped the gate back in place and stepped out onto the verge of the broken macadam and set his steps south.

The closer he got to Coolidge Remson and his secrets, the higher misgivings mounted inside him, the further his vision of himself in the soft, peaceful orchard faded.

When he spied the doctor's shingle a block away, he stopped abruptly. What in hell did he hope to dig out of the old sot anyway and what good would it do him in the present? If he did get any information from him about Maria, how valuable would even the smallest bit be rising back up through twenty-odd years of alcohol? Dear God, wasn't this just a fool's errand?!

How could he have believed, despite all the unknowns, there was even a chance Maria was still alive? Jorge had seen whatever he had seen at the airport day before yesterday, but Jorge had also seen Maria die there six weeks before just as he himself had. Jorge had never doubted that; Jorge had been eager to be convinced his eyes had played tricks on him.

And now he knew the whole Rundqvist family had disappeared seemingly without a trace over twenty years ago and there seemed no way to link then to now. There seemed no way to trace the times and places and people between that unexplainable day and the foggy Los Angeles evening last December when he had driven all the way in from Wasco to attend the opening of his friend Joanne Smart's first one-woman show. Because of the press of the crowd in the small gallery, he had rounded a door jamb too short and dumped a double Margarita, salt, glass and all, down the dress front of a lovely, honey blonde girl with great gray eyes and delicious breasts.

He rubbed at his eyes with one big heavy hand, then let it drop. He emptied his mind; he let it coast, eyes blank, ears not hearing.

After a few moments, the reason was there. To know; that was all that mattered. He had to know.

What had Birdie said? Love and the search for

truth were reasons enough for a man to do anything?

That might be one way of saying what drove him, but what truly drove him was what had always driven him: the awful whip of curiosity, the scourge of needing to know.

If he had to put Coolidge Remson in an institution to dry him out or cajole him or even beat him to pry loose anything inside his head that might help him take the first step, he would do it. After that, if he had to walk the entire world, he would until he knew: Was Maria dead or alive? It was as simple as that.

The faded letters on the shingle said first, "C. Coolidge Remson, MD," then beneath that, in the English fashion, which Gamelon thought a little pretentious for Nesset, "Surgery," with an arrow pointing down a weed-grown walk at the side of the house. Gamelon squared his shoulders and started down, picking his way among the hummocks thriving between the broken bricks.

A wide porch ran down the side of the house and across the back, where it was screened. Gamelon could not see what good the screening would do with all the holes in it. At the corner, just inside the torn and rusted wire, Coolidge Remson sat motionless in a battered rocker that could not rock without tipping over backwards. The business ends of its two tines were gone. He looked to be naked except for a yellowed undershirt and he hummed to himself tunelessly. For some unknown reason, the sound brought back the mourning of the black swan to Gamelon's mind for an instant.

He mounted the two steps, and watching for loose planks in the porch floor, crossed to the sagging screen door and knocked softly.

Remson stopped humming, shook his head, sat quiet for a moment, then took a pull at the tumbler in his hand and resumed his monotonous half-singing.

Gamelon knocked again, harder.

Again the doctor fell silent, then his head came up with a jerk. Without turning, he said thickly, " 'm very sorry, n'body here can help you. Doctor's gone away and I cannot help you."

"But, you are the doctor," Gamelon said calmly.

Slowly, as though with excruciating pain, Remson turned his head far enough toward the screen door to be able to see out the corner of his eye if there really was anyone there. His watery eyes, unaided by the bifocals in the chic frames, did not recognize Gamelon. "No," he said, after a long moment, "doctor's on a long journey. May never return. Go away."

That was enough.

Gamelon opened the screen door, careless that it slammed back, and stepped around in front of Remson. He leaned down and grabbed the man's runnelled, sagging cheeks between the thumb and fingers of one huge hand, shook once sharply and looking straight into the pale eyes, said in a low even voice, "Perhaps you're not the doctor this afternoon. Perhaps you never are after noon. But, as far as everyone hereabouts knows, you *are* Calvin Coolidge Remson. It is Calvin Coolidge Remson I want to see. I've come to return the newspaper he dropped this morning." Gamelon slapped the paper down across the man's bare thighs and let it lie.

He shook Remson's head hard once more, then let go. It fell back against the cracked splat at the top of the chair and stayed there as Gamelon turned away, stepped across the porch and leaned against a skinny flaking doric column.

He stared out over the rail into a rich array of weeds. It wouldn't be any good. Remson was too far gone for that day to cajole. One blow would probably kill him, and the nearest place to dry him out was probably Salt Lake City.

His practiced eye spied some pathetic stragglers among the weeds and knew the weed patch must have once been a rose garden. It bouyed him that the plants still tried at the same time it angered him that anyone could have neglected them to this point. With the right care, they could still be saved, he thought. There might even be some rare old varieties there, moss roses, perhaps . . .

Remson put the glass down on a battered table at his side loudly, but with a relatively steady hand, and rummaged there for his glasses. Even after he got them on, it took him several moments of staring and shaking his head to recognize Gamelon. When he finally did, he seemed to visibly diminish inside the confines of the rudderless rocker. Then in a quaking whisper, he asked, "What d'ya want? Why don' you leave me be?"

Gamelon turned his attention back to the old man. Seeing him now, shrunken and shivering in the chair, saliva trickling from the corner of a mouth collapsed in the absence of dentures, pale eyes with yellow whites darting everywhere but to Gamelon's face, he wondered how the man could have called up any human pity in him that morning, much less curiosity. All he wanted now was to get what he could, if he could, and get away.

"I'll leave you be if you'll do me the favor of answering one simple question about one woman. I know you knew her when she was little. I know you attended her when she was two or three years old and very ill. Now that one question—make it two questions: have you seen or heard tell of that little girl, now a woman, Maria Rundqvist, here in Nesset in the last few days, number one. Number two: what was wrong with her all those years back?"

Between gulps from the glass, Remson whined over the rim, "But, I tol' ya, I tol' ya once! I tol' ya that an' a lotta other things weeks back when ya come here with that moody young Indian. Afternoon you 'n' him went in the kit-kitchen . . . went in the kitchen an' took the liquor, then ya perched y'self right there on that rail . . . huggin' one bottle in your arms an' grinnin' at me." He drained the glass and Gamelon saw he was almost in tears. "I tol' ya once. Why do I hafta tell it all again?"

Suddenly Remson's watery eyes became large and he looked straight at Gamelon for the first time since Gamelon had let go of his face. "You're not gonna do it again? You're not gonna take the liquor?"

Gamelon did not signify whether he would or he would not. Let the old drunk think what he liked. But he dropped his head and looked away in disgust and confusion. He could only suppose Remson had laid out all his woes to some wraith of his deliriums some afternoon weeks before when he had run out of booze.

The old man got shakily to his feet and Gamelon saw he was not naked below the waist as he had thought. Beneath the straggling undershirt and drooping belly, Remson wore a ridiculously skimpy pair of black briefs with a jaunty red, green and yellow cartoon rooster stitched on the front right over the penis. Gamelon shook his head.

Remson wove and shuffled through the open door into the kitchen. Gamelon heard the chatter of glass on glass as he poured himself another tumbler of vodka. Then he heard the man start to giggle.

Remson came back to the doorway giggling. He sagged against the frame and between gulps from the glass, went on giggling, eyes and nose running, losing half each gulp out the sides of his toothless mouth. Gamelon wondered why he did not choke.

Finally the silly laughter stopped and he mumbled almost too thickly for Gamelon to understand, "Two questions, huh? Wanted two answers, didja?"

He giggled again and did not seem to notice as the half full glass slid from his fingers and smashed at his feet. "Well, that's them—it. Two. She's two—or three, five, 'leven, eighteen—a hundred by now f'all I know . . ." and his head fell back hard against the wood as he slid down the door frame into a heap, out cold.

A bluebottle buzzed angrily back and forth across one of the few whole stretches of screen. Gamelon watched its frantic efforts to get out for a moment in silence, then he stepped to where it was beating itself to death on the wire. "Come on," he muttered as he cupped his hand, "there's ways out all over the place." He put his hand over the frantic insect and began to move it toward a ragged tear in the screen. "Come on, come on. There're a hundred ways out. Stop killing yourself going back and forth over the same useless territory." His hand came over the hole and the bluebottle droned out over the strangling rose garden.

Gamelon's stomach rumbled. He had not eaten anything since the doubtful fare at the five-and-dime early that morning. His mouth began to water at the thought of Birdie's fresh green beans. He hoped she would not overcook them. He glanced at his watch and saw that he had plenty of time still to make her mandatory sit-down.

He looked down at Remson and wondered if there was any other way of sweeping together enough crumbs of fact to start off on. Remson was useless, at least for today. Maybe tomorrow he would come back earlier in the day and hold the liquor hostage and see what happened.

Head down, he picked his way carefully across the porch and down the rickety steps and back along the heaved and sunken brick walk. As he went, he thought he would come back sometime before he left—to hell with Remson—to try to fight his way through the weeds just to see if there might be some wonderful old rose in the overgrown garden. If there was, he would take some slips. A cross with one of those old fellows produced unusual, sometimes amazing results.

The quickest way back to Birdie's would probably be by way of the east side of the square, he decided. He had just made the turn and headed north when the short beep of a horn sounded behind him. He turned his head, curious, but not anticipating the sound had been made to attract his attention. He was surprised to see a bare arm covered with red hair to the elbow beckoning to him from the open window of a rusty pickup.

He pointed to himself and the bearded head inside nodded while the arm continued to motion him toward the truck. Gamelon shrugged his shoulders, stepped off the high, old-fashioned curb and started slowly across the street, being careful not to turn an ankle in a pothole.

He stepped up again on the square side and walked back along the side of the truck until he was at the driver's window. He bent down and looked through it. At first, all he could see of the man who had beckoned to him was a chewed and stained cowboy hat that had once been fawn-colored and acres of bristling copper-colored beard. Then the beard parted where the mouth should be to smile a broad, lazy smile. One hand came up to shift the hat to the back of the head and Gamelon looked into liquid amber eyes as a deep voice much like his own drawled softly, "It's about time we were getting together, Little Brother."

La Playa, California
August 18, 1984

My Dear David,

I have to admit, I'm astonished. Fräulein Altenbäumer was not able to locate that letter of Gamelon's, the one I promised you a copy of, when she was here last Tuesday. She now has set her teeth and squared herself away at the problem like a Schnauzer determined to get a worrisome rat. Not a file or a box of old manuscripts, not even my reams of blank staff paper will be safe from her ferreting until she finds that letter. Come to think of it, Miss Altenbäumer reminds me of a Schnauzer in more ways than one. I do believe she even looks a little like one, particularly in the stiff gray hair and black beady eyes department.

So, I'm sorry, but I don't have that to forward to you yet. Perhaps it's just as well. If I'm trying to present my "pieces" in some sort of chronological order, what the letter has to add would be premature now.

However, I don't think it would be premature at this point to tell you what little I know about Gamelon's brother, Racklin.

I didn't know until later that Gamelon had believed him dead or anything of the reasons he thought this to be the case. (Why is it I always seem to learn so much of everything after the fact?) But, as I see it now, it must have been at about this point, sometime shortly after Gamelon arrived there, that he found Racklin, as they say, "alive and well and living in (or near) Nesset."

I don't know that I've indicated it before, but Gamelon spoke very little with me about his background or his family. There really wasn't any reason for him to. I do know—from him—that he and Racklin were the only two children, that they grew up somewhere in New England—Massachusetts, I think—and I gathered, were very close as children.

As I recall, Racklin was a couple of years

older than Gamelon and Gamelon once described him to me as "smaller and stringier than I am but almost as tough, cleverer than I am and always the instigator if there was mischief to get into." I gathered that while they were growing up, Racklin was the leader and that Gamelon not only followed willingly but also was protective of him.

Evidently, the two of them had drifted apart in recent years. This, it seemed, was primarily because of long physical separation and divergent professional interests.

Racklin was an anthropologist with a clinical background in medicine—though not an MD. Gamelon led me to believe he had swung away from the medical career and toward the one in anthropology because of an itchy foot as much as anything else.

I also surmised that while Gamelon was the peaceable sort who delighted in discoveries made through patience, systematic study and understanding, Racklin, though also a scientist, was drawn to wildness and strangeness in everything: people, places, even ideas. As it was, he came to specialize in the study of human aberrations: twinning, dwarfism, etc., anything contrary to the human norm, wherever and in whatever peoples he found them.

On the few occasions Gamelon spoke of Racklin, it was always with a certain small, deep warmth. Although, like all of us, I'm sure Racklin had some drawbacks, some character faults, Gamelon never mentioned them. And, I believe, regardless of the protracted separation, there remained a deep affection between them . . .

Gamelon jumped back from the door of the pickup, stopped, legs spread, arms flung wide, tears starting in his soft brown eyes. He stood that way for an instant, then yelled at the top of his lungs, "Little Brother! Little Brother! I'll 'little brother' you!"

He leapt back to the truck in a single giant stride, tore open the cab door, reached one great red paw inside and dragged the bearded man out in a single swipe and into the crush of his heavy arms. The man, only slightly smaller and lighter than Gamelon, threw his own muscled arms around Gamelon's neck and the two of them jumped up and down, turning in circles in the gutter, all the while hugging each other fiercely and pounding each other on the back.

In their dancing, they tripped on the high curb and fell in a tangle on the edge of the weedy square. Heedless of the cockleburs and sword grass, they rolled over and over, wrestling like rowdy ten-year-olds, until Gamelon managed to pin his brother. He panted in Racklin's ear, "Give up! Give up, now?"

The bearded head turned in his grip enough for Gamelon to see one gleaming eye wink slowly through strands of red hair as Racklin murmured, "And it's nice to be close to you again, too, Lon."

A pang of warm remembrance surged through Gamelon even as he felt himself bristle slightly. Sharply, he let go his grip on his brother's neck and shoulders and rolled off his back.

But, the memory of winter nights and summer evenings long ago when Racklin had crept across the room they shared to teach him with mouth and hands bleached quickly in the strength of the joy he felt at finding his brother alive. He sat up and stared at Racklin, silent, the fixed and helpless smile of an idiot tattooed all over his face.

Racklin lay spread-eagle on the grass sucking in air by the lungful until he had his breath back. Then, he rolled over and stared up at the softening high desert evening sky as one hand began to fish unconsciously in a big pocket. He came up with what had been a perfectly good half pack of cigarettes until Gamelon's bear hugging had squashed it all but flat. He poked in it until he found a cigarette that was still whole, smoothed it, lit it and dragged on it in silence, still watching the sky.

Finally, Gamelon could not stand it any longer. "Rack," he said in a low voice quivering with pent-up curiosity and excitement, "where in hell have you *been*?"

Racklin smoked on for a moment, then said in a voice so like Gamelon's in color and timbre they could have been mistaken for one and the same in different moods, "Here, Lon, in Nesset. Where'd you think I'd be?"

Gamelon chuckled. "Where you usually are: some Godforsaken place in the world or other."

"Well, as they say, don't this fit the bill?"

"Lord, I guess it does, but there've got to be other places to get lost in that are a damn sight more intriguing and exotic than Nesset."

Racklin rolled slowly onto his side to face his brother and just smiled lazily at him for a while. Then he drawled, "Ah, child, more exotic, yes. More intriguing, well there's more in Nesset than meets the eye, and 'tis a long story, that."

"So you're Irish this evening." Gamelon laughed out loud. With every fleeing second he was more and more sure his brother was as he had always been, that he was all right. "I'd 've thought you'd choose to be Chinese if there was intrigue involved." He feinted a loving punch at his brother's shoulder. "But stop playacting with me. What in the hell are you doing here and why hasn't anybody heard a peep or a groan out of you in nearly a year? Lord, Rack, you could've showed a little consideration; Dad thinks you're dead—and why the beard?"

Racklin looked down as he butted his cigarette

in a hummock of sword grass. He did not raise his eyes as he went on in his best Irish dialect, "All in good time, m'boy, all in good time. Too much too soon could have too heady 'n effect on ye. Pay heed to the wisdom o' your older and wiser leprechaun of a brother: all in good time."

He raised his head and smiled broadly at Gamelon, then fell back on the grass, arms flung wide, eyes on the twilight sky. "It suits me. Today it suits me to be Irish. We're part Irish, some small part, so I've more of a right to be Irish if I want to than, say, Russian. Yes, today I must be bein' filled with that queer Irish mixture of a love o' life, a love affair with joy and the never-endin' fascination with doom. That must be it and so it suits me today. Tomorrow, if I'm morose, I will be Russian or if I'm incandescently light-hearted and gay, I may move to the south of France.

"After all, you know me: Racklin Waugh, almost-MD, PhD, Chameleon To The People. I am whatever color I find myself against. I am what I am wished to be. I become what is needed for any given moment of any given day.

"Surely you remember all the things I was for you, Lon: brother, playmate, friend, leader, teacher, lover, even pimp once or twice if I remember right, and all because whichever it was was what you wanted me to be at the time."

Racklin fumbled for another cigarette and lit it before he went on, his face turned away from Gamelon. "But, I needed to be all those things more than you needed me to be them. I needed that fantastic flexibility. I couldn't pass up any possibility to be something more and different. I couldn't even pass up a chance to discover everything about something just because it was said to be wrong, too much, too little."

He sat up suddenly and looked straight into Gamelon's eyes, scintillating amber into soft brown.

"And, Little Brother, I've learned a lot over the years, things conscience or convention or fear have kept other men from knowing. Still, there are more things I need to be and I need you to want me to be those things. That, Little Brother, is why I'm glad to come across you here in Nesset. I need you to need me to be what I cannot help. Then, I can do what I must."

Gamelon could not help but smile inwardly. Bright and winged Racklin had not changed. He could still convolute simplicity into a maze, a beautiful, well-kept, leafy maze, but a maze nonetheless, and he could still spellbind Gamelon with it. All he had really said was, "I love you, brother, I always have. I lead better when I have you to follow. I'm glad you've come." He was about to ask, "What do you want, Rack?" when a small unbidden question made itself vocal in the back of his mind: How is it we could both be in Nesset at this particular time?

Racklin began to speak again. The curtain had come down on the Irish act; his eyes almost hissed with intensity. His voice was low and clear and seemingly overcome with awe. "Lon," he said, "I have discovered something here, here in starving, dehydrating Nesset that is so beautiful it makes my soul kneel, so tremendous it could alter the concept of time, so strange it will change what truth is . . ."

Which meant he had come up with something, probably in his work, which was highly unusual . . .

". . . and tomorrow I will share it with you."

Racklin's mood changed like roller-coastering quicksilver. He launched himself at Gamelon and pulled him to his feet, hugging him close all the while. "If we hurry, Little Brother, you can still get a warm dinner at Birdie's," he said brightly, gave Gamelon one fast bump and grind, groin to groin—"That's for the old days"—let him go and started for the truck. "Come on, Little Brother, I'll give you a lift over there. You've had a tiring couple of days. Get a good meal and a good sleep and I'll come for you first thing in the morning." Without a glance over his shoulder at the following Gamelon, he climbed into the cab.

All the four long blocks back to Birdie's the pickup banged and slammed on its axles and Racklin bellowed *I'll Take You Home Again, Kathleen* at the top of his lungs, his free hand and arm out the window beating time broadly and vigorously enough to have kept a symphony orchestra, double choirs and a full brass band cowed and in line.

Yes, Gamelon thought, Racklin is still Racklin. When something was afoot and the objective close, he had always become maddeningly silent or just as maddeningly, but monstrously, boisterous. When he chose to be boisterous, it was doubly maddening when he chose to sing. He could no more carry a tune than Gamelon could execute a *tour jeté*, and the effect was that of a bull with double troubles: lovesick and his testicles caught on a barbed wire fence. If it had not been for the rhythm and the words, Gamelon would not have had the vaguest idea it was *Kathleen* he was "singing." What he did know was that he would get no answers now for any of the lengthening queue of questions in his mind.

They rocked to a stop in front of the rooming house. Racklin shut up long enough to squeeze his brother's shoulder hard and push him out of the cab. "Get some food and rest. See you bright and early." And he was off again, careening among the potholes and wailing on about getting Kathleen back to the fresh green fields.

Gamelon watched the truck out of sight but he

could still hear the banging and the bellowing as he turned and started up the steps toward board and bed.

Birdie had just finished ladling his portions into the covered dish when he entered the kitchen, so he was able to sit to it all still hot—except for the cold ham—after all. They exchanged the most rudimentary amenities and he fell to.

Birdie hovered for a bit, brushing a spotless counter top, collecting invisible crumbs into her palm from the other end of the table. Gamelon knew she was curious about what had gone on between him and Coolidge Remson. But, after a while, when he did not volunteer any information on the subject, she draped her dish rag over the sink spout and sidled out of the kitchen.

Already, the warmth of the food in his stomach was making him drowsy. He knew he would be welcome to rock a spell on the front porch and gab in the last light with Birdie when he finished, but he made up his mind to just be civil by saying good night and get right to bed. Five and a half or six hours sleep in thirty-eight or so just had not been enough.

There were times he damned his curiosity, the need to know what drove him. Two hours later, naked and sweating in the warm summer night, as he turned from his right side to his left for what seemed the ten-thousandth time, was one of them.

As he had stripped and flung his clothes on the chair in the corner of the big room, he had been sure sleep would club him as soon as he fell across the rumpled bed. But the militant knot of questions had not faded under the onslaught of that sleep. Instead, they had fought back hard. He had been through each and every one to its own particular dead end, and still they fought.

Even now, they showed every sign of winning out and leaving him hollow-eyed, stiff and weak in the morning.

All right, all right, he thought finally, hitched himself over, turned on the small lamp on the stand by the bed and leaned down to reach underneath for the old briefcase he always carried with him. He rummaged in it until he found a yellow pad and a chewed ball-point. Maybe he could empty his mind of the questions if he wrote them all down. He flapped the pad on the sheet in the circle of lamp light and began to scribble. It was no matter whether what he wrote was legible.

Why Rack. in Nesset? How long, etc?
  Find out tomorrow.
What has he found?
All part of same thing?
  Find out tmrw.
Why so silent about whereabouts so long?
  Find out 2 above; probably same ans.
How Rack. know I tired?
How know I staying Birdie's?
Was it Rack. in truck outside 5 & 10 this AM?
  (I heard that truck some other time. Where?)
  Had to be Rack.!
Remson confusing Rack. and me?
Why afraid of Rack./me?
  Had to be Rack. in truck!
Was I lured here?
By Rack.?
By Rack. and girl looks like Maria?
How would Rack know about Maria and me?
  Couldn't have. We no see, talk in more than year.
Why Rack. need me?
  Probably same ans. as 1, 2, 3 above.
Should I have another go at C. C. R.?

What's the use? M.'s young life really no use to me anyhow. He not know her probably now if fell over. You were clutching at straws.

DID RACKLIN LURE ME HERE??!!

COINCIDENCE *TOO GREAT* WE BOTH IN THIS BLASTED PLACE SAME TIME!!

FIND
OUT
TMRW!

BUT, WHY?!

TMRW!

Lured here—

BY MARIA?

Could it be she *is* still alive?!
Oh, God!

TMRW!
TMRW!
TMRW!

He shoved the pad and pen onto the floor with one irritated swipe, almost knocked the lamp off its stand in the process of switching it off and rolled over to lie flat on his back staring up into the darkness at the top of the room, more vexed now than he had been before he decided to write the questions down.

Tomorrow, or the next day, or the next, or the day after that . . .

He tried harder than ever to block everything out. Finally the combination of bone weariness and his intense concentration on nothingness began voiding his brain. It stopped roiling unknowns; questions slithered off to left and right, away, amidst flows of colors and swells of blackness.

Just as he was about to slip out of himself, one final swell bore up the vision of Maria's face and then her breasts, her thighs, her whole naked body, to undulate softly in the blackness. His limbs washed in warmth and he began to rise and throb as he remembered somewhere in his near-dream that he had not wanted her or thought of her that way since she died.

He rolled over hard on himself and bathed himself in the coldest water out of the deepest well his memory could draw from: the vision of Maria's death. To hide from that horror, it was no trouble to flee into deathlike sleep.

La Playa, California
August 22, 1984

Dear David,

She found it! Fräulein Altenbäumer found the letter at last just as I said she would. In fact, she found all the letters Lon Waugh ever wrote me! Unbeknownst to me, the always efficent Miss A. had been keeping a neat little file of them over the years. What had happened was the entire file had gone *behind* the filing cabinet drawer. You can see how this might happen, putting it away in haste one Tuesday afternoon, under "W" for Waugh —and I don't correspond with any "X's", "Y's" or "Z's."

I think the letter speaks for itself, David. I have nothing to add to it at this time, so for now,

Best regards,
J. F. S.

David Sorensen slipped the photo copy of Gamelon's letter from behind Mr. S.'s. It was long and written in a hand worse than his own. On top of that, the copy quality was not the best. He began the painful deciphering.

Wasco, California
July 15, 1984

Dear Mr. S.,

Dr. Ching agreed to help me. I've delivered what was needed and am waiting now to hear the results. Thank you for opening the path for me.

After meeting with Ching, I thought to try to see you personally, but I didn't know your schedule and, having driven in from Utah, I was already bushed and still had the hundred and some miles up here to Wasco ahead of me.

Even if I hadn't promised you an explanation on the phone, I would have written anyway. The last week—beginning the seventh, actually—has been the most intellectually and spiritually disturbing period in my life. I must tell someone about it. I could have had a good listener in Birdie David, my only haven of normalcy while I was in Nesset. She would have heard me out, but she would have been upset and confounded by what I had to tell. I can't think of anyone else but you who would not think me completely mad.

We must go back to the day Maria was killed—but you don't know about that and you must if you are to understand the rest. Yes, she was blown to pieces . . .

JULY 7, 1984

Nesset

He thought he dreamt still and that the hand stroking the back of his neck as he lay sprawled half on his back, half on his side, was the fragile, crushed-green smelling hand of Birdie David. Then he knew the hand was heavy and that the odor coming to his nostrils was that of sun lightly mixed with dust and sweat.

The stroking stopped and a deep voice crooned, "Time to get up, Little Brother—hmm . . ." Racklin leaned over him and glanced down. "Seems you already are, and nicely, nicely, or is that just a piss hard masquerading as the result of one last delightful dream?" Racklin chuckled as he stepped away from the bed and over to the window looking out on the orchard.

Gamelon flipped over on his stomach. He batted his eyes against the light and the sleepers in the ducts of them. He was annoyed. Why was he annoyed? He did not like the idea of waking up feeling annoyed.

"What time is it?" he asked the world in general in a sleep-husked voice.

"A little after seven, Lon," Racklin replied from his place by the window. "Birdie's got the coffee on and the sausage in the pan. I invited myself to breakfast, by the way, on you."

"Well, go keep her company," Gamelon said almost angrily. "I haven't had a bath in two-three days, or a shave. I'm not doing anything else until I get cleaned up."

Racklin headed for the door by way of the bed. He smacked Gamelon on his bare left cheek in passing and said, "Don't go back to sleep. Got a lot to see today." And he went out whistling as noisily and tunelessly as he sang.

Gamelon made no move to get up. Why was he annoyed? Before any of the other questions from yesterday got a chance to come trooping back, he seemed to need to answer that.

He hauled himself up and out and stumbled across the room to yank a towel from the rack by the sink in the corner. As he wrapped it around his middle, it came to him: he resented Racklin's seemingly inordinate interest in his sexuality. As far as he could remember, anything of the sort between them had died with early teenagerhood as was normal.

He started off down the hall toward the bathroom. But, why should he resent that interest? He certainly had nothing to hide from anyone of any sex. He was proud of his masculinity; he enjoyed it; he appreciated it when others enjoyed it. He had never sought to capitalize on it or make any exhibition of it to anyone, but he enjoyed it.

He climbed into the tub and pulled the shower curtain around him on its old-fashioned ring. He began to fumble with the taps and almost scalded himself before he found the right combination. Then why did any other's attention to something he himself was proud of, appreciated, enjoyed annoy him?

It was not just any other, it was Racklin specifically. He had forgotten over the years: nothing was sacred for Racklin. He had forgotten that as far as Racklin was concerned, everything that happened to interest him at the moment for any reason was Racklin's to view, use, comment upon, assess and interpret. What any particular something or possessor of something might happen to feel or think about the process mattered not in the least to Racklin. And, Racklin's interpretation was always his own, regardless of what the truth might be, and even if facts militated to the contrary. And, when he was through viewing, using, interpreting, whoever or whatever had been his interest was stripped, no privacies left.

He finished toweling down, restowed his soap in the toilet kit and headed back toward his room to shave. That was what he resented: with Racklin around, and no matter how brilliant, charming and fascinating he might be otherwise, there were no privacies. Everything was grist for his cool, aggressive brain.

He did not know what Racklin had said to her, but he had Birdie chuckling over her griddle and a growing stack of pancakes as Gamelon came into the kitchen. Then, Racklin stepped up close behind the old lady, squeezed her around the waist, put his face in the crook of her neck and burrowed it from side to side as he whispered something in her ear. Birdie gave a whoop and elbowed him away.

The swinging door creaked as Gamelon let it go and stood looking quizzically at the two of them and thinking, ". . . no matter how charming he might be . . ."

"I asked him why he wore that great big beard in all this heat," Birdie said to Gamelon by way of explanation for all the fun. "He said it was so's he'd fit into the surroundin's. Now, to my way o' thinkin', if that beard was short an' scraggly or lank or gray, I could see that maybe, but as it is, he looks like a walkin' brush fire!"

"That wasn't good enough for her," Racklin went on, "so I had to tell her the truth."

"Had to feed me a string o' sweet apples!" Birdie rared back, one hand on a hip and whooped again. " 'So's nobody'll have any doubts I'm a man,' says he, as if anybody would," she said, mimicking Racklin's deep voice and raking him from head to toe with one appreciative glance, " 'and because all the beautiful ladies like me love men with beards.' "

Indeed "a string of sweet apples," Racklin sweet apples, Gamelon thought as he remembered how vehemently Maria had once threatened to leave him if he so much as contemplated a moustache.

But, the light mood prevailed as the two men "sat to it" at Birdie's direction and started to plow through big pads of spicy country sausage, golden eggs, fresh from the hen and sunnyside, wheatcakes, cold milk and coffee, fresh ground and brewed with sweet well water. Birdie stirred around the table, replenishing here, refilling there, and let the men eat in silence, except for one question of Gamelon which was more a statement. She stopped beside his chair about mid-way through the meal and said flatly, "You didn't say you had family livin' in these parts."

Gamelon felt a little silly when he had to admit to her that until last night, he had not known he had either.

As he swirled the last of the egg yolk from his plate with the last wedge of pancake and lifted the fork to his mouth, he was glad for one thing: he had an answer for the beard: "sweet apples" as Birdie said.

It was just another of Racklin's devices to keep from talking when he suggested Gamelon take the Fiat and follow him and Gamelon knew it. All he had offered as reasons were, first, a shrug-shouldered, "Who knows, you might want to see more of the country on your own later," and then, "and who knows, that relic of mine could go anytime. Be nice to have another set of wheels available in this country if that happened."

Gamelon had not come to see the country and now he felt Racklin knew that. Regardless of the condition of its suspension, Gamelon's ear had already told him Racklin's truck ran as smoothly and effortlessly as a hunting cheetah. And, Gamelon knew that as it had been so many times in the past, especially when they were young together, he was not in control. He had not been since he had clasped his brother to him the evening before. At the same time, he had a submerged feeling—that finding out about Maria was somehow one warp woven into the entire fabric of his brother's doings.

He sighed and shrugged as he cranked the old Fiat then gunned it until it was more or less hitting on all four. As far back as he could remember, when Racklin decided to mount the driver's seat and take the reins, there was nothing he could do but climb aboard the wagon and try to see Racklin did not fall off and hurt himself.

He u-turned the car in the middle of the street, coming down hard once, twice, in the process, having been unsuccessful at avoiding two potholes, pulled in behind the truck, tooted the nasal little horn. Racklin's bare arm out the window waved him forward and they were off.

Gamelon tried to follow as closely as he could in Racklin's meandering tracks as the truck headed out of town to the south, then turned east on a decomposed granite road. Racklin seemed to have a radar-like ability to foresee holes and avoid them, but, to anyone looking down from on high, they would have appeared a drunk dung beetle following a stoned cockroach home after an all-night debacle.

Oh, what the hell, Gamelon thought to himself and smiled. It was another crystalline high desert morning. His brother, whatever his eccentricities, was alive and well. He would find out what he would find out about Maria today or tomorrow or the day after that, if he found out anything at all. He had to admit his never-failing curiosity *had* been piqued about what Racklin had discovered that made him so mysterious. That same curiosity, now briefly back to being horticultural, was already engaged in wondering how many thousands of gallons of water per acre, how many tons of what fertilizers it might take to make the increasingly arid country they were weaving through bloom like his own lower San Joaquin Valley.

Ahead, he saw Racklin's arm come out the window to begin to conduct as vigorously as the evening before. He wondered what words he was howling to himself this time. Then, he found a song of his own to fit the beat and smiled to himself at his subliminal choice as he tuned up in a mellow baritone, "You do something to me, something that simply mystifies me . . ."

He was vaguely surprised when they rolled past a heavy carved wooden sign standing alone in what looked to him like just another barren, scrub-covered spot that informed him they were entering the Dixie National Forest, that firearms, open fires and camping, except in designated areas, were prohibited.

It was a beautiful morning. He was more rested, he realized, than he had thought he would be after the bout with the unknowns last night. He felt like he had enough of Birdie's good, wholesome food packed away inside to last him the whole day if need be. Let the rest of the morning, the rest of the day take him where it might. He was ready.

Ahead, brake lights flashed and Racklin's arm stopped beating time and signaled broadly for a right turn into what looked to Gamelon to be no better than a dual goat track through the scrub and stones. Nevertheless, he dutifully turned the Fiat in the wake of the pickup.

No sooner had they turned than they began to jounce and sideslip down. Gamelon fought to keep the Fiat right side up on its small wheels while ahead, Racklin made the old pickup roar as he rammed as dead straight down the steep incline as he could. Once or twice when he glanced up to gauge his distance from the back of the truck, Gamelon glimpsed Racklin through its rear window, hatless and working his wheel wildly to force the slope as fast as possible. His own teeth clenched, his lips clamped in a thin line, Gamelon grimly imagined Racklin grinning from ear to ear and shouting trite things like "Heigh-ho, Silver!" and "Up, up and away!" with devilish glee.

A hundred yards of this brought them bottoming through a drainage ditch and back onto a road where Racklin swung to the right without a signal and took off in a cloud of dust like a banshee fleeing the dawn.

Damn you, clown, Gamelon thought after a quick glance to left and right made him certain the road they were on now was the same one they had left. It probably had gone on a mile, a half mile, a few hundred yards farther, then doubled back on itself lower down. But you had to take a short cut just for the hell of it, right? You would, Rack, particularly if it was dangerous and broke up your own particular monotony. He downshifted the now even more battered Fiat and headed off into the trailing dust cloud.

For half a mile, the road turned in a lazy half circle that had been chiseled from the base of a high hill. On the opposite side, there was a precipitous fall down to a dry wash where old cottonwoods and live oaks stoically tolerated the dry summer and waited for the winter rains to fill the wash again.

"Leaving The Dixie National Forest . . ." the sign on the right said.

A few hundred yards farther, "Now Entering The Dixie National . . ."

Just as Gamelon realized the road threaded through a ragged edge between public and private land and was wondering how much the taxpayers had had to put out for all the fancy carved signs, his car crested a sharp rise. Right on the other side, the pickup stood idling in a small turnout, Racklin leaning against the rear fender. Gamelon pulled in behind it followed by his own rolling dust ball, stuck his head out the window, coughed, then yelled, "What's the matter?"

Racklin shook his head that nothing was and gestured for Gamelon to get out of the car. When he had, Racklin led him over to the far edge of the turnout high above the cottonwoods and the wash and beyond the swell of the soaring hillside. As they turned and stood facing the strong breeze from the southwest and below, he said to Gamelon, "Pretty, isn't it? Kind of unexpected around here."

Spreading out below them, ever broadening between flaring buttes as it fell away from the pinch stopper of hills where they stood, was a beautiful valley. Every acre of it was plowed or green with orchards or gold with early summer wheat ready for harvesting. Here and there, the dots of farm houses, barns, sheds that looked exceedingly prosperous in comparison with Nesset showed amongst the rich patchwork of the valley floor.

"Around here, they call it Swede's Valley," Racklin went on, "probably because some guy named Larsen or the like settled out here back when anybody who came with an even vaguely Scandinavian sounding name was a Swede to everybody who was already here.

"There's a good hard surface road right up the middle of it coming north and west out of St.

George but it'd have taken us half the morning to go that way around. Besides, it's not half the fun." He slapped his brother on the back. "How'd you like my little short cut?"

Gamelon gave him one flat glance and grunted.

"Thought you'd like to see it—as a horticulturist. The whole valley sits on top of an underground lake. Deep wells, pumps and presto! Eden in the desert! Many aren't aware of the view from here. The shoulder of that hill's in the way of it when you're driving. You'd never have seen it if I hadn't shown you, and we'll be turning off soon." He pointed lazily down the road to where a rickety plank bridge crossed the dry wash a few hundred yards ahead and below. "We'll be home in no time," he finished, climbed aboard his aging Pegasus, clanked back out onto the road and away, down into the top of Swede's Valley. Again, Gamelon followed dutifully.

The plank bridge had no guard rails. Gamelon watched as Racklin pounded the truck across, seemingly oblivious to the fact that his right wheels were only inches from the edge. He turned in and lined himself up more carefully with the center; he had no intention of ending up in the wash after having made it this far. As he started across, it came to him: if this was home, why hadn't his brother asked him to bring his things and be his guest?

At the far end of the bridge, low down, leaning against a boulder, was yet another sign: "Now Entering . . ." He shook his head. Somewhere in the billowing dust, he seemed to have missed the last "leaving."

The small farmhouse was all raw, dry, dull brown curling clapboard except for a new plank here and there, some bright new nail heads glinting in the sunlight and a few streaks of dirty white paint that had hung on despite the years of beating summers and tearing winters. More effort seemed to have been spent on the barn nearby: it looked to be sturdy and tight. Rough-sawn bats had been nailed over gaps between the old vertical siding boards. Where the corrugated iron roof had rusted all the way through, it flashed here and there with odd-sized patches of new metal.

Someone had replowed a row or two of the big kitchen garden between the house and the barn. Some lackadaisical hills of sweet corn were beginning to tassel there, some tomato vines ran rampant and needed staking; something had already begun to make lace out of the hairy, dull green eggplant leaves.

Just beyond the barn, what must have been an open farm implement shed lay in ruins, nothing but a fallen jumble of rotting planks and timbers with the rusted remains of a disc harrow showing through the bones.

The fields beyond the buildings had long since been reseeded by the wind and the birds with scrub and wild blackberries into a low, thorny jungle where even grass had to struggle to make its way.

Gamelon nosed the Fiat into the shade alongside the house by Racklin's truck. As he yanked on the hand brake, he reckoned the Olsens and the Sorensens and the Petersens no longer tilled the land as they once had. And, he supposed nobody at the auction twenty years or so ago had had a need for a disc harrow right then.

He knew where he had to be. It all fit: long-deserted buildings not long patched, the sign, "Now Entering . . ." with no intervening "leaving" sign, the fields gone as much back to nature as lack of water would allow in a semi-desert. Something in him tightened, then steadied, relaxed and set. There might be other deserted farms in Swede's Valley, but he doubted it with the water and the richness of the land, and they had not been bought up by the Park Service and let go mostly back to the wild. This had to be the old Rundqvist place.

For Racklin, with his university credentials to flash at the appropriate moment, and being whatever others required of him on that particular day, it would not have been difficult to get temporary use of the old place for "field work." Gamelon wondered what he *had* been the day he had talked the Park Service into lending it to him for a while—over and above his own manipulative self.

There certainly was nothing Gamelon could imagine in the whole area for Racklin to study, no pygmies, no dwarfs, not even a slight strain of steatopygia in the people hereabouts. Knowing Racklin, he had probably concocted some esoteric grant project, possibly even passed himself off as something other than an anthropologist—an ecologist, perhaps, funded to study how once-tilled land passed back to its natural state. And, knowing Racklin, he could drag that out for years if it suited his purpose.

Discovering that purpose was what had clamped and set in his mind as he put the emergency brake on. That he had found the old Rundqvist farm was of no use to him now he knew. There was no Maria here and there had not been for many, many years. Whatever memory of her he ended up with he could always have and he was not given to nostalgic seizures when in the presence of the past.

Racklin had not gotten out of the pickup, but sat very still behind the wheel, his riotously bearded chin on his chest, staring blankly at the horn button. Gamelon looked across toward him, then got out and went straight around the back of his car and up to the window of the truck. He looked fixedly at Racklin for a while, then said in a strong, level tone, "Now I'm here, Racklin. Now you've got me here. Why am I here? No more feinting and dodging, no more yodeling. No more fun and games. I know all your moods, your tricks. No more wrestling, ass-patting or follow-the-leader down roadless hillsides. No more follow-the-leader of any kind. The follower has followed as far as he's going to until he knows why you're here, why he's here, why, so coincidentally, we're both here and a lot more."

Except to lift his hands from his thighs to grip the crossbar of the steering wheel, Racklin remained as he was, saying nothing.

"Come on, Rack . . ."

"All right, all right, Lon," Racklin said in a husky voice. "You'll get your answers. I didn't bring you all this way for nothing."

At Racklin's words Gamelon's head jerked slightly with the tightening of his neck muscles. *Have I been lured here*? But he could not be sure Racklin referred to anything but the trip from Nesset out to the farm. He forced himself to relax.

Finally Racklin turned his head and looked at Gamelon. Gamelon was so shocked at what he saw in his eyes, something he could never remember having seen there before, that his reflexes yelled for him to step back a pace at the same time his affection dictated he step nearer to caress his brother's head and cradle it. The wide eyes were filled with fear so stark it made the amber seem to shiver.

"Why am I here, Lon?" he said in little more than a whisper. "I know what started it all in the first place but that was so small a thing it hardly matters anymore. I'll tell you sometime. What does matter is what keeps me here, what could well chain me to this Godforsaken place for the rest of my life." On the wheel, Racklin's hands began to tremble. He gripped the bar hard. The knuckles, as big and ruddy as Gamelon's, bled white with the pressure. "I'm afraid, Lon—no, I'm terrified. Sometimes when I'm alone I swear I shake down in the roots of my soul.

"I know I've been playing with you. I didn't know what else to do. I was playing for time, I guess, until today. I desperately need somebody to share what I've found, somebody intelligent, somebody who can be objective, maybe even *somebody who can tell me what I have to do*!" He pounded one big fist on the wheel and seemed near to tears. "I wanted you. I couldn't think of anybody else I could trust or who might understand—but I didn't want you. I love you too much to get you involved in it all. But I had to, I had to do it! Please understand that."

Just as it seemed Racklin had strung himself so far he would fall off his careening wagon, just as Gamelon was beginning to grope about wildly in his mind for the words and actions to break his brother's fall, the hands on the wheel relaxed and Racklin seemed visibly to take himself in hand. The helplessness that had replaced the fear in his eyes faded. He sighed deeply, turned away from Gamelon and leaned his head back against the cab wall. After a few moments, he said in a completely normal voice, "You'll get your answers. All of them. First, I've got a question for you—I don't want an answer now, necessarily, I just want to plant the question."

He turned his head to look at Gamelon again. The amber eyes glittered again with the usual wildness, the drive, the brilliance and—Gamelon's consciousness gasped inside him. Did he see something else in them for the second time in moments—just a touch of madness?

"No answer now, Lon, just the question: what the hell *is* life anyhow? You tell me what you think later. I'll tell you what I think right now. I think life's a fucking joke!"

* * *

In and out among the cornstalks and tomato vines and insect-ravaged eggplant, up and down the old weedgrown furrows of the kitchen garden, circling out and back and all around Gamelon, all the way from the house to the barn, Racklin danced. He danced a cross between a square dance and the dance Gamelon could imagine King David might have done before, behind and all around the Ark of the Covenant as it wound its sacred way slowly up toward Jerusalem. And all the while he danced, he chanted, sing-spoke like a square dance caller or an auctioneer:

"Oh, life's a joke,
Life's a joke!
There's nothin' in the end
Worth *livin'* FOR!

"Well, maybe there is,
And maybe there ain't.
I don't know
'Cause I *ain't* no SAINT!

"Death's a joke.
Oh, death's a joke!
There's nothin' here,
There's nothin' there
That can make it worth it
For a *man* to CROAK!

"And so's the YMCA!
HEY!
So's the YMCA!
Tennis,
Swimmin'
Hikin'

SHIT!
It's one big
Male bor-dell-OOO!
So's the YMCA!
HEY!

Gamelon marveled. Nothing sacred: not life or death or the YMCA. But, he could not keep himself from smiling at his brother's caperings and ridiculous rhymings. He found himself—in spite of himself—feeling the urge to join in even though he did not know where the dance led.

Had Racklin always been this changeable? Had he always been able to flash with light speed from inner terror to utter nonsense? Had he always been able to swing so quickly from one extreme to the other, backstroking easily through several other emotions along the way? Had he always been so capricious?

Yes, yes, he thought to himself as bits and pieces of many a risky, raucous episode from their childhood tumbled helter-skelter through his memory. Yes, but he was older now and the swings, the extremes at either end and the pauses in between seemed somehow more intense.

Was it that they were more intense or only more controlled, more refined, more tools than true emotions? Was it all an act to mask his real motives?

Gamelon cleared his mind, let his smile die and reset himself on the one thing that had become uppermost: what was Racklin up to?

Before him, Racklin bowed deeply from the waist and flung his right arm wide in a princely welcome as he opened a small door in the side of the barn just wide enough for Gamelon to slip through.

A thousand jagged sun shards swirled around and around behind Gamelon's eyeballs in the sudden blackness inside the barn. He dug at his eyes with the backs of his fists.

Behind the dying flashes, huge white squares floated.

He let his hands drop and stood blinking rapidly.

The white squares settled into the emerging dimness and floated just off the ground, their edges swelling and contracting, rippling like the reflections of cube moons in a midnight pool.

He shut his eyes hard.

Beneath his feet was earth, uneven, and trodden to the hardness of concrete, but the feet moved too easily, slipped nearly on the fine lubrication of dusty hay bits settling down from the remnant piles in an encircling loft he supposed to float in the deeper gloom above his head. Wispy bits of old odors came to him: sun-dried alfalfa, sour milk, manure, yet somehow he knew the place was clean as old barns went. He thought he heard the minute shuffle and infinitesimal squeak of a mouse near at hand, inside, outside, he did not know.

He opened his eyes again.

The white squares had solidified themselves into platforms—two, three of them.

The bats over the cracks sealed out almost every thread of light and every questing tentacle of breeze. His skin began to salt and prickle as he began to sweat.

Beds. Three beds.

Each bed was lit by a single shaded down-casting light so dim as almost not to illuminate at all.

He blinked again.

By the farthest bed, a huddled figure sat—on a stool, he thought—forearms on knees, staring at the white covered mound on the white platform that was a white bed without headboard or footboard or sides.

Nothing more.

Three beds.

Three white platforms with mounds upon them, one slender, the others seeming larger.

Three low lamps and a figure.

Nothing more.

Nothing but a silence so absolute he thought he heard his lids grate across his corneas as he blinked his eyes one final time.

A silence so absolute he jerked like a man tied to a post for execution jerks when the bullets strike when Racklin touched his arm and whispered near his ear, "Now that your eyes are used to the dark—or the lack of it—" and then stepped away from him toward the nearest bed.

Some kind of secret ward. Racklin had people here with some strange disease, something that made them hypersensitive to light, something that made them feel the cold even late on a summer morning. Something rare for this part of the country and it was Racklin, the physician, who now controlled.

He moved to stand beside his brother.

Nothing.

Nothing but the head of a plain-faced but not unattractive girl of twenty or so, her long, dark hair fanned around prettily on the pillow. She did not appear feverish or drawn or in pain. That was all he could see; the rest of her was covered. And, she slept.

Nothing. She just slept.

Racklin leaned down and called to her in a soft, loving voice, "Jennie? Jennie?"

Nothing for a moment, then the faintest of delicate smiles tinged the girl's lips and her body moved slightly.

As it did, it was as though the operator of the projector showing the close-up scene before him had accidentally jarred the machine. The retina, too slow to record each finely separated image of the girl, Jennie's, face, saw all of them at once. But there was more: behind the dividing then coalescing images that were that face, he seemed to see in rapid succession a great mound of twisted hair with hollow eyes, a perfect, throbbing flesh-colored cube, a crystal with entrails encased in it as a primordial fly is encased in amber, a writhing mass of tendrils and spikes swimming in deep, watery blue.

He shook his head sharply.

And, there was nothing.

The smile had faded from the girl's face and, she slept.

"What is sh—" He cleared his throat. "Why is she here? What's the matter with her?" he whispered.

"Nothing," Racklin replied. "Absolutely nothing, as you can see. She's just asleep." He turned his head toward Gamelon and even in the dim light he could see the amber eyes were bright, delighted, almost merry. "Come on."

He thought that Racklin would make the logical progression and stop at the side of the second bed in the row, but Racklin passed it by and went on to where the figure squatted on its haunches—he now saw—beside the third. The second mound was completely covered and he could not help but wonder if whoever was beneath the drawn sheet was a sleeper who had died. And was the mound really wider than the one made by the girl's slim body, wider and somewhat longer? He was not sure.

The mound on the third platform was covered, too, but this time, he knew his judgment was true: it was definitely larger: wider, but not quite as long.

As he moved up silently to stand beside Racklin, he caught the sheens of glossy black hair and dark blue sateen. He stood there, sweat pouring from every pore of his body, as Racklin said softly, "Slim Boy, this is my brother, Lon."

As the figure turned its head slowly around and up, he recognized the young Indian who had come into the five-and-dime the morning before. The man looked at him steadily for a long moment, then nodded slightly and returned his attention to the white mound on the bed.

Suddenly, seeming in the silence as loud as a cannon's roar, there was the softest of sounds. It came to Gamelon as nothing more than the deep intake of a breath through pursed lips.

"Guess that's the belly goin'," Slim Boy said to no one in particular.

"What?!"

"Nothing, Lon, nothing. It's all right," Racklin said, then to the Indian, "It's—they're that far along, huh?"

Before Slim Boy could answer, there was a slight zing like a careless brush on the topmost string of a great golden concert harp.

"What was—"

Paying no attention to him, Slim Boy went on, "Yep, the belly. I can tell from where the sound was."

"Maybe it was the chest," Racklin said and made to lift the sheet. At the same instant, Slim Boy's hand shot out and grabbed Racklin's wrist in a stone grip and Gamelon grabbed his other forearm. "Racklin, what's going on?! I want to know—now!"

Racklin shook him off with an angry, "Soon enough!" Then, he turned on the Indian. "Let me go, you bastard!"

Slim Boy made no move to do so. He just cocked his head in Gamelon's direction and asked Racklin calmly, "He know all about this?"

Racklin shook his head.

"Can he take it?"

"Of course he can take it! He's a scientist just like me. He'll see it just like I see it: clinically, objectively, questioning. Now, let go!"

Slim Boy turned his head all the way around to look Racklin dead in his amber eyes, his own black ones unwavering. "OK, if you say so." He shrugged and let go of Racklin's wrist. "He ain't *my* brother."

"No, this is," Racklin grunted, and threw back the sheet.

Gamelon froze. He stopped breathing until the pain in his chest and the unheard screaming of his cells for oxygen forced him to. He did not blink until his reflexes took over and did it for him to protect his eyeballs, drying rapidly in the stifling heat inside the barn. His dripping body became ice cold. His brain ceased to do anything but record the impressions sent to it without either reaction or rationalization.

Slim Boy chortled once. "See? Good thing you didn't bet me no pony or no liquor on it. I been through this once already. I can't say I *remember*, but somehow I know the belly goes before the head or the chest or the prick. Call it ancient Navajo wisdom."

He chuckled again. "I'll bet you the chest goes next!" He turned a glittering smile on Racklin. "Come on, Red Cousin, that nice gold chain you wear under all that hot, dumb beard against nothing from me says the chest goes next. Hurry up, now; he—they're almost done."

Before his last word was out, the fine, tiny wooshing came again.

"See? See! I told you! You watch! It's the chest!"

All Gamelon could do was watch, numbed by double but opposite drugs: complete fascination and near-overwhelming repulsion.

The membrane of flesh alive with tiny red veins connecting the chests of the other two Slim Boys sleeping on their sides facing each other, their thick black hair tangled around their heads and over their faces, began to truncate in the center. It became narrower and narrower and then, as though pinched between invisible fingers, it became only a string, then a thread. Then, a second later, it parted with that almost inaudible harp string sound and the two resulting tags of flesh subsided gently and disappeared into the two breastbones like melting butter fading into hot pieces of toast.

"Damn you for bein' so slow," Slim Boy mumbled at Racklin, "But I'm givin' you one more chance. Your chain says the peter next, my ancient Navajo wisdom says the head."

"OK, OK, why not?" Racklin mumbled in return. "How would I know for sure?"

The small soft wind sound again and then that of the single string and the foreheads parted and the heads themselves lolled away from each other.

And again, as the thin, stretched bar of flesh from groin to groin pinched, sang and separated. Two foreskins slid up to reveal two heads, then slipped back to cover them even as the two bodies rolled away from each other onto their backs and lay as though dead. Slim Boy chuckled and said mostly to himself, "Wonder what it's like with the girls? Wonder if it's like two big pairs o' lips partin' after a big smack? I'm gonna be there when Jennie's time comes." Then he reached out and touched each of the sleeping figures before him on the forehead, the lips and the chest where the heart would be and said softly, "Welcome, Little Brothers," and without taking his eyes from the perfect images of himself, put his hand, palm up, over his shoulder. "Gimme my gold, Red Cousin."

Racklin fumbled at the back of his neck, then dribbled the heavy gold chain into the upturned red-brown palm.

Without a word of thanks, Slim Boy stood up, dropped the chain in one tight Levi's pocket, turned, and stepped in front of the other brothers. To Racklin he said, simply, "Sucker. You can't ever beat old Navajo wisdom," then, "Got to go in and get 'em some food ready. They're gonna be hungrier 'n shit when they wake up. That I *do* remember, even if it was a long time back." And he began to fade into the gloom between the dim lights and in the general direction of the barn door.

Racklin called at his disappearing back in a stage whisper, "How's Frederick?"

Slim Boy's now-disembodied voice replied, "Don't know. Didn't look at him in a while. He's got a ways to go yet anyhow. He just went to sleep this time yesterday. Check him yourself." A rectangle of brilliance sizzled in the gloom as he opened the barn door, the blackness of his figure dulled it for an instant, then all was stuffy near-darkness again.

The sudden shock of light seemed to punch Gamelon back into sense and sensibility. He shivered once, mightily, and felt the smothering heat again. Now it was his insides that were cold, icy, with the hardening of himself against what he had seen, against believing it. He knew he was not as clinical, as objective as his brother had said, he never had been. God, he thought to himself, he became emotionally involved when one of his promising plant specimens ultimately turned out a failure. He had to harden himself to consign it to the compost heap and go on with the others, get on with it. So he hardened himself now. As clinical, as objective, no; as questioning, yes. His brain boiled with the hows and whys of what his eyes had seen and his brain had remembered. His mind was already almost unconsciously marshalling an endless list of separated details about why such human reproduction was totally impossible, could not happen: Simple versus specialized cells and the way they divided, too long a time to divide, wrong temperatures, lack of fluids, no nutrition . . . Something, something larger, something that encompassed all of it. Something. Mass—

"Come on, Lon. The best is yet to come unless I miss my guess." Racklin took him by the arm and steered him toward the center platform, the middle mound. And Gamelon knew the mound was not a sick sleeper who had died; the mound was Frederick. His inclination was to pull back, back before it was too late for the sanctity of his knowledge, too late for the fundamentals of life upon which he had based all of his own until now, but the heels of his accursed curiosity dug in, gripped, and he stood, as close to a picture of a lifeless monolith as he could make himself as Racklin deftly flicked the sheet away.

Frederick would have been tall, very tall, well over six feet, a long-muscled, blond young man in his early twenties, at the physical peak of his manhood. But, at that moment, Frederick was not quite any of those things.

Frederick lay on its back. It was not yet ready to roll half a gentle turn to face itself. Its skin glowed the angry red of high fever or rampant infection. It glistened all over with a fine haze of sweat. Its thick yellow curls, the fur on its forearms, the backs of its hands, were dank and sticking. And it was swelling, stretching, smearing as if it were nothing more than a huge, long lump of hot flesh-colored putty. Only its ears, its hands and arms on the outer edges of the mass pulling slowly, so slowly away from itself were still recognizable as anything human. Its hair was a long, matted gold cap. Eyes were a bulbous line. The nose was a stretched hillock of tissue and gristle. There was nothing recognizable as chin or neck or chest or groin or knees, but connecting what had been its two legs was a third, as long and as wide as both of them had been together and forming rudimentary feet at the bottom.

And the center of the pulpy, indeterminate mass throbbed and grew. It stretched with a terrible unseen tension. It stretched and it squirmed as though under attack by a hundred thousand maggots. It seethed and shimmered as does the water just above when hundreds of piranha do their victim to excruciating death just below the surface. And all about it hung the dull, nauseating stench of a cannibal feast.

Two clod-like rudimentary hands began to form within the center of the horrible, stinking, gelatinous mass just below where the hips should have been as Gamelon jammed his fists into his temples and started to moan and saw again the flashing pictures of twisted hair with hollow eyes, crystals with visible guts and tendril heaps swimming lazily in the depths.

And then there was nothing.

Nothing he had ever learned was valid.

Nothing he had ever believed in deeply was true.

Nothing that had ever been beautiful for him would exist unsuspect again.

"What the hell *is* life?" Racklin had asked. Not what the hell is life all about, which was how he had interpreted it. What the hell is *life*? Life. Life. Human life itself!

And there was nothing.

Life as he had known it had ceased to exist. It had become as Racklin had said: it was a joke.

Dimly through the agony of his realizations and his moaning, he became aware that Racklin was crooning almost to himself, ". . . so strange it will change what truth is, so beautiful it makes my soul kneel . . ."

Before him what had been Frederick continued to seethe and palpitate and squirm its way toward two, and suddenly he knew what had driven Coolidge Remson to drink. He knew what Maria was—had been—is—was—and that they might have given birth to things more dreadful than cases of incurable sunburn. And he was sure that beneath all the other things he was as moments passed, Racklin was quite possibly mad.

He turned and fled, stumbling, once half falling, through the darkened barn, slammed out through the door and retched in one single putrid stinking geyser what remained of Birdie's good, wholesome breakfast.

When the heaving subsided, Gamelon went off around the barn until he found the side where the early afternoon sun struck the least and sat down in the slender shade, eyes closed, his head between his knees, his rump against the rough boards. His brain sizzled and hummed like an old crystal set tuned between stations, nothing framing. He was only conscious of trying to make himself breathe deeply and regularly.

The lush winter grasses, burned to flat tan hummocks by the midsummer sun, muffled Racklin's steps. Gamelon was unaware he had come to stand beside him until he felt the heavy hand on the back of his neck. He jumped at the touch and shook off his brother's attempt at consolation.

Racklin took his hand away abruptly and for several moments there was silence. Then Racklin's voice came low and spitting, "You disgust me! I go to all this trouble to share this miracle with you out of all the hundreds I could have called on and you come off like a squeamish convent girl! You! You: steady, consistent, determined Gamelon Waugh, scientist, geneticist, horticulturist who's spent all his mature life seeking, probing, trying, dicking around with what makes life work!" His voice rose and tightened. "And at the first sight of something utterly new and totally different you run and you stumble and you puke! It's a wonder you didn't piss in your pants, too!"

"Shut up, Racklin. Just for God's sake shut up for a while. I've got to think. It's horrible—ugly."

"What, horrible because it's different? Ugly because it's new?! That's auto-da-fé thinking. That sends uniqueness to the stake and disagreement to the Iron Maiden! Shit! Get off your intellectual ass! Grow up!"

"No—no, it's not the thing itself I don't think, it's—it's the way it happens . . ."

"Did you ever see a child born?

Gamelon shook his head.

"Ugly! Horrible! What's beautiful about a woman in labor being in agony for hours, maybe days? What's charming and delightful about bursting water sacks and umbilical cords and that same woman being stretched almost beyond endurance on nature's little rack?!

"What's so wonderful, for that matter, about the start of things, the way things are? It may feel good—that's surely one of God's little jokes—but, if He's there, He must laugh his butt off every time two "people" fuck. It sure as hell doesn't *look* good! Ludicrous is more like it!

"You may be a scientist, Gamelon, but as of now I see you're country miles away from reality. You've spent too much time in that sweetly scented greenhouse tripping around the frilly edges of life, pondering on meaningless delicacies.

"In there, in that barn is *life*, Gamelon, new life, in a new way, in a new form, life no alchemist could have conjured and no one but some god or other could have conceived and manufactured! You've got a geneticist's dream, a totally new type of life in the highest form we know right behind your back!" Racklin pounded once on the barn wall with his fist. "And you puke and run! Jesus!"

Somehow all of what Racklin said did not quite hang together; somehow, it did. Gamelon raised his head and looked out over the unkept fields. At least where what parts of life might be more important than others was concerned, he might well have been an ostrich until now. Perhaps people were more important than flowers, but then, what was a man without a rose or a lily without a man? He still needed time to think.

He turned down a suddenly quieted and solicitous Racklin's invitation to come in the house, stood up and headed off in a dead straight line for the Fiat. With a shrug and a smirk, Racklin said, "You'll be back," and let his brother go.

As the Fiat labored up the last of the steep incline that ended just past the turnout overlooking Swede's Valley, he realized how intently, yet mindlessly, he had been driving. His shoulders already ached from hunching over the wheel of the car that always really had been too small for his bulk, and he could not honestly say he could see where he was going, the dust was so thick on the windshield from following Racklin earlier.

He jabbed at the wiper button hoping the blades would flip the worst of the grime away. Nothing happened. Some wires must have come loose during the jolting slide down the hillside, during Racklin's shortcut. He tried the lights, the horn. Nothing. All his protective devices seemed to be out.

He thought of the roll of paper towels and the spray can of glass cleaner he always kept in the trunk and wheeled into the turnout. But then, remembering the valley and subconsciously yearning for another view of its peace in the hopes it might restore some of his own, he eased out as far onto the overlook as he could, braked, shut down the engine and leaned back, staring down the valley's length through the dirt.

That did not please him.

He thrust himself out of the car and walked precipitously close to the farthest edge where the earth and crumbled stone began to soften and threaten to drop him, at the slightest misstep, breaking and dying, into the wash a hundred feet down. He stopped short at the warning shot of a few pebbles skittering then disappearing soundlessly into the space below and stood, his hands jammed deep in his trouser pockets, his bright hair blowing back and by in the southwest wind, strongest there where he was at the top of the valley's funnel. Through lids squinted hard against the high early afternoon sun, he let his eyes pull thirstily at the tranquility, the colors, the subtleties spreading away into the rose and steel-blue haze at the valley's far end.

Slowly, the harmonies before him began to have their effect on his disturbed heart and mind and he found himself relaxing, opening enough to begin to wonder, to begin to be curious again.

Here, yesterday, today and tomorrow, it was just going on mid-summer. How changed would the valley be when fall stole in almost unnoticed and the apples ripened and the fodder for the cattle was down? How changed again when winter, seemingly unexpected, whistled up suddenly cold and as steel blue as the top of the summer haze but far less friendly? How riotous would it be with those greens which only early spring could sponsor?

And yet, how unchanging, season to season, lying undisturbed, all in all, between its caressing, protective hills and buttes? Something seemed to tell him that even if the pumps failed and the farmers vanished, Swede's Valley would still be beautiful—it would still change, but so slowly that to the eye of generations it would not seem to change at all.

So with life. All of life. Human life. Every birth a new but gentle mutation, striving upward in an unbroken reach from the slime, changing yet always the same. The how and why of the happening, the pain and the rest did not matter, nor did where it might lead, what it might be a thousand eons from that day.

Perhaps now he had a basis to begin to deal from.

He turned away from the shifting edge and went back to the car for the towels and the cleaner to clear his view from inside the car as well.

He drove slowly, carefully, the rest of the way back toward Nesset. He was even calm and objective enough to let his mind reckon as he went.

No, life as he knew it had not changed at all. Something new had been added, perhaps, but all the rest of it was just as he had always known it, complete with all its beauties and its tragedies and its stumblings.

Maybe what he had seen during those dimly lit moments in the barn was in the nature of a revolution. Man had had his share: agricultural, industrial, communications, transportation. Perhaps Racklin's "twins" were to infuse the race with a new genetics at a time when it was needed, when it was required in order to produce a desired result that would not be known for lifetimes to come.

There were potholes in the road back to Nesset but no invisible stone walls on it. It might have seemed the Fiat had encountered one, however, as Gamelon smashed the brake pedal so hard the front bumper of the car kissed the gravel and sand of the road in reaction to the impenetrable wall his mind had rammed into, suddenly and totally without warning.

That wall was the something larger, the all-encompassing something that had eluded him back there in the barn when his mind was tumbling with impossibilities and then Racklin had turned him toward the horror that was Frederick.

Mass.

He had had all the indicators, all the ingredients then but had been unable to grasp the whole.

Mass. The human reproductions he had witnessed defied the very basis of physical as well as biological law. It was utterly, incontrovertably impossible for anything, *anything* to replicate itself without taking sustenance, without taking matter from somewhere else, matter that once rearranged and recombined in that thing's own particular patterns becomes the atoms, the neutrons and protons of the new thing.

The simplest single-celled creature dividing becomes two of itself, but half the size of the original to start with. But one 165-pound Indian could not become two 165-pound Indians without rivers of water and mountains of food to remake in the process. Mass could not generate an equivalent mass out of nothing.

The Fiat's engine chattered, coughed now and again as Gamelon sat staring at the gritty nothingness of the empty road ahead. Then the cruel lash of his curiosity bit and he thrilled under its sting as the possibility of someday glimpsing the answer to one of the most intriguing questions of the universe loomed up behind his eyes: How to create matter out of nothing.

Yes, Racklin had been right, definitely right in the face of all this: He had too long "tripped around the frilly edges of life, pondering on meaningless delicacies."

By the time he came in sight of the straggling southern edge of Nesset, he was setting up proper standards for observing and recording data in his mind and searching back to his college days to try to remember what tissue samples should be studied.

He rounded the corner into the square short and had to swerve and slam on the brakes again, but this time to keep from running over a bundle of black rags and moth-eaten blankets that looked as though it had been carelessly flung against the horse-and-buggy height curb. He might have steered around it after he recovered had he not seen tiny feet in stained, holed moccasins protruding from the black end of the bundle.

He rammed the gear lever into park and, forgetting the emergency brake, jumped from the car and around to the pile. He knelt down and lifted the blankets to find the taut, sunken face of an old, old woman in a ragged frame of dirty white hair wisps and set with wide black eyes, their pupils going silver with the swelling falls of cataracts.

He stood up and looked around for someone to help, but the neglected square and all the streets and cracked sidewalks around it were totally deserted in the face of the midafternoon heat.

It was only another block to Birdie's. He got the car to the curb, off and braked, then went back and made to collect the bundle in his arms. As he did, the woman struggled feebly against him and strained her head away.

He got her up nevertheless and started off with his frail burden toward the rooming house. As they went, even though the wasted, lined face showed no emotion, the black eyes with the smudged pupils roamed his face unceasingly until finally they seemed to take some decision. Then one old hand with fingers taloned by arthritis gripped his bicep, the withered body relaxed and the old woman turned her face comfortably into his chest.

With his arms full of the old Indian woman, all Gamelon could do was kick the front door to attract Birdie's attention. When she finally responded, she yanked open the door. "What's all the ruckus—" then, at the sight of the ragged, pitiful bundle, she became all brusque, clucking solicitude as he had hoped she would. When he began to apologize, to protest about inconvenience, she nailed him eye-to-eye. "You remember all them drunk cowboys I had to roust? Well, I've home-doctored as many Navajos from chiefs to newborn papooses in my time as I have raised hung-over ranch hands! Get her down into that little room next to mine."

Gamelon navigated along the narrow hall, careful not to bump his light cargo against the walls, then into the plain room with only a ladder-back chair, a wardrobe, a dresser and a brass single bed. He had no sooner laid the old woman on it than Birdie was everywhere, doing, undoing, tidying, plumping, comforting, but mostly shooing him hither and yon out of her path and finally, with a top sergeant bark, into the kitchen for "the basin under the sink full of cool tap water and some clean cloths from the drawer over next to the door into the pantry."

When he had done her bidding, he moved away from the bed and leaned against the wall by the door. Birdie cooed to the old woman in words he could not understand and supposed to be Navajo as she tenderly bathed her face and hands with the cool water. Gamelon could not help but appreciate this new facet of Birdie's capabilities.

The old woman began to chant in a voice as thin and wispy as the scant feathers of hair around her face, first on one tone, then on another not far removed from the first. All the while her withered hands either touched and touched again at a few ragged loops of turquoise beads around her corded neck, their strings knotted and reknotted until there were almost more knots than beads, or waved aimlessly in the air like those of a happy ten-week-old baby.

Who was she? What was her name and how had she come to a dry Nesset gutter a hundred miles or more from the nearest edge of her land, alone and ill by all indications, Gamelon wondered.

Then, a feeling, all at the same time infinitely

warm and strictly exclusive, stole over him. It seemed to emanate from the women, one caring, one cared for. It had crept over leaning, loitering men for hundreds of centuries: his presence was not required but he was also being warned not to stray too far in case it was.

It was a good time to bring the Fiat the rest of the way up the street.

For almost thirty minutes he sat alone in the shade on the top step, absorbing the light and the silence of the lengthening afternoon, easing the reins on his mind to let his memory wander where it would. It roamed the perfumes and half-shade of the crossing shed, touched quickly but warmly on shy Jorge and his absolute simplicity and guilelessness. It caught its breath at the surprised loveliness of Maria that infamous night of the dumped Margarita and almost lost it completely as the recalled joy of making love to her flooded. It smiled recalling an extraordinarily witty reply from Mr. S. to one of his letters. It shunted and twirled, the Blind Man in a game of Bluff, as the happenings of the last thirty-six hours rushed in, taunted, then turned and fled to just beyond reach.

And it kept coming back like a pin to a magnet to the Fiat, slumped a little on the left front and filthy, below him on the road.

He had thought to drag Birdie's garden hose around from the back and hook it up to the tap by the steps and shower off the worst of the grime at least, but he had not gotten any farther than taking off his shoes and socks and rolling up his pants' legs when he heard the screen door open behind him. He turned and watched as Birdie came out, wiping her hands on her big kitchen apron, then eased herself into her favorite rocker. She sat shaking her head for a few moments, then she pinched at her eyes across the high bridge of her nose and muttered, "Poor thing, poor thing—pitiful . . ."

Gamelon swiveled, bunched his knees and clasped them in his huge arms. "How is she?"

"More famished and dried out then anything far's I can tell, but she won't take nothin'. I tried. I warmed her some o' that beef broth I'm holdin' for soup tomorrow. I tried plain tea. I tried water. She won't take nothin'."

"Why not, I wonder, if she's all that hungry and thirsty?"

"I don't know. Poor old thing, she don't make any sense about it neither. All I can get is she won't eat or drink 'less *Nayé nez ghani* or *Tqo bajish chí ni* gives it to her, that if anybody else gives her to eat or drink, she'll die."

"Does she think somebody's trying to poison her?"

"Lord only knows."

"Who are *Nayé* . . . *Nayé nez*—what was it—and the other one?"

"Son, my Navajo's real rusty. There was a day when I spoke it better almost'n English and when I knew a lot of their tales, but now . . . Well, best I can remember right off, they's *they*, all right, but *they* ain't people. Them two was gods of a sort, twin gods, twin brothers."

He did not realize it until that moment, but the word "twin" was like the blatant dive claxton on a submarine. At the sound of it, his mind scuttled below and prepared to track the unknown with all the sensitivities available to it. By the time it was secure within its shell and recording, Birdie had meandered a bit off the subject.

". . . grew up there, stayed right on there till that unusual hot afternoon in the spring of '34 when my Johnny's "T" pickup just stopped about a mile south of my father's trading post.

"He'd just started in to cattle dealin', young, gettin' prosperous—an' handsome, I can tell you that. On his way between auctions, shortcuttin' through the middle of the Navajo nation, he was.

"Took near two weeks for the part of his truck to come. He got it put in and was all set to leave when he asked me if I'd go along, marry him first place we found a Justice of the Peace.

"I loved him so much by then, I just threw everything I owned into an ol' carpet bag'd been my mother's, hitched up my skirts and climbed aboard.

"Never was sorry once . . ." Birdie fell to silent musing.

Gamelon could appreciate the loneliness she had lived with intimately every day since her Johnny had gone. It was softer, perhaps, and crammed with memories muted to pastel by time, but kin, nonetheless, to the emptiness of his own life since Maria.

"I wonder why she's fixed on those twin gods," he asked to get her back on the track.

"Huh—it ain't all as simple as that. The old woman—Old Bead Woman, she calls herself—she seems not only to be fixed on them gods but to have 'em all mixed up with what I guess is some real people. I can't be sure because she goes on about 'em all pretty much the same—switchin' 'em back and forth, as it was, sometimes all in the same breath.

"There's somebody she calls Firehead and somebody else she calls Firehead Again. Somehow they seem to be all one with a Bright Red Cousin and a Dark Red Cousin. You see—"

"Red Cousin?!"

"Uh-huh—you see, with the Navajo, they got three names: a secret one nobody knows but them, a name people call 'em when they talk *about* 'em or when they talk about themselves and one they use when they're talkin' *to* somebody. Now that last one's important. It always has some relation in it, the closer the better, 'cause for them, if there ain't, it's an insult, it means they wouldn't want to *be* related to whoever they're talkin' to—a real insult."

"Who else is drifting around in her pantheon, Birdie?"

"Pan—?"

"Is there anyone else she has confused with the twin gods?"

"Well, yes, as a matter of fact. There seems to be somebody called Slim Boy. Also seems he's the son of her daughter, her grandson—and all of 'em seem to be *Tqo bajish chí ni* and *Nayé nez ghani,* too!"

Before he went inside to see what he could do for Old Bead Woman, he had one more question. "Can those gods' names be translated into English, Birdie? Can you do it?"

"I been harkin' back into my Navajo an' yes, I think so. *Tqo bajish chí ni* would be " 'Child of the Water' " and the other one, *Nayé nez ghani,* that's 'The One Who—' no, better is, 'Slayer of Monsters.' "

As he straightened his legs and stood up, he was fairly sure he was either Bright or Dark Red Cousin and probably Firehead Again. Whether he was also the water baby or the monster killer, he did not know.

He reached down to offer Birdie a hand out of the chair. "Why don't you heat up that broth again, Birdie," he said. "Maybe I can get her to take some."

As he had thought she would, Old Bead Woman sucked eagerly at the broth he conveyed to her lips in a large spoon. Birdie sat on the bed at her shoulders cradling her up to it. Although her old, half-blind eyes, bright now with his presence, never left his face, after each third or fourth sip she would lean her head back against Birdie's shoulder and croon a while. Birdie translated as best her long-unused Navajo would allow.

". . . the Sun said, here are your weapons . . . for you, Elder Brother . . . the lightning that strikes crooked . . . for you, Younger Brother, the lightning that strikes straight.

". . . twins threw the third knife, yellow knife, but it did not harm Yeitso, the Giant.

". . . they hit him with the great white knife.

". . . stop the blood before it runs into the water!

". . . I wonder if the lone eyes are watching me? I wonder if the lone eyes are watching me? I wonder if the lone eyes are watching me?

". . . I am he who has killed the monsters.

". . . The lightning is before me."

Old Bead Woman took the last of the broth from Gamelon's spoon and fell back a final time in Birdie's arms.

". . . All is beautiful behind me."

And she slept.

Birdie lowered Old Bead Woman back onto the pillows, straightened the bed clothes then came around to sit by her in the ladder-back chair. After putting the bowl and spoon in the kitchen sink, Gamelon returned by way of the living room for a stool and came to sit with Birdie. He knew he would have to explain to some extent what he thought he knew and, as a result, they would have to decide together what was best to do with the Indian woman.

Birdie sat in silence for several minutes, then reached out and took one of Bead Woman's hands and began to stroke it as though she could wipe the tortures of the arthritis away. She said as though only to herself, "My Johnny died in this room for a lot of years—of the cancer, you know. Some said it got to him from the radiation on the wind, the fallout from them tests over west o' here in Nevada, the ones weren't supposed to do nobody no harm. But, I don't know. If it got him, why didn't it get me?

"They was good years, nonetheless, happy years. Oh, we cried a lot and we remembered—and we played checkers! Dear Lord, I wonder how many games of checkers we did play.

"Mostly, though, we laughed. We had time to laugh, time to laugh like it seems we somehow never had before.

"And we loved each other like we never'd seemed to have the time to love each other before. We loved each other with our eyes and our fingertips . . . and just, I reckon, with our nearness . . ."

". . . brightness, sunlight all around," Maria had said that last morning, "love nearby—but not right in your pocket . . ."

"And we died together here all them years back. I suppose you might say the cancer did get to me, too, in a way. Johnny, he just died a little more than me and a little sooner." And Birdie lapsed into silence again.

If Gamelon had been drawn to her before, he felt even closer to her now. They had both died some with their loves, only a little less and not so early on. Then, suddenly he felt ashamed of himself. For her, love was gone, irrevocably gone. For him—God only knew how or if or when—there was still the chance to love again if he could just straighten everything out.

He waited for the knot in his throat he had not realized was there until that moment to clear and he was confident he could speak clearly, then, as quietly and simply as he could, without embossing the tale with any of the strangenesses that were so much a part of it, he told her what he knew of Old Bead Woman's grandson—only one grandson—and where he was.

Birdie thought it would be best to either take

Old Bead Woman to him or bring him to her. Navajo kin wanted to be with one who was sick and the sick one usually wanted to have kin around.

Gamelon already knew he would return to the old Rundqvist farm and all the startling, but confusing things within its boundaries, if for no other reason than to prove he could. Uniting the old Indian woman with her grandson would be as good a face-saving excuse as any for him. Then, too, he had no way of knowing which or how many Slim Boys might answer a summons to come to her.

He asked Birdie if she thought it would be safe to take her in the morning.

"If she sleeps through the night an' don't show signs o' fever or anything by then. An' if you can get her to eat somethin' solid, maybe, before you take her."

Then, Birdie, sharp as always, cocked her head in Gamelon's direction and asked, "How *did* you get her to eat anyway?"

Gamelon hedged with, "Oh, something in the way she studied me when I was carrying her here made me think she might trust me. Who knows: in her state and with her sight all but gone, maybe she thinks I'm her Firehead *cum* Child of the Water." He did not like conceiving of himself as the monster slayer.

Without commenting, Birdie continued to scrutinize him as he rose slowly, told her he thought he'd rest until supper and left the room.

JULY 7, 1984

It could not be said she ate heartily, but again with Birdie's help, Gamelon managed to get a soft scrambled egg and some milk into Old Bead Woman. Then Birdie pronounced her fit to travel—not too far and only on the condition someone would care for her at the other end. She held Gamelon responsible in no uncertain terms.

He first thought to take the long way around, down to St. George then up through Swede's Valley. He was about to ask Birdie for a clarification of directions when he thought better of it. It was much longer according to Racklin. He decided to repeat yesterday's route only slowly and carefully with no shortcuts.

Between them, they fitted the frail old woman, well wrapped in her blankets, into the shallow rear seat of the still-filthy Fiat. She seemed content enough as long as Gamelon was near. He climbed in himself and turned to reach over the seat to pat Old Bead Woman's twisted hand, turned back, waved to Birdie standing on the steps and started off.

Almost immediatley, Old Bead Woman began her faint crooning, first on one note, then one higher, then two lower and on and on. She intoned her words and syllables, unintelligible to Gamelon and barely audible over the racket of the engine until he pulled up in front of the ramshackle farmhouse and shut the engine off some twenty minutes later.

* * *

Racklin stood on the farmhouse porch as though expecting him. He had been expecting someone, Gamelon thought, when he realized that in the drowsy stillness which normally enveloped the farm, a car probably could be heard approaching from the time it rattled onto the plank bridge.

Racklin regarded his brother sleepily, hands in his pockets, a half-smile on his face, then said, "Morning. I didn't think you'd miss the day's doings here when all was said and done."

Gamelon ignored the greeting and replied, "Get Slim Boy, will you? I've got his grandmother with me."

Racklin's eyebrows went up. "What the hell's she doing here?!"

"How would I know? All I do know is I found her collapsed in a Nesset gutter when I got back yesterday afternoon."

"How do you know it's Old Bead Woman? Old Bead Woman doesn't speak any English—at least she didn't."

It was Gamelon's turn to raise an eyebrow as he asked, "You know her?"

"I did, years back. I'll tell you about it later. Lord, she must be ancient by now. But how'd you find out it was her?"

"I took her to Birdie David's. We took care of her last night. Birdie speaks some Navajo. She grew up in a trading post on the reservation."

"Huh! Didn't know that."

"Birdie thought it'd be best to get her together with her kin. Not knowing just who or how many I'd get if I put the call out for Slim Boy to come to her, I thought I'd best bring her to—them."

"She sick?"

"Birdie thinks she's just mostly undernourished—and, like you say, old. I guess the only way we could have found out more would have been to try to corral Coolidge Remson in a half-sober moment sometime before noon."

Racklin stood motionless for a moment looking down at his brother, then his shoulders began to shiver with a laughter that pealed louder and louder. "That useless old faggot?! He's not a doctor!"

"Not a doctor? But I thought—"

"That shingle, that prissy 'surgery': It's all a fraud! A complete fraud!" Gasping now from his laughter, Racklin managed to choke out, "Hid his liquor one afternoon—way back—all but one bottle I kept in my hand to tease him with. Time he got through weeping—and slobbering—and groveling to get it back, he'd—told me everything that ever happened around here—in the last twenty-some years—not to mention all about his poor, miserable self—"

As suddenly as it had begun, the laughter stopped. Racklin went on with disdain, absolutely without pity. "He's not a doctor. He was a piss ass male nurse! He came here, as far as he could get from anywhere that counts, to hide after World War II—oh, yes, he was in the service all right, like he tells everybody, but he never saw any more action than the kind that undid him.

"Seems he was off in some linen closet in some big military hospital, wearing nothing but a straight jacket for kicks, getting himself roundly buggered while his top-brass patient slipped out of this world for lack of attention.

"He's been hiding and shying, drinking and paying ever since. He knew enough about babies being born, vaccinations and lancing boils to get away with it until I came along and turned off his spigot for an afternoon. He's fooled everybody else for all this time."

Racklin turned abruptly and disappeared into the house, presumably in search of Slim Boy, leaving Gamelon with new disappointments and a different pity where Coolidge Remson was concerned. A few seconds later, Gamelon heard his voice calling lightly out in the back of the house and soon after that, Slim Boy came around the corner toward him.

Even though he was prepared, it was still a bit unnerving when the second Slim Boy followed, stepping soundlessly in his brother's tracks and, inevitably, the third. Gamelon could tell them apart only by their clothes. Two wore what looked like worn-out castoffs and were barefoot.

The three identical men circled around Gamelon until the mid-morning sun was at their backs, then, seemingly upon a silent signal, squatted down on their haunches and stared up at him unblinkingly. Gamelon collected himself and addressed the Slim Boy in the blue sateen shirt and black hat. "I brought your grandmother with me."

None of the Slim Boys reacted for several moments, then the blue sateen one said, "What you doin' with my grandmother?"

"I found her collapsed in the street in town. I took her to where I'm staying and the lady there and I took care of her last night as best we could. That lady speaks Navajo and that's how I found out who she is to you. That lady also thought it would be best for her if she was with you, so I brought her."

The three slender, powerful young men exchanged slow glances, then one of the ragged ones asked, "What's she doin' here? Long way for an old one like her to come."

All Gamelon could do was shrug.

Again the three were quiet for a while, then there began a conversation that for Gamelon was like listening to a man talking to himself. If they lowered their heads, he was hard put to know which was speaking.

"Followin' me."

"Crazy old woman."

"Hates me."

"Scared to death of me."

"Can't live without me."

"Bet she parlayed almost the last of her beads to get here."

"Stick Leg's greedy."

"Bet she got him to drive her over here in that ol' no-top car o' his."

"Like him to get her so far and dump her."

"Shouldn't have sent no word."

"None at all about where I was."

Blue Sateen Slim Boy stood up. "She's in the car, huh?"

Gamelon nodded and he started slowly past him toward the Fiat as the other two got up. Gamelon put out a hand and touched the young Indian's arm. The man stopped but it was plain he liked neither the stopping nor the touch. The ragged ones queued up at his elbows. Gamelon felt a threatening air, but asked anyway, "What do you mean she's scared of you but can't live without you?"

"She's just old, real old. She gets things all mixed around in her head." Blue Sateen hooked his head toward Racklin who had returned to observe from the porch. "Ask him. He knows all about it." And he made to move on.

"Wait," Gamelon said. "One more question: would she think I was somebody called Firehead?"

Without moving his head, the Indian looked from Gamelon to Racklin and back again, then chuckled, "Got you two all fucked up in her head, too, huh?" He chucked his chin in Racklin's direction. "That's Firehead, the genuine, original Firehead." He removed Gamelon's fingers from his sleeve and went to scoop Old Bead Woman out of the Fiat. He hefted her in his arms and, followed by his brothers, moved off effortlessly, gracefully in the direction of the barn.

When they had gone, Racklin swung casually down the porch steps. "Come on, Little Brother," he said as he sauntered past Gamelon. "Let's take a walk and I'll tell you some more fairy stories."

They moved easily, side by side, down the dirt track that led back to the bridge, much of a height, much of a size and color, two bright, powerful entities temporarily in harmony.

Racklin did most of the talking as they passed slowly from light to shade, from sun into the shadow of a huge live oak and out again. He spoke animatedly but without the excitement or the dramatic emphasis that had powered his thoughts and his voice so many times during the previous days: just a good story teller.

"Well, it goes like this: 'Once upon a time' I did a PhD dissertation, you may recall, on the possible physical origins of Navajo mythology. What I have to tell you, in as neat a nutshell as I can make it, goes something like this.

"In the Fourth World—no, I think it was the Fifth. Lord, it's been so long since I did all that research. Anyway, the Navajo Mythology has them developing up through four unattractive—for the most part—worlds to this one—which is the Fifth. Anyway, there was a time then when that world had become downright unsafe. A man couldn't step out of his hogan of an evening to take a piss, it seems, without risking being gobbled up by some monster or other. Sort of like today, huh?

"There was a string of 'em: giants, huge and very predatory birds—the ones I liked best, I remember, was the huge rock with eyes, a mouth and a nose that would come careening out of nowhere to roll you down and crush your little body if you didn't watch out—can you imagine the number of boogie people a Navajo woman has to sic on her kids? 'An' the Rollin' Rock'll *git* ya if ya *don't watch out*!" He laughed lightly.

"Then the Sun came to the rescue in a roundabout way. Seems that following a lengthy and mysterious courtship, Sun and a very unusual lady called White Bead Maiden, herself of mystical origins, got together and produced twin boys whose job it was to be to rid the world of Rolling Rock and Giant Elk, He-Who-Kicks-People-Off-Cliffs—I always liked him a lot, too—Slashing Reeds and all the rest of the lot.

"The Twins' adventures were long and arduous, but they managed to do all the evils in except what were called The Four Last Ills—let's see—" Racklin ticked them off on his fingers. "—Poverty, Old Age, Death were allowed off the hook for various allegorical reasons—and Lice! Yes, Lice. Isn't that great? Seems picking them off somebody else promoted human compassion, so they, too, were allowed to live.

"The Twins are gods to the Navajo. But, you know what: twins, real flesh and blood twins, among them are considered unlucky. It wasn't too long ago that at birth one would be left to die or killed—maybe it still happens, I don't know. A pleasant paradox, huh: sacred and profane all at the same time.

"Now that I think about it, Lon, it just might have been that human versus heavenly paradox that originally stimulated my interest in abnormalities. Hmmm . . ."

They had come to the bridge. They loitered there a while, then as if by common consent, they turned and began rewalking the road in the opposite direction.

Racklin's tone was contemplative, almost tender when he spoke again. "I was really surprised, shocked almost, at seeing Old Bead Woman again this morning. It's been, what—thirteen, fourteen years since I met her on the reservation."

He became bright, jocular again. "I'd gone there that summer as part of an anthropology field group—I think there're more anthropologists than Navajos on that reservation at times. I was gathering window dressing for the dissertation. As I'm sure you yourself know, one does not dare do anything original for a thesis or a dissertation. All the graduate committee ever wants to hear or see is what's been pumped in through your ears spewed out through your mouth or your typewriter—with a nice shiny coat of high gloss enamel to blind them a little to the fact that all you've learned is how much you don't know.

"One of the customs under scrutiny by the group that summer was the Navajo practice of servitude. Yes, Lon, almost a form of slavery, really. Through their tracking and snooping, the team came upon Old Bead Woman, who, after the death of her husband, being left alone, had been 'given' her daughter's youngest son—"

"Slim Boy."

"Slim Boy."

"And?"

"And I got a kick out of the team's posing and prattling about the subject. God preserve us from the American pride in what he thinks is human freedom and his indignation about servitude! Actually, the Navajo system isn't all that bad. Young mouths that might go empty get filled; old people get looked after.

"Old Bead Woman was a tough, haughty, even vain woman then, in her sixties, somewhat of a recluse, proud of her turquoise hoard, not easy on others and hard to get to. Other Navajos would become silent when her name was mentioned. I didn't know it then, but she was considered a witch by some because of the two Slim Boys—yes, there were two even then.

"I persisted. I'd found out she was the daughter of what had been one of the most famous of Navajo singers, medicine men, and I thought she might be a good source for some of that sheen I needed for the dissertation.

"Finally, she allowed me to come around and loosened up enough once in a while to tell me some of her versions of the old stories."

"And Slim Boy?"

"All the times I went there, I never saw but one at a time, never until the day I was leaving her hogan for the last time.

"I used to park the team's old jeep I had the use of on the highway when I went to see her. I'd walk the mile or so in—couldn't drive in. I was on my way back to it late that afternoon, almost to the road, when an incredibly ancient bus came puffing up the road from the south—the mission bus, I found out later. Lo and behold! Who gets off the bus but Slim Boy who I *knew* I'd just left behind outside Old Bead Woman's hogan.

"He crossed the road, swung up the trail toward the hogan, passed me and greeted me as though nothing was the least unusual.

"I wanted to go back. I wanted to know why this 'twin' had never been seen, never even alluded to, but I couldn't. It was late afternoon and the team was pulling out at dusk so the desert driving could be done in the dark when it was cooler."

"So you didn't know then that they were mutants?"

Racklin turned on Gamelon, his face twisted with a sudden anger. "Don't use that word! They're not mutants!"

"Well, what the hell else *would* you call them?!"

"I don't know. I don't know yet. I don't know

why they have to be labeled with anything but what they are: human beings!"

"All right, all right," Gamelon muttered pacifyingly.

"I despise that term. I always have," said Racklin calming. "It implies something twisted and misshapen. My people are beautiful, beautiful!"

"All right!"

They walked on a distance in strained silence as Gamelon thought, Brother, you have devoted your life to studying what the rest of the world considers twisted and misshapen—at the least, the exception instead of the rule. Have you been at it too long, Brother? True, there's beauty in everything, even death, but could it be that for you, the exception has become the rule and what was the rule is no longer of any consequence?

He thought that, but what he said was, "You told me you were shocked when you saw Old Bead Woman earlier, yet what you've been saying implies you knew what she'd come to in recent years."

Racklin took a deep breath then answered evenly, "Slim Boy told me about the senility creeping over her and with it the delusions, the confusions in her mind. And, I gathered from what was said this morning, she'd laid some of it on you.

"As I see it, she's become convinced all her family and neighbors think she's a witch and have for a long time. According to Slim Boy, she tried to keep the first twinning a secret. The boys took turns every week or so, one going off to the mission school, the other staying around to tend Old Bead Woman, her corral fences and her sheep. That way they were never seen together. What I caught that afternoon all those years back was one coming home from school with the other one due to go the next day.

"But the suspicion that there were two of them grew and Old Bead Woman began to be shunned, isolated. She'd never been all that popular to begin with.

"Finally, with the years and the loneliness, she began to believe she would be killed for her witchcraft—it's been done—next paradox—either because she had made the duplication happen and was condemned as a witch for it *or* someone else wanted to become a witch and by killing her could succeed to her powers. There is belief to that effect.

"She got so she wouldn't eat anything she hadn't prepared herself and later, as she became more and more helpless, nothing except what one of the boys had made for her.

"As for the Twin Gods: she came to believe the Slim Boys were their reincarnation. As such, she 'trembled in their presence,' as they say. Next paradox. Ready? *But*, the Navajo also believe one can prolong one's life by being in the presence of something divine.

"You can imagine how all this could get mixed, interwoven, indistinguishable in her old mind. You can see, too, then, why she would follow the Slim Boys when she found out they were here. Poor old woman, she's damned if she does and damned if she doesn't. She doesn't know whether to go on living or go on dying."

They came around the last slight curve in the farm road's double track as Gamelon asked, "And why did the Slim Boys come here?"

"I asked them to—there's plenty of time to get into that. Right now, I want you to meet my wife."

"God, Brother, is there no bottom to your bucket of surprises?!"

Racklin just turned a smile on him as they went on toward the house where a skirted figure stood near the edge of the porch in the shade of a post and the roof overhang.

As they drew nearer, Gamelon's eyes began to distinguish more of the shadowed woman. Her simple yellow sleeveless house dress stretched into folds at the sides and rose up in front; she was heavily pregnant, near time he reckoned. She wore rubber shower clogs with pink thongs. Her legs were long, well shaped, he could not help appreciating, and she was tall. If not for her condition, she would have been slender, he thought. And, because of that same condition, he was unable to appreciate her breasts; they were no more than heavy sags to left and right of her high belly.

He could not see much of her face; despite the shade, she looked out from under a hand held to her forehead as she watched the men come on. Dark blonde hair was swirled casually up and pinned at the back. Some soft tendrils of it whisked in and back about her cheeks and throat as the gentle breeze do-si-doed unseen around her.

He had long ago learned to discount the "something familiar" feeling he had had now and then about strange women, perhaps coming toward him from a long way off on a near-empty street or in a restaurant or in a shop. He discounted it now. He knew it for what it was: attraction, his own subliminal masculine desire for there to *be* familiarity.

Racklin stepped out ahead, bounded lightly up the steps, turned and stood with his arm around the woman's waist so that the two of them were facing Gamelon. "This is my wife, Lon. This is Marylea," he said just as Gamelon reached the foot of the steps and just as the woman dropped her hand from above her eyes and smiled sweetly.

His mind did not gasp, "Oh, my God, oh, my God." It began a high, distraught keening miles behind his eyes. His heart did not leap up; it all but stopped. But of themselves, his arms started slowly up, stretching toward the woman, then halfway to full reach, stopped, became rigid, as he began to tremble, to shiver all over uncontrollably, loneliness, deprivation, pain sweeping over him, a tidal wave from the soul.

He was looking into the great gray eyes of Maria.

Seemingly unaffected by the awkward weight of the unborn child in her, the woman slipped from Racklin's grasp and came gracefully down the steps to him, stepped easily between his arms, kissed him lightly on the cheek and said in a voice he now could hear only in what had become nightmares, "Hello, Gamelon. I'm so very pleased to meet you at last. I've heard a lot about you as I'm sure you can imagine."

When he made no movement, no sound in reply, she stepped back and stood looking at him quizzically. Racklin came to stand beside her, his face impassive, but with a gleeful look in his amber eyes.

Back amongst the keening, a single phrase intoned mightily, over and over, "It could not have been her, she is with child. It could not have been her, she is with child. It could not have . . .

"What is it, Gamelon?" the woman asked with concern, then turned to Racklin. "Oh, Rack! You didn't tell him. You didn't tell him after all. How could you be so cruel?!"

She turned back to Gamelon and touched his shoulder. "No," she said, "I'm not your Maria. I'm her sister, her twin sister, Marylea. Brothers have loved sisters before, you know. And, you'll see, I'm not much like Maria was except in looks. You'll see."

When again Gamelon did not respond, when still he did nothing but stare into the gray eyes, Racklin took him roughly by the shoulders and shook him hard. "Lon! Lon, come on!"

As Gamelon began to relax, to come to himself again, Marylea turned on Racklin a final time. "Sometimes you carry things too far just to gratify your own twisted sense of pleasure!" She slapped

Racklin hard across the face, turned on her heel and went up the steps. At the top she paused long enough to look back and say, "When the two of you get yourselves back together, come in. There's some lunch." The screen door banged behind her.

Gamelon eased himself down on the bottom step, but Racklin stood where he was, his face stiff, his eyes blind with anger at Marylea's blow. He swallowed hard, almost choked on his private rage, then fought to control it and slowly won.

He plopped down beside Gamelon and said, "I suppose I should have told you, but you knew Maria had a twin sister."

Gamelon clasped his hands hard between his knees and struggled to blot out rising black visions of treachery, incest, even brother and sister orgies. Then, as unemotionally as he could, he said, "No, I did not know Maria had a twin sister. I only encountered the possibility of the fact yesterday. I did not ever expect to see that sister, much less to find that sister was your wife.

"And, yes; you should have warned me. If you know about Maria and me as you obviously do, then you know how much I loved her, how horribly she died and what her death did to me. Yes, it was cruel not to have prepared me, meaninglessly, pervertedly, inhumanly cruel, especially to a brother whom you supposedly love."

As he had spoken, the blandness of his tone had disappeared. Now there was a blindered purposefulness shaded with belligerence to it. The time had come to haul Racklin out of the driver's seat of his life. He did not know how much more of Racklin's reckless, thoughtless abuse his spirit could take and he was not going to allow the limits to be sought.

"I'm glad Marylea struck you. If she hadn't I would have smashed your face in. I've had enough, just plain enough. I'm tired of being jolted like a steer at the other end of an electric prod, of being cast to play devastating walk-on parts in whatever little comedy or tragedy you think you're directing at the moment and for which you seem to be the total audience!

"I am or I have been and hope to be again almost all those things you once said you had been to me, all in my own right and from now on, on my own terms: friend, playmate, leader, teacher, lover. I have never pimped for anyone, and, I warn you, if your—shit—doesn't stop, I'm going to forget I ever was a brother!

"You know I have a temper. You're one of the few who ever saw how huge and vile it can be and that was years ago when I was younger and smaller. Have a care; it's grown with me. It's just as big and coordinated and muscled as I am now. Have a care; don't make me lose control of it. After lying dormant for so many years, an eruption of it might be violent beyond even *your* wildest imagining!"

It was Racklin's turn to mutter pacifyingly, "All right, all right." But, when he stood up and turned to look down at Gamelon, his eyes still glittered in that reckless, almost wicked way. It was as though Gamelon's words had flowed over him as easily as water over pebbles in a stream. He smiled his broadest smile and said, "Don't worry about all those nasty things you just said. Big Brother will forgive you for threatening his life and limb. Big Brother will watch over you. Now come on, let's get that lunch. We've got to get down to the barn to see how Fred and Jenny are doing."

Lunch was simple: big ham and tomato sandwiches on home baked bread, dill pickles, early pears and milk. Aside from the usual please passes and thank yous it went silently and quickly.

Marylea seemed to have withdrawn into herself, her face still fogged with the remnants of her anger with Racklin. Gamelon had never seen Maria look quite the same way, but he could imagine something having induced a similar expression—or lack of it—on her face, so alike had she been to Marylea. Then he remembered: he had seen Maria quarrelsome, "pissed", exasperated, but never deeply angry to the point of striking out as Marylea had been.

His meal finished, Racklin was up and pacing. Finally, he could not wait any longer for Gamelon, painstakingly slicing strips of pear with a knife and methodically slipping them into his mouth. He went for the door calling back on his way out, "Come down when you're through."

He was through soon enough, but he was not ready. He was not quite ready for a putrescent Jennie or a Siamese twin Frederick. Not yet.

From somewhere in her doldrums, Marylea asked flatly, "Was he always like that?"

"Like what?"

"I really don't know the word for it."

"If you mean mischievous, a little wild perhaps and—"

"Selfish is about as close as I can get," Marylea broke in as though Gamelon had never spoken. "Selfish to the point of being hurtful sometimes. It's those times I find it even harder to love him."

"Do I gather it's a little difficult all the time?"

Still staring somewhere over his left shoulder from the other end of the table, her face a sullen blank, Marylea started to nod her head, then suddenly to shake it. She dropped her face in her hands and whispered, "I don't know. It's been like this from the start. Part of me loves him by the hour, by the minute, without a let-up except when I'm asleep and sometimes not even then. I dream about him—I mean I dream about—you know, I want him even deep in my sleep." She took her hands from her face and turned her stare on her own belly. "It's been worse these past weeks. I'm so close. I just can't . . ."

Her spirit seemed to stir itself back to the surface and she looked directly at Gamelon and smiled a little sheepishly at him. "What am I doing?" she said. "I shouldn't be saying things like that to you, Lon, even if you are his brother—especially because you are his brother."

"No, Marylea, it's all right. In all the world, I guess we two know him best. Maybe by talking out what's bothering us, we can help each other. Go on—please."

The sound of her voice, first a copy of things heard only in nightmares, had become a delicate balm for his wounded memory. He seemed to sense already the differences between her and Maria. Marylea, regardless of her earlier anger, seemed pliable, soft, introverted, existing comfortably on banked fires where Maria had been so vivacious, outgoing, changeable, obstreperous at times. Marylea seemed a dreamer in counterpoint to Maria's doer.

Marylea seemed to come to some conclusion. A new smile took over. It had an openness, a tenuously extended welcome for what she evidently hoped would be a friend.

"What does the other part of you feel toward Racklin?" he asked.

The smile closed down slowly and the hint of detachment returned arm-in-arm with a clouding of the gray eyes. "Part of me—dislikes him." Her voice dropped to a whisper. "Even, I think, hates him at times."

Gamelon bristled. "Does he mistreat you?"

Marylea's chin came up and her eyes cleared and toughened. "Yes. I never thought of it that way, but, yes, he mistreats me."

"How?"

"Sometimes, almost all the time, I am let know

by what he does not do, by what he does not say that I am the least important of all the things that interest him. Sometimes, just the opposite is true. He pries into me, never lets me alone, pokes mercilessly into everything I say or think or do until I want to scream and run out into the fields just to be my private self for a few precious moments. He even comes into the bathroom when I . . ." Her voice shut down almost to a whisper again. "I feel like an experiment being done or a germ helplessly trapped between glass slides, my whole life smeared out around me to the thinness of a hair, and all of it—me and my world—being looked at, looked at by an unblinking eye magnified beyond comprehension up at the other end of the microscope tube.

"I feel naked, stripped, nothing that is me is left to me. That's when I hate him."

She was quiet for a time, then she said in a clearer voice, "But that's how it all started. If a part of me hadn't wanted him, loved him and the other part felt—threatened, degraded by him, we wouldn't be here today. But you know all that. He must have told you."

"Told me what?"

"How we met, how—"

Gamelon reached across the table and, but for a moment's hesitation, took her hand. "Marylea, I didn't even know he had a wife until two minutes before we met—much less that she was my Maria's twin sister."

She did not respond for a moment, then she said abstractedly, "Why does he do this? Why does he play God with people this way?" She looked away. "I'm not his wife. Maybe all I am truly is just another of his experiments . . ."

To get her mind away from that, he asked, "How did it all start, Marylea?"

Seeming to project herself back by fixing her

eyes on the coiled steel damper handle of the old wood cook stove, she began.

"He had been in Borneo studying God knows what, whatever Racklin would find fascinating in Borneo. He'd been hot and sticky for months on end, he said, and so had his dreams—imagine that at his age. When he headed for home finally last November, all he could think of was a white woman as warm as Borneo had been and other than that, cold. Cold and snow. He dreamed wide awake of frozen streams and drinks made of nothing but ice. He wanted days of everything on the rocks from breakfast coffee to a brandy nightcap.

"Utah was on the itinerary anyway. He'd read a colleague's paper on the possible relationship of fallout to birth defects in this area and he planned to stop in Salt Lake to visit the man and learn more if he could.

"But why not a few days at Alta or Park City first? Even if he didn't ski, he could run in snow, dance in it, wallow in it. He could cool down everything; after all, he said, there was no such thing as a ski resort without its fair share of warm panties and heavy breathing.

"I was in Park City to ski. I'd come to love the crisp, vital aloneness of it over the years. And, I'd come mid-week when the rates were cheapest and the people least."

She brought her eyes back and around to Gamelon. There was a resigned half-smile on her lips. "Do I need to tell you what he's like when he sets his cap? I was whisked around in an Irish jig, cajoled with ancient Chinese love logic, plied, charmed and on my back with my legs in the air in no time, before I knew what hit me.

"Part of me fell for it all, reveled in it. I'd never met so thrilling a man. But, right from the first, part of me felt unwillingly propelled, used, losing control of what was me.

"When he asked me to tag along for a while, part of me strained at the leash. The other part, by then, kind of flung its hands up in front of its face and started backing off—fast.

"I asked for a while to think . . ."

"It's obvious which part won out."

"Well, no, not really . . ." Marylea sighed heavily. "Both parts did—to some extent." Then she got up purposefully and started to collect the dirty plates and crumpled paper napkins around the table.

Although he had listened carefully to everything she had said, recorded, pieced, responded, still his mind had been vaulting ahead. He could not help ricocheting off the unfinished point she might have made to, "I met Maria in late December. So you didn't know about me then, me and her."

"No. In fact, I didn't know until spring—who you were, that is. Maria began to allude to "an affair" she was increasingly pleased with when she called or wrote to me. She didn't actually mention your name until the last note I had from her when she also said if you asked her to marry you she would and if you didn't soon she was going to take the offensive herself.

"She was dead by the time that note got to me. I was already mourning her. You, too, for that matter, even though I'd never known you. I remember wondering, but being sure almost, if you were kinder, gentler . . . less sporadic than Racklin. And, I remember, too, being mad, feeling cheated Maria and I would never get to compare notes."

"How did you find out she was dead?"

Marylea shrugged as she gathered unused clean spoons from the placesettings. "Very simple: I'm her next of kin. Mother and Dad are both gone now."

"And all you knew, Racklin knew."

"I don't know what you might call it. I call it his twentieth sense. Even though there may not be a whiff of the fact that you know something he doesn't, he knows. It seeps in through his pores or settles at the base of his hair follicles, I don't know. And after that, try to keep that something from him."

"I know what you mean."

Marylea put the spoons in a drawer then picked up the stack of dirty dishes and took them to the sink. She came back to stand over Gamelon, her hands crossed placidly over her stomach. "I'm not relying on Racklin, this time, Gamelon," she said to him. "There's something more you should know.

"Marylea Rundqvist, age nearing thirty-five, Social Security number, 698-068-031, is a violinist in the Utah Symphony. She's a very good violinist, a very complete musician. In fact, she's so good she's going to be one of those auditioned in a few weeks for the assistant concert master's chair which will become vacant this fall.

"We decided it was best that way. There wouldn't be any disturbances. Things could go on in Salt Lake City as they had been.

"I asked for a while to think, remember? When I'd thought, although I sometimes rue the day, I decided that the part of me that wanted Racklin could have him and the part that was afraid of something about him, in him, could do very well without him. There was no real winning either way, just losing something on both parts."

It was tomorrow or tomorrow or the day after that. Gamelon's head dropped forward and he asked flatly, "If he wanted me here, why didn't he just call me and ask me to come? He knew where I was. He knew I would."

Gently, sympathetically, but with a drop or two of deep bitterness, Marylea replied, "It would have been too simple, it wouldn't have been any—fun."

"Why would—she do it for him?"

"There's that part of her even after almost a

year that loves him, still is fascinated by him, still aches for him in her sleep. And Gamelon . . ." She reached down and lifted his chin until his brown eyes had nowhere else to look except into her great gray ones, ". . . she's coming here tomorrow."

All he could do was ask why.

Again, she could not keep a slight harshness out of her voice. "He wanted her to. He asked her to. He thought it would be nice for you—'fun' for you to have another 'go' at another Maria."

She dropped her hand from his face and walked away to the window on the farthest side of the kitchen. She grasped the curtains in her hands and stood looking out between them at the raging bright nothingness of just before one o'clock. When she spoke again, her words almost did not reach Gamelon. "When we're together, which is almost never, and I expect from now on will be even less, just to keep things straight, she is Marla."

There was no tomorrow or the next day or the next or the day after that.

Maria was dead.

But would the constantly appearing reminders of her ever be?

Gamelon decided on another walk, perhaps as far as out to the bridge, perhaps just to the great live oak and back—however long it took—but this time alone.

He crossed the kitchen to where Marylea stood staring out the window and put an arm around her shoulders. They stood that way for a moment or two, then gently he took her hands away from the curtains and turned her toward him. "I'm going to walk a while, just down the lane. It's one of those times I know you can appreciate when I need to be by myself."

Marylea looked into his eyes and simply nodded.

"I don't expect I'll come to any new conclusions

while I'm gone. I think they're all already made. I just need that little stretch of solo time for those conclusions to solidify into resolves.

"But before I go, there're some things I want you to know. I want you to know how much I appreciate your telling me about yourself, about yourself and Maria and—Marla. Now that I know about her, I can't think of any more disturbing surprises Racklin could have in store. Knowing him, though, I'll never completely discount the possibility and I'll be prepared.

"You should know, too, that you're not alone anymore. I'll be around—maybe not right on the premises, but around. You'll know where you can get me and that I'll help you in any way I can if you want me to.

"The most important conclusion I've come to, Marylea, is that I have to be around. I don't know why Racklin is playing organizer, pusher, kingpin—whatever—with life the way he seems to be doing, what hold he has over those out in the barn—Jennie, Frederick, the Slim Boys—but I'll have to find out—all that and more. You might even be able to help me."

Again Marylea nodded.

"Everything else aside, all the wonders of you and those like you and the rest, I have to be in it because I just might be the only one who can put a bit in Racklin's mouth and keep it there, the only one who can control him. I can't put down the suspicion he's—overreaching, that he may be paddling on the edge of an undertow when he shouldn't have gone out beyond the breakers in the first place. I feel it could harm him in the end and I don't want that to happen. He's still my brother and I love him.

"To do that, to help him, I must know more. I shouldn't have any problems now; he's not pulling my strings any longer. I've already served him notice and even though he sloughed it off in his usual way, I think he knows I mean it."

Marylea relaxed, seemed almost to sag with relief at the knowledge she had indeed found a friend who knew it all and was as concerned as she.

Gamelon took his hands from hers and smiled. "I just wanted to let you know those things while we had a little of that privacy that's so difficult to come by around here. Now, I'm going for that stroll."

She stepped along with him as far as the sink where she stopped. She put the plug in the bottom then went to the wood stove for a big pot of water with steam wraiths whisking about on the surface. "You go on," she said as she trudged back to the sink with the pot. "I've got to get these dishes done and put together another lunch. It should be about time for the Fredericks to put in an appearance."

She dumped the water in, set the empty pot on the wooden drainboard then turned toward Gamelon. "You know," she said musingly, "it just might come to something with you and Marla. That one part's still in love with Racklin, I know, but the other, the other might find you very appealing, might like you, just as I do. And, Lord knows, it wouldn't hurt either of you. You've both got your fair share of ghosts to exorcise. Funny, that other part of me getting a chance I never will . . ."

Hairy double blond giants stood, feet wide apart, pissing double streams against the side of the barn. Each had a sprawling tan birthmark high on the left buttock. Each cradled not inconsiderable semi-soft penises identically in identical left hands. Both stopped at precisely the same instant, tilted heads back briefly, shivered, pissed a final stream, shook themselves vigorously, let themselves drop and turned like a precision drill team of two to take

Levis from a waiting Racklin. As Gamelon stood where he had stopped at the sight on his way around the barn to the door side, his walk over, twin furry broad backs bent, right legs, then left were hoisted in unison, the giants squatted a little, heaved up the Levis, stuffed genitals down the right leg with left hands, zippered and turned to follow Racklin's gaze, beyond them, toward Gamelon.

Gamelon recognized premonitions, inklings, rabbits-over-the-grave and other human animal responses, but he never accepted one, acted on one, reacted to one without some rational investigation. He accepted this one and reacted to it without question: he instantly and intensely disliked the Fredericks. They were too big. They moved with a breadth of action that spoke of a careless disrespect for others' space. There was a slackness about the mouths, a vacuous disregard in the too-close blue eyes and when left thumbs went to left nostrils, chests heaved then clamped to shoot snot out the right ones, he knew why without having to ruminate about it: meanness, meanness of both kinds, the meanness that was thoughtless cruelty and the meanness that was cruel thoughtlessness, not inconsiderateness but a totally disregarding, purposeful thoughtlessness, a knowing doing designed to offend. Without so much as a nod of recognition for Gamelon, they lumbered past him, step for step, heading for the house.

Racklin came along slowly in their wake toward Gamelon. He stopped akimbo from his brother, his eyes glowing, still following the forward march of Frederick and Frederick and asked, "Well, dammit, tell me how you like them?"

"I don't like them. Am I supposed to?"

"Of course you're supposed to!"

"Why?"

"You mean the Fredericks."

"Yes."

"Fuck the Fredericks, per se. I'm talking about the whole thing. Like any intelligent human being, regardless of rank or station, knowing what you know and all you don't, you're supposed to be awed, trembling at the mystery of it all. You're supposed to be wildly applauding my efforts to date and begging for more."

"You're beginning to sound like God waiting for cheers from the bleachers for his dirt and spit act with Adam."

"Oh, Jesus, Lon, when are you going to quit stalling and face the beauty of it, the wonder?"

"Right now I think that 'wonder' is something to be taken under study by the finest minds the world can muster."

"No!"

"Then you're going to have to give me yards of goddam good reasons why not, starting now."

"Take my word for it. That mustn't be done."

"It must be and it can and I won't take your word for anything else about these—people that I can't prove to myself!"

Suddenly, Racklin was all total cooperativeness. He put his arm around Gamelon's shoulder. "Fine, Brother," he said, "now we're getting somewhere. Let me share everything I know with you. You're all the mind I need besides my own. That's why I wanted you here to begin with. Nobody else I could trust not to blab to the world and ruin everything.

"Marylea usually makes something cool about this time of the afternoon, iced tea, lemonade, something. Let's go 'set 'n rock a spell,' as they say and have some—if Frederick and Frederick haven't scarfed it all down by now."

Between pulls at what turned out to be cola, which Gamelon had turned down, Racklin, beginning in Borneo as Marylea had done, told their story much as she had with one notable difference. In Racklin's recounting, she had fallen in love with him, true, but what he had felt for her, still evidently felt for her, had never gone beyond the end of his penis and the top of his brain. Gamelon found himself scratching the first notch in what was beginning to become an entrenched dislike of his brother that had come unbidden to roost beside his affection for him.

"Why do you put out the fiction of being married to her?" he asked Racklin with no show of the emotion he felt.

"It makes her feel better."

"It sounds to me as though you don't really care how she feels."

"I don't, when all's said and done, but I have to make some effort to appear to. I need her."

"For what?"

"For the child."

"What's so important about the child aside from the basic importance of every child?"

"Lord, Brother, I'm beginning to think your ability to imagine, to project has deserted you! Can't you see? No sooner had she come back to me in Salt Lake City and I'd gotten the whole astounding story of the twinning out of her than it was the first obvious thing!"

"What?"

"Jesus! You of all people, twiddling with your stamens and pistils all day, every day; you should see it right off: crossing! What would you get by crossing a regular human being with one of these—super humans? More of the same? Part? None? Are the genes of one lethal to the other? Considering the length of time it would take to find out all those things, wouldn't you say it was one of the very first experiments to be begun?"

Racklin had said it and the notch cut deeper. She had said it, and that is what she was, an experiment, although he knew he would do everything he could to keep her from ever knowing.

He parried in a bland, studied voice. "And when it's over, you just quietly send her away?"

"You really are being limited, Lon, or just willfully stupid. Hell, no! What happens when you cross two roses?"

"I get hips, then seeds."

"And then?"

"I separate the seeds and plant them."

"Oh, please spare me all that plodding, step-by-step Gamelon crap and get to the meat of it! What do you get?"

"Widely differing offspring, mostly duds, but the rare chance of something new, different, beautiful, strong."

"With better disease resistance, for instance?"

"Or longer bloom life or stronger stems or—"

"Well, there you are!"

Yes, unfortunately he was there and the notch bit too deep to ever be erased from recall. Marylea was Racklin's brood sow, nothing more.

"Even beyond that, I—we might want her to multiply herself again for study purposes, maybe one for control, one for experimentation or to be able to impregnate with a different man, even you, Brother. God, Lon, the possibilities are endless!"

Yes, he had to admit they were, if you could deal with human life that inhumanly, totally without recognition of those emotions which made that life human to begin with. The Third Reich's soulless attempts at a super-race slithered up out of memory and into his consciousness. But before that could parade all its grossness and falseness before his mind's eye, Racklin interrupted with, "But let's get back to that 'longer bloom life' for a minute. When was Maria's birthday?"

"What's that got to do with the price of cheese?"

"A lot, Brother, a lot. When?"

"If I remember right, March twenty-sixth—yes, she was an Aries."

"And, in a roundabout way, so were Marylea's and Marla's."

"So?"

"Frederick's is March twenty-eighth, Jennie's, April first. And the best I can figure—they can figure—Slim Boy's was late in *Wozhchid,* 'the month when eaglets chirp in the shell and mountain sheep drop their young, the Blue Wind moves over the earth and the first leaves come.' Late in March."

"Not enough to prove anything more than a coincidence. It couldn't have done anything more than intrigue you—"

"It intrigued the hell out of me when I found out the year."

"All the same?"

"Yes, and that's fascinating enough in its own right, but *what* year? Come on, think back."

Gamelon did, but he could not remember what year Maria had been born. The more he rummaged, the more he had to admit she probably had never told him and he had not ever really cared. She had always been a fresh twenty-one or twenty-two to him. There had been times, he recalled, once or twice, no more, when he, at thirty-four had had a slight twinge of dirty old man, but never for long. He had loved her too much for anything like age difference to worry—"Marylea Rundqvist," she had said, "age nearing thirty-five, Social Security number . . ."

"The year, Brother, the year of miracles, the year of conceptions more sanctified than Christ's was—1950!"

"But—I've seen them all, Maria, Marylea, Slim Boy, the rest—"

"Not much more than twenty, right?"

"The skin tone, the clarity of the eye whites, not a sign of wrinkling, even around the eyes. All of them, all at the peak of physical development, not even starting the long downhill run—"

"Exactly."

"But you're telling me they've all already turned thirty-four!"

"Exactly."

"What *are* you telling me?"

"It's obvious. Along with their other strange gift, they do not seem to age beyond full physical maturity. They may well be—"

"Immortal?!"

"And right now—God only knows, but you and I have got to find out—what more."

Until that moment the fact these strange but apparently normal people had hidden within their minutest atomic structure the ability to create matter out of nothing had been his prime deep-seated fascination. That and their ability to replicate themselves as they could zoomed into obscurity in the face of this newest possibility. Gamelon was glad for the study Racklin lapsed into, for the silence that went with it.

Immortality. It took a while to ingest and encompass that the most eternal dream of all might at last be a reality, at least for some and someday possibly for all and that God would die then from rejection and a broken heart. Then there would be no need for an intermediary to eternal life.

The small sounds of life as it yet was filtered to him, but linked now to new visions. The old icebox door in the kitchen closing: Marylea, one of the blessed. A fork scraping repeatedly at a plate: one Frederick or the other, another of the chosen few. From somewhere behind the house, the steady, near-rhythmical thud and rip as logs were reduced to faggots to fit the wood stove: Slim Boys, one, two, even three of them perhaps, gods in themselves, gods come back to life for their people, none of whom knew it yet.

What of all the teeming rest? What of the Racklins and Gamelons, the Freddy Sevrinskys, the Jorges, yes, even the Sam Colemans? In exchange for even the slenderest chance of immortality for themselves, would they reduce the Maryleas and Jennies to serum, boil them down to essences for injection into their own dying veins?

Or would scientists trap them and dissect them to study them under a thousand electron microscopes, searching, searching for their secrets?

Could soldiers come and secure them behind impenetrable fences while politicians and judges argued their ownership forever?

Might women so crave the possibility of the ultimate gift for their children that all the diamonds and saffron of the world would be laid at the feet of gilded-caged Slim Boys and Fredericks in return for a single hour alone with them? And, might the Slim Boys and Fredericks eventually waste away from fornication, their own gift of immortality overcome in the end by being forced to try to perpetrate it?

Could a world come where an immortal, concubine or stud, exhibited caged, its human rights gone completely, was the quintessent medium of exchange?

What of the child to come, half man, half god? Would he have to know the same plagues, the same tormented fates as his Greek forerunners of the same kind or would he be caught in the middle, torn both ways as half-breeds are, loving both, hating both but hating himself most of all, caught in an endless war of likes but unlikes?

Perhaps it would not be Sam Coleman specifically, and certainly not Jorge or Mr. S., but the world the new ones lived in, that surrounded them, would rip and tear and claw their dignity to shreds and them along with it. He thought he understood now why Racklin had reacted so sharply to his threat to bring in that world.

He felt something of that awful fear Racklin had revealed the morning before when he had said sometimes he shook in the roots of his soul. And he knew that, like Racklin, now he, too, might well be chained to this Godforsaken place for the rest of his life. What choice did servants to gods ever have?

The clattering of silverware on plates had stopped but the tap in the kitchen sink ran. High overhead, twin trails sprayed from an invisible jetliner, eastbound, headed over the Rockies. The ax thudded, the wood splintered. And again . . . again . . . again . . .

A long-drawn, down-dying scream of agony came suddenly in the stillness after the last thudding. Racklin ejected from his chair, slammed open the screen door and bulleted through the kitchen heedless of the startled, rising Fredericks, bouncing off one's bulk, then recovering, Gamelon behind him almost running up his spine. Gamelon saw Marylea, her rump against the sink, petrified in place, her wet dishrag to her throat, its dripping unheeded, as he tore past her after Racklin and out through the back of the farmhouse.

A ragged Slim Boy stood by the woodpile, a hatchet at his bare feet, gripping his left wrist with his right hand, staring at where his left thumb should have been but where now there was nothing but blood, dripping on his toes, falling in bright gobbits on the chopping block where the thumb lay.

Racklin ran for him ripping off his shirt as he went and already preparing one long sleeve for a tourniquet. "There's bandages—tape—in the kitchen. Go back!" he shouted to Gamelon as he reached the ragged Slim Boy who was already beginning to shiver and start into shock. Gamelon did a tight end cut back and raced to do as he was bidden. As he went, out the corner of his eye he saw the other Slim Boys pelting up from the barn at top speed.

Marylea had come loose from the sink and was already tugging the first aid kit and bandages from a cabinet over the drainboard when he ran in again. The Fredericks stood laconically watching the goings on out the window, one picking his teeth with a broom straw. There was no time for thinking of them. He flung out again, took the back steps at a leap, came down light and running and met the other Slim Boys beside their injured brother in a dead heat.

Racklin had the tourniquet on and twisted tight with a hefty kindling twig from the woodpile. The blood from the Slim Boy's wound had slowed, almost stopped and the pink and white bone end showed. Together, the other men eased him to the ground in what little shade the woodpile afforded and Blue Sateen was off at a lope at Racklin's command for a blanket to wrap him in. His teeth were chattering.

The blue sateen one was back it seemed almost before he left with a heavy Indian blanket he handed to Racklin. Then he just stood looking down with cool eyes and an expressionless face as Racklin and Gamelon got the blanket under his brother and wrapped up to his chin. He did not even breathe hard from the triple run.

Racklin worked furiously not neglecting to ease the tourniquet now and again. He had the tape out, a thick bandage ready, when suddenly he snarled, "Dammit! The antiseptic's not here! I've got to put some on to keep out the infection until we can get him down to the hospital in St. George. Lon, get it, will you?"

But Marylea had already realized the lack and was on her way across the yard with the bottle in her hand as fast as her laden belly, the uneven ground and her pink-thonged sandals would allow.

Strangely enough, it was the other ragged Slim Boy, who with his brother had been mostly silent since their twinning, who spoke as Marylea thrust the bottle into Racklin's outstretched hand, not the contemplative, hawk-like Blue Sateen. "Why you takin' so much trouble?" he asked the little group in general. "Soon as he gets over the shakes and the paleness goes away, he'll be all right."

Blue Sateen grunted and nodded. All heads turned toward him, even those of the Fredericks who had sauntered down like twin blond bulls slightly curious about a possible conquest in the next pasture over.

"What d'ya mean?" Racklin rasped out. "If he isn't properly treated, he could bleed to death or die of gangrene or God knows what other complication if not from the shock itself!"

The whole Slim Boys, ragged and sateen, just shook their heads and continued to stare into their own considerations.

Racklin loosened the tourniquet for a long moment, tightened it again, sopped away the new blood and began to sprinkle the antiseptic powder on the raw gash preparatory to binding it up. But Blue Sateen reached down and stayed his hand, then gripped his shoulder hard. "Stop puttin' that useless white man's muck on 'm. He'll be all right, I say."

Racklin flashed, "He'll be all dead, I say! He'll bleed to death!"

"No he won't." The blue sateen one stepped back a pace and motioned the ragged one to come around to him. "Still don't believe much in ancient Navajo wisdom, do you, Red Cousin, even after I took your chain off you. Navajo wisdom covers a lotta things. You just gotta believe. Now, take that rag off his arm an' quit messin' with him."

Racklin scowled at him, tried to stare him down, but to no avail.

"Do it."

Angrily, Racklin let the tension off the tourniquet and yanked the shirt sleeve away. "All right, you stupid— Now we'll all just stand here and watch him fade away!"

The released pressure made the blood spurt, but almost at once its pumping slowed, then stopped.

The faces in the circle looked dumbfounded, one to the other, then back to the stump already beginning to crust over. As Gamelon whispered, "I don't believe . . ." he saw that even Racklin, for once, was gape-mouthed.

"Course you don't," Blue Sateen said without emotion. "Still, somehow I think you'll come to an' with more sense'n Firehead here. Someday, maybe." Then he turned to his ragged brother and said, "Tell 'em."

"See them?" the ragged one said pointing down at his right foot, its toes wiggling. "Long time ago, I ended up in a small corral with a pretty big horse. Horse didn't like me bein' there an' he starts to snort an' rear up an' dance all around. Well, he dances around, me cuttin' and jumpin', till he dances right on that foot. He comes down on it so hard, he smashes the toes. Smashed the three little ones so bad, mission doctor, he cut 'em off."

There was total silence as all of them stared at Ragged One's flexing foot. The silence lasted until one of the Fredericks said in a stringy voice seemingly apropos of nothing, "That's nice."

"So, see, don't bother about it," Blue Sateen said. "Blood's stopped. There's a scab an' that thumb'll grow back, a month maybe, maybe a little more til it's back nail an' all."

One Frederick piped he was ready to go now and when Gamelon asked where, he said, "Back to prison." Racklin had to supply that Frederick was a guard at the county farm down near St. George and Gamelon was unable to suppress the suspicion that he was probably a sadistic one. The other Frederick allowed as how he'd hang around the farm a while and Gamelon wondered how soon he would eat Marylea out of house and home.

Blue Sateen Slim Boy demanded money he said Racklin had promised for new clothes for the Ragged Ones, held out his hand until he got it then ensconced himself in the back of Racklin's truck, regardless of the fact that the stores in St. George would be on the verge of closing when they got there.

Gamelon accepted the invitation that came now to get his things and stay at the farm, but only after it had been strongly seconded by Marylea. He rejected making that pickup as part of a roundabout return from St. George via Nesset and opted for the Fiat, a shorter trip and an evening to himself except for a soothing, uninvolved hour or so of Birdie.

Through all of this, Gamelon poked and prized into the recesses of his memory trying to coax back knowledge long ago consigned to uselessness but that now he suddenly needed.

He told Marylea he would be back by midmorning, then added casually, "When you took my chin in your hand and leaned close to me a while back, I noticed you wore contacts."

His heart lifted then settled quickly as she turned a questioning glance up toward him that was exactly the way Maria had looked at him when she was not only curious but also suspected there was more to it than met the eye and replied, "So?"

"Farsighted?"

"A little bit."

"Maria, too."

"I know."

Gamelon smiled. "But she wore glasses and she hated for me to see her with them on. Whenever I surprised her wearing them, they went straight up onto the crown of her head. What do you clean the lenses with?"

"On occasion with a special cleanser but most days just with the same saline solution they're stored in. Why?"

"Can I get some in Nesset?"

"I doubt it. I get mine in St. George."

"Do you keep any extra on hand?"

Marylea nodded. "Wouldn't you if you were way out here?"

"Can I borrow your extra bottle?"

She continued to stare at him for a moment, then she shrugged. The Waughs had one thing in common: if they did not want to supply information, they would not. She went into the house and came back a few moments later with a brightly labeled white plastic squeeze bottle in one hand. "Don't worry about replacing it," she said. "I'll tell Racklin to get me some more while he's in town if the drugstore's still open."

He kissed her lightly on one cheek by way of thanks and goodbye, then went off to take his place in the two-vehicle caravan that soon was rattling across the bridge.

At the far end, the truck with Racklin and a Frederick in the cab and a Slim Boy in the bed swung south, down into Swede's Valley, down toward St. George. The blue sateen one stared back at Gamelon until the dropping hill and the trailing dust obscured the Fiat from his sight.

When the truck had disappeared, Gamelon turned north toward the bottleneck of hills. He was too busy reviewing what he had dredged up from all the way back in undergraduate days to take much notice of how difficult it was to turn the car to the left. He thought if he acted quickly, the saline solution and the little freezer in Birdie's old Kelvinator would do it. Originally, the freezer had been designed only for making two trays of ice cubes. According to Birdie's grumblings one evening, "it wouldn't quite do even that anymore and sure wasn't up to keepin' Mr. Birdseye's stuff more'n a day or so."

Before his interests had swung to botany and the like, some biology textbook or lecture had given the formula: submerged in a one point five sterile saline solution and almost freezing but not quite should keep the cells and tissues of the thumb, hastily retrieved, wrapped in his clean handkerchief and deposited unnoticed in his pants pocket, alive for as long as it was possible to keep such things alive.

Naturally Birdie balked at having a pickle relish jar, already boiled out and being saved for her upcoming peach preserves, put in her freezer with a thumb floating around in it. But after a bit of self-reckoning as to how she never used ice, even the mushy variety her freezer provided, in her tea or anything even in high summer, with all the fresh things in, she hardly, no never brought home any of Mr. Birdseye's vegetables or fruits, she finally agreed. She probably did not open the freezer that time of year more than once every two weeks or so when she defrosted.

Gamelon promised to have the thumb out and gone by the time that chore came around again. An hour later at supper, the sequestered thumb seemed to have been forgotten and Birdie was demanding what news of Old Bead Woman. Because of all that had happened that day, Gamelon could not really say after late morning and he had to embellish his report a bit with conjecture to satisfy her.

He was glad when the supper was ended. There

was plenty of light left and getting some of the dirt off the Fiat was a perfectly valid excuse for getting away from Birdie's questions.

As he stood there, the hose at full power deluging his small dilapidated horse, he thought the sagging in the front seemed more pronounced. Whatever was wrong, there was probably no help for it short of St. George. Not only did he think there probably would not be time for it tomorrow, tomorrow was Sunday anyway; nobody available to see to the ill. He would just have to trust to his luck getting back to the farm tomorrow and hope the luck held for Monday and St. George.

Again, Gamelon lay naked on the turned down bed staring up into the darkness at the top of the room, but this time his mind was a small placid sea of answers instead of a maelstrom of questions, the worst of which had been whether there would ever be any answers. He did not fool himself; he knew the calm was temporary. Out beyond the present calm, new swells were building. When the answers to the questions those swells represented revealed themselves, he knew there might never be true peace or stillness within his mind or soul again. He suspected there might be precious little time before those swells curled into raging breakers and came crashing down on him. He had wanted this quiet night with nothing in it but the smell of ripe peaches to be alone before standing out to meet those breakers.

Maria's death had forced cracks and gaps open in who he was and who he would have become. The openings would have filled in of themselves with time's passing, but just when time had been given the chance to work its soothing magic came Jorge with his eyes that played tricks. Then, the crevices could not fill; heavy wedges of doubt and false hope had forced them to remain open and time's ministrations had been blown aside by the off-color questions that rose and swirled.

So much had changed, so many things had come to light or been snuffed out forever in such a few short days. He needed that night alone to pry the wedges out and let the answers he now had run in slowly and fill the gaps. Then he had to let time catch up and cement them over with only the best of memories and age the scars to the soft patina they should have shown weeks before. Who he had been would not matter then, but he would have to take another look at who he was and who he might be.

The night wore slowly to its center, its stillest time, embellished now by a mockingbird doing its best to imitate a nightingale. It fooled no one, but was having a magnificent summer midnight of it nonetheless.

Even when the agony of Maria's death had been so integral a part of him, he had known he would be different, but not how. Now, after casting back over himself these past weeks, he knew he was both harder and softer. He knew he would be chary of loving so completely, so innocently again, but he also knew he could love again. He knew, too, that he would never be so imperviously happy and content with everything in his small world. That world would never be so small again and now he had no choice but to be suspicious of the things in it, at least for a while. And, he knew he would be far more sympathetic to the crackings and splittings in others and the degrees to which they had or had not been able to heal them.

That left him with what he might become and that concerned him the most. He knew there was a potential for an even greater change in himself than that which he had already undergone, more drastic, counter, perhaps, even to what he was now. That possibility stemmed from Racklin—not what Racklin had discovered. He could handle that now.

In retrospect, he was surprised how quickly he had responded to Racklin's accurately placed blows about getting off his intellectual and scientific butt, yet evidently he had. His actions with the severed thumb that afternoon seemed proof enough of that. Now, even in the face of more incomparable discoveries about those strange and—how had he himself thought of them—"blessed" people, he was sure his curiosity bridled by his training, his self-discipline, would remain in control. He could approach the whole thing with the proper detachment but without losing the awe and wonder that must always underlie any honest research.

It was Racklin himself who might stimulate that deeper, possibly counter change. He had to return to that far more disquieting question: who was he capbable of becoming?

He knew the answer but he rebelled against acknowledging it. Unlike those great inactive portions of his brain he so often longed to make use of, he did not relish perhaps having to make use of the great dormant portions of Gamelon, the animal.

He despised the thought, but it might come to that. He had to face it now, now before the reality of some moment to come might obscure not only what must be done but also his power to do it.

The past three days had gone by like a tiny comet flashing from periphery to periphery of the mind's eye between blinks. Before he could cross the perilous bridge from who he was now to who he might become, he had to separate Racklin from all the rest of what had happened and stick him against a plain white background. He had to create a single, honest picture of Racklin, uncluttered with love and fond memories. From who Racklin had been, he had to proceed to who *he* was and from there to who *he* might become.

Racklin was as mercilessly curious as ever, as relentless an investigator of whatever interested him, but the blithe, breezy disregard he had used to exhibit had changed to an unthinking, prying disrespect.

Even as a boy, Racklin had loved surprises and surprising, even shocking. Now he seemed addicted to sensations, his own sensations, the thrills he derived from jerking the lives of others about and without even a passing thought for what it might cost those others.

His involvement in anything had always been intense. Now it had become manic and excluding of everything and everyone except those he needed to pursue his ends—Gamelon included, Gamelon had to admit to himself. Everyone had become a white mouse for Racklin.

Whether or not he had stated his position on any given matter, his reaction to anyone who, even unknowingly, stood to the contrary was violent, instant, uncompromising. There was no room anymore for debate, much less disagreement; to learn from an alternate point of view was impossible for him.

Racklin had always dived and soared through the range of emotions like a hummingbird in its ritual mating flights. Now he dove deeper and hung longer at the zenith as though unaware the ground was so cold and hard at the bottom and the air so rare at the top.

Yesterday, as Racklin had crooned over the shivering mess that at the time had been Frederick, he himself had judged his brother possibly mad.

Today, he had begun to disfigure the love he had always held for his brother, his patience with him, with notches of aversion.

If tomorrow distrust got added to the changing formula . . .

And if, the day after that, the incipient madness

cracked its fragile container and spurted out as violence . . .

Gamelon shivered with a sudden chill he knew had not been caused by any errant night breeze blowing over him. Parts of Old Bead Woman's ramblings crept coldly through his brain.

". . . for you, Elder Brother, the lightning that strikes crooked . . .

". . . for you, Younger Brother, the lightning that strikes straight . . .

". . . stop the blood before it runs into the water!"

He had told Marylea he might be the only one who could put a bit in Racklin's mouth and keep it there, but could he? If he could not, he knew Younger Brother would have to unsheath his lightning, that Gamelon, the animal, would have to do whatever must be done to keep the blood from mixing with the water.

That final vision of what he could become was not pleasing, but it was faced and recognized. It could be put aside now to await a call he hoped would never come. He could sleep.

For the first time since mid-May, he slept a clean, clear, unembellished sleep, the mockingbird's continuing recital notwithstanding.

JULY 8, 1984

He overslept.

A little after ten, Birdie's rapping brought him to the door to show enough of himself to satisfy her he was awake. She got off a burst about the disgraceful time it was to be getting up and departed martially for the lower regions.

No matter how he might hurry, he could not make it out to the farm by mid-morning. There was no phone there; he could not even call to say he would be late. But, he did not suppose his absence would disturb anything until lunchtime came around. Even taking time for a light, late breakfast, he could be there easily by noon.

Birdie insisted on that—even for slugabeds.

He made a valiant try for just a bowl of cereal and a glass of juice, but Birdie would hear of nothing less than eggs, bacon and coffee. He found himself beginning to fidget while the bacon was frying. By the time the three minutes for the soft boiled eggs came around they seemed like three hours. It was not that he had forgotten what he might have to contend with in the coming hours and days, but that his curiosity had refreshed itself—twofold, it seemed—with that same long, peaceful sleep that had renewed his body.

So much would happen today. If Racklin would just stay on his perch, it might all be nothing short of wonderful. Jennie would be coming in today—coming in two today. Racklin had to be pinned for every detail about the "blessed" people, including all that he even conjectured about them. That had to be the day's primary goal, and not just to gratify his own driving need to know. To control Racklin, at least where the Blessed People were concerned, he had to know everything, absolutely everything Racklin knew about them. And, there was Marla.

He took his old briefcase with him and the big shoulder bag with his toilet kit and the scant changes of clothes he had brought, but not before Birdie had ordered every dirty sock, undershort and Levi out of it to do up for him. "Part and parcel with the room, like the meals—for special paying guests." He moved out for all intents and purposes, but he kept the room and paid two more days for it in advance. He did so as much to give himself the feeling of a ground he could call his own to fall back on as to repay Birdie somewhat for becoming the temporary surrogate custodian of the thumb.

By the time he breached the pass at the top of Swede's Valley, he was fighting to keep the car from pulling itself and him over the edge and down into the bottom of the wash amongst the live oaks and cottonwoods.

The welds that held the top of the left front spring to the fender must have broken or one of the bolts in the lower control arm that yoked the wheel to the frame. The left front tire was getting increasingly out of balance, out of camber and out of round. With that and no wipers, no lights, no horn to boot, tomorrow, St. George.

At the far side of the bridge, Racklin almost jogged with impatience. As the limping Fiat came abreast of him, he yelled to Gamelon, "Keep going! Keep going!" yanked open the right front door and fell in. Before Gamelon could open his mouth,

Racklin went on, "Where in the *fuck* have you been?! You were supposed to be here ten, ten-thirty, and it's past noon! God damn! I thought I could count on you, at least!"

Gamelon slammed on the brakes. Racklin straight-armed the dash just in time to keep his forehead from smacking it. Even if his brother's uncalled for vehemence and allegations of unreliability had not made his temper show a single flaming tongue, he would have made up such a reaction. No more. From here on, Racklin would be met vehemence for vehemence, clamp for wildness, damper for madness.

"Off!" Gamelon growled. "Off my case and stay off! There's something you want from me and it's not out from under the rock yet. One more uncalled for cussing for anything just because it doesn't happen to suit you, one more disagreeable second out of you and I stop even considering you and what you may want! Clear?! Say it!"

Racklin massaged one wrist with the fingers of the opposite hand. "You crazy ass. You almost made me break it."

"Say it!" Gamelon shouted.

"Say what?!"

"Say it!"

"Clear," Racklin mumbled.

"Now what the hell's the big rush?"

"Jennie."

"What about her—them, by now, I guess."

"Yeah, 'them,' but half of 'them' isn't—right and I think it could die. I don't want it to die, but I'm not sure how to save it."

"All right, let's go see. Maybe I can help." Gamelon let up on the brake and the Fiat bounced down the track toward the house. He did not stop there but skirted the garden patch and drove on toward the barn. There was a sassy, bright red lift-back in his usual parking spot anyway, a local rental car placard on the door. Marla must have taken an early flight from Salt Lake City to St. George.

He did not have time to think further about that. Racklin was out of the car before it stopped and headed for the barn door still wringing at the sore wrist. He flung an urgent, "C'mon!" over his shoulder at Gamelon.

It did not take quite as long, blinking between squints, for his eyes to get somewhat accustomed to the darkness inside. Today, unlike the days before, it was overcast and the threat of wind and storm amplified in an air heavy and still.

In the farthest corner of the barn, her face and upper body just visible in the inefficient glow of a small kerosene lamp, Old Bead Woman sat, her back against the wall. Her half-blind eyes stared. Her gnarled fingers plucked at her turquoise now and again as though to reassure her it was still there. Her lips moved slightly and Gamelon could only suppose she sang to herself still of strange things, for no sound reached him.

As before, Slim Boy, guardian of the miracle, sat his post on the stool by the bed, but this time, his attention seemed to be elsewhere. His face was turned away from the sheeted mound before him.

Racklin had gone directly to the bed where the divisions of Jennie lay beneath the spread sheet but had made no move to expose them by the time Gamelon came to stand beside him. He stood looking down at the double form pulling at the end of his nose as though it itched.

"Five minutes ago," Gamelon said evenly, "you were throwing a fit because we weren't here. Now we are, what are we waiting for, particularly if you think part of the woman's dying?"

"We've got some time." He looked over at Slim Boy who now had turned his vacuous gaze on them. "They haven't started the final division yet."

The Indian nodded in confirmation, then asked in a low voice, "You gonna take the cover off again?"

"Not yet, not yet," Racklin answered. He took his hand from his face and turned his eyes on Gamelon. "What is abnormality?" he said. "I've studied abnormality, quote, unquote, all this time and the more I have, the less I'm satisfied with what it really is. I have to find out, I have to. Do you know? Can you tell me?"

He obviously did not really care right at that moment what thoughts Gamelon had on the subject. He went straight on with his rhetoric. "I've thought it was different things at different times. One year it was high asses and short waists on groups of black people in Africa. Another year it was tiny people in Borneo. But they're just variations on a theme. But, aren't we all, all the time? If I have a cold, I'm not normal. I'm even less normal if I've had my appendix out. Woe, woe is me if I've lost an arm! God help me if I was born autistic, but still, I'd just be a variation!

"When you get right down to it, I'm abnormal if I have a corn. I'm abnormal the instant a zit pops out on my chin or when the day comes I need glasses. Is there any such thing as a normal human being?"

This time he seemed to want Gamelon to answer. This time he waited looking deep into his brother's eyes.

"Maybe the theme is an ideal, and maybe, like beauty, that ideal will remain forever undefinable. Maybe we're all variations on an ideal, some to a greater degree than others."

"Maybe the ideal is a vanity, a conceit on Man's part that he's made in the image of God and, of course, he can only see God as a perfect man. I told you life was a joke!"

"Maybe."

"Maybe you can give me some idea of how great a variation on your ideal this is."

Gamelon lowered his face into cupped hands as much to steady the hands' trembling as to hide the sight of what he had seen when Racklin had gently and slowly removed the sheet over the Jennies. He was only vaguely aware of a sudden shuffling and Slim Boy's voice spitting fast and low, "Damn you, Red Cousin! I don't wanna look at that thing again!"

He took a long, shuddering breath then let it out slowly as he thought how nice it would be sometimes if the human eyes were more reptilian, saw things in slits, a band at a time, like a snake, instead of in such vast, all-encompassing swathes. If he could have made his eyes work that way, he could have scanned over what lay on the table a slice at a time, his brain could have worked additively and the sudden strain on credulity might have been far less.

He had assumed all he might discover further about the Blessed People would be incomparable, but incomparably more than, greater than. But, dear God, what more that was supernormal could be piled onto self-restoration, self-replication, the creation of mass from nothing, and immortality?

Something had gone wrong with the Blessed People. With what had seemed his ill-timed little dissertation on abnormality, Racklin had tried to prepare him in his own way. If the Blessed People could be seen as representing a quantum leap into the human future, that future might be one of not only more than, greater than, but also other than. Where did variation stop and a whole new theme begin? He took his hands away and forced himself to look again, long and steady.

Jennie on the left was Jennie, the same plain-faced but not unattractive girl who appeared to be only twenty or so, long dark hair spreading around her head on the pillow and veiling her eyes. Except for the minutest lack of final definition at the nipple, the fingertips, the end of the nose and for the taut strip of flesh alive with veins that still connected her to her sister from forehead to groin, she was just as Gamelon remembered her.

Jennie on the right had the same plain but not unattractive face, the same dark hair swirled around her head, face and throat. Her legs, hands, arms, feet, all were the same and she, too, lacked that detailing in the same places as her sister. But where Jennie on the left curved above full hips into a noticeable waist and a slightly protruberant belly, widened again at the base of the rib cage and flared toward the shoulders, Jennie on the right was grotesquely slim. Her waist could not have been more than twelve or fourteen inches around. Gamelon could have almost encircled it with one of his big hands. The hips stuck out from either side of it like knobby flanges on a large pipe.

There was no belly, no place Gamelon could conceive of for the yards of intestines, the liver, the stomach. The trunk broadened only slightly as it rose toward the shoulders until just at the very last, it flared out to meet them like the bell on a tuba. The generous breasts seemed too close together, even separated as they still were by the band of flesh. To Gamelon they looked like pink balloons with rosy centers grafted to a skin-covered phone pole. Considering the bones, the malformed, greatly reduced rib cage that he could see, the backbone that he could not and the muscles and cartilage that had to be there for the whole thing to hold together, there was hardly cannister enough for the heart. The lungs needed almost all the room in the human chest. Where could the lungs fit?

Almost simultaneously, he noticed two other things for the first time: the creature's skin had an unhealthy cast, a bluish hint to it and its mouth was pursing and relaxing as though its lips reached out again and again to kiss a lover only dreamed of.

"It's starting," Racklin said and pointed to the Jennies' midsection. The center of the flesh strip there became more transparent by the instant until it disappeared and became a tiny but steadily widening open circle.

"That's right, Brother," Racklin went on, "put it all together, the color of the skin, the working mouth and this." Racklin's hand went up and very carefully brushed the dark swirled hair away from the throat. "She's not getting enough oxygen. What little she is getting now is being carried through the veins still in common with her sister, still running through that connecting strip. When it separates completely, even before that, as the veins divide, she'll die of asphyxia.

"We don't dare move them. It might cause the flesh strip to tear and for all I know that might kill them both. But we've got to do something—now. This creature is so fantastic I will not let it die!"

"Trash bag," Gamelon said.

"What?"

"Big plastic trash bag. Have you got any?"

"Yeh. We haul all the stuff that won't burn in the incinerator to the county dump in 'em every couple weeks."

Gamelon looked over into the darkness where he knew the Indian lurked. "Slim Boy, go to the house. Get two—three of those bags from Marylea. Put 'em one inside the other. Hurry!"

"How—it won't work!" Racklin challenged.

"Go!" Gamelon hurled at Slim Boy and he disappeared through the flash of light that was the opening then closing door. Then, to Racklin, "We've got to move them when the time comes, exactly the right time. Leave them now. Come on!"

Gamelon went quickly to the bed at the center of the barn, the bed where lately Frederick had slept and multiplied. "Get on the other side," he told Racklin. "Help me move it—come toward me—that's far enough. Now, over until the foot's right up against the head of the Jennies' bed."

When half the empty bed was snugly fitted just above Jennie on the left's head, Gamelon looked across at Racklin and said, "Now just hope the separations are in the same order they were with Slim Boy."

"They were with Frederick: belly, chest, head, genitals."

"But this is a female and very different. You can't be sure the sequence will be the same."

"What's your plan?"

"It'll be a close thing, but the best I can think of to do without risking ripping any of that connecting tissue before it's ready to part of its own accord.

"When the heads are about to part and the genital area's all that will remain connected, you take the left-hand one, I'll take the one on the right. We pull together until the one's head and neck are on the other bed and—"

"Got it, I've got it," Racklin said. "Where is that Indian?! Look!"

There were more transparencies, more small holes opening in the connection between the Jennies.

In their concentration, their urgency, neither brother had noticed that Old Bead Woman had risen on tottering legs. She stood with her back against the barn wall, her hands covering her throat and her precious remaining beads. She had sensed the excitement; she could not understand but a few words that had been said: Indian, head, go. Her wondering, casted eyes could make out only the twin giants with glowing fire about their heads moving, bending, apart, together, in and out of what for her was less light than moonlight from the small suspended bulbs. Her divine ones, her gods going about their unending task of keeping the world, the world of her people, The *Dîné*, free of monsters. She trembled with the awe of seeing them at work.

The door flashed again, longer this time as Slim Boy, moving to the accompaniment of crackling plastic, came through with a Frederick, Marylea and Marla behind him. All of them passed close to Old Bead Woman but without notice of her. Old Bead Woman gasped in wonder. Who could it be but White Bead Maiden, pregnant yet once more with the avenging Twins and her holy mother and father! Ah, that she should see such things!

When Gamelon saw the women heading toward the bed he said, "No, Marylea—ah, Marla. This isn't very plea—"

Racklin interrupted with a smooth, "Why not? Come see, all of you. You've been like this at one time. Why shouldn't you see what it's like?"

Just as the faces came to ring the bed, the first of the soft wind sounds for the Jennies came followed almost immediately by that of the single plucked string. The bellies parted.

The women gasped together, averted their eyes and stepped back. Then, sobbing, Marylea stumbled across the gloomy barn and back outside. After a few moments, Marla's head turned slowly toward the bed again, but she did not move nearer. She was swallowing hard and her chin trembled a little, but the great gray eyes were steady.

Frederick stood an impassive ground at the side of the bed, his only condescension being to mutter, "What an ugly fucking thing," as the chests whooshed, sang and divided.

"Now, get ready," Gamelon commanded. He and Racklin quickly changed sides and Gamelon found his way blocked by Frederick. All he said to the hulking blond man was, "Move!"

He took the doubled plastic bags from Slim Boy and bent down to slip the open end under his

Jennie and as far over her head as the flesh connection there would allow. He straightened up and grasped her shoulders firmly, careful not to turn her even slightly. The blue tint of the skin had deepened markedly. Across from him, Racklin copied his hold on the other Jennie.

Suddenly, Gamelon threw up his head and cried, "Water! Somebody get water!"

"The trough! Slim Boy! Frederick! The pump on the cattle trough! Bucket should be there! One of you fill it quick and bring it here! The other one stay there and keep pumping!"

The pump clanked and water was sloshing at Gamelon's elbow almost at once. "What do I do with it?" Slim Boy asked in his ear.

"In the bags, pour it in the bags," he answered, freeing one hand to hold the plastic away from the Jennie's head, "then fill it again and again and pour it in until the bags are full."

The slight sounds of it masked by the working of the pump, the heads parted and Gamelon called out, "Now!"

Together the brothers pulled the Jennies up, trying desperately not to twist them, not to put any special strain on the membrane still tying the groins together.

On the right, Racklin's Jennie's head dipped back as it crossed the depression where the bed edges met, then slid onto the foot of the second bed. He continued to pull and the neck followed, then the shoulders started across the depression. His eyes worked constantly back and forth so as to make sure he pulled not a millimeter farther than Gamelon and kept the angle between the two bodies constant.

Slim Boy came with the second bucket just as Gamelon's Jennie's hair tumbled into the trash bag. He just stood there, his eyes turned up.

"Pour, damn it, pour!" Gamelon said.

"Bag's in the way!"

"Christ! I can't let go! Pour with one hand and hold it open with the other!"

A hand, delicate and long-fingered, Marla's hand, not Slim Boy's, came into Gamelon's concentrated range of vision to pull the mouth of the bag wide. Slim Boy poured directly over the Jennie's face as, blue and ghastly looking, its lips working furiously, it tilted back off the bed edge and began to disappear slowly inside the dun green plastic.

The slim fingers shook but kept the bag open as the extraordinarily long, thick neck began to curve, then arch to follow the head down toward the dirt floor, down into the water at the bottom of the bag. The wildly fluttering flaps of delicate flesh from jaw to clavicle, finely ribbed with gristle and hinged just behind the trachea, steadied and took on a rhythm as Slim Boy poured the third bucket over them. Under Gamelon's steady strain, the gilled neck went out of sight but he went on pulling, in concert with Racklin, until his Jennie's shoulder blades were over the bed edge. They stopped together and held. They held until the groins parted and the two beings rolled apart.

Two more buckets and the amphibian Jennie's gills were covered and Gamelon could take over holding up the sides of the water-filled sack from Marla. As he replaced her hand with his, he really saw her for the first time. A firm gaze returned his own for a moment, then she rose and started to move away.

"Thank you," he said to her.

She nodded and replied only, "Marylea may need me," turned and left the barn.

The wind had begun to gust from the west southwest. It took Gamelon a little by surprise after the relative stillness of the barn. He had to lean some on the door to hold it open for his brother. After Racklin had passed through, he held on as he closed it to keep it from slamming. The brothers trudged off together but apart across the kitchen garden toward the house, Racklin, head down, his hair in his eyes, his beard parted neatly by the wind, Gamelon, his face thrust into it, his hair slicked back by it. Each thought his own thoughts and kept them to himself.

The blue had dissipated quickly once the gilled Jennie's throat and head had been submerged in the water-filled bag. As soon as the skin had returned to something like a normal flush, with the Frederick's help—Slim Boy flatly refused to touch the strange creature—they had carried her to the long, half-filled watering trough and lowered her into it. Frederick had returned to his pumping until it was full.

Racklin sent Slim Boy to the house again for an extension cord and to string the garden hose from the pump head, through the barn and into the trough. The water in the trough must be constantly replenished. Even cold and sleeping, the gilled Jennie would deplete the oxygen in the trough's water in no more than several minutes. When that was done, they swagged one of the low-burning lights across to shine down into the trough. Beneath the still water, the part of Jennie, more than or less than, shimmered, still asleep.

Frederick had sauntered out with a single passing comment: "S'past dinner time."

Slim Boy went to pat his frightened old grandmother back into place and soothe her in low Navajo. Satisfied that she was all right, he, too, left the barn, presumably to fetch food for her.

Alone, the Fireheads stood side by side in silence staring down into the dimly lit trough, once the watering place for snowbound cattle, now called into service after years of dust and dryness as an aquarium, until Gamelon asked, "How long will they go on sleeping?"

"About another hour, a little more if everything runs true to form."

"I'm not worried about that one over there," Gamelon ticked his head toward the bed behind them, "but what about this one?"

"What about her? She's still Jennie only with a different breathing apparatus. Fascinating!"

Gamelon leaned forward a little and turned his head to look at his brother's face. Racklin's eyes were wide and darted unceasingly up and down the length of the trough. His lips were drawn back to show big white teeth, but the pulling at the corners of his mouth was not a smile.

Gamelon reached across Racklin's chest to grab his shoulder and turn him sharply to face him. Racklin had no chance to resist and came around, his face suddenly blank, the amber eyes bewildered. "Wha—what's the matter?"

"You just said it, but I don't think you realize what you said?"

"What?"

"She'll still be Jennie."

"Yes, I know."

"You don't want to see, do you? You just don't give a damn outside your selfish curiosity!"

"And what do you see, Oh Almighty Eye, that I don't?" Racklin wrenched his shoulder out of Gamelon's grasp and stepped back.

"Exactly what you do, if you will—maybe even more than you see with your knowledge of biology and medicine! I see that she—it—is only part fish, the part that takes in oxygen and expels carbon dioxide. I don't even want to start thinking yet about how such a thing could be possible. I—"

"How such a thing could be possible and what will come of it's all that interests me!"

"You did not feel that her skin is no different

from yours and mine? She can't live in water forever. If I'm right, within a few hours, her skin will begin to break down and if she touches anything or anything touches her, it will just slough away."

"I know that."

"What happens then?"

"With the skin gone, this being fresh water, her body will take on water. The body will begin to become electrolytically imbalanced, the brain will swell, and finally cardiac arrhythmia, the heart will begin to act irregularly and soon stop altogether."

"And you're just going to stand there and watch it happen?!"

Racklin answered with disgust, "What would you have me do? Drive a merciful stake through her heart or whatever mythical thing one does to rid the world of fish people?"

"You're just going to observe, then?"

"Of course. That's my job."

"You don't care that the brain, the memory—the soul of a woman is going to wake up in an hour or so underwater, terrified, totally disoriented, suddenly transferred into a form vile, repugnant to them?" It was Gamelon's turn to retract a step: "Did you know, did you suspect something like this might happen sometime—to one of them?!"

Racklin smiled benignly at Gamelon and said in the manner of an absolving priest, "One must never feel bad if one is naive, Little Brother. Of course, I suspected it! I hoped it would happen. Wouldn't the nature of all the other things about my people suggest a genetic instability capable of producing even greater wonders? Haven't I the right, then, to be ecstatic, overawed that my theory has been proved?!"

The confirmation of the fact out of his own mouth that his brother was consciously playing with creation just for his own amusement without any controls or restraints or system or sense of responsibility hit Gamelon hard. His control of himself and the situation deflated dangerously for a moment until he forced himself to remember his commitments of the night before. He took hold and asked almost in an offhand manner, "How will she eat? She will be hungry when she wakes up. What will she eat? What will we feed her, live goldfish?"

Racklin metamorphosed instantly from pontiff to dervish. He threw his hands in the air and began to snap his fingers. His eyes burned like those of a bacchante in hot pursuit. He wagged his head from side to side and began to sing full bore without a melody as he stamped his feet and slowly turned this way and that.

"Oh, blessed be the hungry little Jenniefish," he bellowed, "who will never thirst, for I shall satisfy her—"

"Stop it, Racklin."

Racklin paid no heed except to look dourly at Gamelon as he belted at him mockingly, "And blessed be my foolish baby brother who is *so* pure in heart he thinks he knows better than God!"

He began to twirl faster, to stamp harder.

"Blessed, oh, blessed be my people, meek, strong, merciful or mournful, for they shall inherit the earth!"

"Stop it!"

Racklin stopped the whirling at least. He came close to Gamelon and snapped his fingers right in Gamelon's face as he sang, low now, and with menace, "But, woe unto men who shall revile me and persecute me and say all manner of evil against me for my own sake!

"Whosoever shall look down on his brother as a lost soul is in danger of hellfire!

"I am not come to destroy, but to fulfill.

"I am the light of the world!"

Racklin was too close even to try to sidestep.

Gamelon's fist smashed into his jaw. The raw power somersaulted him over the end of the trough. He came down hard on his hands and knees. He stayed that way, shaking his head as though expecting something to rattle. When he finally lifted it to stare unfocused at Gamelon, Gamelon thought he saw the streak of a tear on one cheek.

Gamelon made no move to help him to his feet. He stood his ground across the trough looking down at Racklin and said, "And whosoever calls his brother *Raca*, fool, without just cause is in danger of judgment!

"Wipe the blood off your mouth and let's get out of here for a while."

Marylea was not feeling well. She was resting and Marla had pitched into her duties. She worked gamely over a sizzling griddle trying to keep up a steady flow of grilled cheese sandwiches for the six men around the table. What had been a mounded bowl of marinated three-bean salad was already reduced to near-leftovers.

Outside, the wind strummed the downspouts and gutters. One thunder growl after another lumbered up out of Swede's Valley close on the trail of its lightning.

No words crisscrossed the table; all eyes and all attention were on the food and the business of eating it, except Gamelon's. His alternated between the fare and the figure at the stove. He knew Marla and Marylea had only been separate entities about a year but he felt already there were distinctions between them. He could not put his finger on precisely what those distinctions were yet, but he was aware they were there.

Under the stress of the moment in the barn, Marylea had turned and fled while Marla, though obviously frightened, repelled, had stuck, had forced herself to help. If it had not been for her condition,

Marylea might have done the same, but somehow, he thought not. He thought the softer, introverted, dependent side of what had once been a single Marylea dominated in what was Marylea now. She had said the part of her that wanted Racklin could have him, and that part would have had to be willing to subordinate the whole to another, to leave independent thought and action behind.

Her actions in the barn were only an inch marker on the yardstick that was the total Marla, but taken together with what little else he knew of her from Marylea, he thought what had been the stronger side of the original Marylea still controlled in Marla. The aspects that controlled the present Marylea would still be there in Marla, but not in the ascendant.

Up until early last winter, then, it would seem, the original Marylea and Maria would have been much more alike, the one quieter, perhaps, different surely in many small ways, but nonetheless a fuller, richer person, more exciting, more desirable.

He forked the last kidney bean into his mouth.

But in dividing, had Marylea taken all the softer side with her, leaving Marla to be only strength, drive, ambition, action? Had Marla been drained of that certain tenderness, fragility, moodiness that were the especial province of a woman? He did not think so; he hoped not. No matter who or what else they were, without those things women ceased to be women and became not men but neutered, merely persons. No, those characteristics were still there. In the barn, the strength had had to consciously take the upper hand. That which rounded out to woman was still all there in Marla.

He felt sorry for Marylea, sorry that she had had to so submerge that stronger side of her to have Racklin that that side had finally atrophied and died, it seemed. Such a thing had happened untold millions of times, he knew, but that in itself was no justification. No one had the right to dilute the self-esteem of another—and that was what it came down to—in the name of love, but especially when it was just that: in the name only of love. His dislike for his brother deepened.

He looked across the table to where Racklin watched him with guarded eyes and said, "Let's talk."

There could be no stroll to the bridge with the tearing downpour threatening. Racklin went to the far side of the kitchen and opened a door into a part of the house Gamelon had never seen.

He followed Racklin down a dank, narrow hall where wallpaper with faded roses and trellised ivy peeled and tan stained plaster puffed through and flaked. At the end, Racklin opened a second door. They went into what had been the formal parlor of the old house. More peeling roses, more stained plaster. Bare wide plank floors creaked under their steps and let cold air rise around their ankles. The room was empty except for two rickety ladderback chairs, their tattered rush seats moldering. Two tall, curtainless windows, their panes blurred and streaked with grime, looked out on the north and nothing.

Racklin motioned Gamelon into one of the chairs. It whined under his bulk as he sat on it. Racklin himself went to stand looking out one of the windows, his back to Gamelon, his hands clasped behind him. The fingers worked hard at each other; the knuckles were white.

Gamelon waited. He had called the parley, but the first move had to be Racklin's. It could lead either to a truce of sorts or to open warfare. Gamelon was prepared, now, for either route. Only one thing was sure: before the conversation ended, he would have to be sure that Racklin knew who Racklin was and what he, Gamelon, was prepared to do about it.

Racklin broke the long silence finally. "You really don't care, do you?"

Gamelon recognized the tack immediately and refused to be sucked in by it. He would not be put on the defensive. He did not answer.

After enough time had passed to qualify for a dramatic pause, Racklin went on, "Not only don't you care about me, you don't care about what I'm here to do, what I *must* do. You've decided to actively oppose me, haven't you?

Again, Gamelon held his silence.

Again, Racklin waited. His shoulders rose and subsided with a deep sigh but the hands still worked. "You hit me to let me know that, didn't you?"

"Now that you mention it, I suppose apprising you of that possibility was part of it."

"What was the rest of it?"

"First of all, I've told you I don't know how many times in the last few days that I wasn't going to be jerked around by you. It didn't seem to have registered. There's been enough happening otherwise to keep anybody off balance without your contributions. Sometimes sudden violence is the only way to make a point. I hope I made it—finally.

"Then there's this: an hysterical person I would slap, then soothe. When one is verging on insanity, there are two choices. Sedatives, psychiatrists and straight jackets weren't handy, so I took the second option: shock."

Racklin's hands stopped working, parted and fell to his sides. "You think I'm crazy?"

"Off again, on again, increasingly on, it seems to me."

Racklin turned away from the window but stood his ground there. "If that's what you think, why are you hanging around? Surely it would be better to live out your life in the cozy security of your little greenhouse with fond memories of a brilliant, beloved brother than to hang around watching the disintegration."

"Again, there're a multitude of reasons. You want me to stay. One of the first things you said when we met a few days ago was that you lead better when you have me to follow. You need me around to appreciate your show. The problem is, this time I don't like the act you're putting on and I'm coming to dislike the you that's performing.

"Then, I'm not going to stand around and sigh and tut, tut, as you disintegrate. I'm going to stop it if I can. If I can't, I'm going to control the result."

"What makes you think you can do either?"

"I don't think, I know. I will. Marylea can't; she loves you too much. Marla probably doesn't know how far you've gone. Neither of them have the you of the past that I do for a basis of comparison. The others? The Slim Boys, the Fredericks, the Jennies? I don't know yet what touchstone of theirs you own, but I feel that left alone, you'll ruin them all in one way or another, sooner or later."

"It sounds like you're setting battle lines."

"They're already set. You've set them. Only you can change them or eradicate them altogether. I don't think you're capable of that anymore, though."

"You're saying I'm not in control anymore, not in command of my mind, my scientific experiments, my world in general?!"

"Come on over here and sit down before I answer that."

Racklin came, warily, and sat opposite his brother.

Gamelon longed to slip down, stretch his legs out, but the ladderback chair would not allow for it. He leaned forward instead and put his elbows on his knees.

"You're in command of your mind, all right," he

said quietly to Racklin. "The question is, what kind of mind?

"Let's look at it this way. 'Scientific experiments,' you said. What is your method? Where is your statement of it? What are your goals, what are you out to prove or disprove? Where are all those meticulous records of dates, times, places and events that are required if an experiment is to be 'scientific' and if the scientist involved hopes to prove or disprove his 'something' to others? I haven't seen even a raw journal of happenings concerning these people and what's been going on here. I don't think there is—"

"I haven't had time—"

"A scientist would have *made* time before he went ahead. And I know you know how to do what I'm talking about.

"I'm saying, true, you're experimenting, but not scientifically. There are no records—"

"The people themselves are the—"

"There *are no records*, and without records, you cannot prove *anything* to *anyone else*. If you can't, at best you're guilty of intellectual masturbation, at worst you're playing—in this case, with life itself. As with any uncontrolled experiment, it can explode in your face—has, in a certain way, with the gilled Jennie.

"You're not in control of this experiment because there is no experiment. Whatever it is is in control of you."

"That's not true. You—"

"Shut up, Racklin. I'll tell you when it's your turn."

A bolt of lightning struck so close it seemed to have come down within the room and its thunder crashed before its flash had fully died.

Gamelon sat back again in the stiff chair. "Speaking of that mind, Big Brother: taking into consideration everything I've said, wouldn't I have to find such a mind suspect? A mind that sees itself doing a particular thing for a particular reason, but where none of the methods of achieving the end are in evidence is a mind that's fooling itself. That mind has partially ceased to deal with reality.

"And, when the moment comes, Big Brother—as I think it already has for you—when no other aspect of life has any uniqueness, no separateness, no value in and of itself except as it relates to that thing being done, then dealing with truth, with reality of any sort has become impossible. Then, a man is mad.

"Then, Big Brother, the only way another man can help sometimes, and sometimes as a last resort, is with his fists."

Gamelon leaned forward to look closely into his brother's eyes. "You see, Racklin, when all's said and done, a man's final responsibility is to himself. In the end, he must protect himself.

"Someday, true, his own special, individual madness may bear that man himself off to his own heaven or hell or oblivion on its own particular wings, but he cannot, he must never allow himself to be borne away by another man's madness, not even his brother's.

"Perhaps I cannot stop your flying, Racklin, but I will not climb aboard with you. If you try to make me, if you try to deprive me of the thrill of whatever my own madness is to be, I will shoot you down."

The lightning flashed, the thunder roared even closer, it seemed, than before and a barrage of rain grapeshotted the windows. The thunder died away and over the din of the rain came the sounds of stamping feet in the kitchen, running feet in the hall and Marla's frantic voice screaming, "Gamelon! Racklin! Come quick! Hurry! Oh, God, please hurry!"

* * *

". . . whosoever calls his brother *Raca*, fool, without just cause is in danger of judgment!

"Wipe the blood off your mouth and let's get out of here for awhile."

Gamelon turned away from his brother on the other side of the trough and slipped, almost fell as he did. He looked down. The water was seeping out of the trough into a widening puddle. A layer of fine hay particles covered the puddle. He became aware that the buffeting winds were dislodging near-constant showers of the dry bits and pieces from hundreds of unseen crannies in the loft above. He saw that his shoulders were heavily dusted with them as though he had just walked briefly through fine falling snow. The loft over him creaked as the old barn worked in the wind. He wondered if it would still support a man's weight.

The water level in the trough had dropped with the seeping. As Racklin got slowly to his feet in the darkness on the other side, Gamelon turned back—carefully—took the pump handle and worked it until the water in the trough began to run over the top. Then he went off down the center of the barn rustling his hair with his fingers to rid it of hay.

He waited a moment at the door for Racklin who came toward him through the gloom feeling his way along the wall.

The wind had begun to gust from the west southwest. It took Gamelon a little by surprise after the relative stillness of the barn. He had to lean some on the door to hold it open for his brother. After Racklin passed through, he held on as he closed it to keep it from slamming.

Old Bead Woman had covered her eyes in horror when *Tqo bajish chí ni* struck *Nayé nez ghani*. Or had it been Slayer of Monsters who had struck Child of the Water?

What did it matter which of them had struck the other? The holy Twins fought with each other and that should not be! And she thought one of them had killed the other. The struck one had turned over in the air and disappeared even as she watched.

It could not be. One could not work without the other. Had it not always been as The Sun, their father, had said to them: "You must act together." And, after they had planted the four prayer sticks and the four hailstones in their mother's hogan, did not Younger Brother have to remain to watch the medicine sticks while Elder Brother went out against the monsters? Did he not have to watch each day, faithfully, for if one of the sticks began to burn it meant the enemy was getting the better of his brother? Was it not he alone who could draw the smoke from the burning stick into his mouth and blow it out again on the sticks, the stones and then in the four directions to keep his brother from harm?

If one of them, whether the Elder or the Younger, was gone, the monsters would overrun the world again. What would become of The *Dîné,* her people? What would become of her?

When the pump began to rasp and the water to splash for the second time that day, she summoned enough courage to part her hands and see what she could with her clouded eyes. All she could make out was the blurred back and glowing head of one Twin, its arm working up and down. The other was nowhere in sight.

She closed her eyes and let her head fall back against the blankets. Her hands dropped to finger her turquoise. Tears trickled down the runnels in her ancient cheeks. It was true. One of them was gone. Nothing could save the world from the monsters now.

The pumping stopped. She felt the presence of the one God moving nearer to her, then away. She quaked with fear. She did not dare move even the little it took to raise her eyelids so she could see him.

She heard the door open. The God must be there now, far enough away so that he would not notice if she chanced a look.

He was there, alone, leaning his weight against the door. When he did not move on out, she shut her eyes again quickly. He might yet turn back and find her watching. If he did and remembered she was there and might have seen him kill his brother, what might he do to her? It would be so easy for him to loose whichever kind of lightning was his.

Again, it was a felt thing rather than one seen or heard, but she knew the door had been closed and the God was gone, but she counted twelve beats before she opened her eyes again.

She lay propped against the wall, her old mind in a petulant turmoil. Out of that chaos the thought finally arose, perhaps from the fervent wish that it was so, that perhaps The Slayer of Monsters had not killed the Water Child—or the other way around—after all. Had she not heard the one God speak even after striking the other? She had understood one or two of his words. She had understood brother and fool.

Although mighty, the doers of great deeds, they were really little more than boys. Perhaps they had just been playing! Oh, she had seen it so many times, boys grown into men, but still boys in their hearts, still children in their games, but with the power of men.

That must be it. Such beings would not harm or kill each other. When the one turned over in the air and then disappeared it had been all part of the game. He had disappeared to her eyes, true, but then, he was, after all, a God. His brother could still see him, of course, and he had spoken to him. What he had probably said was, "Brother, you can't fool me. I know you're there. You think I can't see you, but I can!"

Old Bead Woman's eyes began to twinkle. A crafty little smile parted her lips and let her toothless gums show. She wondered, she *just* wondered if *Tqo bajish chí ni* or *Nayé nez gahni* was hiding over there. Now the Twin Gods were become nothing but obstreperous boys for her suddenly and she very much wanted to join in their game. She wondered if she could find the vanishing one if maybe he would do it for her again. She clapped her old hands together once with delight.

Bit by bit, bracing herself against the wall, she got to her feet. She picked up the lantern; if she were to find the vanishing Twin, she would need light.

Still grinning, she started off across the barn toward the trough two or three quick mincing steps at a time. As she went, she sang to herself in jerky, tuneless little snatches. She sang the song Monster Slayer had sung as he neared the mountain of *Tse ná hale,* the giant birds, and interspersed it with little taunts for the hiding God.

"I wonder if the lone eyes are watching me?

"I wonder if the lone eyes are watching me?

"Where are you, Slayer of Monsters? I know you are there.

"The lightning is before me—"

She came to the trough and, stooping almost double, began to make a circuit around it, her lamp held high, peering this way and that into the gloom all around.

"I will find you Water Child.

"The lightning is before me—

"Come out. I know you are there.

"The lightning is before me.

"All is beautiful behind me."

She came around the other end of the trough and straightened up, her free hand at her back. The light from the lantern abetted that from the single bulb from the ceiling. The extra glimmer attracted her attention enough to make her turn her head a little. She took her hand from her back and twiddled the fingers in the water.

Ah, she thought, I know now! Her gummy smile broadened. She tottered along the side of the trough crooning, "I will find you, Child of the Water."

She stopped a little way down and holding the lantern as close to the surface as she could, she leaned down until her nose almost touched the water. "I wonder if the lone eyes are watching me," she teased.

And the lone eyes were watching her, but it was all right. The lone eyes were not those of *Tse ná hale*, the giant birds. They were those of her Water Child! Where else would her playful disappearing God have hidden but in his own water?!

"You see, Child of the Water, I have found you. You are not clever enough to hide from Old Bead Woman, not for long. You did not fool your brother and you cannot fool me!"

She straightened up and began to back away, wagging a naughty-naughty finger at the trough. "You cannot fool me!"

The surface of the water heaved. The God rose, its head and torso flinging water. Its hands grabbed onto the trough sides. The wave its rising had set up rolled the length of it and slopped hugely over the end.

Old Bead Woman staggered and cried out to it, "No, Water Child, it was only a—"

At the sound of her voice, the God's head snapped in her direction, its lone eyes wide, and water spewed in a solid jet from its mouth as it screamed. But its terror was silent, never to be known to anyone else. It had no lungs to bellow air across its constricted vocal cords. Even after the water stopped spurting and came out of its mouth only in swells as it went on screaming, no sound came.

Then the God began to fling about from side to

side in the trough. The lone eyes screwed up as though weeping, but if there were any tears, they were invisible on its wet face. Slowly it released its grip on the sides of the trough. One trembling hand went up to touch and explore its throat. Its mouth had stopped the silent screaming now and worked as though kissing again and again a lover only dreamed of. The hand fell away from the throat and into the water with a limp splash. The head drooped. Then slowly the God lay back and disappeared again into its hiding place beneath the water.

In the end, it was not Old Bead Woman's choice to make whether she would go on living or go on dying. The God's lone eyes had clamped on her and the water, his own lightning, shot out of his mouth toward her. The lantern was flung wide, fell and smashed as one of her hands went to clutch her breast and the other her turquoise. Her heart failed her in one monstrous clap. In the last brilliance of the God's devastating lightning, she thought, "—it was only a game."

The wind, still rising, buffeted the silent barn. The bits and pieces of straw and old alfalfa rained and scattered down, some to form a delicate frosting for Old Bead Woman's body, some to almost unite with the flickering pool of kerosene from the shattered lantern as it widened on the dirt floor. But those sifting through the air above the hot pool ignited and rose up again with the rising heat. As they soared gently, they attracted like remnants and generously bestowed their fire on them, too.

For a few magnificent moments, the inside of the barn was like the bottom of an early summer evening aglow with the cold pinpoints of a thousand fireflies. But unlike fireflies, the light of the shimmering pieces was not cold. Only a few of them had to impart their heat after reaching the loft. Small piles of old, dry fodder became instantaneous miniature fireballs and sent tentacles of flame scurrying around the loft and up the dehydrated walls toward the roof with the fleetness of terrified mice.

The growing fire gulped air. Most of it inside the barn went quickly and all that was sucked in through the cracks was consumed by its ravenous appetite. So it was that the Jennie on the left instead of her gilled sister was the one to die of asphyxia just before her eyes opened on her world again.

The driving rain came too late to slow the burning. Above the corrugated iron roof, the heat was so intense any drop nearing it converted to air and vanished. The ones pelting the walls had an instant longer to exist as steam before they, too, disappeared.

Inside, one end of the tired loft came down in a single searing, flaming sheet and smashed the trough and its contents beyond recognition and set to cremating them long before the water could come to a boil.

Nothing could be done to save the barn. One of the Slim Boys, a rain-soaked blanket thrown over him, made one attempt to help those inside. He ran to the door and grabbed the handle, but yanked his hand away. The iron was too hot to touch. He gathered a dripping corner of the blanket and clutched at the handle again. He pulled hard and the already buckling door came open hard.

He was almost swamped by a huge billow of flame. Only the sodden blanket saved him as he staggered back, fell, then crawled from the fire's lick until he was far enough back for his brothers to drag him to his feet and hurry him away.

The women stayed in the scanty protection from

the storm the front porch offered, Marylea, roused by the scrambling and shouting, the howling wind molding her dress around her belly like tissue wrapper on a fancy citrus, Marla, less mindful of the rain, one arm around a pillar by the steps, a hand shading her eyes from the elements.

The men formed a ragged line of helplessness, their backs against the storm, their face to the tower of fire the barn was quickly becoming now that it had the open door for a massive vent. Frederick rocked back and forth on his heels, working at his back teeth with the ubiquitous broom straw, seeming thoroughly amused by the spectacle of destruction. Racklin and Gamelon stood side by side, Racklin staring unswervingly into the heart of the inferno, Gamelon only now and then raising his head to mark the progress of the disaster. The Slim Boys watched impassively for a while, then turned away slowly, one at a time, and single-filed against the wind around to the protection of the back porch.

They had disappeared when the barn, exhausted with age and riddled by fire, sagged, corkscrewed itself slightly on its foundations, then slowly collapsed in a single motion in upon itself with hardly a sound. The rain began to have a little of its way with the pyramid of flaring timbers and plank ends, and one by one they began to surrender into a glowing smolder, though the smoke and steam would rise for hours.

Marla and Marylea rousted out every towel in the house and, keeping only sufficient for themselves, gave over the kitchen to the men and went upstairs to dry themselves and put on fresh clothes.

Racklin was the last to come into the locker room after stripping his soaking clothes into a draining pile on one porch or the other as all the rest had done. Except for calling up undemandingly to Marylea to throw him down some dry clothes as he toweled himself, he was silent. All of them were silent except for Frederick, who chuckled, "Some show, huh?" He might have added to that but for the three pairs of black eyes in high-cheekboned faces that turned on him and held.

In dry jeans, an old cotton flannel shirt and sweat socks, Gamelon came out of the small pantry where Racklin had put a cot for him, crossed to the back door and opened it quickly to retrieve his wet shoes. He took them to the warm wood cook stove and slid them underneath to dry. As he straightened up, he felt a hand on his shoulder. He turned to see Racklin, dried and dressed, beckoning him with eyes and a tilt of the head to follow him.

Again they crossed the kitchen, went down the hall and took up places opposite each other in the parlor's stiff chairs. Again Gamelon knew the play was not his and studied his brother's calm face in silence. Racklin did not look at him but seemed to peruse the space above and beyond Gamelon.

The violence of the storm's leading edge had moved with it toward the east. The gusts came less frequently. The rain had settled into a steady deluge.

When Racklin finally spoke, his tone was distant, emotionless; and he still held his eyes away from any revelation or commitment to Gamelon's. "I wasn't expecting that," he said, "but I suppose it solves part of the problem."

"The fire?"

"Yes."

"How?"

"The gilled Jennie: there was no way out for the gilled Jennie. You were right—about that and a lot more. She would have died an unpleasant death no matter how you look at it. Maybe the fire was a more merciful way."

Before Racklin was into his second sentence, a warning alarm went off inside Gamelon. It was a dual-toned chime. One reminded him again of Racklin's habit of shrouding himself in either obtuse silence or raucous boisterousness when he had locked on an objective and it was close. The other bell signalled wariness. Racklin's words of last Friday were suddenly there in his mind undiluted by the intervening days: ". . . Chameleon To The People. I am whatever color I find myself against. I am what I am wished to be. I become what is needed for any given moment of any given day." Gamelon extended his antennae to the fullest as he replied, "It might have been for the gilled Jennie, but what about the other two? Was it 'merciful' for them, too?"

Racklin leaned forward, put his elbows on his knees and let his big hands dangle. His head drooped and he said softly, "I'm sorry about them, Lon, you know I must be."

"I know nothing of the sort."

Racklin sat up and jammed his fingers into his hair and looked Gamelon in the eye for the first time since they had returned to the seclusion of the musty parlor. "God, Lon, you've got to believe me." He let his hands drop limp in his lap. "I know I've been difficult these past few days, but—"

"More than ever before in your life."

"—but, Lon, you know the pressure I've been under."

"Not really."

Racklin stood up and began to pace the length of the near-empty room. "Lon, I meant it when I said I was glad you were here. I'm sorry about the way I went about getting you here—"

"A phone call would have done the trick."

"I couldn't risk even that much that might reveal where I was. It was too late."

"Why?"

"The Slim Boys were getting restless. Frederick and Jennie were already here—"

"Bullshit. To have Marla pull it off took a lot of planning over a period of time."

"All right, all right, but everything was ready and I wanted you here for the results.

"Still the strong odor of bullshit, but for now, how did you work it? I'm curious."

"When Maria found out you were going to be away collecting your awards, she wrote to Marla—Marylea—in Salt Lake City and said she'd like to come for a few days' visit while you were gone. Marla always sent Maria's letters on here for Marylea—no, Maria never knew about the second division. She didn't know about me.

"She said she was going to come on a Thursday, the Thursday following the Sunday you were to leave. She was going to have your man pick her up on his way to the airport so she wouldn't have to bring her car in and leave it there while she was—"

"On his way to the airport Thursday," Gamelon interrupted, "almost every Thursday in the late winter and early spring with the cuttings for the eastern growers, always a Thursday so they would arrive at the beginning of the work week and the grafting could be done promptly."

"Yes, but the first Thursday Marla flew down, your man didn't show."

"Late in the grafting season, even for the eastern growers. We have very few shipments in early summer.

"She had to fly down the second time."

"How would Marla know 'my man'?"

"Maria was very fond of him and his family. She'd written a lot about them, described them. Besides, you'd be one businessman in a million if you didn't use your truck panels or your van sides to advertise."

"And it all just happened to coincide: Jorge's

arrival and departure and the departure of the flight to Salt Lake via St. George?"

"It was the flight Maria had planned to take and she'd picked it because of the time your man always arrived at the airport. By the second try, it *was* almost too late. Frederick and Jennie had only so much time away, and the Slim Boy was getting lazier and sleepier by the day."

Racklin came up behind Gamelon's chair and put both hands on his brother's shoulders. "Lon," he said in a soft, impassioned voice, "I really needed you." He came around and sat opposite Gamelon again. "I said you were right about a lot of things. I was playing with a fire worse than the one that killed those poor creatures in the barn, and that fire was burning me, consuming me.

"I don't think I realized it at the time, but that's why I wanted you here. Some part of me was screaming for help and that same part knew you were the only one who could.

"So you came and you tried to steer me with all the love and patience and understanding only you could have for me and still I fought. I couldn't admit what I was doing, that how I was doing it was illogical, unprofessional—wrong."

Racklin seemed to have forgotten that Gamelon had taken countless confessions from him over the years, had witnessed the seeming contrition that followed the recklessness. Now, just as his flights had seemed higher, his repentence seemed too abject. Superficially, Gamelon accepted what Racklin had to say but he did not relax his watchfulness. "Are you admitting it now—finally?"

"Yes."

"Then you shouldn't mind the following proposal: Let me take over. Let me direct not only what happens here in future but you as well until I'm satisfied everything, and most of all you, is back on a realistic path again."

"Well, I—"

"If everything holds steady, gets done right, I only want to be a part of it, really. There's so much that's precious to an infinite degree about these people. It must be discovered systematically and assessed as scientifically as possible, agreed?"

"Yes—agreed."

"And you must agree to this, too: Marla, Marylea, all the rest of them, plus who knows how many more with similar traits, are first of all feeling human beings and *will* be treated with the dignity and respect due them as such. No more trampling. No more handling them like test tube specimens with no regard for their needs, their emotions."

"I—we have to be dispassionate, objective—"

"Objective, yes, but not unaware, disregarding them as human beings."

"I'll try."

"Yes, you will. Now, if the storm's passed in the morning, I'm taking the Fiat to St. George for repairs. The front end's going to pieces and the wipers and the horn don't work. While I'm gone, I want you to sit down and synthesize everything that's happened so far into a rough journal."

"If I can."

"You know damn well you can. You've been doing it on other research projects for years. Just *do* it!"

"OK, OK."

"And, while I'm down there, I'll make some phone calls."

Racklin's head, which had hung in seeming, if reluctant, subjugation all through Gamelon's dictation of terms, came up with a jerk. His eyes had gone ice cold. "And just who will you be calling?"

"Look, Rack, just as I'm not going to step into even the hard edge of your glory spotlight when the time comes, I'm not planning to reveal your findings to date to the world. I'm going to try to arrange for the only logical next step: a proper genetic study in a laboratory by the best cryogeneticist I can get to work with me."

"You will not!"

"Stuff it, Racklin! It's what you've wanted out of me all along, isn't it? That kind of work's way out of your line but you need to know *how* they work or everything else is meaningless."

"It's too soon for that yet."

"If there was only one human being in the world with these attributes, it could never be too soon. As it is, complete findings could take years. Have you even considered what the byproducts of such research' might mean in the world of human suffering, the cures for disease, cancer—Lord knows what else might be discovered from understanding how these people's genes differ from yours and mine—as they must?!"

Racklin got up and walked away from Gamelon, his hands jammed deep in his pockets. At the windowed end of the room, he turned to face his brother squarely. "I was wrong!" he said. "Up to a point, I was wrong, but I'm alright now! This is *my* project, *my* study, *my work* and I'll stay in control of it! It's too far too soon! I'll say when we go into the lab!"

Gamelon had had his legs crossed. His feet slammed down on the floor and he was across the room in two strides. He grabbed Racklin by the shirt front and jammed him into the narrow wall between the windows and held him there with his greater weight. He swallowed once hard to try to damp the anger rising in him but that did not keep it from raging in his usually soft brown eyes. "Listen to me! Listen to me for the last time! You are not in control here anymore. You never will be again except as far as I let you be.

"Never forget, Racklin, never, that I hold the key to the whole thing. 'Your people' do too, but they wouldn't use it. Marla wouldn't use it. Marylea surely wouldn't. Frederick's too stupid and the Slim Boys don't care. I do. I will use that key if I have to, if you force me!"

Racklin tried to pull away but at the first hint of motion, Gamelon pressed him even harder against the wall. "All I have to do tomorrow in St. George, or any day in any asshole of the world like Nesset, is to call one hick weekly or one local television station with just the scantiest of tantalizing facts and the world will be all over you and 'your' people!

"If you force me, my promise not to reveal your findings won't hold. Professional ethics won't muzzle me. Not even the pitiful little bit of love I have left for you won't muzzle me if you don't back down and do things the way *I* want them done!"

Gamelon shoved himself away from his brother and out of the room in almost a single curling motion and without a backward glance.

Racklin stood where he was as Gamelon's heavy tread traversed the length of the hall, the breadth of the kitchen, and the door into the old pantry *cum* guest quarters slammed. He leaned slowly out from the wall then and turned again to look out through the rain toward the north and nothing, his big hands working, this time easily, behind his back. Deep within his amber eyes, the wild fires kindled and flamed for a few moments and he smiled to himself a sloping, crooked smile.

The slam of the pantry door behind Gamelon was like the single stroke of a hammer that drove a single word into the dead center of his mind: coward.

In the small, dim room with but one high window, its meagre light dulled by the weather outside, the rest of his mind asked with surprise, why that word, who is a coward?

I?

Am I a coward?

Was I?

I was—no.

I might have seemed to be from another's viewpoint when I was buried in the greenhouse letting the world go by without choosing to see its realities. Not now.

A man can seem a coward to another when in truth he's not aware there is a problem to face, a challenge to take up, a battle to fight. If it's laid out for him and then he refuses to rise to it with his best or his worst, shirks it, ignores it because he fears the consequences to himself, then, then he is a coward.

Who is a coward?

The answer came slowly in a tattered string of reminiscences and realizations. With the arrival of each, Gamelon felt as though his body disintegrated a little, as though its molecular glue was giving way a bit at a time.

I am as guilty as anyone. I have conceived of him, named him aggressive, bright, wild, winged and stood in awe of him for being all those things and more and considered them wonderful, and felt myself less because I was not all those things.

But, he told me, he said to me—when was it, so little time as three days ago—'I need you to want me to be those things. I need you to need me to be what I cannot help. Then I can do what I must.'

Who is he?

Who is Racklin?

I don't know. I never have. I see now.

He has never been anything but a change of costume, his life nothing but an endless masked ball.

Who is my brother?

I have no brother.

I have never had a brother. There has never been anything there but another entity disguised as a . . .

'brother, playmate, friend, leader, teacher, lover' . . . boy, man, scientist . . .

Coward.

The most craven, despicable kind of coward. The kind of—man—who cannot, will not face the only truth that matters, that he is like every other man: absolutely unique no matter how dull, usual, normal he is otherwise.

Racklin isn't.

Empty costumes dancing through a phantom ball.

How do you deal with someone who isn't?

How do you grapple with someone who has the coward's freedom to be anyone or anything he wants to be?

How can you know who or what it is you love or hate or want to nurture or want to destroy?

I am guilty, more to blame than all the others for letting the costumes use me, for following the hollow dance. I have failed this man since we were young together by applauding the masquerades instead of booing and hissing him into facing the uniqueness and dullness of a real self.

And now, he has made use of me to the ultimate and it is my own fault. He has made me take the responsibility. Now, no matter what happens, it will be my fault, not his.

And now, having done that, I cannot back away. I understand the challenge now—completely. If I turn away, I am a greater coward than he will ever be.

I am my brother's keeper or my brother's killer.

Gamelon crossed the small room in two steps, threw himself on his cot, rolled on his side, hugged himself and stared at the wall.

JULY 9, 1984

Gamelon expected to make the trip by himself to get the Fiat repaired, but was inwardly pleased when, at the breakfast table, Marla asked to go along. Marylea, not feeling up to the jaunt, had quite a grocery list and there were still some things she needed for the baby.

Racklin, otherwise quiet and withdrawn, contributed where Gamelon could hope to get the car fixed, how to find the place and that he was bringing the remaining Frederick down around midday and would swing by the repair shop to see how things were going—in case for some reason they needed a ride home.

As they were walking to the car, Gamelon remembered the battered briefcase with his address and phone book in it, ran back for it, and he and Marla were under way a little after eight.

Before they had left the breakfast table, Gamelon had decided to turn left at the end of the bridge and make the short climb—God and the Fiat willing—up to the deep fold in the pass and the view of Swede's Valley. Except for the few words of request and explanation concerning the morning's trip, Marla, too, had been quiet and withdrawn. There were the shadows of sleeplessness under her eyes and her face seemed tight and stretched. He remembered what a restorative the sweeping view had been for him and thought it might be a help to her, too, after all she had been plunged into from almost the moment of her arrival the morning before.

There is no clarity like that of the high desert air after a storm has passed. It is as though in and of itself, its very nothingness glints and glistens while all it surrounds is left clear of softening shadow. The sky's blue is blue all the way down to the earth. Greens, reds, even tans and listless browns are so intense they stand as progressive flat surfaces and do not blend with whatever color may be adjacent. Even where the horizon far in the distance begins its almost imperceptible rollover, there is no haze.

Gamelon stood a little away from Marla, his hands in his pockets, rocking up on the balls of his feet and back, breathing deeply. He wanted to leave her alone with herself and the view for as long as she needed, but he could not keep his eyes from cutting to her, a yard or so away, again and again.

How could three women, three identical women, be so different?

Maria's hair had been very long and straight. Marylea's was wispy and careless, tucked and gathered only where her pins finally were able to collect enough to finally take a hold. Marla's was neatly trimmed, waved in and then away from her face and fell just to her shoulders.

He had to suppose where Marylea was concerned, but the bodies outwardly were all the same, the long, lovely legs, the flat stomachs, the full breasts—and yet, they were not. Marla's was as subtly different as the others' had been from each other. Without turning his head, he flicked his fifth glance in a minute toward her.

Even at rest, Maria's body had been energy ready to burst forth in all directions. Marylea's? How could he put it? Even in motion, it was softness ready to slacken. And Marla's? Marla, her body, everything about her he realized now had a thrusting up and forward, a power, but under strict control.

He wondered if the bonds were loosened . . .

She turned toward him and he saw, as always, the great gray eyes . . .

She smiled and the smile said all the genuine 'thank you' to him that was necessary for having brought her to the top of Swede's Valley. "I'm ready now, Lon—" she said, "—I may call you Lon?" and seeming to assume concurrence, started for her side of the car.

As he turned to follow, a black, totally unanticipated thought flew through his mind: not so long ago, part of this woman had been in love with Racklin and his brother had made love to all of her.

Just as they passed the end of the bridge back over the wash to the farm, Marla began to sing softly to herself: "La, la, laaaaaa, la la laaaaaa, LAAAA, LA! LA! LA! LA! LA! hmmmmmm, la, la laaaaaa . . ." and Gamelon noticed the fingers of her left hand moving precisely in accompaniment on her thigh.

After a moment or two, he asked, "What's that?"

She turned to him and smiled lightly. "I'm sorry. It's the opening of Beethoven's 'Spring Sonata.' I'm preparing it for a recital in late September."

Gamelon glanced at her hand and she added, "Oh, that. I'm trying out some new fingerings for that passage. Just practicing."

"How did you turn out to be the musical one?"

"Of the two—three of us? Well, Marylea still is, of course . . ." Marla turned her face to the window. "It's just that she doesn't play anymore. She didn't even bring a fiddle with her when she came down here . . ."

Gamelon decided not to prompt, to wait and see if she would continue on her own.

Marla did in a few moments. She turned back to him and said, "Maria was, too—musical. She loved music, but you must know that."

He remembered *The Swan of Tuonela, Rodeo,* 'love nearby—but not right in your pocket' and the *Liebeslieder Waltzes* . . .

". . . and having known her as you did, you must have realized that practicing wouldn't have been one of her long suits. She liked more immediate results and drifted away toward drawing, painting and finally graphics. She was content with that form of expression and to let the practice room drones produce her music for her."

"Your whole life has been music, then."

"Except for a few interruptions—like Racklin—I've been playing steadily since I was six."

'Like Racklin' was said with no more special intonation than 'please pass the salt,' but it was out and acknowledged between them.

"Prodigy?"

"Lord, no. Talent, but not genius. Talent, will, and a certain joy now and then in the doing. What more can one ask from one's profession?"

He would have been able to agree wholeheartedly if life had seen fit to leave him buried in his own, but he declined to pursue the matter. Instead, he said, "Maria never told me much at all about her young years, her growing up. Will you?"

Marla looked at him steadily for a moment or two, then seemed to decide he had some right to know her family's past, and launched a simple, offhand exposition of it, starting where she supposed the start should be made.

"Although both Maria and I had some vague recollections about it, we didn't know for certain about the first dividing until five years ago. We were almost as hazy about having lived on the farm and why we left. None of it was ever discussed at home and if one of us happened to touch on an aspect of it, it was either ignored or put down with some placebo of an answer. Then, when Mother found out she was too sick ever to recover, she told us.

"At the time, I don't think either of us really believed her, even though we both knew she was far too rational and pragmatic to have invented such a wild story. I don't think Maria ever believed it. Of course, with the arrival of Racklin upon the scene, Marylea—I—had the whole thing rather dramatically proved."

"Both of your parents are gone Marylea said."

"Yes, Dad died of cancer about eighteen months before Mother—she died of cancer, too—a different form."

"From the farm, then, the family went to Salt Lake City. I take it your father never went back to farming."

"He didn't. At first, he worked in a hardware store, then he sold farm implements. When Maria and I were old enough to look after ourselves, Mother went back to nursing. She stayed with it even when she was slowly dying. I think now it must have been some sort of penance for her . . ."

"A penance for what?"

"For having given birth to a freak."

There was so much bitterness in her answer, Gamelon felt bound to try to counter it. "Not 'freak,' Marla, 'special,' 'supernormal,' if you like, even 'miraculous.' " But even as the words formed and sounded, he could not help but remember Racklin's question, "What is abnormal?"

"Freak," Marla repeated flatly and turned away from him.

Gamelon fought the Fiat and let her have her silence.

A mile farther down the valley, she broke it and

said musingly as though to herself, "The person with a club foot or a hairlip is lucky. They have some outward manifestation that at least pulls in a little pity. They have the sustenance of knowing it's there for them in others even if it isn't expressed.

"Maria, myself, Marylea, the Slim Boys, we have to live without pity, with the knowledge forever bottled up inside us of how strange, how malformed we really are. Who would feel sorry for us if we told them? Who wouldn't kill us if they knew—except a Racklin, or perhaps—a Gamelon?" She turned a faint hopeful smile on him.

All Gamelon did was smile back and go on battling the car.

A mile farther still, she murmured, "I wonder. Ever since last winter, I've wondered . . ."

"Wondered what, Marla?"

"I've always wondered whether whatever made me and the others the way we are isn't the same thing that eventually caused Mother and Dad to die of cancer.

"I wonder if all of us aren't really some form of cancer."

And a mile farther still was St. George. Marla would leave the bagged groceries at the market to be picked up on the way out of town. They chose a likely looking coffee shop to meet in after their errands were done and Gamelon let Marla out.

As he drove the remaining two blocks to the garage, he felt Marla had shared more of her deep concerns, her misgivings, herself, with him than she had with anyone in a long, long while, perhaps ever. Regardless of how bleak some of her thoughts had been, the realization of that sharing warmed him and he was glad.

"Can't see no problems whatever with the welds. Got to be one o' them bolts." The mechanic's nasal voice seemed to rise like an oracle's through the

Fiat's upended radiator grill. All that showed of him beneath the car was a belly so rotund it would not go under, overall-covered ham hock legs and heavy work shoes so battered the steel showed in places on the toes. As always, it made Gamelon nervous to see a mechanic lying so casually half inserted on his backboard with nothing between him and a third of a ton of uncaring metal but a single jack.

"Hump! Should've spotted that right off. Bolt's gone. Front one on the control arm. Sheared clear off." The ham hock legs kicked and the mechanic's red-nosed balloon face slid out from under the car. He lay blinking tiny washed-out blue eyes at Gamelon towering above him for a moment, then said simply, "Ain't got one."

He rolled clear, grunted and got to his feet with great effort. Even though Gamelon was not inordinately tall, the man hardly came to his shoulder.

Priests wash their hands in nothing. Great beauties flaunt them at anything. Unless their hands are otherwise occupied, mechanics must wipe and wipe at them with the filthiest rag within reach or they cannot talk. The bulbous man dragged one from his hip pocket, scrubbed it between his palms and began. "Them things don't often break, Mister, almost never. What kind o' hill'd you come down anyway?"

Gamelon lived again the shortcut behind Racklin's truck, but said nothing. No answer was required.

"Like I said," the man went on, " 'ain't got one. This here's 'n older model—what year'd you say?"

"Seventy."

"Yeh, seventy. Well, we got one o' two possibilities to keep you on the road till you get where it can be done proper. Got a couple Eye-talian wrecks out in back. Maybe suspension's the same. Never had call to look up to now. If neither of 'em is, I'll have to go with whatever's the closest thing to it I got t'hand. Neither way's it gonna be good as new. You see to it soon's you get where you can, you hear."

Gamelon nodded that he had absorbed his instructions, accepted his risks and asked, "How long'll it take?"

"Depends. I got them fuses to replace—hope that's all it is—so them wipers and the rest'll work. You got errands?"

"Uh-huh."

The mechanic grubbed in a top pocket of his coveralls and produced a card personalized with his greasy fingerprints. He handed it to Gamelon who read, "Herbert's Any-car, Any-time Repair," an address and a phone number. Herbert, or so Gamelon had to assume as there was no one else in evidence in the shop, tapped the card and said, "Gimme a call in an hour'n a half, two hours. We'll see where we stand."

The only errand Gamelon had was to try to get through to Mr. S.

The coffee shop cashier obviously did not appreciate parting with five dollars' worth of her precious change, but Gamelon pried it out of her drawer with a hung head and what he hoped was his most winning smile. He headed for the public wall phone at the end of the almost deserted lunch counter, styrofoam cup of change and briefcase in hand. He was glad it was between meals; the ongoing kitchen din would be enough in itself to make communicating on the unenclosed phone trying.

He never knew what Freddie Sevrinsky's schedule was. He decided to try him at home first in hopes he might be in his study working that morning. He was in luck. Mr. S. answered on a half ring. After an exchange of genuinely warm pleasantries, Gamelon got to the point. "I'm calling to ask for your help if it's possible, Sir."

"Naturally, naturally, my boy. Whatever is possible, I'll always do for you. Say on!"

"Who's occupying the genetics chair these days?"

"One Dr. E. V. Ching. Why?"

"Do you know the doctor well enough to recommend me?"

"Isn't that strange?! Yes, I know Dr. Ching—have for years—but we've never spoken. But, in answer to your question, yes, I think so. What is it I am to say you want?"

"Just—just that I have a problem in genetics with which I would deeply appreciate help. If Dr. Ching agrees to at least hear me out, then I'll call direct. Mr. S.—"

"Yes, Lon?"

"I realize I'm being evasive, but I just can't talk about what I'm into from where I am now. I promise you'll get a complete explanation just as soon as it's humanly possible—"

"Lon, Lon, you don't ever have to explain yourself to me if you don't want to. You know that."

"Believe me, Mr. S., I want to. I need to."

"When you get to it, then."

"Yes, Sir. Do you think Dr. Ching will help me?"

"I don't think there'll be any question of it when I say who you are."

"What does who I am have to do with it?"

"From all reports, Dr. Ching is an avid—no, totally involved rose fancier. What's the name for such a person? I forget."

"A Rosarian."

"Well, need I say more?"

Gamelon sat on the lunch counter stool closest to the phone nursing an iced tea and trying to ignore his gnawing stomach until Marla joined him and they could have lunch together. The counter was otherwise empty except for two trim elderly men in flannel shirts with trout flies in their hat bands a few seats over. Both the iced tea and the wait for the phone to ring were boring and without really meaning to, he found himself eavesdropping on the men's conversation without recording much of what was being said.

". . . always said we wouldn't be caught dead out here this time of year."

"That storm yesterday was a pip, all right, but I don't know, after all those summers of watching the Gulf of Alaska low run into the subtropical jet stream and dump on this area on paper just as predictable as sin and Christmas, I think it was kind of a lark to experience the reality instead of just isobars and gradients and flows."

The two men broke off as the waitress brought them breakfast. Either they had been driving all night and into the late morning or fishing somewhere since dawn, Gamelon surmised. He sipped at the stale-tasting tea.

A few moments later, one of the men stopped, fork in front of mouth to say, "How long *had* we been talking about this trip anyway, Roy?"

Roy chewed his Canadian bacon and ruminated. Then he swallowed and chuckled, "I can tell you the exact date we started! How could I forget? The night we first mentioned it was the same night I got home to find Rachael sitting on the stoop with her bag waiting for me to take her to the hospital to have Harry! That would have been—July 27, 1949. Harry was born the morning of the twenty-eighth."

"I remember, I remember. The tests were going on then. You'd briefed the MIC for Yucca Flats just before I relieved you."

"Yeh—and I was still dreaming of moving to the Virgin Islands some day. A fishing trip in southwestern Utah was really the least attractive thing I could think of then, I remember . . ."

Gamelon could not put his finger on it right then, but the date, July 27, 1949, interested him and he listened as intently as he could to the ongoing conversation without appearing to, until the phone on the wall rang.

By previous arrangement with the spindly counter waitress, he answered it. From La Playa, Mr. S. reported that Dr. Ching was awaiting his call and at what number.

Although the connection between St. George and Mr. S.'s study in La Playa had been clear but for a distance hiss, the one between the coffee shop and Dr. Ching's office at the university was extremely poor. After the amenities and Gamelon's brief and minimally informative explanation of his needs, Dr. Ching gave him a short list of the specimens that would be considered basic for a proper investigation. They agreed on a time and place for delivery, and brusquely courteous, Dr. Ching rang off.

Gamelon hung up, nodded thanks to the counter waitress and turned from the phone to find a smiling, heavily burdened Marla standing behind him. He hastened to relieve her of her parcels and she headed for the nearest vacant booth without any consultation with him.

Gamelon filled the inside ends of both booth seats with bags of diapers, formula powders and the like and they slid in opposite each other. For a few seconds they sat smiling at each other, then, with a flustered little laugh, Marla asked, "Success?"

"Success," Gamelon said more to the gray eyes than anything. "You?"

"Everything on Marylea's list plus a few things that weren't." She leaned across to one of the bags and began removing items one by one.

"A little dress for the baby." She shook the tiny garment out for Gamelon's inspection, then put it aside.

"For me, this. I've been looking all over for one this color. Imagine stumbling on it in St. George of all places!" She held a severe sleeveless blouse in rich Prussian blue under her chin for a few seconds and Gamelon understood why that particular color. It complemented her eyes wonderfully.

She folded the blouse neatly and put it back in the bag and lifted out the last of her treasures. "And this," she said to Gamelon with a mischievous smile, "is for you. I couldn't help but think of you when I saw it—your build and coloring—and all."

All he could make of what she held across the table toward him was a loose handful of deep green strings. "What is it?" he asked, truly at a loss.

Marla shook the strings out into a pattern and held it out delicately with two fingers of each hand. "Now I was *really* surprised to find *this* in St. George—Los Angeles, San Francisco, oh, definitely San Francisco—but St. George?! One *does* have to wonder what really goes on around this sleepy Mormon town, doesn't one?"

As she stretched and pulled the thing this way and that, Gamelon's brown eyes went wide. It was a string swim suit of the scantiest and most revealing kind. It did not look big enough for him to get his balled fist into much less those parts of him that were supposed to fit into it.

He felt himself actually beginning to blush as only redheads can blush. She saw the color rising and took one hand from the skimpy suit first to point a finger at him and then to stifle her laughter.

Suddenly, he guffawed, grabbed the thing in one swipe and stuffed it in the handiest bag. "What in

God's name made you think of something like that for me?!" he chortled.

She got her mirth under control, breathed deeply, then, gray eyes shining, she said, "First of all, from what I can gather, it's been too long since anyone exhibited any interest in you just for yourself, in Gamelon, the man, just that. Second, it appears to me it's been too long since Gamelon, the man, had a good laugh. That's all."

He knew he would never even try to wear the thing, but still, it was his turn just to let a genuine smile say all the 'thank you' that was necessary.

A lunch of surprisingly good tuna salad—with french fries for Gamelon—went quickly and without much commentary from either of them. They both seemed to have wordlessly acknowledged there might or might not be more to come between them and were satisfied for the moment to enjoy each other's company.

Gamelon called Herbert, and yes, the Fiat was ready. The cashier agreed to stow Marla's parcels for a bit behind the register and the two of them strolled leisurely back to "Any-car, Any-time Repairs," pausing now and again in front of a shop window if something caught one or the other's eye.

"Man in a pickup stopped awhile back inquirin' after your car, mister," Herbert announced as Gamelon and Marla came through the shop's high, rolling doors. "Didn't say who he was but he looked tolerable like you if you had a beard."

Gamelon explained briefly who Racklin was and why he had come in.

"Won't keep you," Herbert said. "Let's settle up. Let's see now, oh, fifteen dollars'll do it, I reckon and you can be on your way. Oh—that's an old American made bolt in there. Don't fit exactly. You get it changed soon's you can, you hear?"

Gamelon promised, handed Herbert a five and a ten, thanked him, and he and Marla were off to make the rounds for parcels.

The Fiat's side mirror had a rusted, inflexible down cant. As the car labored up through Swede's Valley, he had to duck now and then until his chin was almost on the steering wheel to check behind. The rearview mirror was totally blocked by the bags and boxes mounded in the rear seat.

Gamelon and Marla had not had much to say to each other since leaving St. George. He had been concentrating on the feel and the reactions of the car with its wrong old new bolt. She had kept to herself except to hum a few more snatches of the "Spring Sonata" while trying the fingering on her knee.

A mile or two out of town Gamelon felt satisfied the makeshift repair would hold. He relaxed after a duck and a study of the road to the rear and turned to the silent Marla. "Now that I seem to have the time to let it," he said, "something bothers me."

Offhandedly she asked what.

"Why isn't Marylea planning to go down to the hospital in St. George to have the baby? It's only a little over thirty minutes from the farm."

Marla neither looked at him nor replied for several moments, then she turned completely straightforward eyes on him and said without emotion, "Having seen the gilled Jennie, need you ask?"

The so-young and healthy Marylea, the so-strong and vital Racklin; foolish of him, but, yes, he had gone right on assuming until that moment that the child would be normal, although usual people gave birth to deformed children occasionally.

He sighed. "Having the baby at the farm would fit Racklin's druthers."

"It would," Marla replied, "but it's Marylea's

wish as much or more than his. I don't think she's told anyone but me, and then only yesterday after the fire, but she is deeply afraid of giving birth to something warped, horrible in some way. That's why she ran out of the barn after one glimpse of the gilled Jennie. Seeing that poor creature was almost like a confirmation of her worst fears, a tangible example of what might have been growing inside her all these months."

Gamelon said nothing for a while, then asked himself as much as Marla, "What do we do if it isn't—right?"

"After yesterday, I have made myself accept the strong possibility that it might not be. I'm trying to steel myself so that I'll be able to do whatever's necessary if anything is. I don't see that either of us can do anything more now."

Gamelon simply nodded.

The car pulled on at a sedate forty-five. An empty stake side overtook and passed them on a straight stretch, the occupants of both vehicles rendering each other lazy, quasi-regal waves. As the truck disappeared over an easy rise ahead, Gamelon said casually, "Marla, I overheard some men talking at the lunch counter while I was waiting for my call. I couldn't help putting what they said together with something you said on the way down."

"What did they—what did I say? Who were they?"

"From what I got, I assume they were two old friends here on a fishing trip—a long-planned, long-delayed fishing trip. They're evidently retired now, but they must have been meteorologists, I gathered, for the government. They seemed to know an awful lot about the seasonal weather patterns around here."

"So?"

He altered the train of the conversation somewhat. "You remember saying this morning that you'd wondered if whatever made you the way you are might be the same thing that was ultimately responsible for your parents' deaths?"

"Yes."

"And you know what cancer is?"

"Yes and no—I don't think I ever really understood."

"Well, as simply as I can put it, a cancerous cell is one whose genetic mechanisms have gone awry. It's considered a retrograde cell. The gene count's always off from a normal cell, sometimes more, sometimes less, so it doesn't function, doesn't do its job like a fellow blood cell or bone cell or whatever other form of specialized cell it might be. It's retrograde and it's a rogue with a faulty time clock for multiplication."

"At the risk of being thought testy, again I ask, 'so?' "

And again, Gamelon veered the conversation. "Birdie's husband died of cancer. Came down with it in the early '50s, evidently, but didn't actually die until some years later."

"Who's Birdie?"

"Never mind right now—when was your's and Maria's birthday? March the—"

"March the twenty-sixth, 19—50. Really, Lon, I'm not following this—"

He raised one hand to gently silence her, then dropped it back on the wheel and started ticking off with his fingers as he computed backwards, "March, February, January, tuh, tuh, tuh, tuh, August—July! Late July, 1949! That's what he said!"

"What *are* you talking about?!"

Gamelon did not reply at once. He did not say anything until Marla turned in her seat and said to him firmly, "What, Lon?"

Still his answer did not come right away, then finally he said quietly, "It's all come out now, but back then nobody knew how dangerous it was to live in this part of the world. In the late '40s, early '50s, all hereabouts were assured and reassured there was absolutely no danger from the atomic testing going on west of here in Nevada. Nobody understood fallout or how the weather carries it—or they didn't want to.

"Then, some years back, people in places like Nesset and St. George—especially St. George—began to put two and two together. The death rate from cancer around here was way out of proportion to the norm they felt. It wasn't long before they tied that to the Nevada tests.

"They probably know now, too, but I'll wager back then, back in late July of 1949, those two meteorologists didn't know all of what was going on. They knew that in high summer the prevailing winds are from the west and that one air mass meets another and produces wild thunderstorms and tons of rain—like yesterday—over southwestern Utah and northwestern Arizona—"

"When were the others born?" Marla interrupted in a voice barely audible over the chunk of the engine.

"Very late March, very early April."

"So, taking individual differences into account—"

"All of you were conceived at approximately the same time. All of you were at approximately the same stage of fetal development—"

"And there must have been more than just Maria and Frederick and—"

"Yes, who knows how many? Do they know even to this day what they are?"

"Some of them are probably beginning to suspect part of it anyway."

"What part? How?"

"The whole human race is vain, but is there a woman alive in her mid-thirties who wouldn't be aware that she doesn't look a day over twenty or twenty-one?"

"I see."

"Well, there's something I don't see."

"What?"

"How are you making the connection? What makes you so sure it was radiation at some critical moment in early fetal development?"

"The two men in the coffee shop, Marla, the meteorologists: they were trying to recall when they first thought of coming out here for the sight-seeing and the fishing. They finally agreed it was one night in late July of 1949. One of them was sure because his son was born the next day. He also recalled having briefed the meteorologist in charge of the Yucca Flats Project that same night for a test that was scheduled to take place the next day. And he remembered because it had always puzzled him why the record of such a test on the day his son was born had never shown up in the public record even to this time thirty-five years later. Could it have been so filthy a bomb the government's never admitted it?"

They came up on the plank bridge and Gamelon wheeled the Fiat onto it. As they rattled across, Marla said flatly, her eyes straight ahead, "Then I was right."

Gamelon knew what she would say; he had already reluctantly arrived at the same possible interpretation, but he asked anyway, "About what?"

"What did you say about a cancer cell, that it is a rogue with a faulty multiplication clock?"

"Uh-huh."

"Well, I was right: the others and I are just another form of cancer, a total cancer."

The Slim Boys were strewn, hunkered or slouched, in the shade on the front porch. They made no move to go out and help with the parcels until a burdened Gamelon mounted the steps and said harshly, "You're eating half the food around here. The least you can do is bring it in."

Blue Sateen looked at him for a moment then shifted his gaze to Marla coming up behind Gamelon. To her he said casually, "You're to go up. The pains've started." Only then did he rise and start off toward the car at a frustratingly casual saunter.

After a brief visit to Marylea to reassure herself that all was as well as could be with her, Marla came back down to the kitchen. She and Gamelon got all the food put away more or less, she surmised, where Marylea would want it.

She had put a kettle on before they began on the groceries. Now, she made bouillon for Marylea, who had not eaten since breakfast, instant coffee for herself, and balancing the cups expertly, disappeared up the stairs again. The second Frederick had evidently gone as per plan. The Slim Boys had melted away as only they could. Racklin had not put in an appearance. Gamelon was alone.

The afternoon was clean, the sky cloudless, a little cooler after the storm and very peaceful. Thank God, Gamelon thought as he went out onto the porch, for once, how quiet and peaceful. He sat down on the steps and pulled off his shirt to let the strong July sun heat his flesh and softly pummel his thick muscles like a thousand lilliputian masseurs. He knew he should find Racklin and go over what Dr. Ching had told him among other things, but he had all afternoon.

He remembered Birdie's aroma-filled orchard. He wondered if she was starting on her preserves with the first of the peaches. He smiled to himself: he would have to retrieve that thumb and free up her pickle relish jar. He stretched. Again it was a time when he could have dreamed and let the day go its implacable way and end without him. He nodded in the glorious warmth and dozed.

He did not realize he had dropped off until he woke with a start, his head snapping up. How long had he slept? Not long. The light did not seem to have altered. Long enough, though, for Blue Sateen Slim Boy to materialize and squat on his haunches at the bottom of the steps and stare at him from the deep shadow of his hat brim.

Gamelon blinked once or twice, then not knowing what prompted him, he smiled at the Indian man. To his surprise, Slim Boy smiled back. Gamelon realized he had never seen him smile before and thought again how strikingly, oddly handsome the man was.

The smile on Slim Boy's lips faded but stayed on his eyes as he said, "I ain't scrawny, but you are one big red devil, you are." His eyes flicked in true appreciation over Gamelon's deep, massive chest, his heavy sloping shoulders. "I sure as hell hope it don't ever come down to cases 'tween you an' me. Always thought I could handle Firehead, but I ain't all that sure 'bout you."

Gamelon said easily, "I don't see any reason it ever should. You know something I don't?"

Slim Boy shrugged slowly, dropped his eyes and let it go at that for a few moments. He made a twisted finger ring from some of the brown grass at his feet, then looked up at Gamelon again and asked, "You wanna talk?"

Gamelon knew it was he who wanted to talk. He shrugged in his turn and grunted, "OK with me." He reached behind him for his shirt, mindful now that the sun not only warmed, it burned—him in particular.

"Firehead get you up here?" Slim Boy asked after another lengthy silence.

"In a roundabout way, yes."

"How long you stayin'?"

"I'm planning to leave in the morning, but it depends on several things, the baby being born, collecting some—things I need to help Racklin and so on."

"What kinda things you need?"

Gamelon was about to explain Dr. Ching's requirements and the reasons for them but thought better of it. "Racklin'll tell you when he's ready, I think. It's his game here," he lied. "I'm just an interested party."

Slim Boy nodded and went back to twisting grass around his finger. Then he asked, "Once you go away, you plannin' to come back?"

"I think I'll have to, at least once more."

"If I was you, I wouldn't."

Gamelon felt his hackles start to rise. "What's it to you whether I do or not?"

Slim Boy sensed Gamelon's feelings. He let go of the braided grass strands and raised a pacifying hand. "Look," he said, "it don't make shit to me one way or t'other. Let it ride."

But Gamelon knew there was something behind Slim Boy's words. The warning—or threat—had been blatant. He needed to know why it had been rendered. He decided to come at the reason from a different, perhaps obtuse angle. "Seeing as we're having a talk: fair's fair. Racklin got you here, too. How?"

The fingers of Slim Boy's hand rubbed together: money.

"He paid you?"

Slim Boy nodded.

"How much?"

"Food 'n a place to sleep an' a thousan' each."

"One for you, one for your brother?"

"An' one for every one more o' us we can make."

"There's more to come?"

"That's the plan."

"When?"

"At a thousand bucks a copy? Soon's somebody can get sleepy enough."

Gamelon's curiosity shouldered the thoughts of the threat or warning aside. "How do you do it?"

he asked. "I mean, how do you just 'get sleepy' so the division will happen?"

Slim Boy appeared to consider for a moment or two, then replied, "First time all I can remember was bein' lonely. You never been a six-year-old took away—give away—from his ma 'n pa 'n brothers. You never been six an' sent off for days—weeks at a time t'follow around behind a bunch o' stinkin' sheep, wintertime, summertime, it didn' make no difference. That's lonely, man, that's lonely. I know there was one day I was so lonely I hurt inside. I guess if I'd o' stayed awake long enough, I'd o' cried deep in the night when Old Bead Woman was asleep or when I was out on the range alone with them fuckin' sheep. But the more I thought about it the more I hurt an' the sleepier I got till I couldn't hol' my head up.

"From what I heard tell, it must've been what it's like when somebody takes too many pills. It's like drinkin' too much an' startin' to pass out but no dizziness an' that kinda thing—I know how *that* feels." He chuckled to himself.

"But this last time, when your brother went to sleep: what made it happen that time?"

Slim Boy gave him a warped smile and rubbed his thumb and fingers together again. "Seems if you want somethin' so bad it hurts, you can get sleepy if you're like us. That passin' out feelin'll come over you if you want it to."

"How often can you make that feeling come over you—I mean how soon again after you've divided can you do it again?"

"Sooner'n you might think—when you want something bad enough."

"How soon?"

Slim Boy cocked his face up to the sun, his eyes closed and counted on his fingers. "Four days since my brothers woke up, s'been, what, six since the one went to sleep. Week before that, he started gettin' lazy." He dropped his head so that again the hat brim shaded his eyes. "One of em's gettin' lazy now, so, what d'ya figure? He goes to sleep again in a week, less maybe? That's how it was last time."

"How many times're you going to try it? How many times do you think it'll work before something goes wrong like with Jennie?"

"As many times as Firehead's got thousands o' dollars, an' who cares if one or two go wrong? Just kill 'em. There'll always be more right ones, fast as we can make 'em."

All Gamelon could visualize was an overview of the entire earth with normal people being pushed off the edges by an unending, undying supply of Slim Boys. But he said, "I should be back in time to see what happens when your brother divides again—if it goes like you think it will."

All traces of involvement with anyone or anything vanished from Slim Boy's face and eyes but his words belied this. "I dunno why I should give a goddam," he said, "but there's somethin' about you I like. I like you like I liked my grandmother when all was said an' done. She was tight, she was hard, she was picky, she was even mean sometimes, but she saw things real, she was right about most things most o' the time until she got old an' funny in the head.

"Ol' Navajo Wisdom tells me you're like her in that. When it comes down to it, if there's a turd on the trail, you're gonna see it an' smell it an' know it for what it is an' kick it out o' your path. Nobody's gonna be able to persuade you it's a wild flower or a pot o' jam no matter what they'd like you t'think or what they'd like t'think themself.

"Firehead, it ain't like that with him. He can look at anything an' see nothin' but what he wants to. Worse'n that, he's a witch. He can make other people see it same as he does."

Slim Boy stood up effortlessly, his back perfectly straight, only his legs unfolding. "Ol' Navajo Wisdom tells me, too, things're gonna get worse around here in not too long. If they do, you gotta know I'm on the side o' the money, I'm with the man payin' the dollars."

For the first time since Gamelon had known him, he saw Slim Boy's eyes catch alight and smoulder. "I—we want out. An' we—part o' us—wants in. Th' outs want off that fuckin' desert they call a reservation. That takes dollars. Th' ins wants to sit on the tribal council an' deal like A-rabs with th' U.S. for all the gas an' oil that's under that desert and make 'em eat it for everything all the way back t'the first goddam covered wagon! That takes dollars!"

The embers in Slim Boy's eyes faded. He stood looking just over Gamelon's head for a long moment, then said, "Like Bead Woman, you're right. I like you for it. Don't come back." And he turned and moved off around the house with that same beautiful flowing stride that Gamelon remembered all the way back to the five-and-dime.

When he had gone, Gamelon got up and went into the house. His briefcase was where he had left it leaning against a leg of the kitchen table. He felt around in it until he found one of his old ballpoints, a yellow pad and his portable desk calculator and headed back outside again. Halfway out the door, he realized the bright sunlight would make the calculator's red LED numbers almost impossible to read. He returned and settled down at the old scarred table and started to make notes on the pad.

Given: A 'blessed person' can divide every fifteen days.

Assumed: There will be no Jennie-like malformations.

He switched on the calculator and began punching buttons, noting the results on the faintly ruled paper.

365 Days ÷ 15 days = 24.33

1- 2 × 1 = 2
2- 2 × 2 = 4
3- 2 × 4 = 8
4- 2 × 8 = 16
5- 2 × 16 = 32
6- 2 × 32 = 64 . . .

13- 2 × 2,048 = 4,096 . . .

17- 2 × 32,768 = 65,536 . . .

22- 2 × 1,048,576 = 2,097,152 . . .

24- 2 × 4,194,304 = 8,388,608.

In 360 days, just short of one year, one 'blessed person' could theoretically become 8,388,608!

Assume: 25 such people multiplying at the same rate.

25 × 8,388,608 = 209,715,200!!!!!

Gamelon raised his eyes from the pad and stared into space. Out of habit, his right hand moved to the calculator to cut it off. Out the corner of his eye, he saw the appalling, silent 209,715,200 wink out. It should have been flashing, he thought, in numbers a hundred feet high across the sky to the accompaniment of a thousand screaming sirens. The vision behind his blank eyes narrowed. It was no longer one of a world with Gustave Dorè sinners screaming and kicking as they were pushed off into the abysses of Danté's hells. Now it encompassed only the continental United States. Twenty-five multiplied into over two hundred million and along the coasts, the Atlantic and the Pacific filled up as body upon body was squeezed off into the seas. If there were twenty-eight, he thought, thirty maybe—three to five more—just as short work could be made of Hawaii and Alaska in the same short year.

From above, the wordless murmur of the two sisters' voices filtered down now and again. A bluebottle that had blundered in during one of the many openings and closings of the screen doors buzzed in erratic patterns between them now or bumped into a window pane trying to find a way back out.

Gamelon tried to blank out everything in his mind to let it rest a little. Even as he did, he realized he had been unable to accomplish this refreshing trick, had not even thought of trying it for days. He was unable to accomplish it now: the red numbers would not shut off inside his head as they had on the calculator. The gilled Jennie would not stop floating there, nor would the swelling, sweating, dank, dividing Frederick, the sodden Remson. The memories would not leave him.

Almost unconsciously, his eyes began to follow the jerky flights of the bluebottle back and forth across the kitchen. Slowly some words came across his mind as if on a ticker tape, words he did not at first recognize as having been his own only a few days before: "Come on, there're ways out all over the place. Come on, come on. There're a hundred ways out. Stop killing yourself going back and forth over the same useless territory . . ." He had mumbled that admonition to a frustrated bluebottle then and the frustrations of another bluebottle had recalled it. But, as the words circuited through, he knew that then as now the words were as much for himself as for the trapped fly.

He followed the bluebottle's search until it lit on the screen of the front porch door, got up, went to the door, opened it and shooed the fly outside. Perversely, after one lap around the porch, the insect returned and lit on the outside of the screen almost opposite Gamelon's face. "You don't know when you're well off, do you?" he muttered.

Nor had he when it had still been possible to heed his own counsel. It was too late now. The memories of all that had happened in the just passed days and the people in them were no longer memories. They had become responsibilities, his responsibilities. He had cut off his own last escape route the afternoon before when he took the mantle from Racklin.

The consternating certainty enveloped him again as he turned away from the door: it was exactly what Racklin had wanted him to do. Racklin had had his own way again. Whatever Racklin did from here on would be laid at Gamelon's door. He had given his brother an open ticket to wear whatever costumes he chose and to call whatever mad dance piqued his fancy of the moment. If he had unconsciously harbored any small hope of getting out, that hope died now. There was no way out.

As he went back to the table, he had to admit that still underlying everything else was his accursed insatiable curiosity—derailed, almost stifled at times in recent days, but still there and throbbing.

He sat down and began to add to the notes on his pad.

Racklin had taken down the door between the parlor and the hall and set it across two old scarred sawhorses which fortunately had not been put back in the barn where they belonged before the fire.

He had put the makeshift desk in front of the windows; there was no electricity in the parlor for a lamp.

Gamelon found him ensconced there, a cigarette in one hand, a pencil in the other, busily writing in a loose-leaf notebook. When he looked up as Gamelon came into the room, pad in hand, his face was set to show annoyance at being disturbed. Gamelon disregarded whatever his brother's feelings might be, dragged the second ladderback up to the door-desk and sat down. Racklin put down his pencil but went on smoking as he said coolly, "Well?"

"Dr. Ching has agreed to do the lab work."

"What's required?"

"I'll get to that. First I have some questions I want answered—none of them are earthshaking, just gnawing."

Racklin said nothing. He just looked steadily at Gamelon as though from some distant retreat of his own making. This aloofness gave Gamelon an uneasy feeling but he shunted it aside and went on. "How did you find out about Frederick and Jennie to begin with?"

Racklin said, almost condescendingly, "There is a courthouse in this county with its resident bespectacled squirrel duly recording the momentous occasions in its history. I knew Marylea's date of birth. I had the clue of 'late March' for the Slim Boys, and assumed the year. Allowing a latitude of a few days each way from the last day of March, huzzah: Frederick and Jennie! Brilliant, huh?"

"And no others?"

"Not recorded in this county, but there are other counties between where the original Maria and the original Slim Boy were conceived—half a state, in fact."

Gamelon told him of his radiation theory, then went on to ask, "Then you contacted them?"

"When I was ready. The barn was a mess and Marylea flatly refused to have any of what I was planning happen in the house."

"How'd you approach them? How'd you convince them they might be what they were?"

Racklin came back from his self-elected private place long enough to give Gamelon a wry smile. "God, Little Brother, after all these years, don't you know I can get a hive of bees to make a special honey just for me if I want to?" The smile switched off.

"Did you pay them—like you're paying the Slim Boys?"

"So you know about that—would have, but I didn't have to. Jennie was a spinster with a puritanical, tyrannical family. She was ready to grasp at any straw that might provide her with even a partial escape from them. Frederick, ah, Frederick: part of him thrives on his job as a prison guard. He's got a cruel, vicious streak as wide as—once I was talking to him in his yard. While I watched, he systematically delegged a beetle without missing a word in the conversation and I'm sure, whatever I or anyone else might have thought of what he was doing never wandered through his head. I think he's the only person I ever encountered who is absolutely without social consciousness.

"Now Frederick's other part considered itself an expert gambler and something of a stud. Add to the mixture a wife and kids he can't stand . . . Anyway, the possibility of becoming two people was the chance for part to go on cracking the whip at the prison farm and part to tear up Vegas and Reno and the ladies as well as for the parts to swap off whenever they liked. Nice, huh? Wouldn't it be fine if all of us could be all the things we'd like to be without any interference from all those other parts we're unfortunately bound up with?"

Gamelon could not help but note that Racklin had achieved that goal in his own way, serially instead of separately, but he said, "How will you explain Jennie's disappearance?"

Again Racklin shrugged. "Not my problem."

"What about her family, her friends? Won't anybody send out the posse, so to speak?"

"Who cares?"

"Damn it, Rack, I told you we've got to care!"

"You care, then," Racklin said emotionlessly as he ground out his cigarette in the cracked saucer at his elbow. "I've got better things to do."

Gamelon felt his anger rising and swallowed it back down. "New subject: are we going to make any attempt to get the remains of those three—women out of the ruins of the barn and give them a decent burial somewhere?"

"Why bother? All you're talking about is a few charred bones which as far as I'm concerned are as 'decently buried' as they need to be. And, who's to say which bones are whose? Why dig them up and bury them all over again? It would be nothing but a sweaty exercise in worthlessness and futility."

"Won't the Slim Boys want to take what's left of their grandmother back to the reservation?"

"If they do, let them dig and sift and do the sorting. Except for dividing for me they're not much good for anything except eating. It might give them something to do to keep them busy."

Gamelon sat silent for a few moments, his lips compressed tightly, then he forced himself to say evenly, "Back to Jennie for a moment: won't you have to be worried about your tracks being covered? You are responsible for her death in a way, you know. What if somebody comes looking for her?"

"Nobody will. It was part of the deal when she came here—Frederick, the Slim Boys, too, even though one of them broke their word in telling Old Bead Woman where they were. None of them could say they were coming here. They could say they were going anywhere else in the world, but not here. Jennie'll just come up never having made it to wherever she said she was going."

"There's no way you could ever be suspect?"

"Of what—now, do you have any more questions, Torquemada, or can we get to the lab requirements?"

"Just one more: Racklin, do you have enough experience to tend Marylea when that baby comes?"

"A *bit* more than your average, run-of-the-mill midwife," Racklin answered sarcastically.

"And—and what if the child's not—right?"

"Another Jennie-like manifestation, you mean?" Racklin leaned sideways in his chair, waved one hand languidly and feigned being blasé. "Well, let's see, I might plunge it into a formaldehyde-filled gallon mayonnaise jar, without ever slapping its little bottom, to preserve it for future study, or, I could pounce on it like the mad scientist I am and cut open its little gullet to see what makes it tick, or—"

"Good Lord, cut it out, Racklin! Forget I asked," Gamelon said with disgust.

"Now can we get to the lab requirements," Racklin said, again all coolness and detachment.

Gamelon went through the short list, revealing in the process his preservation of the severed thumb and surmising it should supply the desired bone and connective tissue samples Dr. Ching had requested. When he was through, Racklin said, "I have needles and test tubes here. We can make slides out of window glass—not the best but it'll do. There're some pieces of broken pane out back and a glass cutter in my tool box. You can do that. I don't have a trocar, though—"

"What's a trocar? What do you need it for?"

"It's like a big thick horse needle. To take a liver sample from a living human being, you stick it right through the flesh and draw out a sample of liver material—" Gamelon shivered in spite of himself. "—and I don't think I could get any of 'em to let me do it even if I had the trocar or the proper local anesthetic. Probably have to do without that one. When are you going?"

"In the morning early if everything's settled down here and you've got it all together. I told Dr. Ching I'd try to be at the university mid-to-late afternoon tomorrow, if not, the day after, and so on."

"Not wasting any time, are you?"

"There's no need to," Gamelon replied meaningfully, "now that we've agreed it's to be done."

Racklin stared at Gamelon balefully for a long moment, then without another word, picked up his pencil and returned his attention to what Gamelon supposed to be the beginnings of the rough scientific journal. Gamelon decided to go upstairs and look in on Marylea before he attempted the slides.

JULY 10, 1984

It would have been easier if Marylea had had a Caesarian section. It could have saved hours of agony and screaming for her. Racklin had been willing to try the operation with a scalpel honed from a kitchen knife, but Marylea had refused. "No! Nooooo!" she had cried between contractions. "If—it—doesn't want to be born, there must be a reason! If it won't come on its own, I don't want it!" She did allow Racklin to try to manipulate the fetus, to better position it to have an even chance of finally being born. Still it was nearing one in the morning before it was.

Gamelon and Blue Sateen Boy had kept the kitchen vigil throughout the soft summer evening as it grew later and cooler until finally they had to close the doors and windows. Gamelon tended the cook stove fire, kept the needed water hot, the coffee made. Slim Boy replenished the wood box without being asked as that was required, but otherwise, the vigil was a silent one for the most part. Only once did the lean, handsome Indian speak. On toward midnight he looked up from where he hunkered by the door and said, "Remember what I said. Don't come back if you don't hafta."

Gamelon replied almost with resignation, "I don't have any choice, Slim Boy. I have to."

"On your own head, then," Slim Boy said, his deep eyes holding Gamelon's.

"Yes, I know."

Except for Marylea's cries and whimpers and an occasional murmured exchange from above, all was quiet again in the kitchen until the sounds of slapping followed by one long squall served notice that the child had at last condescended to be born. A moment later, Marla's weary voice called from above for Gamelon to come up.

He started up the stairs and, without being invited, Slim Boy set his hat over his eyes, rose from the corner and padded along behind him.

As Gamelon came into the room, he caught Marla's eye as she stood at the washstand cleaning the newborn with a warm damp cloth before swaddling it. She managed a weak smile and a nod for him and he knew the child was "right" at least to all outward appearances. He went past her toward the rumpled bed and Marylea but Slim Boy proceeded directly to the washstand without a glance for anyone else in the room. He stopped there and stood, his hands in his pockets, staring down at the infant boy. After a moment, he removed one hand and reached out to touch the child delicately on the forehead, the lips and the chest where the heart would be and whispered, "Welcome, Little Cousin." Then he promptly turned away, left the room and went back downstairs. Gamelon was subliminally aware of the back door's opening then closing.

Marylea's eyes were closed, her hair and face damp with sweat. She appeared nearly bloodless and breathed shallowly. Gamelon took her hand and pressed it very gently. Her head rolled slowly toward him and the lids of the great gray eyes lifted heavily. When she saw it was he, she managed an indication of a smile.

"Marylea," Gamelon said in little more than a whisper, "it's—all right. You have a perfectly normal—well," he chuckled, "I don't know. What is it?"

Marylea whispered so softly he had to lean down and also watch her lips to catch what she was saying. "A boy—but, Lon, you're right. What is it—really?" She turned her head away to stare at the wall on the other side of the bed.

Gamelon patted her hand and silently cursed himself for his careless, thoughtless choice of words. Then he said to her, "That's not to be worried about now. Rest. Just rest awhile."

Marla brought the baby then for Marylea and Gamelon to see. All he could see was a miniature pink old person, its crown covered with a pink-blond dusting. Its eyes were closed. He knew that now they were blue but wondered whether months from now they would shade into amber or into gray or into somewhere between the two and found he could not imagine such a blend.

At first, Marylea would not look at the child, much less take it from the proferring Marla. It was only after much coaxing from her sister that she finally allowed the tiny thing to be laid on her breast.

Gamelon sighed as he turned to leave her bedside. Even that helpless infant, no matter what he ultimately turned out to be, was now his responsibility, too.

From his subconscious, Gamelon resented being forced awake and resisted the undercurrent of movement shuffling within the house that was disturbing him. But when the door to his cubicle was opened softly and the light from the lamp on the kitchen table threw a strap across his face, he had no option but to come back from his restless sleep.

"Wha—who is it?" he mumbled trying to shade his eyes from the light and make out the fluorescent hands of his wristwatch all at the same time. The watch said 4:48 and a voice from the doorway said, "It's Racklin, Lon. Marylea wants you."

"Me? Why?"

"I don't know. All I do know is she's dying." Racklin's words were tired, flat, absolutely without feeling.

Gamelon sat up with a start. "She's dying! But she was all right a few hours ago. What—"

"She's bleeding to death. She has been ever since the child was born. I didn't know. She didn't want me to know. Marla just called me and told me a little bit ago."

Slipping on his pants was not easy. His body was still clumsy with sleep. "Racklin, women don't bleed to death as a result of childbirth anymore."

"They still can," the flat voice from the doorway said. "In a difficult birth like hers, especially, small parts of the placenta can break off, not come out. Then the uterus can't contract completely and clamp off the broken vessels in the endometrium. In a hospital, the surgeon could just reach in with his hand and clean it out—"

"Well, if you know that, why don't you do it?"

The black figure in the door leaned across from one side of the jamb to the other. "Because she won't let me. I've decided not to force the issue. There's another copy."

"Dear sweet Christ! Not even you can be that detached and callous!"

But Racklin was not heeding him. He had already turned away and started across the kitchen toward the front door. He was just going out when Gamelon hopped out of the pantry on one foot still pulling a sock onto the other. "Racklin," he yelled, "come back here! We've got to *try* to do something!"

Racklin stopped in the half open door but he did not turn back to face his brother. With a bitter, lackluster laugh, he said, "Save her? Save her in spite of herself, Mr. Dogood? She doesn't want to be saved, don't you understand that? She wants to die and she wants you there when she does, not me."

Gamelon stood in his stocking feet watching his brother's back departing into the outside blackness with more frustration and deep anger than he could ever remember having had descend upon him all of an instant before, then he turned and took the stairs two at a time.

Gamelon tried to convince her to let him get Racklin, to let Racklin do what he could to try to make the bleeding stop.

The flesh between the unblinking gray eyes wrinkled and the white-lipped mouth laboriously formed a "no."

Then he remembered the scabbing stump of the Slim Boy's severed thumb and he begged her to try to stop the bleeding herself.

The head with its matted, tangled hair moved almost imperceptibly from one side to the other and again the pale lips framed a "no."

Marylea's body went slack and her eyelids dropped slowly and for a moment he thought she was gone. He was gathering himself to confirm it to Marla when he felt the limp fingers in his own tighten, then grip. He looked down at them and then up again to find her eyes wide and shining. She stirred slightly and said in a small but strong voice, "Marla? Sister, where are you—where am I?"

Marla came up from the foot of the bed to stand at Gamelon's shoulder where Marylea could see her easily. Her countenance was almost as haggard as Marylea's. When she came into Marylea's range of vision, Marylea said almost brightly and with more smile on her face than Gamelon recalled having seen there since she had come down the steps to greet him that first time, "I would like some music. I would like to play . . . I cannot . . . I would like to hear the Bach I—we love so. Will you play it for us, Marla? We've got the fiddle, I know we do. We never go anywhere without it."

Marla's head fell forward and in her closeness to him, Gamelon could feel her struggle to control her emotions. After a moment, she nodded once, then turned and left the room, her head hanging, her body seeming to trail slightly behind her dragging feet.

Marylea lay dreamily smiling on at the space Marla had vacated until the sounds of the violin being tuned came from the adjacent room. Then she turned the smile toward Gamelon and said softly, "Ah, ah-ha, that's right—a little higher-ah. We have perfect pitch. Maria did, too. Did you know that?"

He shook his head as the first rich double stops of the *sarabande* from the *Partita In D Minor* for violin alone bit deep then leapt, then bit again, then soared in the surrounding silence of pre-dawn.

Marylea's face twisted like that of a consternated child and tears started in her eyes. She gripped Gamelon's hand as tightly as her weakness would allow and spluttered, "Oh, no! Lon, tell me, please tell me, not the *sarabande*. It is too lovely. It tears my heart. The *gigue*, Lon, tell me—her to play the *gigue*. After all of this, let me have something lilting to die by—please."

He left her long enough to relay the plea to Marla, standing alone, playing with a deep fervor, tears leaking from closed eyes. Marla nodded and without breaking off, shifted to the light, springing, endlessly spinning triadic melody of the *gigue*.

When he returned, Marylea's face had softened again. "That's better, isn't it, much better," she said, mostly to herself, then to him, but not to him, "You must take him, Lon. Racklin must not make a white rat out of him as he did of me. Name him blessed, name him damned, name him after yourself, but never after Racklin, never . . ."

She stopped a moment as though casting about

for the strength she needed to say what she felt driven to say before she died. A moment later she went on in a hurried, slowly fading voice, "I knew, Lon, even before I overheard him tell you on the porch that first day, tell you I was good for nothing but an experiment in breeding . . .

". . . knew, already decided . . . couldn't kill myself then . . . couldn't kill the child whatever . . . it was . . . couldn't . . ."

The bright *gigue* danced relentlessly on . . .

". . . take him . . . he could have been yours and Maria's . . ."

Up and up, arpeggio upon arpeggio, higher and higher . . .

". . . no choice for me . . . this part—I still love him, still want him deep in my sleep, but . . . I will never have him and . . . I will not let him use me to play with life . . . anymore . . . so he can use the world . . ."

The final notes of the *gigue* showered down in a brilliant broken chord and ended on a long-drawn, vibrant single tone.

Gamelon released Marylea's lifeless fingers and turned away from the bed. In the doorway, Racklin, his eyes vacuous, his face expressionless, confronted him. His arms hung motionless at his sides. In his right hand he held something loosely wrapped in a checkered table napkin. As Gamelon moved toward him, Racklin's eyes snapped back into focus and acknowledged Gamelon's presence, but nothing more. He stood his ground, blocking Gamelon's exit.

For a slow ten count, the two men faced each other, their eyes waging a silent pitched battle, then Racklin said, "You will not have my son." And with that, he gave way, stepping aside and into the room. "Now, leave me alone with her for a while."

Gamelon, knowing full well he probably was only crediting his brother with the emotions he wished Racklin might be feeling at the death of a woman beloved, squeezed his brother's shoulder tenderly and passed out of the room. The door was closed behind him.

Marla still stood in the center of the next room, but now the violin hung, a seemingly unbearable weight, from one hand, the bow from the other. He took them from her, put them on the bed and gathered her to him. As his big arms went around her, she all but collapsed. He had to hold her up, keeping her from slipping to the floor as she wept her losses, her emptiness, her futility into his chest.

Gamelon steeped the tea strong, brought it to Marla where she sat, her head in her hands, at the kitchen table and insisted she drink it. When almost all the tea was gone, they talked a little.

He doubted she had heard Marylea's desires about the child over her playing, just as he knew Marla as Marylea's only living relative should have some say in the matter. He recounted what Marylea had said very simply to her.

He had already accepted a responsibility for the child along with all the others but had never anticipated it would be so large a one as her death and her dying wishes had made it, nor did he delude himself about what he might encounter in trying to keep his faith with the dead woman. He could use all the help he could get; he needed an ally in Marla and so he did not omit Racklin's statement from the end of the telling.

Marla drank the last of the tea and said in a weary, tremulous voice, "I can stay a few days longer, a week perhaps to look after the child. We'll talk about it some more in the meantime and decide what to do. I think we can make Racklin see, if nothing else, he can't properly care for a motherless newborn infant. Even he should be willing to see that."

"I wouldn't bet on it."

"Lon," she sighed, "I'm so tired. I've had nothing but uneasy cat naps since the night before last. The next few days don't promise much better than that with the child to care for. Can we please go on with this later?"

"It'll have to be several days from now. I haven't had the chance to tell you, but I'm leaving in an hour or so."

"Leaving . . . leaving?" It was as though she did not want to understand what he was saying.

"Yes. I did arrange to take the samples for study down to Dr. Ching at the university, you know, and the sooner the better."

"But—*so* soon . . ."

He leaned across to touch her hand. "You'll be all right here for a few days, I'm sure." But he could not convince himself as he sought to convince her. He could not ignore the fact that she was the only known female of her curious species left, and, above all, he could never be sure of Racklin. Yet, he knew he had to go; it was basically for him that Dr. Ching had agreed to perform the laboratory investigations. He had to present himself—at least this once—along with the specimens, to bind the agreement.

He was about to pay out a string of logical assurances to her when Racklin came down the stairs into the kitchen. He crossed the room without a word or a glance for either of them. He opened the ice box and placed something wrapped in the red and white napkin inside. His back was to them as he side-stepped to the sink, rinsed something under the tap and left it there. He turned toward them drying his hands on a kitchen towel and when neither of them did anything but stare at him with cool curiosity, he said, ostensibly to

Gamelon, "Well, you needed a liver sample, didn't you? I told you I didn't have a trocar or the right drugs—"

Before Gamelon could even begin to react to his words, Marla was out of her chair flying across the room, her hands already claws going for his eyes, screaming hysterically, "You bastard! You cold, hollow bastard! Ghoul!" She caught Racklin with his hands still twined in the towel and her nails raked his cheeks. The parallel furrows began to seep blood almost at once. He managed to rid himself of the towel in time to grab her wrists before the talons could strike again, but she went on screaming, "Goddam you! Goddam you! Not even the dead can escape you!" And she went on twisting and kicking until Gamelon got behind her, grabbed her, spun her toward him, slapped her hard across the face, then cradled and soothed her as she collapsed sobbing.

Racklin's eyes, suddenly hot and spilling over with anger, did not leave her for a moment even when he squatted down to retrieve the towel and began to pat at the oozing welts on his cheeks. They did not waver as Gamelon scooped the whimpering Marla up easily in his arms and headed for the stairs. They did not blink as Gamelon paused at the bottom, turned back to him and said, his voice almost cracking with an anger more than equal to his brother's, "There was a way to do that. There was a way, just a little longer, with a quiet expression of need, a calm, genuine explanation, a pinch of consideration, but that way never even came up for consideration, did it? Or, if it did, it wasn't your style, never has been, never will be. She was right. If you are capable of being anything, anything except an act, it is a cold, hollow son of a bitch!!" By now, his temper bellowed and roared within him. He had begun to tremble so violently, Marla raised her head and put a hand intended to calm on his chest. It was well that she did. If the flues had opened another millimeter, he would have dropped her and proceeded to beat his brother to death. He swallowed hard, flipped his head once from side to side, and still shaking, turned away and carried her up the stairs.

It would have been nice, he thought, to swing by Birdie's and pick up the things she would have laundered for him by then, but it would be too early and unnecessary miles out of the way on a day he had so many ahead of him to drive. There were fresh clothes in Wasco.

He stuffed the last dirty sock, then the toilet kit into the shoulder bag, collected the old briefcase and went into the kitchen. Outside, the eastern sky was rapidly lightening. It prophesied a clear day for the run all the way across Nevada and southern California to the Pacific coast and the university a few miles north of La Playa. A searing promise, too, for a midday crossing of the Nevada desert, and the Fiat was not air conditioned. He hoped the ice in the picnic chest on the kitchen table would hold through the trip, but he could replenish it along the way—just before and just after the desert, for—

Damn, he thought, the thumb! I have to go by Nesset anyway! Oh, well, what's another forty miles when before the day's out, I'll end up pushing six hundred?

He would have liked to say goodbye to Marla, but she was sleeping, he hoped. He decided to leave her a note instead, that last reassurance, as it were. He opened the briefcase, got a pen and tore a page from one of his yellow pads.

Marla—

I hope not to be gone more than a few days. If Dr. Ching's work is going to take more than that, I'll come back here then return to the coast when she's ready with her findings. Maybe we'll all go together, you, me and the child. I'm sure everything will be all right here while I'm gone—perhaps not your joy and laughter thing, but all right . . .

He paused, his pen lifted, then he wrote with an accepted appreciation of the basic and most uncomplicated meaning of the word where she was concerned,

Love,
G.

He started to leave the note on the table for her, thought better of it and went up the stairs as quietly as his weight on the old complaint-filled steps would allow.

She slept deeply, sprawled almost as he had left her an hour before. Beside her, the child, bundled up and in a small plastic laundry basket, slept still, too. Without really being aware of what he was doing, he let one thick forefinger trail first across the boy's tiny cheek and then just as gently across her flushed one. Then he folded the piece of yellow paper and put it on the pillow beside her head.

As he left the room, he sought to reassure himself: she was strong; she was a fighter—more of both than either Maria or Marylea had been. She would certainly be all right, just for a few days . . .

The Slim Boys, one or all of them, it really did not matter, had provided the blood and the Buccal smears, under what promise or coercion, Gamelon did not know and Racklin did not volunteer. There was the liver sample, and of course, it was up to Gamelon to retrieve the thumb.

When Gamelon with shoulder bag, briefcase and

cold chest started down from the porch, Racklin stayed where he was without an offer to help or even a goodbye. At the bottom of the steps, Gamelon turned back, looked up at him and said plainly, "I do not need you to be anything for the next few days. Nobody needs you to be anything for the next few days. There won't be an appreciative audience while I'm gone. Please, just be nothing until I get back." And he went off toward the car.

Blue Sateen Slim Boy was there. He helped Gamelon stow his luggage and the chest and held the door as Gamelon got in, then closed it firmly behind him. As Gamelon turned the ignition switch, he leaned down and said through the window, "I really like you. Don't come back."

The engine caught as Gamelon looked up at the Indian. "Thank you," he said, "but I don't have much choice—now less of one than ever. I'll be back."

As the car started down the rutted dirt track to the bridge, Slim Boy sauntered around to stand below Racklin. Together they listened to the slowly fading clatter of the Fiat, then Racklin asked, "You cook?"

"Some bacon an' eggs, maybe."

"Why don't you get enough together for you and your brothers and me. I want us to be in town no later than nine."

Slim Boy nodded and moved past him up the steps leaving Racklin alone to listen to the car rattling across the plank bridge, alone listening until there was nothing to hear but the birds' ecstatic exaltation of the new day.

Nesset, Utah

Coolidge Remson had to have an eye opener. He had to have a drink every morning right out of bed before he could even piss or fish his dentures out of the squat glass on the kitchen sink and rinse them off, much less get them in his mouth or put on his pants or tie his tie so he could parade the short distance to the decaying Kresge's for his only real meal of the day.

That first drink first thing in the morning on an empty stomach would have made almost anyone but the total alcoholic he was vomit. For him, it was the high point of the day. It was the only drink of the day he truly relished. It was the only drink of the day he tasted, if one can really taste vodka. It was the high point of his day and he honored the occasion each and every morning by drinking that drink from a very special glass.

Each afternoon, before he became too drunk to risk it, he went to the cupboard by the sink and took down an extraordinarily delicate, long-stemmed Orrefors claret glass in the Prelude pattern, the only one he had ever owned, polished it gingerly with a linen napkin and set it on the counter, well back, behind the denture glass, on a gaily decorated paper cocktail napkin. He then filled it precisely, almost to the rim—the equivalent of about four shots—reached in the cupboard and took out a square of window glass just large enough to cover it, polished it and placed it on top of the goblet to keep out itinerant insects and wayward dust during the remainder of the day and the night to follow.

Never, even if he drank everything else in the house during that remaining day and its following night, never, even if his disability pension check from the Army or his Social Security were late and he had to shiver through abstinent hours, never did he drink the contents of that elegant glass until its appointed time. And when that time came, before he could even piss, and he stood wheezing and hawking at the sink after downing those contents without swallowing, he carefully rinsed and wiped the fragile wine glass and its cover and replaced them in the cupboard until the ceremony should begin again sometime, sometime, sometime in the afternoon.

The serious business of drinking, the part of the job he really did not enjoy all that much, began about ten when he shuffled back from the five-and-dime with his half-read *Deseret News* under his arm. How many times had he recalled, how many times had he forgotten then remembered again what his father had said about one's profession—fortunate is the man who loves his work, but even then, ninety percent of it is drudgery—that was it.

And the part of the job he found more drudgery than not was by the tumbler-full. Tumbler-full by tumbler-full until he had to give up trying to finish reading the paper. He never finished it, it seemed. That was when, if it was hot, he stripped to his underwear, filled the tumbler yet another time and went out to sit on the back porch and sing to himself.

And, he always cut his work out for himself before he left the house for breakfast. He poured out the first tumbler-full, draped a linen napkin over it last thing before he went out the door so he would be able to get right to it when he returned.

He stumped into the kitchen and across to the sink. He lifted the napkin. It took several seconds to penetrate his alcohol-tunneled brain that there was no tumbler under it. The panic started. He knew he had filled the glass, as always, before he went out. No, no, maybe this one time he had forgotten. Hadn't he forgotten once or twice before, at least, in the past five years—or was it six—eight?

He opened the cupboard on the opposite side of the sink from where the sacred morning vessel was kept. The tumbler, his primary working tool, was not there.

Glass smashed out back of the house.

Remson whirled around and backed up hard against the counter edge. He began to shake as though palsied from head to foot and he knew what was happening, happening again even before Racklin's voice reached him, disembodied, as though through a ship's speaking tube.

"Out here, you old fairy sot. I've got your precious glass out here. Come and get it."

Remson just stood where he was, trembling, tears starting in his eyes.

"Come on out here and get it, I said!"

Remson began to make noises like those of a kitten crying close at hand or a sea gull screaming far overhead as he wrung his hands and started toward the back porch barely able to make one foot step out ahead of the other and take him there.

He did not see them. He did not have a chance. Two Slim Boys, one Red Sateen, one Black, now grabbed his arms as he came mewling through the door and pinioned them cruelly behind him. His eyes slewed in terror from one to the other of them, then to Blue Sateen standing by the railing casually tossing his liquor, bottle by bottle, onto the rocks that bordered the weed-gagged rose garden through a huge rent he had made in the rotted screen, and finally, like those of a petrified but mesmerized rodent to its cobra killer, to—

The other one! The one without the beard! But he had the Indian—the Indians—God, how many of them were—

Remson would not have noted the strongest difference between the brothers in the past, the color of the eyes. Nobody much would have when what had so markedly set them apart had been his flaming bush of a beard. He counted on that. But the eyes that appraised Remson now with complete disdain were amber.

"God," Racklin spat at him in a low, gravelly

voice, "You're disgusting! I've got the strongest stomach in the world, but just looking at you makes me want to puke!"

And in his terror, Remson did—at Racklin's feet, splashing gobbits of half-digested sausage on his shoes and the bottoms of his trousers.

The amber eyes went wild with fury. Racklin threw the glass full of vodka in the face of the now-limp, still heaving Remson, then, very calculatingly, he lined up the liquor bottle he had held in his other hand all the while with the porch rail. He made a few preparatory passes, then brought it down sharply. The bottle smashed leaving only the neck in Racklin's hand with a vicious, trowel-shaped wedge attached to it.

The razor-edged glass glinted in the light as he turned it this way and that, contemplating it. Then, seeming satisfied, he nodded and turned his burning eyes on Remson again.

"I've got your records. We cleared them out before you got back, but I can't trust you—"

Remson screamed just the once, when Racklin rammed the wide glass knife into his gut with so much force it went through all his fat and almost to his backbone.

"You'll tell anybody—"

In the side of the neck—

"A sheriff or a reporter—"

In the liver—

"Anybody who takes your fucking booze away—"

The groin—

"And I can't have that—"

And in the chest, into the left side of the heart and there the glass knife stayed, jammed irretrievably between two ribs and the breastbone—

"I won't have that—"

Red and Black Sateen heaved Coolidge Remson through the great gash the Blue One had made in the screen and he died in the weeds and thorns and bottle shards wondering who had let his rose garden come to such a sad pass.

"But—you just left here! What're you doin' back—oh, it's you, not him," Birdie said. "Well, what can I do for ya? An' what's become o' that fine beard o' yours?" She chuckled. "Don't need it t'titillate the ladies no more?"

"I'd just like to talk to you for a minute or two. May I come in?" He smiled at her ravishingly.

She studied his face for a moment or two, then shrugged and said, "I reckon so. Come on back. There's still some mornin' coffee on the stove an' if you're here long enough, till it's full brewed, there's sun tea makin' out on the back stoop . . ."

JULY 13, 1984

Near La Playa, California

E. V. Ching brushed by the medical student who had leapt from his seat to hold the door and flounced out of the lecture amphitheater angry with everything: the student, the lecture, the amphitheater and the flouncing itself.

The student was a third-year exchange from McGill. He was as tall as a young Blue Spruce and as full and regular and handsome and pacific. He had not missed a session of 386-BG, the Molecular Biology of the Human Gene, and, evidently finding Southern California quite warm, had never worn anything but a T-shirt, jeans cut off almost at the hips and sandals. And, he had never crossed his legs, which meant that the farther down in his habitual seat right in front of the lectern he slid, as he always did, gradually, during the hour, there was never any telling how much of his spruce branch and other masculine accoutrements would squeeze out below the stringy bottom of his shorts, millimeter by millimeter. He had never seemed to notice. Today had been no exception and the show had been just as disconcerting to Dr. Ching. Damn thoughtless Canadian clod! Gorgeous, superbly hung Canadian stud!

The lecture had been the last of the summer session for 386-BG on the last Friday of that session. It had been riddled with more restlessness and uninvolvement than usual right from the start. Dr. Ching had only agreed to conduct the special segment of the course during the summer because the chairman of the university biology department had been properly obeisant when he had come to beg last April. He had promised a good turnout what with "makeups and so many pathologists who need 'continuing education fillers' to keep their licenses." When it finally got down to registration, the class had numbered a big seventeen, most of them ill equipped and lacking in genuine interest.

Seventeen—more like ten for any given session—had been lost in the goddamn amphitheater and E. V. Ching absolutely refused to condescend to the folksy behest for them all to come on down front family style. Dr. Ching detested that amphitheater for its vastness not to mention its sterility. It could seat a hundred and fifty not counting the riser-like stairs and it was whiter and brighter than the inside of a burning light bulb—except for the floor covering which was a raging magenta only a gay decorator could have loved.

The lectern was a consternation with wand attached. One needed to be licensed by the FAA to operate it! Switches, buttons, LED's, microphones; it could do everything from counting responses—correct and incorrect—to controlling black lights that made fluorescent chalks of more colors than Joseph's coat visible on a myriad of appearing and disappearing boards.

Dr. Ching *really* loathed the attached pointer with its own monstrous little set of controls. Inevitably she would press the button to light up its little red tip and send her slides tumbling instead. As far as she was concerned, the thing could have been the primary working tool for the Wicked Witch of the West!

And the flouncing; Elizabeth Vetsera Ching, PhD, cryogeneticist, ensconced very firmly in the Thomas

Hunt Morgan Chair of Genetics, disliked herself exceedingly when she flounced. She only did it when she was angry and that made her even angrier and *that* made her flounce even more. Flouncing made her angry with herself because she could imagine how absurd the broad *schlagobers* ass she had inherited from her Austrian mother, which was so unjustly slung on her otherwise slender, diminutive body, must look to anyone walking behind her.

There were two things she would never forgive her sweet, sentimental and sometimes dolorous Austrian mother for: her ass and her name. She had been called Elizabeth in memory of Franz Joseph's tragic empress and Vetsera for the equally tragic and just plain stupid Marie who had done herself in with Rudolph at Meyerling. Since before high school, therefore, she had made it patently and consistently clear that she was E. V., that's all: E. V. Well, there were those rare occasions when it came out "Evie," like when Charlie, her current pacifier, having achieved the proper balance between his propensity toward premature ejaculation and the booze he took to offset it, was about to come massively with his whole marvelous body. She did not mind that.

"Ms. Dr. Genes," as the students called her in the Commons or on the lawns and in other out-of-earshot places, with her silver-threaded, mouse-brown bob, her slanting black eyes magnified to startling proportions by myopic goldfish bowl lenses, and her mouth habitually compressed into a pink line to mask its natural rosebud, came off as a dyky terror to student and colleague alike. She liked it that way. That way she could get her teaching and her research done without having to suffer the stammerings and tremblings of the perennial med student in love with an older woman, or the pattings and pinchings of the household variety lab grabber. That way, too, she could leave the university behind her when she left it, leave herself free to pursue her two great avocations: tenderly nurturing prize-winning roses and wearing out men, one at a time, about one every two years. She was a staunch supporter of the separation of business and pleasure, the wheat from the chaff, and the men from the boys.

In her office, the flouncing thoroughly nullified and contained by her massive armed desk chair, she pulled on a brown Sherman—another of her effective anti-university humanity tools—and let the other angers rise with the smoke and dissipate in the air conditioning. She shuffled her notes and checked her calendar the meanwhile to see what was left for the week before she could get on home to roses and a healthy spate of Charlie with good conscience. As she had expected, there was nothing that could not wait until Monday, which left her free as planned for her initial look at the Waugh material, enough of a look so she would know what further might have to be done off and on next week between work on her own research. If any additional preparations were needed, Clarence could take care of them over the weekend.

She leaned back in her chair and put her hands behind her head. Her lips loosened enough to allow for a tight little smile. It would serve Clumsy Clarence right, she thought, for no other reason than that she disliked the post-doctoral fellow who was her lab assistant. And, she disliked him for no other reasons than that (a) he *was* clumsy, and (b) his fellowship was funded by the American Poultry Grower's Association. That she, brilliant person and descendant of emperors—or so her sweet-opium smelling grandfather had always used to tell her—should have been saddled with a fellow whose project was to attempt to alter chicken genes so the chickens would keep the teeth they formed in embryo on the fifth day—a passing trace of some primordial chicken ancestor—and now lost on the sixth! So what?! Teeth couldn't possibly make chickens plumper. They would probably just make them meaner once they realized they were better armed. Fruitless research!

She wondered if the research she had agreed to do for Gamelon Waugh would turn out to be as fruitless. She had only agreed to undertake it at all after finding out he was to the magnificent rose what Gregor Jacob Mendel had been to the humble sweet pea. Taking a bit of pity on the unfortunate Clarence, she half hoped she would not find anything unusual after lunch and have to make him give up all or part of his weekend. Poor Clarence. He could not help it if he had been born a klutz and some minds, no matter how bright, were foredoomed, it seemed, to chicken's teeth.

She slid down out of the great desk chair and went into the tiny connecting office to ask her secretary to get her the usual from the cafeteria, but, yes, today she would have Thousand Island instead of just lemon juice and a little dribble of oil. To hell with it, she thought, it's Friday and between the roses and Charlie, I'll work it all off by Monday.

She returned to her big chair and leaned back with eyes closed to await the arrival of the paper plate sagging with lettuce and bean sprouts and whatever else Mattie decided to heap it with that particular noontime. Her lips relaxed into a genuinely pleased smile as she recalled the afternoon a few days back when John Frederick Sevrinsky had telephoned.

It took her a few moments to place him from the "Freddie Sevrinsky" he identified himself as. Then she remembered the tiny man with the walk of a teenager, seemingly all on the balls of the feet, the shoulders of a miniature tackle and the face of a benign dried fig. He had always nodded and grimaced at her across the room at the Chancellor's annual cocktail party for the faculty élite and invariably stopped, hands together prayer-like, to bow deeply for her when infrequently their paths crossed around the university grounds. Yet, until that day, she had never heard his voice. It was surprisingly deep and musical and she could not help but think of the old saw about what the good Lord sawed off the top of a short man's head he made up for by sticking it back on between his legs.

"Let me say right at the outset, Dr. Ching, that I apologize for bothering you. I know your schedule must be as packed as my own and where I have a backlog of commissions to fulfill, I am sure you must have research projects, in process or contemplated, that claim nearly all of your time and effort. However, I have a small favor to ask—not for myself, you understand, but for someone very dear to me in a way—and I would deeply appreciate your condescending to at least hear me out."

Vociferous, courtly little bastard, aren't you, she had thought. Perhaps it was just as well they never had gotten into conversation. She had felt he probably knew very little about her work and she did not like what she had heard of his music: too romantic. Everything between Mozart and Stravinsky was pretty much sonic mush as far as she was concerned and Beethoven bored her. What would they have talked about? Still, she owed him a hearing because (a) he had her on the phone, and (b) he occupied an endowed chair equivalent in stature to her own, the Edward MacDowell Chair of Composition.

Even so, she might have pled the press of work in the face of his request had it not been for his talk of Gamelon Waugh and what he had done. Sevrinsky had even named some of the varieties Waugh had developed, all of which she had cultivated with awe and great joy. She had wondered after hanging up how the hell Sevrinsky had known she loved roses so and marked how clever it was of him to use that to get to her.

If she had known how absolutely gorgeous, how fabulously built, and, if she read all her private indicators right, how opulently endowed Gamelon Waugh would be when he had finally arrived in person late the previous Tuesday afternoon, Sevrinsky could have forgotten all about roses.

Although her dark eyes remained general and her voice and attitude courteously distant all through their brief meeting, her secondary thoughts about him had raced, bit in teeth, panting, imagining how delicious it might be with the man with the riotous hair, lovely skin and huge hands. When he spoke to her from the doorway of her office in his deep gentle voice, this time without a crackling, no-fidelity phone line between them, she had to consciously suppress a little shudder of delight that jangled her spine.

"Dr. Ching?"

"How do you do? Yes, I am E. V. Ching."

"I'm Gamelon Waugh."

He came to her across the office, so lightly she noticed for such a wonderfully heavy man, and placed the small picnic cooler on the corner of her desk. "Here are all the samples you requested; saliva from inside the lower lip in smears, three of them—on slides made from window glass, I'm afraid, but made sterile before they were used—blood, liver and—for bone and connective tissue, a thumb that was cut off in an accident.

"The saliva, liver and blood samples are between seven and nine hours old. The thumb is, ah, about three days old now, but I've kept it in an isotonic borate and sodium solution—" He smiled. "—all that was handy: sterile saline solution for cleaning and storing contact lenses—and I've kept it as close to freezing without freezing it as I could.

"All of it's been packed in ice," he tapped the cooler, "since I left for here early this morning. I hope they're all right."

"I'm not sure about the thumb. It may have been too long. Won't you sit down for a moment, Mr. Waugh?"

As he took the chair next to her desk, he said, "Please, Doctor, Gamelon or Lon."

She did not dare.

Rather coolly she said, "Ah—Mr. Waugh, it would be nice if I had a bit more information than has been supplied me so far. To begin with, what is it I'm supposed to be looking for?"

"You already know from our phone conversation that my brother's field is anthropology and, within that, the study of the abnormal. He has discovered an abnormality in a group of people in a certain geographic area and would like to know if you can find in routine investigation anything genetically or metabolically different which might point to the cause of that abnormality."

"Describe the abnormality to me. It might point me a little better."

Gamelon dropped his eyes. "I'd rather not say, Dr. Ching."

There was silence until Dr. Ching said with some annoyance, "That's all then? That's it? I'm to work in the dark?"

Gamelon leaned forward and put one big hand on the desk near her childlike one. "Doctor, I'm a scientist. Sometimes I've had to be vague, evasive in order to protect my work. That's what my brother is doing now. You must have done the same thing on occasion yourself."

She nodded. Openness had caused the kudos for more than one great development in science to go to the wrong person after years of labor. Still, she balked a little at being given the equivalent of a first-year medical school laboratory species identification project. But she said, simply, "That would explain to some extent your brother's reluctance to use his own academic connections for what he needs."

"Yes. And we both ask that you be as discreet with your findings—if there are any unusual ones—as you can." Gamelon leaned back in his chair, a conspiratorial smile hovering on his lips. "I understand you are a Rosarian of no little standing as well as one of the world's most eminent geneticists."

Dr. Ching just stared at him from behind her thick lenses but thought, *Boy, you're going to touch all my soft spots, aren't you?*

"I've come up with the most unusual new rose the world has ever seen, if I do say so myself. I'll see you have the first well-grafted and rooted specimen, if you like. Oh, yes, the offer to assist in the lab still holds."

She would not dare.

"How long has it been since you were a lab monkey?"

He smiled broadly and she felt passingly ravished. "With any regularity? Oh, fifteen years, I suppose."

Even though he did not look it, that put him *pushing* her age—from a distance.

"I still do a bit of work now and then—" He chuckled. "—on rose roots."

"Leave it to me then."

"I think so."

"Now, will you at least tell me this: are all the specimens from the same individual?"

Gamelon hesitated just an instant before replying, "No. The liver sample is from a different individual."

"Sex?"

"All male except the liver sample."

"Race?"

"Again, Doctor, I'd rather not say."

"Age, then?"

"Approximately thirty-four—all of them."

"Sick? Healthy? Can you tell me that?"

"To all outward appearances, healthy."

"Anything else."

"I'm afraid not—well . . ." Gamelon dropped his head, appeared to muse, then smiled conspiratorially at Dr. Ching and continued, "Well, perhaps there is just one other thing, something you could do for me personally . . ."

She would not dare.

". . . something I suppose, really, you might just stick in the back of your mind while you're going about your investigations."

"And what is that?"

"The problem of the creation of matter, in this case, more the question, how matter, new matter, might be created out of nothing."

"That's patently impossible. Even you must know that."

"Yes."

"That's all? Just put the question out there in the ether?"

"Yes—please."

"Well, I suppose what little you've told me—plus that intriguing tidbit—will have to suffice for the time being."

Gamelon smiled at her again. "Thank you, Doctor." He rose and made to leave. "When shall I get back to you?"

"I'll call you when I'm ready." She flipped through her telephone card file. "You'll be at this number you gave me when you called—in Wasco?"

"Until I hear from you."

"Hopefully that won't be more than a few days.

The samples have to be prepared for study and then I have to set aside the time to study them. You understand."

"I do, and again, Doctor Ching, thank you. My brother and I both appreciate what you're doing."

Mattie brought the salad. E. V. Ching leaned forward to stab at the bean sprouts drowning in Thousand Island with a plastic fork as she remembered how she had thought how much she would appreciate his getting out of her office. He had been (a) peeving with his reluctance to share even fundamental information that could save her hours of effort, (b) something close to infuriating with his vague mumbo jumbo about matter being made out of nothing, and (c) altogether too goddamn attractive.

She really was not looking forward to a Friday afternoon reliving Microbiology 1A, but the time set aside for it was at hand. As soon as she finished the salad, it would be time to see what little mysteries the beautiful redhead and his brother had brought her to discover. As she chased a slippery cherry tomato with a hide that seemed invulnerable to the plastic fork tines through the Thousand Island, she thought how nice it would be if the unknown brother was as attractive as the known. Lord, two of them! What a lovely rainy Sunday afternoon in January *that* could make!

She kept her teeth clenched, her smile tight and her nods curt as Clarence shuffled and droned his way around the laboratory ahead of her from incubator to incubator. Here in this one, on this shelf, centrifuged out from the blood samples, were the white cells in the appropriate culture broth in three wafer-like petri dishes. Here, on another shelf, neatly labeled, were what Clarence felt were viable cells from the liver sample in their medium, in their dishes.

He caught his thumb in the incubator door when he closed it, stuck it in his mouth and forgot to take it out as he explained the samples in the next one. Fortunately, aside from the locations of the various cultures, Dr. Ching did not need to hear all the commentary on their preparation. Knowing Clarence, however, he would recite the process with each and every one. She resigned herself as he shambled and mumbled on.

"Bone . . . shavings from—here—" he tapped two petri dishes, "—periostium, here—" he tapped two more, "—marrow, both from right at the severance point.

". . . fibroblasts separated out from . . . big muscle . . . base of thumb—" He stopped and stood looking vacantly around him.

"Buccal smears," Dr. Ching prompted.

Clarence took his painful thumb out of his mouth long enough to say, "Sterile box," and stuck it in again.

"Somatomedin and fetal calf serum in the ice box?"

Clarence nodded.

"All right, set up one of the smears on the electron microscope, put a wet slide from the white cell culture in the microscanner and get the hell out of here. You make me as nervous as spit on a hot griddle! I'll take care of everything else myself."

Clarence managed to do everything he was told, including hightailing it without once falling over his own feet, much to Dr. Ching's amazement.

Perhaps for no other reasons than (a) she was standing closer to the electron microscope than to the soft laser microscanner and (b) she wanted to get on with it as quickly as possible so as to get on with the weekend of roses and Charlie, Dr. Ching decided to look at the smear first. When launching a blind search for a "genetic or metabolic" aberration, it was more or less Hobson's choice between the dead cells in the smears and the live ones in the white cell culture. Alive, the cheek cells reproduced themselves faster, more frequently, than almost any other specialized cells in the body and it was easier to catch more of them at any given instant, dead or alive, in the act of dividing, when the chromosome strands in the cell nucleus were all nice and neatly spiraled up and easy to see.

It was because of this high rate of mitosis, this frequency of division, in the lining cells of the mouth that it did not really register on her first scan that there were even more in the mitotic state than would be usual. She was not counting anyway; she was looking for a cell right at the proper point in the act of dividing, where she could see chromosome structure the clearest.

She found one that suited her, scrutinized it steadily for a while, then murmured under her breath, "Poor bastard. I don't know what, if anything, else is unusual about you yet, but I'd bet my weekend you've got squamous cell carcinoma."

Aneuploidy.

She was sure of it: more than the normal twenty-three pairs of chromosomes in the cell nucleus. She could not get an exact count, but there were more on each side, not many more, and not the same amount, but more. A cell gone genetically haywire, a cancerous cell if she had ever seen one. She investigated two, three more. They exhibited the same characteristic. Three more, the same.

She swiveled her chair away from the microscope and noted in her laboratory journal on the table behind her what she had seen, adding, "No apparently genetically normal squamous cell noted of seven investigated. Odd, even in advanced carcinoma. Investigate further."

E. V. Ching, it was true, did not believe in mixing business with pleasure, but there had been once when such a juxtaposition had paid off—scientifically, at least. The personal side had ultimately ended in too little of the things that count and far too much of the things that should not have amounted to a hill of beans. But, some time back, two frantic years of sleeping *and* working with an outwardly lethargic, inwardly lecherous laser expert had produced the prototype of the computerized soft laser microscanner, the CSLM. It was in no small part due to this pioneering outside the bedroom that she now occupied her prestigious chair at the university. What or whom the laser expert had gone on to occupy, she could not have cared less.

She closed her journal, stood up and crossed the laboratory to the microscanner, casting a critical eye over the settings on the computer in passing.

She brought herself up short. She was letting the weekend press her. She really should do a gross investigation of the white cell culture before trying to get the microscanner's computer to paint complicated pictures of the individual cells' chromosomal structure.

She brought a culture dish from the incubator and before preparing a wet slide for close study, put the dish under the regulation light microscope and focused on its center. If Clarence had done his job right, the culture would have been begun there, allowing for it to grow its maximum, to the perimeter of the dish, where it would automatically stop. At their characteristic rate of growth, the white cells would have multiplied very little in the three short days in the growth medium. She might have to search around a bit.

Clarence came in for a round of silent, sarcastic applause: he had hit the center for once and Dr. Ching looked at perfectly normal human white blood cells, alive and well as far as she could determine. She slid the petri dish a little to the left, a little to the right, up, down under the microscope: more of the same.

Too many of the same.

She moved the dish until she was looking at one edge of it and quickly realized that she was having to focus up and down, in and back. She was looking through two, perhaps three layers of cells there, mounded up and already growing back toward the center again.

She raised her head from the microscope eyepiece, slowly replaced her glasses, then went for the two remaining white cell cultures in the incubator. She studied each in turn and found in both the same phenomenal rate of cell growth. "Poor bastard," she whispered again. "How could he have said you were 'to all appearances, healthy?' You may well have leukemia, too."

She returned all but one of the cultures to the incubator and was returning to the microscanner with it when she stopped suddenly midway across the room and began talking to herself out loud. ". . . even in the standard fluid growth medium, too high a replication rate—even for a cancerous cell unless . . . it is some new form of white cell carcinoma . . ."

She wheeled around and headed for the refrigerator, roses and Charlie paling in her mind in the light of her unanticipated findings.

Somatomedin, synthesized in the human liver in the presence of the pituitary growth hormone: 25 mg in solution used frequently in the laboratory to stimulate more rapid cell growth in cultures. She applied the carefully measured amount to the white cell culture, then quickly, with a skill generated by vast experience, prepared a wet slide from it, placed it beneath the light microscope, removed her glasses and put her eye to the thousand times magnified view below.

She managed to keep watching steadily between blinks, but she had to fight to keep the trembling that came over her under control. The knuckles of her diminutive hands gripped the edge of the laboratory counter and went white.

Beneath her eye, every cell that had been bathed in somatomedin stretched, pinched and divided simultaneously again and again and again and again . . .

After a time, the frenetic mitosis subsided and finally stopped. She stepped away from the microscope and just stood there, alone in the center of the laboratory, feeling very small, infinitely small, smaller than she had ever felt in an entire life of being small. Her face shone with perspiration; her armpits dripped under her blouse and smock. Her soul litanized with itself in weird, brittle harmonies, "My God . . . My God . . . My God . . ."

Between 1:33 pm, Friday, July 13th and 5:00 am, Sunday, July 15th, Dr. E. V. Ching left her laboratory only four times.

She needed no more than the extraordinary cell reproduction under the stimulus of somatomedin to tell her she was dealing with something unique. If she needed any confirmation of that, it came when she perused the structure of a living white cell from one of the untreated dishes with the CSLM. The chromosomal banding patterns, different, but not radically so, were the same as she had seen in the Buccal smears and had at first suspected indicative of squamous cell carcinoma. There was no doubt left when the scanner's visual computer readout showed the same patterns in the liver cells' chromosomal structure. It was then that she had to admit to herself that she was indeed involved in a species identification, but that this was no Microbiology 1A, no first year medical school laboratory project. Although she was still on the marches of it, she was moving toward the isolation and identification of something either so magnificent or so monstrous it would tax her genius and press her credulity to the threshold of collapse. But, if anything, her curiosity was greater, more merciless than Gamelon's and could make her forget everything else when it sunk its great nails in her and soared.

As she returned the petri dishes to the incubator temporarily, she felt everything but her need to discover, to know, slipping out of control into a no-man's land of sorts around her as that need gathered wattage unto itself deep in her mind, began to burn, then glow.

It was 4:06 Friday afternoon when she left the laboratory for the first time. She crossed the hall on the long diagonal to her office. She told her secretary to take the rest of the day off and wished her a nice weekend. She had already forgotten that Sunday was Mattie's fiftieth birthday and that she had promised to come for cake and ice cream in the afternoon. She stuffed her lab smock pockets with jars: freeze-dried coffee, powdered cream substitute and artificial sweetner, then she phoned Charlie. When he began to "Aw, Evie" her and pout about her possibly not getting home until very late, she let him have it. She told him to go fuck himself—literally—and slammed the phone down. She picked it up again immediately and called him back to order him, on pain of castration without the benefit of surgery, to see the slow hoses were rotated throughout the entire rose garden if she had not appeared by morning.

She went to the ladies' room, then returned to the laboratory and locked herself in.

* * *

Elizabeth Vetsera Ching also sat in her university chair because of her masterful work in the definition of the functions of GFG: Growth Factor Gradient. It was this mysterious process which told a severed flatworm's tail to grow another head or the stump of a salamander's leg to grow first a new leg and then a new foot and not vice versa. Theoretically, the same could apply in *homo sapiens*. Theoretically, GFG would tell an arm severed between the elbow and wrist to regrow the lost arm portion first and then the hand.

She had never seen it occur as yet and her experience to date certainly had not included the reverse. She could be wrong, but in her heart she knew she was not. In her gross observation of the thumb, she found (a) no evidence of Clarence's removal of the miniscule bone shavings or muscle tissues from the *flexor brevis pollicis,* (b) that having been brought back to normal body temperature and maintained there for several days now, the cut had healed over and (c) the bone end under its tissue covering was rounding up, budding like a salamander's incipient regenerating leg.

Dr. Ching made one other phone call between early Friday afternoon and early Sunday morning. At 4:46, she called the university Cell and Serums Bank for 100 cc of human pituitary growth hormone in solution. When the hems and haws about providing it so late on a Friday afternoon started to come from the bank supervisor, she let him have it, too. She left no doubt in his mind about exactly who she was as well as offering a threat almost as potentially devastating as the one made to Charlie if the solution was not in her lab before the bank closed at 5:00 pm.

It was obvious, even under the light microscope, that the bone shavings in culture were no longer shavings. There were no unevennesses, no raw cutting marks. All were smooth, regular and appeared larger than what she supposed Clarence would have removed for the purpose.

She took her eye from the light microscope, blinked several times and leaned down again. She was convinced that the near-transparent fibroblasts from the muscle tissue were spreading, growing, on their twin beds of fetal calf serum.

Investigating a mitotic white cell with the microscanner, she thought that as she watched, the banding pattern along the chromosome changed, shifted dark to light to dark again. Had she witnessed a DNA repair sequence? She could not be sure.

During the late hours of Friday night, Dr. Ching tried every method known to damage or disrupt a DNA strand. She exposed the white cells to X-rays. Even as she watched, the strand broke and immediately repaired itself. So with the liver cells and so with both when subjected to the injurious effects of ultraviolet light. She introduced various endonuclei, enzymes which could nick the DNA. The nicks were at once repaired.

SV-40, Epstein-Barr virus, associated with Burkitt's lymphoma, known to disturb human DNA, had no effect. The white cell's DNA set about modifying it into a harmless viral form. Even recombinant DNA techniques did not succeed. She managed to insert a plasmid from E.coli bacteria into one strand, but it had corrected the defect and returned to what for it was normal.

By 2:00 Saturday morning, Dr. Ching could hardly manage to focus the microscopes, much less coax her weary, red myopic eyes to cooperate with them. For the second time, she left the laboratory. She walked stiffly across to her office, set her Rolex Oyster to sound at four and threw herself on the leather couch.

At 4:40, she sipped distilled water coffee heavy with fake cream and sugar now and again as she prepared all new samples, new cultures of all the materials, blood, liver, fibroblasts, bone, all in differing growth mediums, all in varying degrees of concentration, but all stronger than those in which Clarence had prepared the originals. She added adrenalin to two of the new bone sample cultures. Almost as an afterthought, she submerged the thumb in a small beaker of pituitary growth hormone, covered it and put it in the incubator. After carefully labeling each culture and meticulously noting in the journal what she had done, she returned all of them to the incubators and herself to the CSLC to try one last and very difficult thing with the white cell DNA. If she succeeded, there would be no question that what she had come to suspect was true.

By 11:30 Saturday morning, she had succeeded. It had only been done up until then with the cells of mice.

At the precise point in the anaphase stage of division when the cell nucleus has divided and contains only half the normal paired set of chromosomes and had not yet begun creating the other half, she extracted that nucleus from a normal human white blood cell and inserted it into one in the exact same state of division from those with which she had been working.

The single DNA strand in the newly divided cell did not reject the strand from the normal cell nucleus. It did not neutralize it by rendering it harmless. It quickly renovated it into a mirror image of itself.

Over the years, the forms, the actions, the exquisite complexities she had observed in her work from time to time had made her think, if only for an instant, only very definitely in passing, that there might be such a thing as the hand of, for lack of any better terminology, God, at work in the limitless macrocosms and particularly, the microcosms of the universe. Now, there was no thought of hand. Elizabeth Vetsera Ching was in His awesome, total presence, be it ever so minuscule.

She had discovered an indestructible cell; she was in the presence of an immortal genome and more.

For several moments, her soul bowed double in that mighty presence and then she left the laboratory for the third time.

She walked in the nearly deserted Saturday corridors of the university Human Sciences Building for almost a half hour, ignoring, not even registering the occasional respectful greeting from some passing student or colleague. She walked until out of the wasteland of shunted daily things, hunger cried so loudly she could ignore it no longer.

She took the next elevator she came to down and fled out into the gorgeous mundanity of grass, sunlight, concrete sidewalks and the immense prolonged fart of some departing student's Harley Davidson.

At the cafeteria in The Commons, with what few Saturday students and faculty who were there exclaiming *sotto voce,* unheeded by her, about her totally unfamiliar presence, she gorged on orange juice, greasy bacon, fried eggs and rye toast.

She made a long stop at the ladies' room which included icy water for face, hands and the back of the neck, then returned to the laboratory to immure herself again behind its locked doors.

The bone in somatomedin plus adrenalin was changing.

The bone in increased fetal calf serum plus adrenalin was changing.

The liver cells in pituitary growth hormone had outgrown the petri dish.

Where necessary, she began again—with the liver cells—but with even higher concentrations. Where not, she simply upped the amount, then returned to her microscopic studies. It was 12:45 Saturday afternoon.

At 5:07 in the afternoon, she put distilled water in a beaker on a Bunsen burner to heat for coffee and went to check all the incubated samples.

She forgot the coffee; the beaker eventually boiled dry and splintered unheeded over the flame.

She had to dredge her memory, but, yes, one bone sample in adrenalin had taken on more the aspects of pectoral fin material. The other had come to strongly resemble the bone at the tip of an amphibian toe more than anything—tiny, like that of an embryonic alligator.

The fibroblasts had altered also but she was not sure just how.

She terminated the cell replication experiments after duly annotating her journal. They were getting messy, flowing out onto the incubator shelves. She scraped them, dishes and all, into sulphuric acid and wondered as she watched them smoke away what made her think she heard an angel scream.

As of 7:13 pm, she noted that the thumb apparently had not responded to growth stimulation in any way. She could not intensify the growth medium it was immersed in; there was nothing stronger.

She was so tired, she had to rest, if only for a few hours. Again, she made her way to the couch.

At 9:37 pm that Saturday evening, she told her journal: "Bone fragment, P. dish #1, appears to have become small pectoral shoulder bone, approx. four times longer than wide. Cannot identify species, however, resembles possibly *cross opterygian,* primitive lobe finned fish clavicle. Confirm: this class of fish in direct line to amphibian leading evolutionarily to *homo sapiens?*"

At 9:42: "Bone fragment, P. dish #2, appears transmuted into reptilian vice amphibian toe. Rudimentary scale-like sheathing covering large end away from apparent nail or claw. Resembles that of some lizards. Species unidentifiable."

From 10:01 Saturday night until 4:42 am Sunday morning, she made no further entries in the journal. From 10:01 to 4:42, she smoked Shermans until her tongue and palate became seared and insensitive. She stopped drinking coffee when she realized it might be hours before she would dare leave the laboratory to go to the bathroom.

For six hours plus, she sat on a high laboratory stool at the counter and watched as the center of the thumb became a pulpy, indeterminate mass that throbbed and grew, that stretched with a terrible unseen tension, that stretched and squirmed as though under attack by maggots until there were two thumbs, connected only by a thin membrane of flesh, both cut ends broadening into what would sooner or later be a hand.

At 4:33, the membrane began to truncate in the center. It became narrower and narrower and then, as though pinched between invisible fingers, it became only a string, then a thread.

At precisely 4:35, the membrane parted and the two resulting tags of flesh subsided gently and disappeared like melting butter fading into hot toast.

At 4:39, she threw the thumbs, jar and all, into the acid and waited by the tank until 4:41 to be sure they had boiled away without a trace.

At 4:42, she wrote: "Severed thumb not responsive to massive growth stimulus. Specimen destroyed in concentrated H_2SO_4."

She put her mechanical pencil in the breast pocket of her smock and closed the journal. From 4:45 until 5:00, she sat on the laboratory stool and sobbed like a bereft, deserted child.

At 5:01, still dabbing her eyes with a lab towel, she locked the laboratory behind her and went to the office and her final telephone call of that deeply disturbing weekend. She punched in the 1, then the 805 for Wasco, then Gamelon's number.

JULY 11-15, 1984

Wasco, California

After his brief meeting with Elizabeth Ching late on Tuesday afternoon, a meeting both would have admitted was not the most satisfactory, Gamelon had thought to look up Freddie Sevrinsky for a long, comfortable, unburdening talk. He felt the need of it as strongly as any tormented soul feels the tug of the confessional. As usual, he had no idea of Mr. S.'s schedule for that particular day and he was still drained from the near-solid ten hours of driving from Nesset to the coast with only two stops for ice, gas and urination. Almost two more hours of hypnotic freeway still lay ahead of him to Wasco. He had opted for pouring out the tale of his days in a long letter, contorted his big frame into the Fiat again and left for home.

A long sleep had kept him gently snoring until near nine o'clock. He had awakened into a flawless Wednesday morning, deeply glazed with layer upon layer of different perfumes from thousands of roses.

He got out of bed naked, but cloaked in a newly recognized sense of the security he felt there among his flowers. He had always taken it for granted before.

He showered, as much in the sweet peace and tranquillity of the place as in the warm water, and lingered longer than usual under the caress of both.

As he had tramped through the day, Jorge at his side, up the length and across the breadth of the growing fields, through the crossing shed, inspecting every specimen closely, around the test gardens, studying the progress of every plant, it was as though he had been away for months instead of days. Everything seemed to need rediscovery and every discovery was a sheer joy for him. Several times that day, he had found himself just standing, feet apart, hands on his hips, head back, smiling and taking long, slow, deep breaths. Thoughts of Nesset, Racklin, even Marla and the child had come in poor seconds to his initial happiness at being back where he belonged.

His sense of rightness, his happiness did not long endure. He had not been sure exactly when it began to erode under the constant washing of the knowledge coursing deeply, irreversibly within him that everything in his life had changed beyond restoration. It could have been as early as mid-morning Thursday, when he sat silently listening to his accountant project the year's income for his nurseries and submit ways of avoiding the taxes. It could have been as late as just after lunch on Friday when Jorge came into the crossing shed where he was noting his morning experiments in the cross list.

Jorge shuffled at his elbow and cleared his throat. Gamelon completed his entries and looked up at his small, swarthy friend with a smile. "What's up?" he asked.

Jorge relaxed a little and replied, "Couple o' things. *Numero uno*—an' it better be, or my Maria, she cut off my evenin' bottle o' *Carta Blanca*—it's been a long time."

Gamelon chuckled as he set to prompt Jorge around one of his typical circular narrations. "What's been a long time?"

"Since *mi hermano* brought up the *langosta contrabanda* an' the real strong *cerveza Bohemia.*"

"And he's going to?"

"Sí."

"And?"

"Maria, she says its been a long time, too, since you come to us for *una pequeña fiesta.*"

"I am to come?"

"Sí."

"When Jorge? I'd like to very much. I haven't done *Cuervo* and *sangrita* with you and your family since—Lord, I can't remember when."

"*Mi hermano,* Luis, he gets here from Ensenada with the stop at Puerto Nuevo for the live *longosta,* oh, say, four, five, six, maybe, Saturday. Six *està bien?*"

'*Si,* Jorge. Six will be fine. And you tell Maria what I'm really looking forward to is her *tortillas.* Nobody makes them like she does."

The little man's smile went almost too broad for his face. "She still grindin' the corn herself. *Hay muy pocas mujeres* that still do it the old way." Then the smile faded and Jorge looked troubled.

Gamelon prompted again. "There was a *numero duo,* I seem to recall."

"Sí Señor."

"Well?"

"Well, you don't ask about it an' I'm not sure you want to hear about it, if you even care no more."

"About what?"

"About the Maria Waugh, about *la rosa azul . . .*"

And Gamelon realized he had not seen the fabulous rose in his inspections. "Where is it, Jorge?"

Again Jorge seemed to go roundabout. "Well, you know, way back, before you went away, I took some cuttings an' I try 'em on different root stock?"

"I remember."

"I'm the best at graftin', *Señor* Lon, you know that," Jorge said almost defensively.

Gamelon boosted his pride with, "There is no one better."

"*Están rechazados.*"

"The root stock rejected the cuttings? I've never heard of such a thing."

"I know. An' I'm the best grafter. You said so." Jorge dropped his eyes, and again Gamelon felt the need to prod. The small man did not reply right away, then he said, "Day after you go away, Maria Waugh just up an' die. I dug it out careful an' wrapped it in plastic for you to see when you come back."

It took Gamelon only a cursory examination of the withered plant to see why. The natural root structure was extremely weak. That was usually the case with hybrids and the reason all were grafted to hardier root stock. But he could also see the roots were crimped, dessicated with disease. He knew the signs so well he could have drawn at the moment what he would see if he looked at them under a microscope.

He cut off one branch and told Jorge to wrap it in wet cotton and seal it in plastic and then consigned the remainder of the dead bush to the compost heap. Perhaps when all the other was done and said, he could prevail upon Dr. Ching in the name of her love for roses to try to seek out what peculiarities of its genetic structure had made it at one and the same time so magnificent and so foredoomed.

By Saturday morning, he knew without doubt that he was no longer comfortable, satisfied. As he began his long letter to Freddie Sevrinsky, he knew that he was no longer at ease with this life among the flowers, that no matter how gratifying, how exciting all his future endeavors with his roses might be, he would never have the total sense of fulfillment that had been his, every day, until just so few weeks before.

Wasco, California
July 14, 1984

Dear Mr. S.,

Dr. Ching agreed to help me. I've delivered what was needed and am waiting now to hear the results. Thank you for opening the path for me.

After meeting with Ching, I thought to try to see you personally, but . . .

. . . would say the sum total of all of this was like witnessing God in the process of creating Eve from Adam's rib, seeing the resurrection of Lazarus, hearing a misdirected Jesus preach a drunken Sermon on the Mount and Sibyl predict the fall of Rome all in a single twist of some demonic kaleidoscope.

The effects of all this on me have been profound, I know. What I do not know yet is the true extent of the change in me those effects have caused. I know I am no longer the man I was, the man you have known all these years—more a man, less, I'm not sure. I don't believe my fundamental values have changed; it is as though I've had to rejuggle their relative weights and I'm not sure which has come up the heaviest. One sleepless night in Nesset, I was able to admit to myself what I might ultimately have to become, but I'm still not at all at peace with that image.

In your seminars so many years ago, Mr. S., and whenever the subject's come up in conversation since then, it has always been assumed, it seems to me now in retrospect, that whatever Man, in his infantile wisdom, has deemed beautiful was always automatically right and vice versa.

Could it be, my very dear friend, that there is an infinite wisdom that does not necessarily relate the two, right and beauty or wrong and ugliness? Could it not be that the only true beauty is time, the orderly progress from the infinity of beginning to the infinity of ending, both of which will remain forever beyond human comprehension? Could it not then also be that the only lack of beauty, the only ugliness, the only wrong, if you will, is the disturbance, however slight, of that progress?

Perhaps someday we'll get a chance to discuss this. For now, I must close. I have been invited to a very special dinner of lobster smuggled out of Mexico and excellent, high potency Mexican beer with all the accompanying rice, beans, *tortillas,* tequila and singing, which is sure to follow.

Thank you for hearing me out.

Affectionately,
Gamelon

Sing they had. After the *langosta,* split, smothered in fresh parsley and garlic and grilled, the *tortillas,* the Cuervo chased with shots of the watered-down tomato paste called *sangrita,* Luis Gonzales' oldest boy, a would-be *mariachi,* had gotten his battered guitar and they sang—*Guadalajara,* and the old revolutionary song, *Adelita,* and *La Paloma* and more that Gamelon did not know.

Near midnight, Gamelon, who rarely drank, had stumbled along the rose rows, stopping now and then to bay a chorus of *La Paloma* at the stars, until he reached his cottage near the crossing shed where he tumbled into bed with his socks and his shorts on. He was asleep before his eyes were fully closed.

So it was that the phone rang for almost a full five minutes shortly after 5:00, before he managed to get to it, corral it, get the right end to his ear and grunt his confirmation of the fact into the mouthpiece.

"Waugh?" a raspy female voice at the other end said. "Waugh, get down here."

"Who—" He cleared his throat. "Who is this?"

"E. V. Ching."

"Oh—ah, yes, Doctor. What did you say?"

"I said get down here to the university. I want to see you."

"Yes . . ." He squinted at his wristwatch, longing for his bed like a lover. "I'll leave here about nine—"

"Now. I haven't had any rest to speak of for three days because of your investigation. I'm damned if I'll cool my heels waiting for you until pushing noon."

"All right, Doctor. I'll be there, seven, eight at the latest—"

The crash of the receiver at the other end made him yank his own from his ear in pain.

JULY 15, 1984

Near La Playa

E. V. Ching stood, her hands clasped behind her, looking out one of the down-canting, porthole-like windows on the far side of her small office. As Gamelon entered, he wondered what, if anything, the tiny scientist could see outside; her nose came just barely even with the bottom rim of the ultra-modern window.

He stopped just inside the door. "I'm here, Doctor," he said, although in his still somewhat hungover, unbreakfasted state, he was not sure all the best of him was.

"Sit down," was all Dr. Ching offered in the way of a greeting.

He did so without replying. He lolled in one corner of the leather sofa through several more minutes of silence waiting for her to speak. It had been intimated on the telephone and it was obvious now just in her two curt words that she was immensely weary and just as immensely tense, perhaps even angry. He did not press her.

Finally, without turning away from the window, she said in a thin voice, "I do not appreciate being used, Mr. Waugh. I do not like having any part of me used, my body, my mind or my—spirit, for lack of any better word. I feel at this moment, however, Mr. Waugh, that I have been viciously used, every aspect of myself raped, as it were, by you and your brother—"

"Dr. Ching—" he interrupted trying for the interpolation of some propitiating word.

"Oh, please keep your mouth shut for a while longer. I'm not ready for anything you have to say yet, and when I am, whatever you do say had better be the absolute and complete truth.

"I'm sure as a geneticist—of sorts—you had some suspicion of what I might encounter doing your investigation and yet you and your brother would do nothing to prepare me. You left me to stumble about and discover all this—terrifying information alone. I did you a favor and it has come near costing me my sanity. I shall always resent you for that, Mr. Waugh, you and your brother. The slightest manifestation of trust could have prepared me."

She fell silent again and Gamelon studied the backs of his hands on his knees for a while before saying anything. When he did speak, it was in a soothing way. "I see now, Doctor, that we should have taken you more into our confidence before involving you—I should have. It was I who insisted what we'd observed in the field be corroborated in the laboratory and I who involved you specifically. In light of what you've just said, I feel I should fear for the overall well-being of anyone who becomes involved. If my apologies will make any difference at all, you have them."

A rigidity seemed to melt away from the small woman's back. She turned slowly away from the window toward Gamelon. The look of her face, her haggard eyes, confirmed for him how exhausted she was. She went to her big chair, climbed aboard and sank into it. She took off her glasses, let her head fall back and closed her eyes and stayed that way as she spoke further to him. "So that there is no misunderstanding, Mr. Waugh, I want you to know something: you asked for my confidence at the outset and, no matter how badly I feel I may have been used, you still have it—so far.

"Now, although I have destroyed that—thumb and most of the cell and tissue cultures, I still have some very strange bone samples. I have white blood cells and liver material as yet uncultured. If, as I said, when I ask for it, I do not get complete and absolute honesty from you, I will make three or four telephone calls. One to the Sorbonne, I think, and one to the editor of *The New England Journal of Medicine,* an old and dear friend. Another to Stanford, for certain.

"At my beck, Mr. Waugh, two or three of the world's most eminent cryogeneticists will assemble here within twenty-four hours. My laboratory will be sealed to all but them and my friend, the editor, who will be here to jury their investigations. Within a week, I would say, the whole world will know what I know now and the hunt will be on for your—people. Clear?"

Although he could not blame her for what she said, he rebelled nonetheless at the threat of a sort of blackmail. All he said was, "Clear."

"Very well, then, and before I outline my findings for you: from the beginning and leaving nothing out, what *have* you and your brother observed—everything, start to finish, dates, times, and yes, damn it, places."

Gamelon told her as quickly and concisely as he could while not omitting any detail he thought could be of value to her. He found in the doing that the telling was a good thing for him. He found himself being as objective about the total thing as he had ever been able to be.

He was able to be objective about it all until he got near the end, to Marylea, Marla and the child. His tone did not alter but he became aware, vaguely, of a waxing sense of uneasiness, a furtive concern.

As he neared the end of his recital, Ching's eyes,

which had remained closed until that instant, flipped open with the startled look in them of one who had been slapped across the face.

He fell silent and waited. The turn was hers. When a minute, two, then three had passed and still she only stared into the space left of his head, he asked evenly, "What is it, Doctor?"

Her eyes flicked to his, then she whispered, "I didn't know . . . I forgot all about it . . ."

"Forgot about what?"

"The mass, the replication of mass, the creation of matter out of nothing." Something of her assertiveness seemed to return. "In the end," she said coolly, "that may turn out to have been the cruelest usury of all, Mr. Waugh."

"My having planted the possibility in your mind—"

"Full well knowing how relative it was to everything I might discover and also knowing—if you took the time to think about it, which I doubt—that nothing I would do in the laboratory would point to it. Only your observations would reveal so astounding a thing.

"In every one of my experiments," she went on, angrily underlining her most important words with slaps of her small hand on the desk top glass, "I *supplied* the necessary ingredients for these people's molecular structure to reproduce itself: the fluids, the nutrition, the incubation, so that the little bits of them *I* had could reproduce—God knows, not normally—but reproduce under what I would consider usual conditions . . ."

Her voice trailed off; she shook her head from side to side, then muttered, "But one full-grown being producing another of itself without food, or water—and in so short a time . . ." Again she fell silent.

"It is impossible, is it not, Doctor?" Gamelon asked firmly.

Silence hung between them until at last she shook her head slowly and ventured in a small awed voice, "There is one possibility, but it is so abstract, so abstruse . . .

"Once, years ago, when I was involved in some studies at Princeton, just for the intellectual hell of it, I audited a seminar under a man named John A. Wheeler. He was—is—perhaps one of this century's most brilliant physicists.

"The whole seminar discussion centered around the mathematical construct of the Energy of the Vacuum Field—"

"You're already losing me, Doctor."

"Yes, well, to put it as simply as I'm able, the theory proves that all the universe contains minute vacuums—too many billions in your earlobe alone to even conceive of, for instance—and that these vacuums are in a constant state of fluctuation.

"What Wheeler had 'proved' mathematically was the existence of enormous energy densities in those electromagnetic fluctuations—no, it's too much even to consider."

But what she said had clicked for Gamelon. He said in pure amazement, "Are you theorizing that somehow the—the—atomic structure of these people is capable of converting the energy of those vacuum fluctuations into matter?"

She brushed away any further conjecture with, "It's not possible for me to hypothesize any further at this point. I'm weary—perhaps sometime I'll discuss it with George Dorfben. He's a friend and an expert on the whole matter. Not now." And she abruptly changed the subject: "So there are, at present, the five males and only the one female left alive—known to be alive—at this time?"

He resented somewhat her impersonal use of just gender in speaking of them but said only, "Yes."

"Perhaps not . . . but, to your senses, again, how do they appear, how do they act?"

"Just like you and I, like normal human beings."

"But, of course, they are not." Dr. Ching continued to sit motionless, unresponding for some time, then she said, swiveling her chair to face him as she spoke, "Any discussion of normalcy is not valid in this situation. It would be an exercise in futility."

She replaced her glasses and her dark eyes, fixed now on Gamelon's, leapt into swimmy globes. "Mr. Waugh," she said, "you are aware of the quantum leap theory of evolution as opposed to that of slow, steady, almost imperceptible change?"

Gamelon nodded.

"Until this weekend, I have not particularly subscribed to it, but after having had my nose rubbed in it up to the eyes . . .' Her voice trailed off and she looked away and sighed. "No, Mr. Waugh, normalcy or the lack of it has no place in our talk. What these—people—are not is human. They are not *Homo sapiens*. They are an entirely new species, destined, I'm afraid, to eventually replace *Homo sapiens* just as *Homo sapiens* replaced his genetic predecessors—and with all their capabilities, possibly within just a few lifetimes, unless for some reason they themselves are eradicated. From what we know, that would be difficult."

Gamelon was stunned "But how? It took *Homo sapiens* thousands, perhaps hundreds of thousands of years!"

"They have so many ways to survive as a species, so many ways to reproduce themselves. I strongly suspected everything you've reported about the self-replication, the regeneration, and so on, but there are two more things I know you could not possibly have discovered outside the laboratory.

"First, the regeneration works in reverse, as it were."

"The thumb—"

"The—thumb was growing another hand before I—killed it. Theoretically, it would eventually have produced another total being given time and nutrient enough.

"But, Mr. Waugh, to my mind, what qualifies these beings as a new, more powerful species is this: not only are their genomes indestructible except, perhaps, from some form of oxygen deprivation—I haven't tried that yet—but also the DNA contained in those genomes is correcting."

"What do you mean?"

"Simply this: in the mating of a *Homo sapiens* female and a male of this new type—or vice versa—at the instant of conception, the DNA of the new type will correct, adjust that of the *Homo sapiens* half of the zygote to mirror itself, and any offspring, however garden variety human in appearance, will not be. It will be *Homo superbus*, or whatever you might wish to call them—the new type."

As though issuing from an old recording, Marylea's words floated back to him. ". . . a boy—but Lon, you're right. What is it—really?" He felt as though someone had begun to slide ice cubes down his spine one at a time. He realized his feet were cold.

"I haven't done any arithmetic, Mr. Waugh, but say there are only the five males—there will be six in, say, fifteen years when the boy reaches puberty—and that the world knows their offspring will be immortal. Suppose each male spawned only one child a week for—well, ostensibly forever as they do not age, do not die . . ."

Now filtering through the gauze of days was a chanting of his own words ". . . women so crave the possibility of the ultimate gift for their children that all the diamonds and saffron of the world would be laid at the feet of gilded-caged Slim Boys and Fredericks in return for a single hour . . ."

His thoughts came back to Dr. Ching as she removed her glasses again and put her hands over her eyes. ". . . add to that their ability to multiply themselves on their own and so on . . . As I see it, Mr. Waugh, we, you and I, *Homo sapiens* is a doomed race." She laughed bitterly. "And I always thought we'd blow ourselves off the face of the earth."

She took her hands from her eyes and turned her nearsighted gaze on Gamelon again. "There's one more thing I know—I strongly suspect, rather—that you do not. It's probably a small issue, comparatively speaking, but perhaps not."

"Yes?"

"There is another theory I always thought it fun to philosophize about. It hasn't any basis in proof, and up to now, I most definitely did not subscribe to it. It holds something to the effect that within our genes, on our genes, each and every one of us carries the entire evolutionary history of the race from mote of star dust through primordial bacteria, fish, lizard, ape, right on down—or up, if you will have it that way—to what we are today.

"Now, the bone slivers I treated with various growth stimulators did just that: they grew—slowly, but they grew. Why I did it, what made me think to do it, I really can't say, but two other slivers I elected to submit to growth stimulation *plus* the stimulation of adrenalin," and she went on to recount the strange transformations.

When she had finished, she sat silently watching Gamelon as though expecting a reply, at the least some reaction. When neither came, she went on with a trace of condescension, "Mr. Waugh, I am not a wild conjecturer, but having seen what happened with those samples, I—I feel like a fool even expressing it—I—you know what adrenalin does to the human body, of course, basically speeds everything up making the body capable of surpassing its regular ability to perform for short periods of time.

"If the huge pituitary gland I suspect I would find if I could brain scan one of these—people—is capable of stimulating the immense quantities of growth hormones that must be present to explain the super-rapid cell division and thus the regeneration and the replication, could it not also stimulate the release of immense amounts of adrenalin or some other speed-up chemical peculiar only to them in times of extreme stress?"

He had already caught the drift of where Dr. Ching's words were leading and his brain began to race, back through the past ten days, darting into dim corners, poking in the dust wiggles under beds of superfluous information, searching for something of immense importance he could not recall.

Dr. Ching had raised her eyes to the ceiling. "I know it sounds ridiculous," she went on, "but the bone bits, what you tell me about the one Jennie; I just cannot escape the feeling that in times of extreme stress, these beings can retreat back along the evolutionary chain to take a clue from it and change into something else, take another form that would better suit their need for self-protection at that moment. Say one of them was in imminent danger of drowning . . ." Her voice trailed off.

Twice, came to Gamelon. Twice he had seen or heard or thought whatever it was he could not find now.

Two times.

Two.

Twin.

Jennie.

He was back in the barn. Jennie, deep in sleep, had stirred slightly. He saw her face, but there was more: behind the dividing and coalescing images that were the face, he seemed to see in rapid succession a great mound of twisted hair with hollow eyes, a perfect, throbbing, flesh-colored cube, a crystal with entrails encased in it as a primordial fly is encased in amber, a writhing mass of tendrils and spikes swimming in deep watery blue.

Twice.

Frederick.

That same morning. He had started to moan and saw again the flashing pictures of twisted hair with hollow eyes, crystals with visible guts and tendril heaps swimming lazily . . .

In his turn, he covered his face with his hands and began nodding his head. Dr. Ching caught his actions out of the corner of her eye and turned toward him. "There's something you haven't told me," she said with a bit of knife in her tone.

"I just remembered it," he replied between the butts of his big hands, then he tried to explain what his mind had registered during those nearly forgotten moments.

When he had finished, she said, "Mental impressions under stress, but the indication would be, to me, at least, that perhaps they actually pass through the entire evolutionary history—very quickly—many times during the act of dividing. If so, then what I suspect has a very good chance of being true."

Gamelon dropped his hands between his knees and sat staring at the carpet between his shoes. Neither of them spoke for a long while. But his mind's eye saw anything but dun carpet. It was all of human society in chaos for millenia as the new species rose to dominate the old, as the old made gods of the new and the new, slaves of the old until the old disappeared completely or were herded onto reservations to be kept alive, to be bred like any species in danger of extinction. He saw a day when a mortal human was put on exhibit and great fees charged to come and watch it in its death throes, to see it die. And God would have died long before that of rejection and a broken heart.

During the long silence that warming summer morning, the last of what had been the springtime Gamelon died also. Deep within his soul he became aware of what seemed to be a distant whirring.

At last, Dr. Ching broke the silence and asked him, "What will you do now?" When he neither raised his head nor answered, she said, "What about your brother? What will he do now?"

"By way of answering that, Doctor, let me tell you what I think you're going to do now, have already begun to do in your mind, at least.

"I've answered all your questions, fed you all the information you wanted, so you won't be cornered into making good on your threat of bringing in the world. You didn't want to have to do it anyway. If I'd forced you to make good on your blackmail, you'd have summoned the world with dragging feet.

"It is crucifyingly clear to me now that what you say is true: these beings are not human, but a—I will not use the word, new; it implies good somehow—they are a different species and not necessarily good . . .

"And yet they love in a way I understand, and fear and hate and cry the same style tears as you and I . . .

"They are different and in that very difference, they are the ultimate realization of the human dream, but they themselves are not human.

"Not only are they not human, Doctor, they are the doom of the human race and what it might have become during the eons to follow.

"I need not ask what view you have of them, Doctor. You've already chosen to see this different species as wonderful and as inevitable. It was you, after all, not I, who named them *Homo superbus.*

"But, Doctor, when the dream comes true, there is nothing left to dream. And, with their immortality, their replication, their immunity to everything except perhaps asphyxiation or starvation, there will someday be nothing on this earth but replicas, sames, identicals. There will be no truly new individuals, no new ideas. There will be no better, no best still to strive for. There will be nothing to dream.

"What will my brother do? What is he already doing, Doctor? Much the same as you but in a different way.

"I believe that after I leave, before you totter off to get some sleep, you will put your laboratory journal under lock and key. Bright and early tomorrow morning, you will transfer all the remaining sample material to the Cell and Serums Bank. With "E.V. Ching" on the labels, no one would dare so much as question what they are.

"Time will pass and you will stew and fret. Then you will return to the research. You will become increasingly cloistered and secretive until, in the end, the power your knowledge can wield, the "first" that could shed its radiance on you, until your pride drives you to publish your findings. If indeed, the human race is doomed, you will be the first to recognize it, define it and proclaim it, and one of the first of that doomed race to have the all-transcending thrill of going out with a blaze of glory while there's still an audience left.

"You share several things with my brother. You share the lure of that audience, certainly. You share the love of the power that elite knowledge can bring. And you share what to my mind can be the supreme human curse: brilliance. Brilliance breeds a dangerous kind of boredom, Doctor, boredom with the usual, with slowness, with what the brilliant see as useless, wasteful repetition in all things. They have a tendency to come to look down on the world and everything in it. If someone does not check them or they do not check themselves, the brilliant may leap at anything—for its own sake and without regard for the consequences—that is unusual, above the normal human ken, and faster. It's just a slender side-step from there to falling victim to that yen for power that the control of special knowledge can bring.

"In the boredom brought on by your brilliance, you and my brother both have given up on the human race.

"Marylea's last words to me were, 'I will not let him use me to play with life anymore so he can use the world.' The full meaning of those final six words, 'so he can use the world,' is just coming home to me.

"My brother Racklin, too, has harkened to the herald angels' singing out the doom of the human race and in the particular boredom growing out of his particular brillance—unlike you, who will gét your glory cravings satisfied by the earthly proclamation of that doom—Racklin has decided to hasten it just for the selfish, insane pleasure of witnessing it, to ride the black high horse of it all the way as far toward his race's obliteration as he can before he himself dies."

All through this, Gamelon had not raised his voice, but his tone had become increasingly impassioned. Dr. Ching, whose eyes had chilled, whose mouth had gone hard when he began to expose her to herself with a clarity she could have conveniently ignored forever, had not taken her gaze from him, nor had she outwardly winced. Now, as he stood up, his great frame seeming to occupy all the available space in the cubicle of an office, she cringed down into her great chair and avoided direct contact with his intense brown eyes. As he went on with what he felt driven to speak out, a low anger, a bitterness came into his voice.

"I don't have the ridiculous blind assurance of a fundamentalist concerning the nature of God, Doctor, nor do I ponder daily on His—Its existence. I do not spend any time begging It, trying to con It or giving It credit for everything, good or bad. But this morning, I thank It for one thing: that I am not brilliant, not like you and Racklin.

"I like the human race. I like the newness, the fresh promise of each child born of it. I like even the uncertainty of where that race is going if for no other reason than it leaves me with something to dream.

"I will not live in a sterile world of samenesses. I do not believe the mutants are *Homo superbus,* Doctor. I don't believe their ability to clone themselves, heal themselves, to be immune to sickness, to nullify other genes and chromosomes or adjust them to mirror their own represents a quantum leap forward in evolution. For me, it represents a quantum leap backward, backward to the ways and days of the simple cell. For me, the mutants are not the ultimate rendering of humanity. They are humanity's terminal illness. They are the cancer that will destroy us, not the God Children destined to replace us."

In his soul the whirring had become a wind-rushed beating that grew, mounted, until it emerged as tolling words inside his mind that almost obliterated the ones his mouth went on forming: *Someday . . . a man's own special, individual madness may bear that man off to his own heaven or hell or oblivion on its own particular wings . . .*

"If those herald angels are proclaiming what God truly wants—if there is a God to want—then I have no choice but to be an unwilling Lucifer and fall from heaven and grace to do what I must do.

"I will try to stave off the end of Man awhile, long enough to give Man time to catch up, to become whatever he inevitably will become. If—if the human race wishes to destroy itself, that's part of that inevitability. But, I will not stand by and see it supplanted without having had an even chance."

The thrill of his own madness wrapped its shrouding wings about his soul then, and rose toward oblivion or hell. He sobbed once, hugely, with tears in his eyes, but he finished in a strong voice that belied his torment. "And if I cannot control the cancer," he said, "I will destroy it. I will find and kill every one of—" Again his voice broke badly. "—'my people' and anyone who stands in my way of doing it . . . even my brother."

La Playa
7/15/84
8:45 AM

Dear Mr. S.,

Please forward the enclosed to Jorge (Gonzales) at the nursery . . .

He leaned on the top of the Fiat in the nearly deserted parking lot outside the Human Sciences Building scribbling on a yellow pad dredged out of his old briefcase. The sun scooped highlights by the handful from his bright hair as the rising morning breeze from the sea tossed it lightly now and then.

. . . Box 43, Wasco, 93062. He won't be there today, Sunday, so I can't call him and there's no phone in his house. It's just to let him know I'm not returning to Wasco right away—if, God knows, I ever do. Wasco is out of my way. Indeed, I think Wasco will always be out of the way from now on, just a well-remembered place in an all but forgotten time.

Again, because it is Sunday and early, I'm not going to try to contact you personally, but, like any poor soul heading into the unknown perhaps never to return, I'd like for someone to know I've gone, so that some single comrade in the human race might remember me.

I'm going back to Nesset. Adding what Dr. Ching has discovered to what I've already told you about in my long letter mailed from Wasco yesterday, I think you'll agree I have no choice. When you've had adequate time to think about it all, I think you may even understand.

As quickly and simply as he could, he summarized the famous geneticist's findings and her extrapolations.

. . . know that other members of the race may someday come to curse me for what I may do. They will surely label me insane, a homicidal maniac. But, Mr. S., therein lies the tale. If I am forced to it, it will not be *homi*cide I commit. Human genocide, slow and relentless over the decades, is what *will* occur if I don't do what I must. It may happen anyway. There are surely others of this different race which I don't know about. I see I'll have to do what has to be done now and then go on to find them, all of them.

I will try to control the cancer, limit it so Man has an even chance, so that the social upheaval that would be inevitable when what they are became known can be avoided or minimized. But, if I cannot control it?

Something has overtaken me, Mr. S., and now drives me like my curiosity, my creativity never did. It is love, Mr. S., a fierce, relentless love akin to nothing I ever felt for another single human being, not you, not even Maria.

It is a love I thought always in the past only saints and prostitutes capable of. It is a love scathingly humble and mountainously prideful all at the same time. It is love for that laughable beast, Man.

Affectionately,
G.

He rousted out one of the cheap envelopes he always tried to keep in the briefcase, addressed it simply, "J. F. Sevrinsky, PhD," and dropped it in the intra-university mailbox outside the campus post office on his way off the grounds.

He set the car running east the few miles needed to intersect the northbound freeway that would take him eventually to Swede's Valley and the doing of whatever he had to do in the name of his new-found love.

The summer session at the university having come to its conclusion, Freddie Sevrinsky had departed promptly for the Marlborough Festival in Vermont and two weeks of participation in the music-making there. The long letter, which Gamelon had addressed to him at his home, was waiting when he returned.

Fräulein Altenbäumer had planned to visit her cousins in Düsseldorf for only the last two weeks of July, but, at their urging, stayed for three.

Freddie had no reason to go to the university upon his return from the festival and had happily secluded himself in his studio at home. There was a little suite, a frothy trifle for small orchestra, closing with variations on *Bring in the Clowns* that had been singing brightly in his head for weeks.

In the quiet moments after a gratifying day of *glissandi,* grace notes and springing meters, he pondered on Gamelon's long letter and what it said as well as what it implied in the broadest terms. But it was not until the second Tuesday in September, when the ever-efficient Miss A., five pounds heavier from too much *sauerbraten* and *kalbskeule* and *strudel,* cleared the university mailbox on her way to Mr. S.'s for a scheduled stint, that Freddie received the last note ever to come to him from Gamelon.

Just before noon, as the Fiat started down the interminably long, slow drop from the Cajon Pass to the desert floor, he swore to himself that no matter how deep his madness led him, he would not harm either Marla or the child. He was sure that when he got to sharing all he now knew with her, no matter how many lifetimes she lived, she would see to it that she produced no offspring, even by accident. During the coming years, under his tutelage, the boy might be taught a sacred obligation to do the same. The risk of oblivion for humanity could be reduced without violence, he thought, by at least that much.

Passing Las Vegas, he completed a letter in his mind instructing his attorney to sell all his plant patents and the nursery, with the stipulation that Jorge be kept on by the new owners, and went on to wonder where in the world there was a place remote enough to collect all these new beings, if he could do it, so as to isolate them from humanity and keep them under his eye for the rest of his life.

Midway between Las Vegas and the Virgin River Gorge, he prayed silently to nothing or no one in particular that the boy could be made to understand as he grew that his would have to be the eye once Gamelon's own had dimmed and at last gone out.

* * *

Deep in the gorge itself, he admitted he could not stave off the inevitable forever. He could only dedicate himself to the grandest play for time ever made, time for Man to have his chance. He wondered then, too, if he could not reverse the whole thing. Why could he not band together a small army of men who saw things as he did to help him, to keep the other species in check, contained for all the thousands of years it would be necessary? He began sloughing off the thought almost before it had finished forming. He would be the slave-owner then, the zookeeper. Anyway, the lure of immortality would always prove too strong, even for the strongest of his beloved laughable beasts. His pilgrimage would have to be a lonely one.

Crossing through the brief wedge of Arizona between Nevada and Utah there was barely time, but time enough, for him to remember one last time, as though they had existed for him in some former life and reincarnated themselves for him now, loosely, more in his heart than in his mind . . .

. . . tripping around the frilly edges of life, pondering on delicacies . . .

. . . the foggy evening last December when he had rounded a door jamb too short and dumped a double Margarita, salt, glass and all down the dress front of a lovely, honey-blonde girl with great gray eyes . . .

. . . Maria, his head held tightly in the circle of her arms, her hips locked against his, purring, "Lon—don't go yet . . ."

. . . brightness, sunlight all around, a baby's breath of a breeze, the sound of water trickling in a fountain, rich, black coffee, love nearby—but not right in your pocket and Brahm's *Liebeslieder Waltzes* . . .

* * *

As the Fiat rolled into Utah, it came to him with no more strength than that of a clarifying afterthought: he had never received his honors and now life held no promise of any ever again.

Five days from the summer solstice, the sun was only reluctantly beginning to set as St. George began to go by like a sliding, somnambulent postcard. With the sun lowering behind its butte, the Temple seemed no more than a structured hole in the butte's blackness. Only the gilded, trumpeting angel, Mormon, on the Temple's spire still caught the light and seemed to float in it above nothing.

Gamelon grimaced as he realized he was having feelings of homecoming and that they were anything but joyous. Then he smacked the wheel once and muttered, "Damn!" as "home" reminded him he had not followed Herbert's stern instructions; he had done nothing about having the bolt in the suspension replaced.

Although the gloaming had yet a while to linger in the western sky beyond the hills and buttes, between them, at the top of Swede's Valley, it was already dark. A hundred yards below the bridge, he switched off the Fiat's headlamps and crept forward with only the weak yellow gleam of the car's parking lights to help him stay on the road. Soon enough, he made out the bleached planking spanning the wash. He pulled off a few yards short of it, shut down the car and got out, closing the door behind him with only a tap.

He stood beside the car for as long as it took his eyes to become so adjusted to the blackness that the faint light which exists even within it made the ground blacker than the crowns of the live oaks across the dark matte gray bridge and the sky a grade more luminous than the trees.

He went forward lightly. He crossed the bridge at a lope, careful to keep above one of its horizontal supports all the way. Even so, the warped crone of a bridge complained once or twice under his relatively light weight.

On the other side, he stopped beneath the limbs of the oaks, tendering their foliage like old servants with arthritic arms offering around dark salads. Ahead, up the curving double dirt track, he thought he could make out a light in the house, only one, high, and guessed it came from the room where the child had been born and Marylea had let her life drain away rather than live with fear and degradation.

He stirred and made to start up the rut toward the house, then stopped and stood quite still listening carefully to the silence all around him. Suddenly, his mind was asking itself when he had last walked here. The night became a brilliant forenoon shaded heavily here and there beneath the oaks as he and Racklin sauntered and Racklin winningly told the old Navajo tales of rolling carnivorous rocks and He-Who-Kicks-People-Off-Cliffs, of The Sun and Twin Saviors. Then, just as suddenly, it was later the same day. The big ham and tomato sandwiches on home-baked bread, dill pickles, early pears and milk were finished, Maria was dead, he had promised Marylea she would never be alone anymore, and he had gone to walk, perhaps just to the great live oak and back—however long it took—but this time alone. He needed time for his conclusions to solidify themselves into resolves.

It was then he had last walked here. Alone. He had made his real resolve then; all seemingly taken since then had been nothing more than blocks built on that foundation. It was that resolve, taken then, which had condemned him to be alone for the rest of his days. And now, as with all who finally admit without qualification to aloneness, he felt the wall he had built which his back would be forever pressed against.

He started forward, stealthily, slightly crouched, his head swinging slowly from side to side as his eyes sought to dig out of the darkness on either side of the path anything that did not rightly belong in it. He had gone only a dozen yards when a sudden thrashing in the underbrush almost beside him froze him in mid-stride. He whirled toward the sound, his heart jerking, as whatever thrashed went on getting out of his way until it was satisfied it was far enough from him to be safe and the sound stopped as abruptly as it had begun.

Still he did not move. He wondered what other creatures, great or small, watched his passing, and Old Bead Woman chanted again from her own particular heaven or hell or oblivion . . .

"I wonder if the lone eyes are watching me . . . I wonder if the lone eyes are watching me . . ."

He turned his steps up the track again, still moving carefully. Again the silence of the moonless, windless night was total, so complete it seemed unnatural, the silence of the inside of a suspended soundproof box. Even his boots did not seem to make any sound as he went on. He thought he only imagined he heard the press and release of each step on the packed earth.

Under the great oak, he paused again. The view of the house from there was unobstructed and he saw he had been right: the only light showing was from the window of the room where Marylea had died and it was low, dim.

A scratching, a shifting in the low branches over his head, flattened him against the great oak's trunk and yanked his eyes upward . . .

"I wonder if the lone eyes are watching . . ."

His eyes searched in the morass of limbs and twigs and leaves as he waited for an owl's sad oohing or the great crash of its wings as it rose, a lost soul departing, dense and solid black against the high twinkling of the evening's first stars.

Nothing.

No mourner's bleat.

No beat of striving wings.

Nothing.

"I wonder if the lone eyes . . ."

Then there came what sounded to be no more than a hint of a whisper, an articulated sigh with malformed syllables.

He lowered his head and rubbed at his strained eyes. He was imagining sounds now in this overbearing silence.

The whisper breathed again.

All his great muscles curled and drew taut. He eased himself very slowly away from the tree and even more slowly studied the darkness all around.

From above, the sound settled on him once more. Someone, something tried to speak his name as though through bruised and swollen lips, "—am . . . eh . . . on, —am . . . eh . . . on . . ."

His eyes, all his attention strove to see into the tangled growth above him. "Yes," he hissed, "yes, Gamelon. Who is it?"

Again the disembodied whispers reached him, slurred, their patterns broken as though returning with difficulty to memory from some long forgetfulness. "—ar . . . la. Mmmmm—arla."

"Marla! In God's name, why are you up there?"

". . . mmm . . . am—s—safe up here."

"From whom? Racklin?!"

"Awww . . . all of them . . . but y-you."

"Marla, come down. Let me help you—"

"N-no! No! I can't come down. I can't let you—don' wan' you to see—" and the whispered, barely comprehensible words dissolved into short, stifled sobs.

"Marla, I'm here now. I won't let any of them do anything to you. Please come down. Please."

There was no reply but the sobbing and then the shuffling, scratching sounds began again as among the thick leaves he saw a faint whitish shape materialize and begin to move backwards along a branch, on hands and knees it seemed, toward the bole of the great tree. It disappeared around the massive trunk and a second later, Gamelon heard a soft thud on the far side of the oak.

He stepped into the undergrowth and moved to round the tree as quickly and as quietly as possible, his arms already prepared to cradle, hold, carry her, whatever was required.

She huddled in the gloom at the base of the tree, a naked mound, her head between her knees, her arms gripped tightly around her drawn-up legs, still sobbing as though for everything the world had ever lost. He stepped past her and squatted down facing her. When she did not move, did not acknowledge him in any way, he reached out and touched her shoulder lightly. At first, she shunned that touch, but he persisted. He stroked the back of her head, her neck, and slowly the crying subsided, then stopped after one deeply-drawn, shuddering breath. But still she did not raise her head, did not look at him. Gingerly, but with all the firm tenderness his big hand could relay, he lifted her chin until he could see her face completely.

Although the night had stolen their color, he looked into the great gray eyes, still brimming with tears, then his hand fell away. He sat back on his heels, staring. "Oh, my Dear God," he said, his voice trembling even in whisper. "What have they done to you?"

Wednesday, Thursday, Friday, Saturday and the morning, noon and early afternoon of Sunday had been all much the same. She ran the house as best she could. She cared for the child better than she would have thought herself capable of.

Thursday at lunch, Racklin had made a desultory attempt at conversation by dredging up some sordid crumbs of their days and nights in Park City. She had squelched it in the most offhand of styles. The men, pausing at appointed times to eat, coming, going, had, for the most part, otherwise passively ignored her. That suited her. At best, she was ill at ease among them.

When wet diapers or ham and eggs did not demand her attention, she took long walks around what once had been a farm, what once had been home, or spent hours in her room practicing. She was beginning to be satisfied with the *Spring Sonata* and the other pieces for her recital were coming along. It would be time to start working with her accompanist when she got back to Salt Lake.

Friday, after she recounted a few critical items that were needed, Racklin told Blue Sateen Slim Boy to run her into Nesset and asked her to stop by Birdie David's long enough to pick up some promised jars of new peach preserves. The stop had extended to forty-five minutes of sun tea and gossip with the lonely, curious, angular old lady and Marla came away somehow disturbed by the news of Coolidge Remson's violent death.

When he had not come in for breakfast Wednesday morning after all the endless march of mornings he had helped open the doors, the cook at the five-and-dime had sent the thin-haired, thin-shouldered boy to check on him. The boy had returned fifteen minutes later, his mouth finally open, in hysterics, babbling. It had taken the cook and the store manager another fifteen to get enough that was coherent out of him to understand that the county sheriff needed to be called. It had been the sheriff's coroner, it seemed, over coffee at the five and dime later, who had established that Remson had been murdered somewhere one side or the other of noon the previous day.

The news of Coolidge Remson's death disturbed her because she seemed to connect it with something. What she should have connected it with was Birdie's report of Racklin's visit to her about the same time as Remson had been killed, a visit during which he had charmed Birdie so, that she herself had not realized how skillfully he had pumped her for anything she might have learned about the happenings at the farm from Gamelon—over and above her limited involvement with Old Bead Woman—pumped her until he was able to convince himself she did not require killing.

Saturday afternoon, yesterday about this time, Red Sateen Slim Boy had gone up to Marylea's room, stripped, laid down on the bed and drifted off to sleep.

A little after four o'clock, she put the child's bottle on to warm and the big water pot on to heat so she could have at least a shallow bath in the tub later.

In the sun by the window in her room, she fed the child, then patted and murmured it to sleep. She put the tiny boy in its makeshift laundry basket bassinet, took off her dress and slipped into a short, light robe. Towel over her shoulder, she went down to the kitchen.

The water from the big pot amounted to little more than a finger or two in the bottom of the old claw-foot tub, so she did not dally. She sponged, rinsed, dried herself and pulled the plug posting a mental reminder to come in and scour the soap ring later. She left the door to the bathroom, next to the pantry *cum* guest room, open so it would air out and went back upstairs to dress.

The blue sateen shirt hung on the post behind his head. His Levis were in a denim crumple on the floor. Slim Boy lay propped on an elbow on the bed smiling at her, his penis at that indecisive state between something and nothing. He lifted his free arm and lazily waved her forward. "Come on in," he said. "Just gonna' do a little work for some more o' Red Cousin's dollars." He patted the bed beside him. "C'mon."

At first, she was just disgusted. She stayed where she was just inside the door and said to him contemptuously, "Get out. Get your clothes and get the hell out of here." But her disgust changed to fear and the fear to terror before she could whirl around as the door closed behind her and the lock clicked.

Racklin and the Black Sateen One stood there, their arms folded across their chests. The Indian's face was impassive, his eyes vacuous, indifferent, but Racklin's face was taut, strangely pulled back as though any second he might begin to giggle and be unable to stop. His eyes flamed and seemed to jump about in his head. He put out one hand, grabbed her by the arm and yanked her hard against him and held her there. The other hand set to stroking her hair. His voice shook as he said to her as though to a naughty child, "Come on, now, Little Sister, you're all God has to play with at the moment. You're the only one left and I've got to get you bred, bred to one of your own kind—"

She tried to fight him, but to no avail. At a nod from Racklin, Black Sateen stepped around behind her, pulled the towel from her shoulder and ripped her robe from neck to hem. But even as the robe fell about her ankles and Racklin began to press her back toward the bed, even as she gasped, "No! No!" and then screamed, she became aware of something totally unfamiliar beginning to happen to her. It was as though every molecule in her body had set to simmering and with every passing instant were rising closer to a ferocious boil. She tried to scream again, but all the air seemed gone. It was as if she had been transported in a single shot from the seacoast to the top of a high, high mountain. And she was warm, too warm . . .

They held her down, Black Sateen on one side, Racklin cackling repeatedly now on the other, an arm and a leg each, and Blue Sateen, nothing about him now even vaguely indecisive, was on her and in her, ramming cruelly, in an instant.

In a space of only moments, with a single sharp cry followed by fading rhythmic grunts, he came. Then his hips stopped and he opened his eyes just in time to see the butt of a large, strangely tendoned, powerful hand ramming toward his face.

The disbelief of what he had seen beneath him, the low-browed, flared-nostriled face with its underslung jaw and thick, snarling lips did not even have time to register on his face before that hand hit his chin, jammed his head back so hard the bones in his neck cracked and separated and he found himself flinging up and off her backward. He tumbled left, over Racklin, who still managed to swing onto one long arm, just as his spinal cord severed below the base of his skull. He hit the floor flat on his back, his head twisted weirdly up and to the side, dead, for all intents and purposes, irreparably dead.

Had he not let go of her, had he not backed away against the nearest wall to leave her to roll up onto splayed feet at the end of thick, bowed legs and dance there, snarling viciously at him, Racklin would have shared the same fate. As it was, he managed to slide along the wall to the door the Black Sateen One had left open as he fled the room, get through it and slam it in her face as she came for him in one single lunge all the way from the bed. He locked the door and held it until the pounding on the other side ceased, then he raced down the steps carooming off the walls.

She rolled back and forth across the room, arms dangling, until she came upon Blue Sateen's naked body. She stood looking down at it for a moment. She kicked it once. Then she bent a little, picked it up by the shoulders, shook it so violently its disconnected head whipped around like a steel ball in a pinball machine, then flung it like the rag doll it had become into a heap in one corner.

She went out the open window easily and onto the porch roof. She was across it to the edge in two strides and, without the slightest hesitation, shimmied down one corner post to the ground where she took off with a queer gaited lope toward the line of oaks. She knew she would be safe in the trees.

The eruption came then, the one he had warned Racklin of once, and it was violent beyond even his own wildest imagining. It was not only what Racklin had done to her—that the Blue Sateen Slim Boy had been the one who actually raped her counted for nothing now, only Racklin, Racklin—it was not only what he had done to her, it was what he had made her do to herself, the degrading bestiality Racklin had forced her to confer upon herself out of fear of him, that finally released the magma of his temper, his huge, vile anger. But the magma, distilled by his own particular madness, became a concentrate of liquid ice spewing from the depths of his soul and coursing out along every vein to every capillary of his mind and heart. His anger was a vaster, colder thing than the space between stars, with no light of its own to guide him. All he had to find his way by now was the reflected light of others: the piteous, broken light of Marla, the terrible but wonderful light of the infant boy, the greedy but beautiful and effortless lights that shone relentlessly and without remorse from the remaining Slim Boys, the near-blinding light from the center of the renegade star that was Racklin.

He ceased to feel. She had not even completed her stumbling, thick-tongued, whispered tale before the icy distillate racing through him froze the last spore of compassion or consideration within him and left him capable of but one thing: to act.

In a low voice so bereft of any warmth it made her wince, he told Marla to stay where she was until he returned and he set off up the path toward the house, he began on the road that would lead to nothing less than Racklin's death. Nothing else could satisfy him now.

She had told him the pickup had clattered down the track soon after she had taken to the oak tree, but she did not know whether anyone but Racklin had been in it. She was sure he himself had been; she had seen one elbow and red-haired forearm out the driver's window as the truck had passed beneath her. She thought it had turned right at the end of the bridge, south, toward St. George. He thought to move his car, hide it more thoroughly, thus masking his presence from anyone in the truck if it returned before they could get away, before he could get Marla and the child away. He decided on speed instead; there was no question of purpose.

He slipped from trunk to trunk until there were no more oaks to shelter under. He stood a moment beneath the last one, long enough to take off his boots and to convince himself there was no one in the lighter open hundred yards between the oak and the house, then he sprinted the distance to the shadowy steps up to the porch.

That brief run raised the chances a hundredfold of his encountering the waking Slim Boy, the Black One, if he was there. He went up the steps and across to the door with the stealth of a gliding, hunting tiger rounding its prey to put the wind at its back.

At the door, he strained his eyes into the dark kitchen through the door's mullioned panes as his brain clicked off like a computer all the places where the kitchen floor squeaked.

Nothing.

He was careful to lift slightly on the door as he opened it, then closed it noiselessly behind him. With the old, sagging places in the floor showing red like small towns on a secondary road, he followed his mental map through the darkness to the bottom of the stairs without making a sound. He paused there only long enough to send his senses on a scouting mission into the lighter darkness above.

They reported back. Nothing.

He started up on all fours keeping close to the wall side where the stairs were still the firmest.

The death smell stopped him halfway up, the dull nauseating stench of a cannibal feast. The sick-sweet odor made the icy magma in him flow at top speed and he began to creep upward again.

At the top, he came upright slowly. The dim light coming through the open door of Marylea's room was enough for him to assure himself finally that if the Black One was on the premises, he was not in the house.

He went into Marla's room, whipped a quilt from the bed, scooped up the sleeping child, laundry basket and all, and took them out to the head of the stairs. Then he started into Marylea's room where, even from the hall, he could see the glowing, swelling, stretching line throbbing and growing down the length of the sleeping Slim Boy, squirming as though under attack by a hundred thousand maggots.

He did not feel the cutting, only a stinging as Black Sateen's knife glanced off his bottom rib, but the force of the powerful young Indian's sideways thrust from where he stood concealed just inside the room sent him into a scrambling heap in the corner past the door. He was on his hands and knees and coming up almost before he finished falling, some of the wind knocked out of him. He crouched, panting, squared against the Black One across the open door, blood-smeared knife in hand.

"My brother said, in a way, he liked you," the Indian ground out low between clenched teeth framed in a bloodlust smile, "but I don't like you *any* way."

He took one jumping step toward Gamelon. "He said, too, he don't think he'd like gettin' down to cases with you, but I don' mind." He moved the knife slowly from side to side in the air before him. "He forgot 'bout the bigges' Ol' Navajo Wisdom here—"

He lunged across the short space separating them, the knife leading his charge. At the last possible second before there would have been no stopping the knife from ripping into his gut, Gamelon swiveled like the most adroit of fencers so the blade started by his stomach instead and he grabbed the wrist that followed it, flipped the off-balance Black Sateen toward him and onto his own weapon. The long steel went into him higher up than he had intended it to tear into Gamelon, up under his ribs and into the bottom of his heart. As Gamelon let go of him, the spin he had started when he grabbed the Indian's wrist went on, lazily now, until Black Sateen, fish-eyed, the hilt of the knife still gripped in his own hand, smashed into the wall by the bed and slid down. His head dropped forward and he sat staring at the hand that seemed unable to unclasp itself from the knife handle.

Without a thought for the gurgling that started in his throat or the red trickle that began at one corner of his mouth, Gamelon turned away from him toward the bed. He yanked the pillow from under the head of the stinking, stretching mass there, jammed it down hard over its face and held it, held it firmly for a long time, until the cancer's dividing stopped, until the piranhas beneath its throbbing center were gone, leaving in their wake only a brown, smirched stripe down its middle, until its outer coating cooled, its angry, high-fever red gone wax white. Then, he shook the lethal pillow out of its case and let it fall back on the dead Slim Boy's grotesquely spread face. He fashioned a pad from the case itself to slip between the gash in his side and his shirt and left the room without a backward glance. He collected the child and the quilt and left the Rundqvist house behind him to hide the terrors and mourn the sorrows it had contained through whatever beating summers and tearing winters it yet had left to weather until it collapsed in upon itself and them and let the woes out into the earth to trickle down to death at last. He would never enter it again. When he came for Racklin, he would lure him out if need be.

Twice they were lucky. Twice, when the distant loom of headlights warned of a car or truck making its way toward them up Swede's Valley, Gamelon was able to find a place to get the Fiat off the highway and out of sight of all but the most intent passing searcher. The first time there was a farm lane on the right dropping steeply down among tall trees. When next the telltale glow showed, he simply bumped off the road over the runoff ditch and in behind a dense clump of wild dwarf cedar.

Between hidings, Gamelon pressed the Fiat to its limits. The battered old automobile roared and sputtered as he held the accelerator without a letup, even downhill. The ranked and martialed trees of orchards, the open ends of parallel furrows running away to an unseeable convergence in infinity, an occasional house or barn set close to the road, sailed by now and again in the periphery of the racing headlights only to repeatedly give way to the flat black green of pastures behind prickly gun metal strands of barbed wire or the gray gold swarming of ripe, uncut grain.

Marla hunched beside him, cloaked and deeply cowled in the Bear Claw quilt. The child, coming awake now and beginning to fret, was in the basket on the floor of the back seat. Nothing but the need to get them to St. George, to barricade them in some anonymous motel room with food for a time, drove him, and so the car, at breakneck speed. Then he could return to face Racklin.

Luck was not with them the third time. Gamelon cursed under his breath: he remembered this particular stretch of road. It was a high spine and would be so for another mile at least. The onrushing high beam lights were already on the opposite end of the backbone between the sunken fields on either side. There was nowhere to turn off, nowhere to hide if he could have. There was not even a shoulder here on this dike between two irrigated plateaus. He jammed the accelerator as if to force it through the floor and hurled the car against the oncoming scream of light. At the last moment, he stomped the high beam button in hopes of blinding the driver of the other vehicle, please God, if, as something seemed to tell him, it was his brother, then rammed past at over eighty-five.

The Fiat and Racklin's pickup rocked in the double blasts of displaced air the passing caused. Gamelon fought for dear life to hold onto the car as it swung and danced, but he did not let up on the gas. He knew his last-minute strategy had failed. One flashing glimpse of Racklin's face as he tore by told him his brother had recognized the Fiat.

He needed no confirmation of the fact but he got

it in the rearview mirror an instant later. The pickup's stoplights came on red and yelling danger, and the truck's rear end started to swerve as Racklin tried to spin it. He did not succeed. Gamelon's last good sight of the truck in the vibrating mirror was of it broadside to the road and beginning to back and fill. Racklin would lose precious moments in that maneuver and Gamelon made the most of every one of them. He held the car on at near ninety.

They cleared the end of the dike and the plowed fields and orchards flashed by again. As Gamelon juggled whether to run the race and try to win it or hide again in hopes Racklin and whoever might be with him—a Frederick, most likely—would pass them by and leave them to win it later, luck deserted them altogether.

Gamelon tried. As he tried, all he could see before him was Herbert's bloated face and pudgy admonishing forefinger. When the suspension bolt gave up and sheered under the strain of too many miles as a misfit and too much pounding at insensate speed, he took off the accelerator and tried to brake. That only made things worse. He tried to keep the car going straight, but when the bolt had broken, the left front had dipped sharply, the bumper caught the macadam in a shower of sparks. He tried, but the drag on the left was too much for even his great strength to keep in rein at that speed. As though at last too beaten and weary to take it anymore, the old car rose on its right wheels and lay down on its side, still going fifty. Its abused body met the road and slid on with a tearing and screeching like all the fiends of hell in congress. After a few yards of that, it was as if it did not feel quite comfortable in that position and rolled on over, laconically, to scream along on its top until it tired of the friction between itself and the road and came to a stop, dark and silent, after its engine clanked twice, then gave up.

He thought a puppy cried somewhere nearby, then he realized the sounds were coming from the bundle beside him. Marla. She was alive at least. He managed to twist himself around and gave the door on his side one mighty kick. It popped out, completely. He followed it, feet first, turned and dragged the whimpering bundle toward him over the inside of the roof of the car.

The heavy old quilt had saved her when the car touched down on its doors and the side windows shattered. It had kept the flying shards from reaching her and had cushioned her as she was tumbled about inside. He carried her to the side of the road and well off it into a thicket of juniper, put her down there and went back for the child.

He could not find it.

He never would.

When the side window smashed, the tilting of the car had already rolled him onto it. He was dragged through the opening and smeared to little more than a gristly, bloody remnant among the powdered glass by the grinding passage of the car.

Then all there seemed to be to do was get out of the scalding glare of the nova exploding at him out of the night. He flung himself off the road and into the ditch alongside it just seconds before it struck.

At seventy, the pickup had begun to overrun its headlights. At ninety, it was so far outdistancing their ability to probe the night, Racklin did not see the dark hulk of the Fiat astride the road until the last chance of stopping before the truck smashed into it was long gone. He tried. He stood on the brakes. The wheels locked. Rubber screamed in agony and caught fire. Racklin forced his door open and rolled out just seconds before it struck.

Tires flaming, the truck roared snout first into

the driver's side of the overturned car and the two twisted and turned together on down the road in a mangled waltz. The impact fired the Frederick through the windshield, decapitating him in passing, and what was left of his parts after first the Fiat's and, seconds later, the pickup's gas tanks exploded in twin fiery balls, roasted amongst the fender remains and blackened frames or smoldered greasily on bits of guttering upholstery.

Gamelon dragged himself out of the ditch. His side where Black Sateen had cut him pained him. As he staggered off to where he had left Marla, wagging his head, punchy from the concussion of the double explosion, he put his hand there. His side was sticky with blood and he realized dimly that his dive into the ditch had opened the wound. He kept his hand to it as he went back along the road, a lone, stumbling silhouette against the burning center of the night.

The crashes, the explosions, were certain to spill out the residents of the nearby farms. He wanted nothing to do with them. He wanted not to offer any explanations. And, if anyone saw Marla the way she was they would shoot her or shut her away.

Act. Do it. That was all that mattered. He felt the throbbing in his side, but other than that, nothing.

Nothing.

Racklin was dead. No one in the truck could have survived that small holocaust. So that was done.

The child was most probably dead, thrown from the car and broken. It was for the best. How could an immortal any more than a mortal resist the shimmering lure of immortality in the end? He had been a fool to think he could have ever taught the boy otherwise.

He had to save Marla, help her out of this place.

He did not know why, half-woman, half-beast, and far from laughable, that she had become. He had to, that was all. Then he could begin his plodding throughout the length and breadth of the earth if need be. First, the Fredericks, then the ferreting out and eradication of whatever others there might be. Nothing of them would be left if he lived long enough.

Nothing . . .

Nothing . . .

She was where he had left her in the juniper stand, huddled under the quilt. He held out his bloody hand to her, not even noticing its blackness in the faint light from the dying fires on the road. He withdrew it when she put out her misshapen one to take it and she was left to get up by herself and trail along behind him as he set off without a word. He was driven to help her, but somehow the sight of her hand, so far a cry from the one with the long fingers delicately picking out the *Spring Sonata* on her knee, repelled him. He could not bring himself to touch her.

He calculated they were no more than three miles from the bottom of Swede's Valley, four from St. George. Twice, early on, they had to hide as trucks came out of farm lanes, people attracted by the calamity on the highway as he had thought they would be.

He stumped along the shoulder of the deserted road only half mindful of Marla, now close, now farther behind him. Other of Old Bead Woman's words came back to him. Without realizing what he was doing, he began to chant them under his breath much as she had done, first on one tone, then on another a note or two higher or lower.

"The Sun said, here are your weapons. For you Younger Brother, the lightning that strikes straight."

His voice grew louder, his syllables more emphatic.

"The lightning is before me. I am he who has killed the monsters!"

As he walked on, he began to stamp his feet in time with his own rhythms, hard, harder still.

"I am HE who has KILLED the MONSTERS! ALL is BEAUtiful beHIND—ME!!

"LIGHTning IS beFORE—ME!!

"I am HE who KILLS the MONsters, I am HE WHO KILLS THE MON—STERS!! I—AM—HE—WHO—KILLS—"

"Gamelon! Gamelon!" In his mesmerized insensibility, he almost trampled her over. Marla had run around in front of him as his chanting rose to a bull roar and his tread shook the earth. "Gamelon, stop it! Please stop it! Please!"

He stood before her for several moments, his head down, then without a word, without looking up at her, he stepped around her and started off again down the road, silent.

A half mile farther on, she caught at his sleeve and begged for a rest.

He could see the glow of the lights of St. George on the horizon now. It might be their last chance. He looked around him, then motioned to an orchard on the left side of the road. They crossed over and he held the barbed wire up for her to crawl under, then vaulted over it himself. They wandered a few rows in, then, by unspoken consent, dropped separately at the bases of neighboring trees.

Smell told him what sight on that dark night could not be sure of. He had chosen a peach orchard. A peach orchard . . . He seemed to be looking at a beloved faded photograph from sometime in his youth. In a peach orchard on some summer afternoon, he stretched slowly on the ground and dozed, aware but undisturbed by the sounds around . . . He stretched and dreamed and let the day go its implacable way and end without him . . .

. . . undisturbed by the sounds around: the last bees hurrying about their final collections . . .

. . . aware but undisturbed . . . dreaming . . . letting the day go . . . aware but undisturbed . . .

"Welcome me, Little Brother . . ."

. . . aware but undisturbed . . .

"I've never failed you . . ."

You are dead, Brother. Leave me be . . .

"I am what is needed for any given moment of any given day—for you . . ."

From where Marla sat at the base of her tree, there came a low growling like that deep in the throat of a tomcat, low-slung, creeping forward into battle.

"Surely you remember, Little Brother: playmate, . . . leader . . . teacher . . . lover, all because that was what you wanted me to be at the time . . ."

A sharp hiss across the darkness was all that was needed to tell Marla to keep her place and silence. Gamelon gathered his feet under him and came up, his back against the tree. From somewhere to his left and back a little, the deep rich voice, so like his own in color and timbre it could have been mistaken for his in a different mood, came again. "I've never failed you. For you, I didn't die back there. Not there. You didn't really want that—"

Gamelon's voice was flat, cold, without even a faint aroma of emotion. "I see you, Racklin. I see you even though I cannot see you. You are behind me, but I am turning, and when I turn, the lightning will be before me. I am going to kill you."

"Of course you are. You must try at least—"

Gamelon saw the softer shadow that was his brother swell out then detach itself from the trunk of the next tree down the row.

"—if you can. As I was a friend, a teacher, and all the rest when you needed me to be, now you need me to be a victim, some Judas goat to sacrifice, some ultimate thing to punish for all the misery you've been responsible for—*you*, Brother, not me!"

Gamelon charged across the darkness between the trees. Racklin grabbed a low limb above his head, swung back, and rammed his feet into his brother's chest. Peaches, ready for the picking, thudded around them. Gamelon gulped and tugged for air as he staggered back. His heel came down on a piece of the ripe fruit. He slipped and went flat on his back.

As he fell on him, Racklin snarled, "Victims, Little Brother, even when they're trying to do what's expected of them, are never willing!" His hands went around Gamelon's throat. "You see *me?!* You see *me?!* I see *you!!*" Gamelon grabbed his wrists and with a superhuman strength born out of his driving madness, ripped his brother's hands away and twisted from under him.

Racklin was on his back instantly, one arm locked around Gamelon's neck. "I see the coward, the hypocrite who ambles through life telling the world he is normal and begging in the bottom of his timid soul nobody ever finds out he isn't and never can be!" Heedless of the ridging hummocks and the fallen fruit, they rolled over and over until Racklin was able to pin his brother. He panted in Gamelon's ear, "Normal! You were never normal! But you've made normal, God! Only, like God, you don't know what normal is!"

Gamelon heaved up on his elbows and knees like a humping boar, somersaulting Racklin over his head. Racklin landed on his feet and spun around to face him, spitting words at him now, rapid fire. "You see *me?!* You see *me?!* How can you?! You can't see yourself!"

Gamelon circled him, feinted in now and again.

Racklin turned with him, dodging. "You can't see yourself and so I've had to be you, I am you! I've always been what *you wanted to be* but didn't have the guts!" He began to laugh maniacally between phrases. "I am your thrill in terror! I am your naked lust without a pretense of love or rightness! I am your mindless cruelty, your capacity for bottomless hatred, your uncataracted eye! I am the you who flies without a thought for any other man! I am your true genius! I am your pure joy! I—I am the you that is the real, despicable human being. I am the you that is *normal!!*"

"Nooooo!!" Gamelon bellowed and threw himself at Racklin. He caught his brother around the chest and hurled him to the ground pinning Racklin's arms with his knees. He did not know how the lump of field stone came to hand, but as he raised it high above his head, Racklin screamed, "I am the victim because you want me to be—because you are the vic—" The rock smashed into his face and there was no other sound then but the dull squashing as Gamelon raised the stone and brought it down again, and again, and again.

When it was done, he felt nothing.

Where the road south out of Swede's Valley intersected the one coming in from the equally rich farm area directly to the east, the highway department had put up a prefabricated metal shed for hand tools and wheelbarrows amidst the heaps of gravel stored there. With a single wrench, Gamelon tore the lock off, hasp and all, put Marla inside amongst the rakes and shovels, closed the door and started off alone into St. George.

The duty physician in the emergency room at the small hospital was happy for something to do late on an otherwise quiet Sunday evening, but the nurse told him the big red-headed man outside would not fill in the required forms.

He went into the waiting room to reason with the man, but one look at his face, not to mention his size, convinced him to take the cash in the man's hand and forget about the forms.

The man said only one word while the doctor cleaned and bandaged the obvious knife cut in his side: "Shirt!" Uneasy in the man's presence, the nurse was only too happy to slip away and get an old one from the discards the hospital auxiliary collected for just such purposes.

The last show on a Sunday evening was always so poorly attended, it hardly paid to roll the projectors. But, the percentages held: out of the twelve cars in the parking lot outside the theater, one had the keys in the switch. As the final chords of the theme crashed triumphantly, "The End" confirmed the finality and the house lights came up, Gamelon drove off in the twelfth car.

Through what of the night remained and into the day that followed, Gamelon drove. Down the black abyss that was the Virgin River Gorge, across the dessicated, empty desert, up through the Cajon Pass with its never-ending dervish winds, Gamelon drove the distance for the second time in a single day. He drove all the way to Wasco, Marla cowed and cowled beside him, without a word.

JULY 21, 1984

Wasco

Marla had seldom left the spare bedroom in the cottage since they had arrived early the Monday morning before. She ate alone from trays he prepared for her unenthusiastically. She spoke only when he asked her a question, and her answers were little more than one syllable negatives. Did she want him to try to find some clothes that would fit her: no, what would? Could she see even the smallest sign that, now she was safe, she might be returning to normal: after a long pause, a whispered no. She became a soundless figure glimpsed now and again as a floating Bear Claw quilt gliding down the cottage hall to and from the bathroom.

During those crawling six days, Gamelon had slept much but always awoke unrefreshed. His dreams, distorted, often violent, incomprehensible, and remembered only in bits and pieces gave him no peace. His days were haggard and devoid of joy. The nursery, the flowers, the constantly emerging results of his earlier experiments were of no interest to him.

He, too, spoke little during that time, and only twice at any length, both times haltingly and in a desultory way unlike the Gamelon of springtime. Once was when he dictated the disposal of his patents and the nursery to his lawyer; the second, later the same day when he told Jorge what he had done but not why. The little man's best, most concerned attempts to get that from him met with only, "I must. I have no choice." over and over again. Jorge had finally retreated with halting steps and a burdened, saddened heart, wondering again if maybe *Señor* Sev—, Sev— might be able to help, but knowing that though *Señor* Sev—, Sev— would surely try if he was asked, he could not.

In the heavy, deeply scented silence of the hybridizing house, Gamelon sat alone that Saturday evening, his head bent over the closed cross list. The light coming through the roof was just barely that, but he made no move to switch on the lamp on the desk. He sat alone, staring at nothing, oblivious to the sights and smells about him, even to the single insect tunneling through the quiet.

He was reluctant to become aware of the disturbing shuffling sound at his elbow. He raised his head wearily and glanced out the corner of his eye expecting to see Jorge standing near him. It took a moment for the realization to grow in him that it was Marla who stood there, although it was not she whom he saw but only the faded splays of color on the Bear Claw quilt. With difficulty, he shunted off his useless conjecturing about whether Black Sateen had been able to mend his punctured heart and how many Fredericks there still might be and asked, "What is it?"

She did not answer. He began to think she had not heard him. He was about to repeat himself when she asked very softly in her thickened words, "Will you—will you do one la—something for me, Gamelon?"

He seemed to himself a bored parrot performing out of habit. "What is it?"

"Will you—will you take me to the sea?"

"What for?"

"I—it may seem strange to you, but I've never seen the sea. I've read poems about how it smells, how vast and limitless it is. I've seen moving pictures of all its moods. Up until now, that was enough. Now, something . . . something about it draws me, beckons to me."

"All right. I'll drive you down in the morning."

"No—please, now, while I—now, at night, so no one can see me."

"If no one can see you, neither can you see the ocean. You can smell it at night, hear it, but if you can't see it, you can't grasp its vastness."

Marla was silent, as deeply hidden for several moments within herself, it seemed, as her body was within the quilt. Then she said, "I read somewhere once that even a blind man can appreciate the sea's endlessness, that its vastness is more a feeling that comes over one than what one actually sees, a sort of unheard roaring or throbbing. That would be enough to reassure me . . ."

"Reassure you of what?"

"That it could—" At his elbow, the quilt seemed to shiver. "That it could hide me—if I wanted it to."

There was a dreg of the springtime Gamelon, no more than a stain at the bottom of the empty cup that was now him that stirred him to counter her statement, throw her some pittance of love, some scrap of hope, but he did nothing. What could one who had none of either left offer another?

He said they would go after supper. They would drive to La Playa. There was a long, lovely beach there and they would walk it. She trailed off, out of the dim greenhouse, a swaddled wraith.

La Playa

They had driven from Wasco in the nursery's van. It was the only transport left. The Fiat was junk and, after driving it to a side road by the rose fields and cleansing it of fingerprints, Gamelon had reported the stolen car with Utah plates as seemingly abandoned near his property.

It was the time of the month for the spring tides. The flow of the ocean reached higher, the ebb bared the beach farther out. The flooding light of the full moon helped him steer her shrouded figure in and out among the tangled piles of stranded kelp as they went. And they went slowly and in silence along the shimmering, windless night beach for a long, long while. Now and again, she would pause and turn to face the sea directly as though to contemplate it, as though not only to be sure it was there, but also that it was what she wanted it to be. He could not tell what she might be thinking. She kept all of herself hidden from him, shared no thought with him.

They came at last to the northern end of the beach where great stones, tumbled by some bygone suffering of the restless earth from the cliffs above, barred their passage farther and she stopped. She turned to look out to sea again for a while, then turned back toward him. When she began to speak, her voice came from a small shadowed cave in the quilt; he still could not see her face.

"You must help me, Gamelon," she said quietly, just loud enough to be heard above the sound of the breakers collapsing a few feet from them, strewing their foaming crumbs, then dragging them back again across the glistening sand. "I don't want to go on, Gamelon, not like this, and I know I will never be again what I was." She put one hand out through a fold in the quilt. "I was never beautiful, Gamelon, but that never bothered me. I had my music. These—fingers will never be able to open a bottle much less hold a violin bow." Just a hint of sighing disappointment had crept into her voice. "Then, like Marylea, I have a horror of—of giving birth to a—a twisted, terrible thing—yes—" She seemed to sense rather than see or hear that he was about to interrupt her. "—yes, you can ask how, but I know. I am carrying Slim Boy's child. Being what I have become, knowing about the Jennie—I will not bear it, Gamelon. I cannot.

"But you must help me, Gamelon. I cannot do it alone. I cannot trust myself to go alone. I might become something else in the water . . .

"You must come with me, Gamelon. You must walk with me into the sea. You must hold me tightly. If I become something that lives in the sea, then you must strand me on the beach. Whatever happens, you must not let me live. I am too—too strange, and too sad.

"Give me a stone. Gamelon. Give me a stone to hold me down, and take my hand. Take my hand and walk me into the sea."

At first it was only as the slight stirring of a dreamer at nightmare's onset, but it swelled rapidly into an awful confusion within him. He became the sleeper watching himself in a terrible dream, praying for it to end and knowing full well he had no means to end it. He was unable to do anything but what she asked.

He watched himself probe and search among the droppings from the cliff until he found a stone that seemed the proper shape and size for dying. When he returned to her, she had surrendered the quilt at last. It lay at her feet. White hips too narrow, white arms too long, white legs more knotted tree roots than human limbs, tangled golden hair silver-plated by the showering moonlight, she stood like a cruel parody of an alabaster Venus at the water's edge.

Still, she turned her head away from him as she took the stone and cradled it in one arm as he remembered the art nouveau lady on the stele cradling Nesset's grief. She stood that way for a long moment, then she reached her free hand out to him.

The consternation within him swirled higher and with it now there came a pressure like that at the lead edge of a tornado. Still, he stood aside, it seemed, and watched himself helplessly as he took the white hand with the thumb so oddly jointed. Together they started into the water.

At first the sand was firm beneath his booted feet, but by the time the water reached his waist, it had gone soft and he found it more difficult to go forward. A gentle summer swell swept by him and buoyed him, but it submerged her. When the swell had passed, she cried out, "Hold me, Gamelon! You must hold me!"

He shifted his grasp to her wrist. The pressure inside him mounted. He began to shiver under it like a glass pane before it gives way and shatters under the onslaught of a great wind.

The next swell came, rolled on, and only her head was above the surface. At last she turned her splayed face to him, looked directly at him with great gray eyes and called above the sea's rustlings, "Goodbye, Gamelon. In my way, I loved you. All three of us did—" and she disappeared within the rushing of swells.

There was a struggling beneath him. He grabbed her drowning wrist with both his great hands and held it in a vise grip. He was shaking almost uncontrollably now. Then the great glass between himself and himself shattered inward with a devastating crash and left him alone at the vortex of the whirlwind. He held her down, he held her and screamed up into the placid summer night sky, "Oh, God! Oh, God, please—" an oncoming wave smothered him and filled his mouth with brine. He spewed it out again with his screaming. "—please be there! Someone—" Again his cries were flooded out with salt for an instant. "—something has to tell me what I've done is all that could be done!"

Nothing.

The struggling stopped and his hands gripped nothing but a tugging weight.

Nothing.

And his mouth was salt.

He turned and began to drag the weight through the water with him back toward the beach.

He did not know why.

He dragged it until the sea was shallow enough again for him to pick it up and carry it.

He did not know why.

He stumbled, he fell once as he carried it out of the water and up beyond the tide line and laid it on the sand there.

He did not know why.

Only then did he look down.

What he saw was what Marla had become in death and he understood his blind need to help her. Twisted, tortured, bent; still, she had been his last fragment of love.

What he saw when he looked down was Maria.

There in the shadow of the great stones tumbled by some bygone suffering of the earth, he dropped to his knees. His limp fingers trailed in the sand. His head fell forward and he wept. He wept with soul-wracking agony as only a lost man can weep.

And he knew why.

If he had left on some other day to collect his honors . . .

If he had recognized Marylea's desperation right after the child was born . . .

If he had remembered to replace the bolt . . .

If he had checked his brother's madness with a strong arm around the shoulder instead of a fist in the face . . .

If he had taken Marla's hand before tonight . . .

He wept until all the ifs melted away and left him with but a single reality: everything he had ever loved was dead and he had killed it.

Everything.

And he was left with . . .

Nothing.

Nothing but a curse far more damning than brilliance: love for the laughable beast.

Nothing but that and the shattered remains of a human life, his own.

God had not answered him or blessed his actions, but the sound of the sea came to his ears again, its odor to his nostrils. He was aware again of its vastness behind him and he was quiet.

With what remained of his life, there was still the play for time to make.

He struggled to his feet, Marla's limp body in his arms. He secreted it among the rocks, retrieved the quilt from the ocean's verge and went up the beach and through the scattered chapparal and stone to where the van stood just off the highway.

The back of a blank waybill from the clipboard on the dash and the stub of a pencil connected to the board by a dirty length of heavy twine would serve. He switched on the cab map light and, heedless of the occasional passing car, wrote:

Mr. S.,

This is the last piece of the hell I've lived through these past weeks. Maria's death was the first piece. Yet, it is only the end of the beginning. Please forgive me for leaving it on your doorstep, but I must.

You may not realize it at the moment, but you have almost all that's needed to reconstruct those weeks, that hell, fill in what's missing and fit it all together. And, you have the only mind I know capable of comprehending what you'll find when the patchwork's complete. Whether you'll understand, agree, disagree, I don't know. But someday, someone may have to try to explain, and, as I said in my last note, any poor soul, no matter how depraved, who is heading into the unknown perhaps never to return would like to feel some single comrade in the human race will remember him.

I doubt we shall ever see each other again, Mr. S., and I think you know how much I'll miss that. In the end, all the words and thoughts we exchanged over the years couldn't help me. I had to take my own terrible stand on the meaning of truth, on what beauty really is. Pray for me that what I did as a result was the only thing that could have been done.

With deepest respect and affection,
Gamelon

A shred of plastic from a damaged bare-root rose shipping bag in the rear of the van and the twine from the clipboard served to make a packet waterproof enough to withstand the spray and the mists at the ocean's edge.

He returned to the beach. There, he tied the note to the stiffening left wrist of Marla's body then carried it down the beach to as near as he dared go to the first house above the strand. Gently, he laid it just out of the sea's reach. He stood looking down at it for a moment remembering great gray eyes, then he sighed, "Goodbye," turned away and headed up the beach again toward oblivion and the hell that would be the rest of his life.

SEPTEMBER 24, 1984

La Playa

The clerk shuffled casually through the stack of letters in her hand and equally as casually dealt two onto Deputy Sorensen's desk as she strolled by. He disregarded them until he had finished the report he was working on, then he took them up.

He knew from the handwriting that the first was from his father. He was sure it contained the annual plea for him to give some thought to returning home. He dropped it back on the desk and stuck his pencil into the envelope flap of the second, ripped it and pulled out the letter.

La Playa, California
September 20, 1984

My Dear David,

I thought I had sent you everything I had concerning Gamelon Waugh, but it appears I was wrong. The enclosed had been sent to me at the university and we did not discover it until today. I don't think it has much to add to what we already know but it does serve to explain something I had not quite understood: Gamelon's having said in the note we found on the dead woman's arm, "in my last note, any poor soul, etc." Why not break here and read it, then return to my closing comments?

David did so. He scanned Gamelon's next-to-last communication to Mr. S. quickly, laid it aside and went on to read the rest of what Freddie had to say.

I don't think we will ever know what happened between the time Gamelon left Dr. Ching that Sunday morning at the university and the night we found what I must assume to have been Marla's body on the beach here—that is unless you pursue the matter further and share with me whatever else you may find.

I cannot find it in me to believe he murdered Marla. He seemed to want to protect her. Exactly how and why she died is a mystery to me.

As to Gamelon: I believe he is committed for life to the extermination of the "cancer" as he called it. I had already gathered that before I wrote the first of my letters to you with the first of my "pieces." I doubt I'll ever be able to establish whether what Gamelon did, is doing, was right or wrong. If anything, it was probably both—or neither. That statement should really apply to the stand he took, to what he was willing to do if he had to. There is too much we don't know.

Concerning that stand of his vis à vis the human race: at this writing, I tend to sympathize with him. I, too, am in love with "the laughable beast."

So, my dear boy, with this, I leave you, you and/or your law, to come to your own conclusions, take your own actions. I'm sure you can comprehend it all, but can you understand? Perhaps we'll meet on the beach some afternoon soon and can discuss it further. Until then,

Best regards,
J. F. S.

David sat for a long time staring at the letters on the desk, tapping his upper lip with the eraser end of his pencil.

His father had been urging him, the only son, the only child, to come back to help him with the big dairy farm. It would all be his someday, after all. But his was a true criminologist's mind and it only found real nourishment in the kind of work he did now—or something similar. He leaned back in his chair and pulled open the center desk drawer and looked at the papers there: his captain's glowing recommendation that his request for transfer to the Sheriff's Detective Division be approved. Still, the innermost part of his heart joyed in thoughts of the lazy peace of the farm, the growing and reaping, the changing seasons, the fresh cream and tomatoes right off the vine.

There had not seemed a way until just recently for him to have both. Both and more. If he honored his father's wishes and returned to Swede's Valley, he might be able to satisfy his detective's driving curiosity to discover what had become of Racklin, the Slim Boys, the Fredericks. There was Gamelon, too. David was as sure as Mr. S. that he had returned to somewhere in the vicinity of St. George, at least for starters.

He leaned forward and began to leaf ahead in the pages of his desk calendar until he came to Friday, September 28th. Cribbed on the page in his own painful uphill scrawl was "Begin Vacation. Rtn. 10/15."

He got up and sauntered over to the window. He stood there for a long time contemplating his squad car on the street outside, the village policeman, looking for all the world in his uniform like nothing but an overgrown boy dressed up for a masquerade party. Then, seeming unaware of what he was doing, he reached into his back pocket and pulled out his wallet. He flipped it open carelessly and looked down at himself, poker-faced and unglamourous as one always is in a Motor Vehicles Department photograph. He studied the picture and words directly opposite it, "Date of Birth, March 30, 1950" and wondered what he might make of his vacation that year.

MAY 1986

For this, the world premiere of his latest large-scale work, the composer has supplied . . .

> Who or what is Gamelon? For purposes of *Aubade,* let us just say that Gamelon is that force which insures that life does continue. In doing so, that force, that power recognizes neither light nor darkness, good nor evil, truth nor falsehood, beauty nor ugliness, as Man defines them, but only the necessity for that life, with its peculiar combination of stability and change, to continue its slow upward progress undisturbed.
>
> I have been asked why I chose the viola and the tenor voice as soloists . . .

AUTHOR'S NOTE

Wasco, for example, is real and is the center of commercial rose growing and development in California. DNA, weather patterns, St. George, Utah, the Dixie National Forest, a Fiat, *The Deseret News* and the superb Guarneri Quartet are real.

The Navajo Nation and the beliefs, customs and history of its strong unique people are real. When the fictional triggering is considered, it would have been illogical not to include them in the fictional results. I have tried to depict everything pertaining to the Navajo as accurately as possible within the requirements of the narrative. If I have erred in even the slightest detail, I hope I will be forgiven. The Navajo are story tellers. So am I.

I am deeply indebted to certain experts in genetics, biology, anthropology, meteorology and medicine who very generously shared their knowledge with me so that matters falling within those disciplines could be made as correct as possible—up to my own fictional points of departure. They may not be able to professionally condone those departures and so I thank them, but I shall not name them.

No information available to me records any atomic explosion at the Nevada Test Site on or about July 28, 1949.

La Playa and its environs, Nesset and Swede's Valley do not exist, nor do any of the characters in the narrative, except in my imagination.

There are no blue roses—yet.

The Dîné: Origin Myths of the Navajo Indians by Aileen O'Bryan, Smithsonian Institution Bureau of American Ethnology, Bulletin 163, was my primary information and quotation source for the myth of The Twins and the Navajo calendar.

J. W.
San Diego, California
June, 1984

Here is an excerpt from *Killer*, by Karl Edward Wagner and David Drake, coming in January 1985 from Baen Books:

Rain was again trickling from the greyness overhead, and the damp reek of the animals hung on the misty droplets. A hyena wailed miserably, longing for the dry plains it would never see again. Lycon listened without pity. Let it bark its lungs out here in Portus, at the Tiber's mouth, or die later in the amphitheater at Rome. He remembered the Ethiopian girl who had lived three days after a hyena had dragged her down. It would have been far better had the beast not been driven off before it had finished disembowelling her.

"Wish the rain would stop," complained Vonones. The Armenian dealer's plump face was gloomy.

The tiger whose angry cough had been cutting through the general racket thundered forth a full-throated roar. Vonones nodded toward the sound. "There's one I can't replace."

"What? The tiger?" Lycon seemed surprised. "I'll grant you he's the biggest I've ever captured, but I brought back two others with him that are near as fine."

"No, not the tiger." Vonones pointed. "I mean the thing he's snarling at. Come on, I'll show you. Maybe you'll know what it is."

Beasts snarled and lunged as the men threaded through the maze of cages. "There it is," Vonones announced, pointing to a squat cage of iron.

"You've got some sort of wild man!" Lycon blurted with first glance.

"Nonsense!" Vonones snorted. "Look at the tiny scales, those talons! There may be a race somewhere with blue skin, but this thing's no more human than a mandrill is. The Numidians called it a lizard-ape in their tongue—a sauropithecus."

It seemed as good a name as any for the beast. It was scaled and exuded an acrid reptilian scent, but its movements and poise were feline. Ape-like, it walked erect in a forward crouch. Its eyes looked straight forward with human intensity, but were slit-pupiled and showed a swift nictitating membrane.

"This came from the Aures Mountains?" Lycon questioned wonderingly.

"It did. Came with a big lot of gazelles and elephants that one of my agents jobbed from the Numidians. All I know about it is what Dama wrote me when he sent the shipment: that a band of Numidians saw a hilltop explode and found this animal when they went to see what had happened."